How to Find a Guy in Five Weddings

How to Find a Guy IN Five Weddings

CYNTHIA TIMOTI

Tor Publishing Group
New York

This is a work of fiction. All of the names, characters, organizations, places, and events portrayed in this work are either products of the author's imagination or used fictitiously.

HOW TO FIND A GUY IN FIVE WEDDINGS

A Bramble Book
Published by Tom Doherty Associates / Tor Publishing Group
120 Broadway
New York, NY 10271

www.torpublishinggroup.com

Bramble™ is a trademark of Macmillan Publishing Group, LLC.

EU Representative: Macmillan Publishers Ireland Ltd, 1st Floor, The Liffey Trust Centre, 117–126 Sheriff Street Upper, Dublin 1, D01 YC43

The Library of Congress Cataloging-in-Publication Data is available upon request.

ISBN 978-1-250-34348-2 (trade paperback)
ISBN 978-1-250-34349-9 (ebook)

Our books may be purchased in bulk for specialty retail/wholesale, literacy, corporate/premium, educational, and subscription box use. Please contact MacmillanSpecialMarkets@macmillan.com.

First Edition: 2026

Printed in the United States of America

10 9 8 7 6 5 4 3 2 1

This one is for my mother, Errie Gunawan (1948–2025), who always pushed on even when the odds were stacked against her, and showed me what it means to be strong, brave, and resilient.

How to Find a Guy in Five Weddings

CHAPTER 1

There's No Such Thing as the Perfect Kim

This might be an extremely unpopular opinion, but whoever invented dating apps should be arrested and jailed for life, because thanks to that possibly unhinged individual, I was only a few steps away from the fiery gates of hell right now.

I knew my time for finding a guy was running out, but I shouldn't have listened to my "well-meaning" friends when they convinced me that I should try the internet. Should have stopped them when they went rogue and created a dating profile for me, then convinced me to swipe right on the men that had seemed suitable, because nothing good could ever come out of uploading my picture and personal details for virtual stalkers to salivate over. It only gave them a chance to plan their kidnappings, tortures, and eventual murders—or whatever it was that stalkers usually got up to.

"Gosh, the music is atrocious here." My date sighed. "So, Kimmy, what do you do again?"

I suppressed my own sigh. Nope, I didn't need to find dates online. What I needed was someone to have invented a time machine, so I could skip forward to the end of this dinner. It was online date number twenty-eight, and, by far, the worst of them all.

"Like I said, it's Kim. Please don't call me Kimmy."

At least I should thank my friends for not choosing a serial killer, although my ODOTD—Online Date of the Day—had his own unique brand of torture. Five minutes after meeting Shane, it was obvious that we weren't destined to be soulmates. Not in this life, not in the next one, not even if the universe was imploding and we were the only two survivors the future of humankind depended on. Right now, fifty-two (painful) minutes into the date, I'd rather have a sleepover with a couple of saltwater crocodiles than endure a second date with him.

Shane's dating app profile had proudly boasted that he was a dentist, the owner of a successful, thriving private practice, winner of the highly coveted Best Dental Clinic Award four years in a row. His roster of patients (supposedly) included several well-known celebrities. In hindsight, that should have been my cue to insert a major eye roll before quickly swiping left.

The "thriving practice" was actually owned by his uncle, and the award was bestowed a decade ago. The "well-known celebrities" were: (1) a local lawyer who had gone viral for all the wrong reasons and (2) the mayor's assistant's sister-in-law's second cousin twice removed. The cherry on top: My date was a dental assistant, not an actual dentist. Not that there was anything wrong with being a dental assistant, only if you lied about it.

His profile had listed him as six feet and five inches, so I was expecting a towering, Thor-like specimen. In reality, I stood eye to eye with him; and the last time I checked, I was a foot shorter than that. The smiling thirty-something man I'd seen on his profile, who looked like he'd be a lot of fun to chat with, turned out to be a moody fifty-something with an enormous chip on his shoulder who'd criticized almost everything in his sights from the minute we met: The place was too busy, his appetizer was too small, and the wine I'd chosen wasn't sweet enough. Plus, he was pleasantly surprised that I looked the same as the picture my traitorous friends had posted, because he was convinced everyone lied generously on their dating profiles. Like he did, by posting a photo of his much younger stepbrother. And no, he wasn't at all remorseful about it when he'd confessed that to me.

The only reason I had swallowed my irritation and stayed was because I'd been waiting for six months to eat at this upscale fine-dining establishment. The Orchard at Waterfront was the newest talk of the town, and I was lucky to have made my reservation early on because the waiting list had exploded to over a year now. Its owner and head chef had previously worked at famous Michelin-starred restaurants, so when word spread that he'd opened his own place at Port Benedict, almost everybody I knew had raced to book a spot here. Thankfully the food didn't disappoint, so it was worth the wait *and* this torturous date.

"Kim, yes, you did say that. Sorry, old habits die hard."

I paused, my fork suspended midair, ready to plunge into the last piece of my fancy herb-crusted yellowfin tuna. "Old habits?"

A bitter scoff preceded his answer. "My ex-wife was named Kimberly. Kimmy for short."

"Oh." I stabbed the fish and mopped the lemon sauce with it. No judgment on his ex, but I *hated* that nickname. Obviously, my unenthusiastic one-syllable reply was exactly the invitation he needed to regale me further with his sob story.

"She left me. For our personal trainer. Twenty years together, gone down the drain, just because she wanted to 'explore things'"—he made air quotes with his fingers—"with a guy ten years her junior. Ten years younger! I mean, he's practically still a child!"

I wasn't a genius, but the math sounded straightforward. "Assuming you're the same age as your ex, if he's ten years younger, wouldn't he be in his forties? Pretty sure that's way past the age bracket for a child."

He frowned. "I'm only thirty-one. Same age as you are."

Riiiigghhttt. And I have Mary Poppins on speed dial.

Shane was still waxing poetic about his ex. "She's a great cook, beautiful, and has an amazing body. All the other Kims I've dated since could never measure up to my Kimmy."

Wait, what?

I didn't know how he managed to cram so many wrong things in just a few sentences, but, somehow, he did.

"First of all, that was really sexist. And did you just say 'all the other Kims you've dated since'?" I put down my fork, a precautionary move just in case I had an overwhelming urge to stab something other than the lone piece of asparagus on my plate. I wasn't a violent person, but there was always a first for everything, right? And after twenty-seven failed first dates (give or take) in the last year and a half, tonight might be the time I finally snapped and explored my darker side.

He nodded. "I only date women named Kim and their variations. Kimberly, Kimberley, Kimball, Kimani, Kimiko. One day I'll meet the right Kim, and our love story will be even greater than the one I had with my ex-wife."

Oh boy. Now I *really* wished time machines were real.

To be fair to Shane, we'd chatted a few times on the dating app, and he had always seemed . . . *normal.* He was polite, said the right things, told the right jokes, absolutely nothing weird to indicate an unhealthy obsession with his ex, so I didn't think twice about inviting him to dinner tonight. Or maybe it had been his stepbrother chatting with me instead of Shane himself?

I blew out a long breath. Had I known this was going to happen, I would have asked one of my best friends to dinner tonight, but noooo, they both insisted that I needed to go out, meet new people, and enjoy myself. Well, they can be damn sure I'd be reassessing those so-called friendships as soon as I got home tonight, because there were plenty of other ways to enjoy myself, and none of them included suffering through an awkward, excruciating evening with a creepy, ex-obsessed stranger.

The sound of a chair lightly scraping the floor caught my attention as an elderly woman at our neighboring table got up and smiled at me, reminding me of my late grandmother. It slapped me back into the cold, hard realization of why I was giving up several precious hours of my life doing this. The *real* reason I suffered through this date, and so many others before him.

I steeled myself, vowing to give Shane another chance. Everyone deserves a second chance, don't they?

But my date wasn't making it easier, and things only escalated from bad to epic shit show. He went on about his Original Kim, the other Kims after that, and what he was looking for in his Perfect Kim. I pretended to listen while silently counting the seconds and telling myself to hang on for a few more minutes. My oat milk latte and raspberry mille-feuille should be here soon, then I could leave and be done with this dreadful nightmare.

But alas, the universe had other plans.

"Kim? Is that you?"

I stiffened.

Not just other plans, but the universe also had a peculiar, warped sense of humor.

Looking up slowly, I came face to face with Leo De Silva—my ex-fiancé, the first guy I'd ever loved, looking exactly as I'd remembered him: tanned, lanky, clean-shaven, but this time with the addition of a stunning, very pregnant woman hanging on for dear life to his arm.

"Wow." Leo gave me an awkward smile. "How long has it been?"

"Not long enough," I muttered under my breath, before pasting an overly bright smile on my face. "Hey! What are you doing here?

I thought you moved overseas." Or to another galaxy, somewhere far, far away.

"I came back." He squeezed the hand of the pregnant woman on his arm. "This is Lila, my fiancée. Babe, this is Kimiko Halim. We used to go to college together."

"Oh." A look of recognition flooded into her eyes. "You're *Kim*."

"That's me." I stopped myself from saying that we used to do a lot more than just going to college together, because that would be petty and crude, and my grandparents raised me better than that.

"Lila wanted to move back home so the baby could be surrounded by family." Leo flashed her an adoring smile, and I nearly threw up in my mouth. He pointed to a table at the other end of the restaurant. "It's my dad's birthday, so we're all here to celebrate."

My smile vanished as I glanced in the direction he was pointing. His parents, his siblings and their partners—people I used to regularly talk to—were glaring at me, resentment plastered all over their faces.

"How nice." I returned their glares, then directed my attention to the happy pair. "Leo and Lila. Such a perfect couple name. Are you naming the baby Luke, Leia, Liam, or Lily?"

"You haven't changed." Leo raised his eyebrows. "There's no need for that. We're all adults here."

"No need for what? I was just suggesting some baby names."

"No, you're being passive-aggressive, and you know it."

Fine, maybe I was. Leo possessed this rare ability to extract all the catty, snarky bones in my body and shove them into the spotlight for all the world to witness. It had been several years, so I wasn't still hung up on him. In fact, him cheating was the best thing that had ever happened to me. The reason I was seething was because he seemed happy, and it felt like he was here to rub his happiness in my face, because I was still alone, struggling to navigate the murky waters of online dating. And unfortunately, in the biased eyes of society, that meant he'd won, and I'd lost, because he was checking off all the boxes in the (Ridiculous) List of Things an Adult Should (Supposedly) Achieve Before They Turn [Insert Desired Age].

"I'm Shane. Kimmy's friend." My date, who had been shamelessly staring at Lila's chest, offered his hand to Leo. "Congratulations on finding your person, man. Hold on to her with all you've got, because nothing lasts forever." He raised his wineglass. "To your happy little family. May you be blessed with a long and fruitful union, with many more kids to bring joy and laughter to your household."

What. The. Fuck.

I buried my face in my hands, not even bothering to hide my exasperation. Where on Earth was my coffee and dessert when I needed them the most?

Shane and Leo continued their aggravating bonding while I considered moving to another country to avoid sharing a city with my ex and his new fiancée. Or undergoing facial reconstruction surgery and changing my name, to anything but a variation of Kim. Maybe hiring a team of scientists to wipe my memory so I'd have no recollection of these people. No, why should I be the one making such a huge sacrifice? I'd pay to wipe Leo's memory instead. Better yet, all of *their* memories.

I glanced at Leo's family and felt chills trickling down my spine. His scowling mother, with her eyes trained on me, got up from her seat, presumably eager to share a piece of her thoughts about how, according to her, I'd committed the eternally unforgivable sin of breaking her precious son's heart. I wasn't raised to run away from confrontations and challenging situations, but I'd already been subjected to that highly delusional speech once, so I wasn't keen on a repeat performance now. Or ever.

Grabbing my purse, I got up and mumbled to Shane and the happy couple, "Gotta go. Just remembered I had a, um, hair coloring appointment. Enjoy the rest of your evening."

Without waiting for their answers, I turned around and collided with a solid wall of muscle, smelling faintly like fresh mint and crisp apple. I staggered back a little, and a strong pair of hands gripped both my arms, saving me from falling over and using Leo and his fiancée as safety cushions.

A familiar, amused voice rumbled from somewhere above me. "Sorry to interrupt, Ms. Halim, but your wine tasting session is about to start."

Surprise flooded through me as I looked up. "My *what now*?"

Instead of a friendly, smiling waiter, a pair of hazel eyes twinkled down at me. My own eyes widened at the sight of Rob Carmichael, in his white T-shirt, brown suede jacket, and dark jeans, and definitely *not* part of the restaurant serving team.

Thanks, universe. Go ahead and pile on the humiliation, why don't you?

I took a step back and pulled my arms away. "What wine tasting?"

"The private wine tasting you booked last week." His smile grew bigger. "We're starting shortly. Would you like to follow me?"

I glanced behind me, sighing when I saw Leo's mom getting closer. Time of impact: less than twenty seconds. It was now or never.

"Yes, of course, the wine tasting!" I gave Rob an overly bright smile. "Guess I'll have to cancel that hair appointment, huh?"

"I do love a good bottle of wine." Shane placed his napkin on the table and stood up. "Would you like to join us, Leo and Lila? I've heard great things about the wine cellar at this place."

No, no, no. Over my cold, dead, rotting body. And also, did he really just offer wine to a *pregnant* woman?!

I opened my mouth to protest, but Rob beat me to it. "My

apologies, but the session is fully booked tonight. Please speak to the duty manager if you'd like to reserve a spot at our next one." He glanced back at me, the smile still on his face. "Shall we?"

Yep, I didn't need to be asked twice. I quickly flagged a waiter and told them I'd be at the bar, then bid a hasty goodbye to Shane and the parents-to-be before following Rob toward the back of the restaurant. He rounded the corner and strolled into the connecting building, where the formal ambience of the restaurant was swapped with a more relaxed yet still classy vibe. We made our way toward the bar, a long glistening crystal-white table backlit by warm lights. An ornate wine rack with hanging glass holders and bottles upon bottles of wine and liquor lined the back of the bar, where a couple of smartly dressed bartenders were busy pouring drinks. The place buzzed with chatter and laughter of the patrons, with clinking glasses and the gentle sounds of smooth jazz playing in the background.

Rob made a beeline for the only vacant seat and motioned for me to sit on it. He held out his hand, offering to help me up on the high stool, but I shrugged it off and hoisted myself up.

"You know what's funny?" I said. "I don't remember booking any wine tasting."

"You don't? That *is* funny."

The guy sitting on the stool next to me hopped off, and Rob nodded his thanks as he took the vacant seat.

"Downright hilarious."

CHAPTER 2

Rom-Coms Are Funny (Unless They Cost You Five Hundred Bucks)

I first met Rob Carmichael when Ellie Pang, who is now one of my best friends, leased the store next to mine and discovered that the place was in dire need of some TLC. Alec Mackenzie, Ellie's (now) fiancé, was Rob's best friend and business partner, and Rob was the contractor who had handled the work on her store. On a passing glance, Rob could probably be best described as that popular guy who was everyone's high school crush: tall, fit, with tousled brown hair and friendly eyes that seemed to be perpetually smiling. He moved with an effortless physical grace, was generous with his dimpled grins, and was always quick to charm anyone with a pulse in his path.

But he was also a bit too similar to Leo: confident, too good-looking for his own good, and should probably come with a flashing red light and a warning in big, bold capital letters: CAUTION: PROCEED AT YOUR OWN RISK. I should know, because despite my extensive experience with the dynamite combo of relationships and disappointments, I was once gullible enough to be persuaded into giving Rob a chance, but he hadn't even bothered showing up for our date. And while I might have forgiven him for making me waste forty-five precious minutes of my life, because it was in the past, that didn't mean I wasn't still a little bit wary around him. It was ironic—and *mortifying*—that he had been the one rescuing me from this horrible date.

Rob gave the bartender his drink order, then turned to me, patiently waiting as I studied the drinks menu with a more intense concentration than probably necessary.

"You've been staring at the same page for a few minutes," he finally pointed out. "Have you noticed there's another page at the back?"

My grandmother's voice echoed in my brain, chastising me. *Remember your manners, Kim.* I sighed and looked up at him. "I'm sorry. It's been a long night. Thank you for helping me out just now, but please don't feel like you have to stay and keep me company."

"Oh, not at all. More than happy to be here. I was watching you and your date. It was fascinating to see your face turning into so many different shades of red in just a few short minutes." He flashed me a cheerful grin as I told the bartender what I wanted. "But seriously. That date must have been a real doozy. You looked like you were going to barf at some point."

"I should have. On one of them. Why didn't I think of that?"

He let out a mock gasp. "*No!* You mean the date wasn't a smashing success?"

I chuckled, feeling some of the tension from the date and seeing Leo slowly ebbing away. "Oh, best first date I've ever had. Couldn't keep our hands off each other. Haven't you heard? We're eloping next weekend."

"Congratulations." Rob made a motion like he was hopping off his stool. "Should I go and get him? I'm sure you'd rather spend time with your betrothed than me."

"Don't you dare." My hand shot out to grab his, anchoring him in his seat. "That was one of the worst dates of my life. Although at least he showed up." I smirked at him. "Refresh my memory. I think that's a concept you're not entirely familiar with?"

"I'm never going to live that down, am I?" His grin turned sheepish. "Come on, Kim. It was, what, three, four months ago? And I've apologized at least five times now. I admit, it wasn't my best moment, but my head just wasn't in the right space at that time."

"I know, I know. It's not your fault. It was Alec's fault for setting us up, even though he knew you'd just gotten out of a serious relationship, you weren't ready to move on, yadda yadda." I thanked the bartender as he set down a shiny copper mug of strawberry mojito for me and a bottle of light beer for Rob. "Anyway, I appreciate the assist tonight, and sorry if I derailed your dinner plans."

"I wasn't here for dinner. I was working."

"What?" The mojito paused halfway to my lips. "You don't really work here, do you?"

He took a sip of his beer. "Has it ever occurred to you that I might own the restaurant?"

"No way. *You?*"

"Kimiko Halim. That hurt my feelings." Rob placed one hand over his heart, his expression wounded. "Is it hard to believe that I could own a fancy place like this?"

I raised my eyebrows. "Yes, because you don't own restaurants and bars. You work in construction. And the guy that does own this place is an actual chef who used to work in posh, world-class restaurants."

"You're being extremely condescending." He produced a sad pout, the corners of his lips drooping all the way to his chin. "Maybe I'm a wildly rich secret investor and entrepreneur on the side. Have you ever thought about that?"

"Mmm, I don't really spend my free time thinking about you, to be honest."

"That's too bad, because you're missing out on a lot." His pout was replaced with a chuckle when I rolled my eyes. "I was here to meet the owner about some renovation work for a new place he's opening."

"You're meeting a client on a Saturday night?"

"No time like the present."

"Setting a high bar for workaholics around the world, aren't you?"

His easy smile didn't quite reach his eyes. "If you think I'm a workaholic, wait until you meet my dad."

"So, a workaholic, and you're alone, which means I can safely assume no significant other to spend your weekends with?" I mimicked playing a sad tune on a violin. "Kind of tragic, Carmichael."

"At least I didn't need rescuing from a horrible date."

I grinned. "At least I *had* a date."

"Ha! That's true." He nodded. "Who was the other couple?"

"My ex and his fiancée. We were together five years before he left me for her."

"No wonder you looked like you were ready to claw his eyes out." He cocked his head, assessing me. "Gotta say, his fiancée looks like she could be your sister, though. Tall, brown eyes, long dark hair. He clearly has a type."

"I'm not his type. She is." I took a long sip of my mojito to get rid of the bitter taste of betrayal in my mouth. "They were coworkers, then gym buddies, which turned into fuck buddies behind my back. Next thing I knew, he told me he'd met someone else, but he had the audacity to tell his family that *I* was the one who had cheated on him. And now they're having a baby together." I wasn't usually an oversharer, but it was probably the shock of seeing Leo again after so long that had loosened my tongue.

"That's really messed up." Rob frowned. "Your ex is a dirtbag. I'm sorry you had to go through that."

"Don't be. Seeing the two of them only validated my theory, actually."

"What theory?"

"There's no such thing as soulmates and happy endings. It's nothing but myths, lies, and bullshit, romanticized and fed to the unsuspecting public so they'll buy into the commercialism of it all."

"Wow. That's such a sad way of viewing the world," Rob said. "I think there's a happy ending out there for everyone. Whether they want to pursue it or not, that's another story."

"This, coming from a man who's working on a Saturday night, all alone."

"I'm taking a break from relationships. Doesn't mean I don't believe in happy endings."

I smirked. "Well, my advice is to take your happy endings and shove it—"

Someone cleared their throat before I could finish my sentence. I turned around to see a frowning Shane standing behind me.

"I thought you had a wine tasting session." His tone was accusing. "This doesn't look like one."

Rob didn't miss a beat. "There's been a delay. We're still waiting for it to start."

Shane narrowed his eyes at Rob, then at me. "Right."

"Thanks for a wonderful evening, Shane." I gave him a polite smile, because even though he was the date from hell, my grandparents had raised me to always say please and thank you. "I'll pay for my share of the dinner when I leave. Take care."

"You too, Kimmy." He hesitated, before asking, "Can I call you tomorrow?"

"I think we both know this isn't going anywhere," I said. "Good luck with your Kim-finding quest, though."

His face fell, but he nodded, gave Rob another quick glance, then left.

"Kim-finding quest?" Rob looked amused.

"Trust me, you don't want to know. And that is just one example in a long list of why happy endings only happen in movies, romance novels, and fairy tales. Not real life. At least, not mine."

But even as I said those words, a tiny prick of fear threatened to overtake me. The afternoon of my grandmother's will reading floated into my mind, clear as the bluest sky, as if it hadn't happened a year and a half ago. The two-year period stipulated on the will was quickly running out, so the clock was ticking. Loudly. Reminding me that I only had five months, twenty-eight days, and probably three hours left to do what my grandmother had wanted me to.

If I couldn't find a partner and settle down by the end of that time, I couldn't inherit her store and continue her legacy, which meant I wouldn't be able to repay my grandparents for raising me. If I failed, the business would be sold, and the proceeds donated to a charity specified in her will.

But I knew there was no such thing as happy endings and settling down. It was an old, antiquated notion, but my grandmother had grown up in Asia in the 1960s, and it was what she had believed in. So my plan was to find a man, date him until the store was mine, then gently uncouple from the poor, unsuspecting victim. It was a simple yet brilliant plan, if I did say so myself.

"They do happen in real life." Rob's reply snapped me out of my thoughts.

"Obviously you have a totally different life experience than mine."

"Maybe I do. My parents have been married for over forty years. I have five older siblings, and they're all in happy relationships.

And look at Ellie and Alec, childhood friends turned soulmates. Weren't you cheering them on to get together last year?"

"Because Ellie is the happiest I've seen her when she's with him," I said. "I'm thrilled it worked out for them, but it's just not for me."

"Why not?" Rob slowly sipped his beer, his eyes thoughtful as he watched me. "I think it's wonderful to build a life with someone who has your back, who's going to be there for you through thick and thin. Share a family and kids and maybe a dog or two, and the rest of your lives with each other."

"Aww, how sweet. The way you view the world through rose-colored glasses." I drained my mojito. "Sounds like you need to get on a dating app to find your future partner and start mapping out your happily-ever-after."

"One day." He grinned. "Work's priority right now. I'm happy to wait for the right person to come along."

"You'll be waiting for a long time, because they don't exist." I hopped off the stool. "It's late, I better go. Thanks again for the rescue."

"Glad I could help."

Rob tossed some cash on the bar for his drink, and followed as I went back into the adjoining restaurant to settle my tab.

"Your bill comes to a total of five hundred and forty-nine dollars and ninety-nine cents," the manager said. "Will you be paying by cash or card?"

My mouth fell open. "That can't be right. I had an appetizer, a main course, a glass of red, and a mojito. And a cup of coffee and dessert, which I didn't even get a chance to enjoy. That wouldn't be five hundred fifty dollars."

The manager peered at his screen and tapped a few keys. "I'm seeing here two appetizers, two main courses, two sets of coffee and desserts, a glass of our house Shiraz, one strawberry mojito, and two bottles of the 2012 Fitzgerald Creek cabernet sauvignon."

He printed off the itemized bill and handed it to me. "Does that look right?"

My eyes nearly popped out of their sockets as I scanned the list of items and the eye-watering prices next to each line. Did Shane really buy two expensive bottles of wine for himself and leave me with the *entire dinner bill*? He wasn't kidding when he said he loved a good bottle of wine, was he?

This was why I was not a foodie, because I couldn't afford to eat in exclusive, super-pricey restaurants, and it was just my luck that this one rare time I did, my jerk of a date left me high and dry to pick up the astronomical check. Give me a bowl of ramen or a plate of nasi goreng over this any day, because at least they wouldn't cost me my hard-earned money.

"I know the owner." Rob was scanning the bill from behind me with a frown. "I can have a chat with him and explain the situation."

"He's just left for the night," the manager said, his tone apologetic. "I could try to give him a call, if you like."

I sighed, exhaustion suddenly washing over me, and all I wanted was just to go home. "Don't worry about it." I handed my credit card over, because Shane was my date, and it wouldn't be fair to the owner. He was running a business, not a charity, and if I were in his position, I knew I'd prefer not to give free meals and expensive wines to douchebags who skipped out on their dates.

"You sure?" Rob asked, his frown deepening.

"Yes." I nodded my thanks as the manager returned my card and the receipt. "This, by the way, only proved my point that happy endings don't happen in real life. You don't see this on TV, or the big screen, or in romance novels, do you? Only the smiles and the happy endings."

"Except in really funny rom-coms, maybe," Rob said, before quickly adding, "Not that I think this is funny."

"They're funny until they cost you five hundred and fifty dollars." I gave him a tired nod. "I'll see you around, Carmichael."

I walked away and pushed open the heavy front door, while silently berating myself, regretting my foolish decision to bring practically a stranger to an expensive restaurant. What on Earth was I thinking?

Not only was I five hundred and fifty dollars poorer now, but I was also back to square one, nowhere near what I'd set out to do, and therefore, nowhere near meeting the deadline that was breaking every imaginary speed limit toward me.

Five months, twenty-eight days, and three hours would be here before I knew it.

CHAPTER 3

My Grandfather Has More Instagram Followers than Me

For as long as I could remember, my life had always revolved around the Yarn Fanatics. The store was practically my second home, because I used to spend all my free time there: after school, on the weekends, and during school holidays, helping Oma, my grandmother. Knitting was one of her passions, and she had worked her ass off to turn the place into one of Port Benedict's go-to crafting suppliers, so when I first started running the store eighteen months ago, I knew I had my work cut out for me if I wanted to live up to her legacy.

Sundays are usually our busiest days at the store, so I arrived an hour earlier than our opening time. I did a quick check to make sure all the shelves were fully stocked, then went outside to put up an A-frame chalkboard on the sidewalk, where I'd advertise special offers, new stocks, and sometimes write fun knitting puns—something I'd started a few months ago to bring more customers in. This week's offer was written on one side (10% OFF

ALL CROCHETING SUPPLIES!) and our extended business hours (OPEN 9–6 DURING SUMMER—COME IN AND HAVE A BALL (OF YARN)!) on the other side.

I stood there for a minute, my mind quickly running through our store inventory. I needed to push the DIY animal crocheting kits that hadn't been as popular as I'd expected, so I crouched down, crossed out the 10 percent, and wrote 15 percent instead. Then I wiped the opening hours off the other side of the board and wrote a pun I came up with last night (AT YOUR KNITS' END? KNOT TO WORRY, WE'LL HELP YOU UNRAVEL!).

It was a gorgeous summer morning, and the cobblestone sidewalk was already teeming with people, mostly customers for Twisted Sweets, Ellie's bakery next door. Our precinct, a strip of shops at the back of Port Benedict Plaza, housed around twenty stores, including an organic juice bar, an art gallery, a yoga studio, and a secondhand bookshop. Towering oak trees framed the sidewalk, along with a few antique-style cast-iron benches and vintage streetlights, making the vibe—as Ellie had once said when she first moved into the city—idyllic and charming as hell. My grandparents had bought our brick building many years ago when it was still affordable, because they'd always been big believers in property investing as a retirement nest egg. They'd renovated it, turning the place into its current facade—white painted bricks with a blue doorframe and window frames—while still keeping the beautiful original architecture of the building intact.

Our window display had piles of pastel-colored yarn, bright scarves and beanies, thick knitted blankets, and cute crocheted animals, artfully spilling out of old wooden crates. As customers walked in, the wall to their left would have rows of knitting needles and crocheting hooks. The other two walls had floor-to-ceiling shelves, filled with yarn in every color imaginable, arranged from the darkest to the lightest color. There was a long wooden table in the middle, with baskets of more yarn and piles of knitting books. Everything looked warm, inviting, and aesthetically pleasing, so apart from rotating the window displays every other week, I hadn't reorganized the store, because it was what Oma had done before she was gone.

Because changing it felt like I was somehow removing traces of her from my life.

"Good morning!" Nicole, my grandmother's longest-working (and only) staff member, burst through the front door as I was counting the float in the register and handed me a to-go coffee cup. "Grabbed your oat milk latte. Love the new pun outside, by the way."

"Thanks, Nic." I grinned at her. "It's what I do best."

She drained her own coffee, then shoved her handbag into one of the drawers underneath the counter. "Better get ready, the crew will be here any minute."

Before I could respond, she was already hurrying toward the front of the store, where we'd set up a few comfortable chairs in a small corner nook for Nicole to run the knitting and crocheting clubs. Sure enough, five minutes later, the front door swung open again and a few women walked in as they chatted with each other.

We ran a few clubs a week, and today's club was called Yarned and Fabulous. It was the OG club, the first one that my grandmother had started back in the day, and although it had gone through a few iterations of names and members, the main objective of the club remained the same: to provide a space for people to get together and share their passion for knitting. There were a few other, newer clubs, because when I took over the store after Oma was gone, I had this irrational fear that our regular customers would take their business and loyalty elsewhere (even though the store was doing perfectly well). So I had the idea of starting themed clubs, hoping to attract different types of members to join and bring new customers in.

Thankfully, it worked.

There was one called Knit 'n' Chat, which was mostly geared to beginner knitters and crocheters. The Knotty Tea Society was for those who loved having a drink while they knit, and it didn't really have to be teas, because the rules were extremely loosey-goosey—we'd had people bringing iced coffees, pale ales, even pitchers of homemade margaritas. The last club was our most popular one, called the Fellowship of the Strings, and it was basically if a knitting club had gotten married to a book club. We'd even had a few authors come in to talk about their books while they knitted book sleeves with the members.

"Kim!" Melly, the owner of a women-only yoga studio in our precinct that I sometimes went to, beamed at me. "How's my favorite yoga student today?"

"You know." I shrug. "Just trying to stay *pose*-itive."

Melly chuckled with amusement, while Nicole shook her head from where she was setting up the nook. "She's on a roll this morning."

"You mean like my yoga mat?" I quipped, prompting Melly into another wave of snickers.

"Oh, please." This came from Anahita, who owned a music shop a few buildings away from us. "It's a bit too early in the morning to be trading cheesy puns."

"But you usually love my cheesy puns." I raised a questioning eyebrow at her as they all took their seats around the table. "Something's not right."

"She's been having a rough few days." Selma, the young woman who worked at the secondhand academic bookstore on the corner and sometimes helped Nicole run the Fellowship of the Strings, patted Anahita with sympathy. "You want to tell them about it?"

She waved her hand. "We're here to knit, not to hear tales of my sordid love life."

"Oh, but I *live* for stories of sordid love lives." Melly began to pull out her needles and balls of yarn from an oversized drawstring bag. "Hit us with it."

Anahita sighed. "My boyfriend is leaving next week. For twelve months. He accepted an overseas secondment in Dubai last month and didn't even tell me until four days ago. In Dubai! I don't believe in long-distance relationships, so I'm seriously considering breaking up with him. I don't have the bandwidth to juggle a business, be a single parent to my four-year-old, look after my elderly mom, *and* keep a long-distance relationship alive. It's just too hard. I'm *this close*"—she held her thumb and index finger half an inch apart—"to a full-blown breakdown, and I don't have time for one."

"He didn't even tell you?" I frowned. "Major red flag right there. What's his excuse?"

"He thought I was going to freak out and stop him from going. How pathetic is that?"

"I'd dump his sorry ass if I were you," Melly said. "You deserve better."

"That's what I told her," Selma said as she reached into her embroidered jute bag and took out her own knitting supplies. "The fact that he didn't say anything until the very last minute means he doesn't respect you."

Anahita blew out a long breath. "I know. And I will. But my daughter worships him. I don't know how to break the news to her that he's leaving." She swallowed, looking like she was on the verge of tears. "She's gone through so much the past couple of years since the divorce, and now it's the same thing all over again. She's going to be crushed."

"I'm so sorry." Nicole leaned in and gave her a hug. "We're always here for you. And she's got you, and you're an amazing mother. Whatever you need, you just let us know."

The other two women murmured similar sentiments, and as I watched the scene in front of me, I thought, *This is why I have to keep Oma's business alive.* Because this place was more than just a yarn store. It wasn't just a spot for these women, or the knitters in the other clubs, to meet every week to share their love of the craft, or to learn new techniques, or to be inspired by each other's creations. My grandmother had created a community staple: a safe space for these people to connect with fellow knitters, to share their lives and build meaningful friendships, and support each other in good and difficult times.

"You guys are the best." Anahita wiped her eyes. "I'm truly lucky to have found you all."

And I knew, without a doubt, that if I couldn't inherit the business, and the store was to close, it wouldn't just be hard for me.

It would be devastating for them, too.

That afternoon, after locking the store, I drove to Opa's house, a neat one-story cottage-style home ten minutes away from my place, with white paneled shutters and herb plants overflowing out of the window boxes. He'd been living on his own since Oma was gone, and no matter how many times I offered to move back into my childhood home, he always insisted that he was fine, that I was only a phone call away should he ever need anything.

"Opa? It's me." The smell of something burning greeted me as I walked in with the food I'd picked up on the way.

"In the kitchen."

I followed the sound of music and found him humming to an Elvis song as he pulled out a tray of burnt fish from the oven. He'd been trying out healthier recipes lately, which was great because he needed to watch his diet, if only he wasn't so bad at cooking. So to save us both from food poisoning (because I wouldn't subject anyone to anything I'd cooked either, not even myself), I usually got takeout for dinner.

My grandparents, Thomas and Emilia Halim, were the only real parents I'd ever known. Both Opa and Oma were fifth-generation Indonesian-born Chinese who had lost most traces of their Chinese heritage. Hence "Opa" and "Oma," Dutch for grandfather and grandmother, something that was deeply rooted in Indonesian history, having been a past Dutch colony for three and a half centuries. They had moved to the States when Opa did his higher education degree, choosing to settle down in Port Benedict, around an hour and a half from Seattle, and had my father, their only son.

I'd never met my mom. Hana Sato, my Japanese mother, had had a bright future ahead of her as a reporter for a respected international news channel, which was where she had met and fallen in love with my dad. Their blissful existence was forever shattered when she didn't survive an amniotic fluid embolism during childbirth, leaving my father to be a single parent within hours after I was born. The only mementos I had of her were an old photo album with pictures of my younger parents and her ancient Nikon F3 camera, which was kept in a special dry cabinet at my house.

By the time I was old enough to walk, Daniel Halim had decided that he'd had enough of playing the role of the doting dad. He'd accepted a role as a foreign news correspondent that required him to be roaming all over the world, packed his bags, and left his parents to care for a two-year-old. He'd breeze into our lives once, maybe twice a year, whenever he had time off long enough to fly back home, before moseying out of town again for his next job.

My grandparents used to tell me that my dad had big dreams—to travel the world, to make a difference by telling stories that are important to the lives of many people. That I should be proud of him for doing that. Still, when I was younger, it used to bother me how he was never around. How I was the odd kid at school, the only one without parents—and it didn't help that we'd also lost contact with my maternal grandparents. I used to hate how he chose his job over me, over *us* as a family. How he pretended that things were fine every time he came home for a visit, like he didn't just spend the past few months away from his only daughter, the one person who was supposed to matter the most in his life.

My grandparents were certainly the silver lining of my childhood, though. They doted on me, raised me like I was their own child, and had never once made me feel like I was a burden. Opa would drop me off at school on his way to work, then Oma would pick me up, and I'd stay with her at the store until it was closing time. Even at the age of eight, I'd help her restock shelves and rearrange displays, serving customers and carefully adding up their purchases with Oma's old calculator, while other kids my age were busy having playdates and birthday parties and sleepovers.

It was the only childhood I knew, and I'd loved every second of it.

"Hey, sweetheart." Opa dumped the burnt fish into the trash can, then gave me a hug. "Grilled trout isn't on the menu tonight, sorry. I must have left it in the oven a bit too long."

"That's okay. I brought plenty." I placed the food on the kitchen island, next to my grandmother's vase and her favorite—white calla lilies. "Where's everyone else?"

"They couldn't make it. Their dog swallowed their car keys, so they're waiting for him to pass the keys before they can come over."

He met my eyes, and I gave him a measured look, before shrugging. "Not bad. Eight for content, ten for delivery."

"Thanks." Opa chuckled as he washed his hands. "Lucu, kan?* I found it online."

It was a silly game we'd been playing for a while. After Oma had passed, our weekly dinners would always be just the two of

* Indonesian, meaning: "Funny, isn't it?"

us, with the occasional addition of Jenna Ng, my housemate and one of my best friends, and/or Ellie and Alec. But that had never stopped Opa from getting too much food. We both knew he did it so he could send me home with the leftovers, saving me and Jenna from having to cook for ourselves the next few days. No matter how many times I told him not to, he never listened.

So one day I asked if he was feeding the entire city of Port Benedict and if the other guests were arriving soon. His flippant answer had sent us both into a prolonged laughing fit, and since then, it had become a weekly game of him trying to come up with the most ridiculous excuses for the imaginary guests who were never coming to dinner.

"Got food from Java Spice. Some beef rendang, Balinese grilled chicken, and spicy beef oxtail soup. There's coconut rice and some stir-fried veggies." I opened the takeout boxes from our regular Indonesian restaurant, grabbed plates from the cupboard, and started plating some food for him. "Oom Tanujaya sent his regards. Even gave us some crispy-thin martabak with cheese and chocolate fillings."

"Oom" meant uncle, and even though he wasn't really my uncle, that was how I was taught to address an older man from our background, even if they weren't related to us.

"I'll text him to say thanks. That smells great." Opa sniffed the container of rendang with appreciation. "Make sure you bring the leftovers home."

He came around to my side of the kitchen island, and I helped him up onto his special chair, a comfortable wooden stool with a padded back support. Pulling out his phone from the pocket of his trousers, he took several pictures of the food from different angles, then got busy tapping on the screen, before holding it up for my inspection. "Bagus nggak?"*

* Indonesian, meaning: "Does it look good?"

I understood enough to catch what he was saying, although I could only reply in English. One of my biggest regrets in life was not taking my grandparents' pleas for me to learn Indonesian seriously when I was younger, only making a half-assed attempt to appease them, because my ten-year-old self was convinced that it would be incredibly uncool to speak a foreign language that none of my friends could understand.

Peering at his screen, I nearly choked on my chicken. "Are you posting it on Instagram?"

"Yes." He tapped and posted the photo. "Let's see how many likes that gets."

I swallowed my food and gaped at him. "You have an account? Since when?"

"Since yesterday. Johnny's grandson taught him how to set up an account, and Johnny showed the rest of us. We're going to see who can get the most followers in a week. I have"—he glanced at his screen—"fifty-six followers so far, just from posting photos of my woodworking pieces, you know those wooden spoons and the little chopstick holders I made?"

"Fifty-six? In just one day?" I gave him an impressed nod. "That's incredible. You have probably thirty more followers than me, and I've had my account for years."

"If you hadn't kept it private and posted more than once a year, you'd probably have a lot more. Oh, you need to approve my follow request, by the way."

Opa had always been quick to adapt to new technology, and for someone in his late seventies, my extroverted grandfather still led a very active life, even after he was diagnosed with late-stage kidney failure almost two years ago and now had to sit through regular dialysis in order to survive. On his non-dialysis days, he'd be out with his friends, or hammering away in his garage with his woodworking stuff (the bedside table he'd been making for the past year now had three legs), or getting his hands dirty repotting plants in his backyard (his herb garden was thriving), or trying his hand at one of the recipes he'd copied off the internet (mostly inedible, but A+ for effort).

"Johnny's been posting pictures of his sketches, and he's gotten over two hundred new followers in just one week. He says the key is to post constantly and use the right hashtags. I'm thinking about posting more woodworking stuff, maybe flowers from the garden, and some food photos. Not the food I made myself, of course. What do you think?"

"That's great, but isn't Oom Johnny older than you?"

Opa gave me a dirty look. "That's the problem with you young people. Ageism is so deeply entrenched in our society these days. Is it hard to believe that older people can use social media, or have more followers than younger influencers? Age is just a number, you know."

"No, it's just that . . . I mean . . ." I trailed off. "You're right. I apologize. What I meant to say was, I thought Oom Johnny was the one who didn't even know how to use his new smartphone. I had to teach him, remember? And he's suddenly a social media expert now?"

"He's a quick learner, maybe. I don't know. Anyway, tell me about your week." He put away his phone and peered at me. "Met anyone interesting lately?"

"We spoke about this two days ago when I took you to dialysis. Nothing's changed."

"You need to get a move on, sweetheart. Clock's ticking."

"But you know how hard I've been trying, Opa. It's impossible." I groaned. "You sure you can't intervene and declare the will invalid?"

"You know I can't. I don't know why she had the settling down clause in it, but your grandmother knew what she was doing when she drafted the will. It's ironclad, and the lawyers' hands are tied until the clause is fulfilled. Remember what I always tell you? Nothing is impossible. Except—"

"Humans flying and rising from the dead." It was something he used to say when I was younger, whenever I was feeling discouraged from not being good enough at something. *Keep trying. Don't give up. You can do anything you set your mind to. I believe in you.*

"Your grandmother meant well. She only wanted what she thought was best for you," he said. "Have a partner be there for you in good times and bad times, like what she and I had."

I understood where my grandmother was coming from, but I wished she had discussed it with me first when she was still around, instead of surprising me with it. "That's why it's impossible. I'm never going to find someone, because you and Oma are relationship goals. You two are the exception. Not the rule."

Opa paused in the middle of scooping more coconut rice. "We're not the exception, honey. What your grandmother and I had was special, but there are lots of other couples in happy, long-term relationships."

"I disagree. My parents never got their happy ending. You know what happened to me and Leo. The guy I met on a date yesterday, his wife left him for someone else, and now he's on a mission to replace her by going on a dating spree with women who have the same name as his ex. And why did Oma want me to settle down, anyway? It's such an old-fashioned Asian thing. Am I not enough of a person, or half the person that I am, if I didn't have a partner in my life?"

"You know that's not it. She's just worried you're going to end up sad and alone."

"I can be alone *and* still be happy," I argued.

"I know." Opa gave me a smile. "Just like I know you're more than capable of looking after yourself, but also, a selfish part of me wants to see you settling down, so I can go in peace, knowing that when I'm no longer around, you'll have someone to share your life with."

My reply died in my throat, and just like that, my mood turned somber.

I'd been working my way around the country when news came that my grandmother had had a heart attack and was gone. I returned to Port Benedict for the funeral and hadn't even had the chance to mourn her properly when she gave me the biggest shock of my life at the reading of her will.

A small part of me had quietly raged at Oma then, because she knew about my history with Leo, and how I hadn't been in a serious relationship since. I had considered ignoring the request and walking away, but I couldn't, because she meant the world to me, and I knew how much the store had meant to her. Then I'd learned that Opa's health had taken a serious turn for the worse. My grandparents never mentioned anything during our weekly video calls, because they didn't want me to worry.

That was what had pushed me over the edge: It was crucial I inherited the store, because the earnings could help with Opa's medical bills, since dialysis treatments weren't cheap, and his savings wouldn't last forever. Plus, after spending years hopping between odd jobs that had nothing to do with my accounting degree and not knowing what I really wanted to do with my life, I figured this was my last-ditch attempt at finding my version of a fulfilling life.

So I stayed. Did what I could. I drove Opa to his thrice-weekly dialysis appointments, bought his groceries, ran his errands, took him to brunches, and spent time with him at gardening and woodworking expos. According to Dr. Google, the average life expectancy of someone on dialysis was around five to ten years. I didn't know how much longer I had with my grandfather, so I was going to make every second count.

"Oma only wanted you to keep your options open." Opa was still talking. "She had faith that the right person for you is out there somewhere. All you have to do is find him."

"Finding a tiny needle in a haystack would probably be easier."

"Nothing is impossible, remember?" My grandfather smiled. "Now, tell me more about that date you were talking about. What happened?"

I told him about Shane and how I'd run into Leo. "It was dreadful. Good thing a friend was there, and he helped me escape those people."

"That's awfully nice of him. Is this friend single?"

"I don't know. I don't go around asking people about their relationship status."

"Let's find out." Opa placed his fork on his plate and reached for his phone.

I groaned. "Don't tell me you're going to stalk him on social media."

"What's the point of setting up these accounts if you don't use them to learn about other people's lives?" He opened his Instagram account. "Does this friend have a name?"

I knew he'd keep asking until I answered. "Rob. Rob Carmichael."

He tapped and scrolled for a few minutes. "You don't have him on your follow list. Let's see if we can find him on Ellie's or Alec's profiles."

"You've only joined social media yesterday, and you've already found my friends?"

"Yes. Why, what's wrong with that? Oh, there's a Rob Carmichael tagged in one of Ellie's posts." Opa turned his screen toward me. "Is this him?"

It was a carousel of pictures of Rob, Alec, and Ellie grinning into the camera, the beautiful pristine water of Port Benedict Bay glistening in the background, and Rob's dimples nearly stealing the spotlight.

"That's him."

"Great." Opa tapped on the follow button.

"No!" I tried to grab his phone, but he swatted my hand away. "Opa! You don't even know the guy! Why are you following him?"

"Why not? Is there a rule that I can't?"

"Yes! Because he'll see that you're following him and he might look at your profile and put two and two together and realize we're related, and he'll think we've been talking about him!"

"But we *are* talking about him."

"That's not the point."

"Too late, I've already followed him. You don't have to personally know everyone in real life to follow them, right? I'm also following a few woodworking influencers and a bunch of your cousins in Jakarta."

There was a soft *ping* from my grandfather's phone, and his face brightened. "Oh, he followed me back! He must have recognized you from my profile picture. Let's see if he has a girlfriend." Opa spent a few minutes inspecting Rob's posts, muttering things like "ahh" and "hmm-hmm" every few seconds.

"I hope you're not double tapping all his posts," I said.

"Only a few. Is there a rule against that, too?"

I concentrated on my food, knowing it'd be easier to let him do whatever he wanted.

"Looks like he's single. Although he doesn't post a lot, so it's hard to tell for sure." Opa nodded. "Boleh juga,* Kim. He's handsome, and he has kind eyes. And a friendly smile. Cheeky, but friendly. I approve."

"No," I said firmly. "You're approving nothing. I'm not dating him or anything."

"Didn't you say he's a friend?" Opa patted my hand. "I'm approving my granddaughter's friends. You can never be too careful these days." He set his phone down and picked up his fork again.

---

* Indonesian, meaning: "Not bad."

"How are things at the store? Oh, have I told you we have a new nephrologist at the dialysis center?"

I listened as he told me about his new kidney doctor, but my mind still hadn't moved on from his words earlier and what it had implied: that he might not have long to go, and I shouldn't take whatever short time I had with him for granted.

But most importantly: that he—and Oma—meant the world to me, and I would do anything in my power not to disappoint them both.

CHAPTER 4

Dragons, Unicorns, and Pokémon Are Not Real

Another day, another failed date to add to my increasingly laughable repertoire of Online Dates from Hell.

"Thanks for coming to get me, Jen." I pulled out a chair and slumped down in it. We were at the newly opened branch of Ellie's bakery, located along the strip of restaurants at the Waterfront, a popular tourist area facing the picturesque Port Benedict Bay. The place was full, but we managed to snag a table by the window. The sweet smell of baked goods and the stunning ocean backdrop gave me a chance to finally take a breath after the chaotic lunch I'd just had. "If you hadn't arrived when you did, I was ready to march into the restaurant's kitchen and grab a lighter to set myself on fire." I groaned. "Lesson learned, though. Never arrange a date on the same day my car is being serviced."

My ODOTD had met me at a popular, reasonably priced Thai restaurant for lunch, because I wasn't risking a repeat of the outrageously expensive date last weekend. He was polite, a theater buff, listed his karaoke skills as "the best way to a woman's heart" on his profile, and worked as a sports podiatrist (the thirty minutes

I spent researching him on Google confirmed it). Everything seemed to be going well, until it didn't.

My date had been distracted throughout the meal, and his eyes kept darting to the tables next to us. I thought it was only nerves, but as we were eating, he suddenly stood up, jumped onto his chair, and started belting out *Grease*'s "You're the One That I Want."

Off-key.

Obviously, the hours he'd put in at karaoke didn't do him any favors. Then, to my absolute horror, half the restaurant got up, too, and began dancing in a flash-mob formation. Sure, flash mobs are fun to watch, and I'd been known to belt out '80s and '90s pop tunes at karaoke every now and then. And while I appreciated the effort he'd gone through, it wasn't my most favorite way to spend the afternoon, because the other half of the restaurant had their phones up, filming the scene, and I was absolutely *mortified*. So I called Jenna while keeping the awkward smile on my face. She was loitering in a bookshop two blocks away, exactly for emergencies like this, and within a few minutes, had pulled up to the front of the restaurant. I fled the scene of the crime as the dancing crowd screamed the final note to thunderous applause from the other customers.

"No worries. You're not lighting yourself on fire on my watch." Jenna waved at Ellie, who was serving customers behind the counter. "What do you want? I'll order."

My phone vibrated in my back pocket. "Just an oat milk latte, please."

She went to place our orders while I pulled out my phone. It was a WhatsApp message from my grandfather, sharing a meme about commas saving lives instead of eating grandfathers. Then he proudly announced that his Instagram followers had been steadily climbing (currently sitting at 137) thanks to constant posts of his woodworking pieces, his gorgeous garden, and his strategic use of hashtags, before sending me a link to his latest reel. It even had lo-fi beats playing in the background, and the fact that he knew how to make one was mind-blowing, because I wouldn't even know where to start.

I reposted it to share with all of my twenty loyal followers (who were probably following him at this point anyway), then sent him a reply, reminding him I'd be shopping for groceries tomorrow, and for him to send a list of items he needed. The two blue checks appeared immediately, followed by an animated GIF of a dancing dog shouting, "Okay!"

"One oat milk latte." Jenna placed my coffee on the table.

"Thanks." I took a small sip of the hot liquid, relishing the warmth and comforting taste of coffee in my mouth.

"So. Back to square one, huh?"

"Yeah." I grimaced. "I need to change my strategy. No more online dates."

"At least he chose a great song." Jenna grinned. "Is your grandpa aware of these exceptionally charming men you've been seeing?"

"He doesn't need to know. He's only going to worry."

The front door swung open, and Rob and Alec strolled in. Alec went to find Ellie while Rob walked over to our table and pulled out the chair next to mine. He was wearing a charcoal-gray suit and a crisp black shirt, with what looked like a few days' worth of stubble on his jaw.

"Ladies." He gave us a nod, then grinned at me. "We must stop meeting like this, Kim. This is, what, twice in eight days? Not that I'm counting."

"Sounds like you are." I returned his grin. "Looking sharp, by the way. Got a hot date, or somewhere you need to be after this?"

"No. Went to a church wedding this morning."

Just then, Ellie and Alec came over. She gave me and Jenna a hug, then peered at me. "How was the lunch date?"

I made a face.

"Another one, huh?" Ellie shook her head in sympathy. "Is he alive? Do you need help hiding his body?"

"He's fine," Jenna replied. "He's probably auditioning for a lead role on Broadway as we speak." She was chuckling as she recounted the flash-mob story to the others.

"I thought you don't believe in happy endings," Rob said to me. "Why do you keep putting yourself through the trouble of going on dates with these awful men? Like that guy who made you pay for the entire dinner?"

Three pairs of curious eyes swiveled his way.

"How do you know she doesn't believe in happy endings, Rob?" Ellie propped her chin on her hands, as if she was settling in to hear an interesting story. "That sounds like particularly intimate knowledge to have of Kim. I didn't know you two were *that* friendly."

"More importantly, how did you know about her date making her pay for dinner?" Jenna hummed. "Is there something you both forgot to tell us?"

Oops. I told them about the date with Shane but didn't mention that Rob was there, too, because this was exactly what I was trying to avoid. Ever since Rob became single, Ellie and Alec had been blatantly trying to get the two of us together.

"Kim didn't tell you?" Rob was oblivious to my subtle headshakes. "I ran into her at the restaurant, and after her date, we had a nice heart-to-heart about happy endings and the joys of being in love. Or in her case, *not* being in love."

"But I'm not wrong, am I? You saw what my date did."

"Yeah, but now that I think about it, the guy did exude BDE, so I was surprised you didn't see it coming." Rob gave me a knowing nod when I raised my eyebrows. "Big Douchebag Energy. And you know who else oozes that same energy? Your ex. He looks like a self-important piece of work, and I'm not just saying that because he cheated on you."

"How do you know what her ex looks like?" Ellie's eyes widened. "Was Leo there, too?"

Okay, so I might have also skipped that part of the story. "There was nothing to tell. I ran into him and his fiancée, and Rob helped me escape. End of story."

"Fascinating," Alec said. "Never thought I'd hear the day that Kim Halim would need someone to save her."

"She didn't, really. She was getting up to leave anyway when I came over." Rob turned his attention back to me. "You haven't answered my question. If you don't believe in love, why do you make your life miserable by going on these dates?"

"Because I promised someone important to me that I'd try." I glanced at Ellie and Jenna, who knew about Oma's wishes. What they *didn't* know about was the inheritance clause, because I'd been too embarrassed to tell people about it, even my closest friends. I had considered telling them, more than once, but I never did, because of how humiliating it was to start with; and I knew they wouldn't have agreed with my approach. "My late grandmother wanted me to settle down, to find"—I made air quotes with my fingers—"'my one true love,' and I'm doing this to fulfill her request."

Ellie and Jenna began peppering me with questions about Leo, but Rob was quiet, his hazel eyes thoughtful as he watched me.

"I'm not sure I like that look on your face," I finally told him.

"This is my thinking face. It means I'm contemplating a brilliant, groundbreaking, Earth-shattering thought—"

I shook my head and kept a straight face. "It's not a good look on you."

"—and because I'm a generous human being, I'm willing to share my brilliant idea with you." He leaned forward, his entire body facing mine. "I can help you find your one true love."

"It was my grandmother who wanted me to find true love, not me, but go on."

"I don't know how my mom put up with my dad," Rob continued, "but despite their differences, they're still madly in love even after so many years. It's sickening sometimes. All my siblings have great partners, and, not to brag, but my longest relationship lasted a few years."

I drained my latte. "And are those things supposed to make you a relationship expert?"

"Maybe not, but they give me in-depth knowledge of what to look for in a potential partner, because I'm surrounded by happy, loving couples. So, here's what I'm thinking: I need to go to all these weddings in the next few months. I'm allowed to bring a plus-one, so why don't you come with me? I can introduce you to some single men there."

"What do you mean, 'all these weddings'?" I narrowed my eyes at him. "Let's be more specific. How many are we talking about?"

He silently counted off his fingers. "The one I went to this afternoon was wedding number five for the year, and it's only July. I was a groomsman for two of those, and best man for another one."

"Always the groomsman, never the groom," Ellie said.

"Yeah. Most of my friends seem to be in that phase where they're settling down and starting a family." Rob's eyes took on a wistful look. "Anyway, I still have another five to go to before the year ends."

I gave him a look that said, *You must be joking.*

"I'm dead serious. Weddings can be a great place to meet new people. And here's the best part: Not only can I introduce some eligible bachelors to you, but I can also help you avoid the weirdos and find the good ones. Guys with similar interests. I can curate a series of personalized dates, guaranteed to give you the greatest chance of finding your soulmate." He paused. "Maybe I can even change your mind and make you believe in happily-ever-afters."

"Nobody can, because they don't exist, just like dragons and unicorns and Pokémon."

"That's not a bad idea, Kim." Jenna turned to me. "Remember your disaster of a date earlier? And Shane and all those other guys? You need a new strategy. Just hear him out."

"Okay. Let's pretend for a moment that I agree to this ridiculous idea."

"Not ridiculous." Rob gave me a lopsided grin. "The word you're after is 'brilliant.'"

"Why are you offering? What's in it for you?"

"You'll be keeping me company, so I don't have to turn up alone to the weddings."

"There we go," I said. "Who's going to be there that you don't want to turn up alone?"

Rob was quiet for a moment, the wistful look back on his face, before answering, "Some of the couples are also friends with my ex. If they invited her as well, I'd prefer not to show up on my own."

"Sorry, but I'm not going to fake date you"—I gestured at Ellie and Alec—"like what these two did last year."

"I don't want to fake date you, either. I just want her to see that I've moved on."

"If you want that, it means you *haven't* moved on," I said.

"It doesn't matter whether I have or haven't," Rob said. "My point is, if you accompany me to those weddings, I can introduce you to some single guys."

I considered him. "What are your qualifications, though? Your success rate? Your methods? Why should I trust your so-called matchmaking services?"

Our friends were watching our exchange with rapt interest, their gazes going back and forth between us.

"First of all, I'm a builder, not a professional matchmaker," Rob said. "But I believe everyone deserves a happy ending. Even nonbelievers like you. And I've done this before. I introduced my brother, one of my sisters, and two cousins to their partners, so I know what I'm doing. It's the best kind of feeling when you know you've helped people meet their soulmates."

"How do I know you're not just making things up right now?"

"You can call my siblings and my cousins to check."

"For someone who believes in true love, your approach sounds awfully scientific," Ellie piped up. "What about the excitement and the butterflies in the stomach, those giddy, swoony moments of spontaneously meeting someone new? Wouldn't Kim be missing all that?"

I couldn't care less about butterflies and swoony moments, but I kept my mouth shut.

"Excellent point, Ellie." Rob beamed at her, as if he was a lecturer answering a question from one of his students. "It may seem scientific, but my approach gives Kim a higher chance of finding someone she can truly click with. People with shared interests are more likely to be attracted to each other, and that's where the giddy butterflies will happen. Don't worry, I'll make sure Kim gets her swoony moments."

I still wasn't convinced. "How can you be a matchmaker when you're single yourself?"

"The same way a wedding planner doesn't always have to be married. Or how an obstetrician doesn't always have to have kids. Or a dentist not pulling their own—"

"I get the idea." I didn't want to be intrigued, but I was. "But why should I believe that you can do what dating apps can't do? If their algorithms can't match me with the right person, what makes you think you can?"

"Those dating apps don't personally know those men in their database. But I personally know the guys I'll be introducing to you. I'll vouch for them, confirm they're not creeps, and make tailored recommendations to give you the best chance of finding someone. It's fail-proof."

Jenna did have a point. I needed a new strategy, and this could be it.

"It's worth a try," Ellie said. "What have you got to lose?"

"She's right." Rob gave me an easy grin. "Five weddings, that's all you need. You'll be doing me a huge favor, and I'll help you fulfill your grandmother's wishes while proving to you that happy endings do exist."

"Why is it so important to you, anyway?" I asked. "To prove that true love really exists?"

His face turned serious. "Because I think nobody should ever have to go through what you went through with your ex. One of my sisters was in the same boat once, and it did a huge number on her. It was heartbreaking to watch her go through the aftermath, and it took her a long time to heal and be able to trust someone again." He broke into a small smile. "Look, at the very least, you'll have five fun-filled afternoons guaranteed to wipe that frown off your face."

"It's not a frown. This is *my* thinking face."

"I'm convinced, Kim. It's your decision, but I'd go for it if I were you," Jenna said. "It sounds so much better than going on awful dates with weirdos you've just met online."

Rob *did* sound convincing, and I didn't have much time left. If I couldn't find anyone by the end of the two years, I'd have to give up the yarn store. And I couldn't let that happen. Plus, honestly, I was sick of wasting my time with so many less-than-subpar dates.

Give it a shot, a voice reasoned in my brain. *What other options do you have?*

None. I have no other options, because I'd rather gouge both my eyeballs out with pitchforks than endure another painful online date.

Then do it, the voice coaxed. *Go to the weddings and pick one man that's the least horrible of them all. Date him until the store is legally yours, then break up with him.*

Maybe this could work. At least I knew I wouldn't be wasting time going on one disastrous date after another, and the sooner I found someone to "settle down" with, the sooner I could get this entire ordeal over and done with.

My phone screen lit up, notifying me of a message in the dating app from ODOTD.

HAD A WONDERFUL TIME. TOO BAD YOU LEFT EARLY AND MISSED OUR ENCORE PERFORMANCE. DINNER TOMORROW? 😏 😉 😘

Good Lord. What was even the meaning of those emojis? Did he think the all-caps weren't clear enough to convey his enthusiasm?

See? That coaxing voice reappeared. *Do you really want to spend the next five and a half months jumping from one atrocious date to another?*

I glanced at Ellie and Jenna. "Is it crazy that I'm actually considering this?"

"Not at all." Ellie's face broke into a huge smile. "I think it'll be good for you."

"Just think of all the food at the weddings," Jenna said. "The music, the wine, the dancing. You'll have heaps of fun."

"Rob is an awesome wingman," Alec added. "He'll have your back."

"I am, and I will."

Do it for Oma and Opa.

"I might be out of my mind," I said. "But I'm in."

My friends whooped and cheered, while Rob grinned. "Awesome. I promise we're going to find your Mr. Right in no time."

CHAPTER 5

The Ideal Man Does Not Exist (or Does He?)

A few days later, I dragged my feet to what Rob had dubbed our first "strategic wedding meeting." He was already sitting inside Ellie's bakery, frowning at his laptop, when I stumbled in after lunch. I ordered an oat milk latte and low-carb banana bread, then walked over to his table.

"Give me one minute," he said, as I pulled out a chair and sat down. "Just finalizing a proposal for a prospective client."

"Sure. By the way," I said, "I called your siblings. It felt weird calling literal strangers to ask for matchmaking references, but I figured if I was going to invest the next few months of my life doing this, I owed it to myself to do my due diligence. Make sure you really are the awesome matchmaker you claim to be."

"I bet they told you that I'm super awesome."

"I think your brother said, 'Rob isn't as amazing as he thinks he is.'"

He tore his attention away from his screen, looking pained. "How dare he."

"But they did sing your praises and confirmed that you played a crucial role in introducing them to their partners. Your brother even got a bit sappy and repeatedly said he owed you his lifelong happiness or something like that. It was a bit hard to tell between his sobs."

"See?" He gave me a smug smirk. "Feel better now? Confident you're in safe hands?"

"The jury's still out." I sipped my latte. "Can we make this quick? We're running a knitting club this afternoon, then I have to pick up my grandfather from dialysis."

"This will take us less than an hour. I've got another meeting after this anyway. Okay, sent my proposal." Rob glanced at me, looking curious. "What do you usually make in the knitting club?"

"The people in the club make things like scarves, beanies, blankets, even sweaters and dresses sometimes. I don't make anything."

"Why not?" He raised his eyebrows. "Wait, do you even *know* how to knit?"

"I run a yarn store, Carmichael. Do I not look like someone who could knit?"

"Now that I think about it, you don't." Rob pointed at my cartoon dinosaur T-shirt, faded jeans, and scuffed white Converse. "You don't even look like someone who would *wear* what other people have knitted."

"Insulting, but accurate." I flashed him a grin. "My grandmother taught me how to knit from the tender age of nine, but to her dismay, it just wasn't one of my God-given talents."

"You're very close with your grandparents, aren't you?"

"They raised me. Since I was two."

"I think your grandfather might have followed me on social media," he said. "His profile picture had you in it. Is his name Thomas?"

"That's him. He's a budding social media influencer and content creator."

"I've seen some of his reels. They're pretty good. And you said he has dialysis?"

"On Mondays, Wednesdays, and Fridays. I drive him to and from his sessions. He isn't supposed to drive on dialysis days, because his blood pressure often drops very low after."

"So you're running a business, looking after your grandfather, and trying to find a partner in the meantime." He let out a low whistle. "You're one busy woman."

"I am. That's my talent. Juggling ten different things at once while being in twenty different places at the same time."

He chuckled, before turning serious. "I hope you don't mind me asking, but what about your parents?"

"That's a story for another time. Let's get this strategic meeting on the road."

He didn't push and returned his attention to his laptop. "Before we get started, I've put together a questionnaire to better match you with your perfect partner. It's the same questions I used with my siblings and cousins, to help us narrow down the type of person that would suit you best."

I was secretly impressed. "I wasn't expecting you to have an actual system and structure to all of this. You really are taking this seriously, aren't you?"

"I take everything in life seriously."

"How did you start doing this?" I tilted my head at him. "Did it start as a joke? Or a bet? Was it a side gig? Why matchmaking people, of all things?"

His eyes met mine. "I started doing it because of my sister. The one I told you about. After her partner cheated on her, she was in a very bad place for a really long time, and when she was finally ready to start dating again, I wanted to make sure the guys she was seeing were decent people. Not that she has terrible taste in men, but I felt like I had to do something to protect her, so she didn't have to go through the same ordeal. And it worked, because her current partner is one of the nicest men you'll ever meet and worships the ground my sister walks on."

"Oh." I didn't know why his reply gave me a fluttery feeling in my stomach. "That's not the answer I was expecting. I thought it'd be something . . . less serious."

"My dad would probably say the same thing. Anyway, you ready?"

This was the second time he'd made an offhand remark about his father. "Do I really have a choice?"

"No. Number one. What are you most passionate about?"

I knew the questions were supposed to help him find a suitable match for me. But even though I'd known him for a while, and he was Alec's best friend, I didn't know yet whether he could be trusted or not, so why should I open up and share my innermost thoughts with him?

I bit into my banana bread, trying to buy time. "I have a lot of interests. Don't know if I could pick just one."

"Don't think too hard about it. Tell me the first thing that pops into your mind."

"What about important things like my favorite color, my celebrity crush, or my go-to ice-cream flavor?"

"We'll get to that later. Just answer the damn question." But he was smiling.

"The environment." It wasn't exactly a lie, but it wasn't the truth, either, because I wasn't going to tell him that the only thing that mattered to me right now was looking after Opa and continuing Oma's business.

Rob raised his eyebrows, like he knew it wasn't a truthful answer, but typed it into his laptop anyway. "Any hobbies? Favorite sports? What do you enjoy doing in your spare time?"

"Fighting injustice and helping the oppressed." Again, important things, but not exactly what I did in my spare time, either.

"Nope." He shook his head. "Let's try again. If you went

through the trouble of calling my siblings because you didn't want to waste the next few months with a subpar matchmaker, then the least you can do is give me a serious answer. Don't you want this to work?"

He had a point. I needed this to work, which meant I had to start trusting him, even if just a little. It wasn't like I was handing over my heart and soul to him or to anyone else—that was something I would *never* do, ever again—I was only sharing tiny bits of information about myself, right? Plus, he got a bit personal with the story about his sister, so it was only right that I returned the favor.

"Fine. I like watching movies in my spare time, especially classics, in any genre. I also read a lot of fantasy. It gives me the chance to escape to a completely different world for a while. My favorite series is The Lord of the Rings, and I've probably read them at least ten times, cover to cover. My favorite sport is swimming, and I used to do it competitively when I was younger."

"You used to compete in swimming?" Rob paused his typing. "That's incredible. How old were you?"

"Started when I was eleven. I loved it, although it was a lot on my poor grandfather, because he was the one who had to drive me to the pool every morning at six for practice." I gave him a wistful smile. "Then the training hours got a bit too much, because I was helping my grandmother after school at the store, too, and I wasn't really winning a lot of events anyway. So I slowly lost interest in it and quit when I was fourteen."

"Still an amazing achievement for a teenager," he said. "The only thing I did competitively at that age was probably racing video games with my brother."

I chuckled. "Anyway, what else do you need to know? Oh, I have probably more funny coffee mugs than I'll ever need. I'm a huge fan of ramen, sushi, and bubble teas. There. Is my answer good enough?"

"Great." He kept typing. "What are the most important things you're looking for in a partner? Describe your ideal man, or woman, for me."

"The ideal man doesn't exist."

"Humor me. If you were to custom-build a partner, what qualities would you give him?"

"How long do you have? Because we might be here for a while." At the exasperated look on his face, I grinned. "Okay. He needs to have confidence, kindness, and a great sense of humor. Hard-working. Trustworthy. Someone I could feel safe with, who'd have my back in all kinds of situations. Someone who understands that I come as a package with my grandfather, and if I had to choose between my grandfather and whoever my partner is, I wouldn't hesitate to kick my partner to the curb without a second thought."

He looked up at me, and I thought I saw something closely resembling approval in his eyes. "He's very lucky to have you as a granddaughter."

And because I'd given him a bigger glimpse into my life than I probably should, I decided to mess with him a little. "He must also be a good cook, since I'm not, and I want to be served breakfast in bed every morning. Must be fit, with a six-pack, just as long as he's not a gym rat, because I couldn't tolerate another one after Leo."

Rob had gone back to typing notes on his laptop. "Mm-hmm."

"Being smoking hot wouldn't hurt. Fantastic in bed, because there's nothing worse than bad sex. Debt-free, asset-rich, has a sizable investment portfolio." I thought of other ridiculous requirements I could throw at him. "Finally, must be exceptionally intelligent. I prefer him to have, or at least be working toward, a doctorate."

"Is that all?"

"That's it for now." I popped the last piece of my banana bread into my mouth. "You think that's achievable?"

"I don't know. I stopped taking notes after 'breakfast in bed.'" He scanned his questionnaire. "Next: How would your friends describe you? Serious answers only, please."

"This is starting to feel like a job interview. Am I secretly interviewing for a role in your business? Because I've already got my hands full with the yarn store, and I'm trying to stop job-hopping, thank you very much."

"What do you mean, job-hopping?" He slid me a curious look. "How long have you been running the store for, anyway?"

"A year and a half, and it's probably the longest I've ever stayed in one role."

Rob went back to his laptop and muttered as he typed, "Has commitment issues."

"I just haven't found my niche, is all." I could hear the defensiveness in my tone.

"What other jobs have you done in the past? It might be useful to know, so we could find someone with a shared experience."

"You name it, I've probably done it." I started to check things off my fingers. "A barista, a waitress, a pool lifeguard, a photographer's assistant, worked in a call center, and a brief stint as a morning radio announcer." At the baffled look on his face, I paused. "Should I stop? Because I can still go on, and I'm not even joking."

"Please continue. At least you're telling the truth this time."

"I've been an office receptionist, a cinema operator, a dog walker, and a nanny. Did seven months as a property stylist."

His gaze turned curious. "A property stylist, huh?"

"There were several others, but I can't remember them all. Oh! I was an assistant zookeeper once, but three weeks in, I quit when they rostered me to work in the snake enclosure." A shiver went through me at the memory. "And no, I don't have a negative childhood experience with snakes. I'm sorry if you're a snake lover, but they're just not for me."

"But why did you change jobs so often? Because you didn't know what you wanted to do with your life?"

The answer was probably deeper than what I was willing to share with him right now. "I thought I did, but things change. People and plans change."

"Okay." He glanced at his laptop. "Things your friends would say about you."

Relieved that he didn't press further, I decided I owed him a real answer this time. "They'd call me loyal and supportive. I can be a bit too blunt sometimes, but I've also been known to be the first to lend a hand whenever someone needed help."

"Name two things for which you are most thankful."

"My health. My family and friends."

Rob asked me a few more questions before finally nodding with satisfaction. "That should do it. Let's move on to the dossier."

"The *what now*?"

Instead of answering, he shifted his laptop so the screen was facing me, then tapped open a presentation. My eyebrows shot up toward my hairline as my jaw slowly lowered. It was a thorough rundown of the first wedding we were attending, with information on the bride, the groom, the bridal party, and separate profiles for each potential date.

"Now, obviously we don't have enough time to find you candidates at the first wedding based on your answers, since it's only a few days away, but that will help us with the second one. The guys on this dossier might not be specifically based on the questionnaire, but they're still good men that I know will be attending the wedding, and I've known most, if not all of them, for at least a few years."

I quickly scrolled through the presentation, and he'd covered everything: basic facts on each man—education, hobbies, occupation—and deeper, more detailed information, including history of their past relationships, likes and dislikes, which sports teams they support. There were pictures, lists of social media handles, and links to online interviews and articles.

"This seems a bit excessive. A tad stalkerish, even."

"It's not," Rob said. "It's called being prepared. I have a template from the ones I did for my siblings and cousins, and I already know some of the basic info, so it was just a matter of filling in the gaps that I didn't know, and those were easily found online. There might be overlaps, by the way, since some of these guys might also be at the other weddings."

I glanced at the screen again, and panic started to claw its way around my insides. "Tell me again how you're qualified for this. One long-term relationship and you're suddenly Cupid's prodigy? Why aren't *you* looking for a relationship yourself?"

"Because I'm taking a break from relationships right now, but I know what to look for in a partner." He pointed at the presentation on his screen. "I guarantee these are genuinely nice guys who wouldn't stiff you with a dinner check or shatter your heart into pieces."

My guilt nagged at me. He didn't want to introduce me to someone who might break my heart, but he didn't know that *I* had every intention of breaking someone else's heart. Should I be upfront about my real reason for doing this?

No. Not until I knew how much I could trust him.

I settled for a vague response. "I don't have the best track record when it comes to relationships. Even if I do start dating one of these guys, I don't know how long it'll last."

"You won't know until you try."

"Are you always this optimistic about everything?" I raised an eyebrow at him. "They're your friends. Are you not disturbed by the possibility that I might crush their hearts into tiny little pieces?"

"They're big boys. They can look after themselves."

"So you're saying you're heartless."

"I'm sensible," he said. "They're all adults. Successful, well-rounded, intelligent men. They should know there might be risks to meeting a smart, beautiful woman and possibly falling in love with her. If their hearts do get broken, they'll survive."

"Did you just call me smart and beautiful?" I cocked my head at him, ignoring the sudden somersault in my stomach. "What's with the compliments?"

He shrugged. "Because it's the truth. Anyway, here's the low-down on this weekend's ceremony." He scrolled back to the first slide. "Gracie Platt and Jayden Lee are childhood sweethearts. They have a best man, three groomsmen, a maid of honor, and three bridesmaids."

I gave an admiring murmur when a picture of a gorgeous man appeared on the next slide.

"First candidate. Tony Bailey, thirty-nine, Jayden's best man. He's a criminal defense attorney, and the youngest partner at his firm. Oldest of four boys, grew up Catholic, served as an altar boy when he was younger. Hard worker, smart, and volunteers what little free time he has at his local youth center."

"He sounds like a saint." A hot saint, if there was such a thing. Dark hair, deep-blue eyes, piercing gaze. On paper, perfect. A good-looking, successful man I could date for a few months.

"Hold your horses, we're not done yet. Single guy number two is one of the groomsmen. Spencer Au, thirty-six. He's a financial advisor and has a string of prestigious letters to his name: CA, CFA, CFP, and MBA. Two younger sisters, both married, so his parents have been pressuring him to find someone and start producing grandchildren to carry on the family name."

"Not sure I'm ready to start procreating, but he's cute."

"He rows and plays football, so he's fit. Isn't that one of your requirements?"

I gave a reluctant nod. "It is."

"Next candidate. Seriously, I think you've been looking in all the wrong places, because you're so spoiled for choice right now. Oscar Perez, thirty." A photo of a devastatingly handsome man appeared on the screen. "An actor, one of Jayden's childhood buddies. Had a small role in that hit Netflix action comedy everyone raved about last year. The guy sings, dances, and writes poetry. He's into rock climbing, has a black belt in jiujitsu, and hikes on the weekends. Takes his parents to all his movie sets, so he's close with his family. He's the complete package."

"We can cross him out."

"We can?" Rob raised his eyebrows. "Why?"

"Because he's an actor, so he must have a long line of gorgeous people who are throwing themselves at his feet."

"That might be true, but he's looking for someone outside the industry, who doesn't care about his fame."

"Still, I'd probably go mad hanging around someone that active. I don't even have time for real exercise because restocking the fluffy piles of yarn at the store every week is already strenuous enough."

"Fine. That brings us to the last candidate. Ben Tran, twenty-nine. He's a vet and runs his own clinic, so you can bond over your time working at the zoo. And, get this: He put himself through college by working as a swimming instructor." He beamed at me, looking very pleased with himself. "See how many things you have in common?"

I studied the face on the screen. Ben looked exactly like the kind of guy I could take home to introduce to my grandfather. Tall, a friendly smile, and intelligent brown eyes. Someone kind, who looked like he wouldn't hurt a fly. Someone safe.

Someone I could probably trust, if my circumstances were different.

"Here's what I suggest you do: Study the dossier in your own time, then decide which man you think would be the best fit. I've prepared some date ideas tailored to each candidate based on their personalities, a few conversation starters, and first-date questions to help you get to know them better."

"You seriously did all this?"

"Prepared it after work last night."

"I don't know whether to be afraid or impressed. Either you're a deranged, closeted stalker, or you have too much free time on your hands."

"Neither. I'm just very thorough. I leave no stones unturned. What do you think?"

He'd done the work, like he'd promised. The men he'd suggested were all viable options, people my grandparents would be happy to see me "settle down" with, and definitely a huge improvement from all the weirdos I'd found online.

"You can personally vouch for these guys?"

"A hundred percent. I would never have suggested douchebags."

Maybe this could work after all. "Let me study the dossier tonight."

"Awesome." Rob whipped out his phone and tapped his Calendar app. "I'll send you the dates of the weddings. Let's meet again on Friday for a follow-up. In the meantime, have fun going through those profiles."

CHAPTER 6

Don't You Dare Stand in the Way of Progress

Nicole was serving a customer when I walked into the yarn store after the briefing with Rob. "Oh, you're back." She quickly looked up from the register. "A courier just delivered a letter for you. It's in the office."

I thanked her and went into the tiny office at the back of the store. It still had my grandmother's touch all over it: On the wall were her framed economics degree from Universitas Indonesia and a large cross-stitch piece depicting the sunrise at Mount Bromo, one of the most active volcanoes in East Java. On her desk were a framed photo of her, Opa, and me, taken the day I graduated from college; the large yellow mug she used as a pen holder next to it; and her old monitor screen rounding out the ensemble. I'd been using my laptop to keep the books for the store, but I couldn't bring myself to get rid of Oma's ancient computer just yet.

My attention immediately caught on the large brown envelope on the desk, covering Oma's old keyboard. I tore it open, and my eyes got increasingly wider as I read the contents.

It was a letter from Goodwin Property Group, the property giant that owned Port Benedict Plaza and a few of the storefronts on our strip, expressing an interest in purchasing our shop. The letter explained that Goodwin was in the process of buying all the stores in our precinct, with a view to tear them down and build a multipurpose high-rise building in their place, that would home a boutique hotel, luxury apartments, and prestigious office spaces. They had just finished a revamp of Port Benedict Plaza a few months ago, and by buying all of us out, they were hoping to bring our strip of shops in line with the modern aesthetics of the Plaza. It was apparently a collaboration between Goodwin and the local government, as part of the Port Benedict Urban Renewal Project, which aimed to beautify the city.

There was another line or two about progress and moving toward a better future, but I was already too baffled to register the words.

The legend on the street was that this area had started off as a tiny cluster of shops many years ago, slowly growing larger, until Goodwin bought the vacant land behind our strip of shops and built a massive shopping center around a decade ago. It had provided thousands of new jobs, brought lots of international big-name brands into the city, and turned Port Benedict Plaza into the premier shopping and lifestyle destination that it was known as today. Our quiet precinct at the back of the Plaza was left untouched, so all the shops still retained the old brick buildings, keeping our quaint, charming, rustic vibe. It was common knowledge that in the past year or so, whenever there was a shop front on our strip that had gone up for sale, Goodwin had been quick to snap up the property, and now I knew why—this had been their plan the entire time.

The letter was quick to assure that Goodwin was willing to buy our property at 15 percent above the market price, and the project wasn't expected to start until early next year, so it should, according to the letter, give business owners ample time to plan their next move.

Next move?

There was no next move, because I wasn't even going to consider the offer. This wasn't in the plan. The plan was for me to inherit the yarn store and continue running it, so I could keep my grandmother's legacy alive and earn enough money to help Opa with his medical expenses. The plan was *not* for some big property developer to buy and demolish the place that had been here my entire life and rebuild it into an ugly, soulless high-rise devoid of any charm or personality while destroying my grandmother's hard work and memories in the process.

Nope. I wasn't selling, and that was that.

I was about to crumple the letter and toss it into the trash when my phone vibrated, and Ellie's number flashed on the screen.

"Kim! Did you get the letter from Goodwin? Tell me you're not thinking of selling."

"Don't worry. I'm not."

"Good. My landlord isn't selling, either. But Selma told me the antique store owner next to her bookshop is planning to sell. He's retiring, and Goodwin's offer was too good to turn down. He said he'd be a fool to say no."

"That's not good." My hands tightened around my phone. "He might not be the only one thinking of accepting the offer."

"I don't blame him, though," Ellie said. "Ever since they renovated the Plaza, I've heard some store owners complaining that things have been quieter. I'm sure there are others who are thinking of selling. And the businesses renting their shops from Goodwin won't have a say. They'll have no choice but to relocate elsewhere."

And if the majority of the owners caved in and accepted the offer, it would back me into a corner and I might eventually be forced to sell, too.

"Didn't Alec have some business dealings with Goodwin last year?" I asked. "Is there any way he can help?"

"He did. Alec knows the owner pretty well. I've met her a few times, and she's lovely. I'll see if we can reach out to her and talk about this."

"Let's do that. We should also set up a meeting with other businesses in the area," I said. "We can't be the only ones worried about this. See if anyone has any thoughts on how to tackle this problem."

"Good idea. The more people in the community are involved, the better."

We hung up after a few minutes, but something she said gave me a spark of an idea.

I flipped open my laptop and got to work. I had to do a bit of research before trying to get the other shop owners on board with my idea.

Because there was no way I was letting Oma's legacy be taken from me without a fight.

CHAPTER 7

Everyone Is Perfect in Their Own Way

I didn't want to say anything to Nicole about Goodwin's letter, but she somehow found out anyway, and by Friday morning, just two days later, almost all our regulars had heard about it. I'd done almost nothing the entire day but field calls from customers wanting to clarify the rumors: that we were closing down this weekend, that we were relocating the store across the country, and that all our stock was marked down 50 percent because of the impending move. But mostly, people were concerned because they all said the Yarn Fanatics had been a big part of their lives.

I'd been worried when I first took over the business, because my grandmother's regular customers were used to her warmth, her upbeat personality, and her in-depth knitting knowledge. When I stepped in, none of them were too impressed with the fact that my knitting skills weren't up to scratch. Oma could make cable-knit sweaters and beautiful knee-length dresses and crochet all kinds of cute mini animals, whereas I'd have to consult patterns just to make scarves and beanies—something she could probably have done with her eyes closed. The sad truth was that I was light-years away from being anywhere as good a knitter as my grandmother. I didn't have the patience for it, and as a little girl, the novelty of pretending to be A Very Important Adult managing a store and dealing with customers had been far more exciting than counting how many rows of knit stitches I'd worked on.

But over time, even though I hadn't gotten better at knitting or crocheting, I had—somehow—won her regulars over. Or maybe it was her regulars who had won *me* over, because I hated the thought of having to tell Melly, Selma, Anahita, or the other members of our knitting clubs that we might have to close our doors permanently. And the gravity of the situation loomed like a guillotine over my head: The threat of having to close down my grandmother's store—her legacy—was more than real, and if I didn't do something to save it, the inevitable would happen.

Just then, the bell over the front door jingled, interrupting my train of thought. A young teenage girl wearing a floral summer dress walked in, her eyes darting across the store as if she was searching for something.

Nicole looked up from where she was restocking the shelves. "Hello. Can I help you?"

"Yes, please." The girl brightened. "I'm planning to make the love of my life fall for me by crocheting him a wristband. He's the best tennis player in the world, and it'll be the perfect birthday gift for him."

I glanced at her and raised my eyebrows—even though I knew I wasn't supposed to—in a totally judgmental way. "Um, did you say the *love of your life*?"

The girl nodded, barely able to contain her enthusiasm. "He's my soulmate."

Nicole gave me a pointed look, as if saying, *Shut up and let me handle this*. "Of course. Have you done any crocheting before?"

The girl's eyes twinkled with excitement. "No, but I've watched lots of video tutorials, and by the power of my love for him, I'm confident I'll learn in no time."

Yikes. Had no one ever told her that soulmates and true love weren't real, but tales—nay, *lies*—spun by storytellers, hopeless romantics, and corporate sharks to dupe people into parting with their hard-earned money? (Valentine's Day, anyone? Biggest scam in the entire universe.)

But Nicole was unfazed.

"You absolutely will. It's very simple. If you run into any trouble, feel free to come back into the store and we can help you out." She offered the girl a friendly smile. "I'll show you what you need to get started."

I watched as Nicole expertly—and very kindly, in a nonjudgmental way—explained to the girl which hooks and yarn she needed to get. The woman was a godsend, because the contrast of my response to hers was oceans apart. I could handle the administrative side of the store, but she knew the place like the back of her hand, and on the days I had to drive Opa to dialysis, it was a relief knowing the store was in her capable hands. Twenty minutes later, the girl was beaming as she bounced out of the store with her brand-new crocheting supplies.

"I don't know what I'd do without you, Nicole." I gave the older woman a grateful smile. "Promise me you'll never leave."

"Never. I love this place." A sad smile crossed her face. "Emilia was always so kind to me and my family. She was always flexible with schedules, so understanding whenever I had to leave early for family emergencies. That's why I could never bring myself to look for another job, because no other employer would be as supportive." Nicole reached out to squeeze my hands. "I'm so glad you're continuing the business. She worked so tirelessly for this place, and it's wonderful to know her hard work isn't going to be wasted. I really miss her."

I swallowed the lump in my throat and gritted my teeth to stop the tears that were threatening to flood my eyes. My grandmother had been gone for eighteen months, but that didn't make the pain any easier to deal with. I still found myself going into my old WhatsApp thread with her sometimes, wanting to tell her about my day, or to listen to her messages just to hear her familiar, comforting voice. I'd never known a time when she wasn't around, and the fact that she was no longer in my life often felt like I was in a horrible dream I couldn't wake up from. "Me too, Nic."

And this was yet another reason why I needed to fight for the store, because Nicole still depended on it for her livelihood.

The shop bell jingled again, and Nicole whistled under her breath when she glanced at the front door.

"Who is that, and where do I sign up for one?"

I quickly composed myself and followed her gaze to see Rob strolling into the shop. He had on dark jeans and a white T-shirt, with his hands shoved deep in his pockets as his curious gaze wandered around the space, taking in the wooden shelves stocked full of colorful yarn.

"Seriously? He's probably your daughter's age."

"Exactly." Nicole chuckled. "She's just separated from her partner. Maybe I could get his number for her. I wonder if he's single."

I shouldn't be bothered by what she'd said, because I loved Nicole like she was my own family, but I was, and the fact that I was even bothered was disturbing in itself, because why on Earth would I be? "He is. You're in luck."

Nicole eyed me with curiosity. "You know who he is?"

"I do."

She swallowed her next question, as Rob walked up to us just then.

"Hey, Kim." He nodded at me, then gave Nicole a friendly smile. I could almost see the cogs in her brain working overtime, sprinting ahead to plan his wedding to her daughter and naming their horde of unborn children.

"You're early. Didn't we say a quarter to six?"

"I finished a job earlier than I thought. No need to rush, I can wait." He jerked a thumb over his shoulder to indicate the front of the store. "Did you come up with that pun outside?"

This week's offering was OUR KNITTING CLUBS ARE SEW MUCH FUN, YOU'LL BE HOOKED! INQUIRE IN-STORE TODAY, BECAUSE TIME AND YARN WAIT FOR NO ONE.

"I did." I gave him a proud grin. "You like it?"

"Loved it." He grinned back. "It's pretty punny. Sorry, that was the best I could come up with. By the way, did you realize the handle on your front door is a bit loose?"

"I know." I made a face. "It's been on my to-do list for a while, but I just haven't had the time to tackle it."

"I can grab my toolbox from the car and fix it right now if you want. It'll take me five, ten minutes while I wait for you to finish."

"Oh." I wasn't expecting that. "Thank you, that would be so helpful."

Nicole was standing next to me, listening to our conversation while giving me a not-so-subtle nudge. "Rob, this is Nicole, my grandmother's most trusted employee," I said. "Rob is the builder who worked on Ellie's shop last year."

She shook his hand, recognition in her eyes. "Of course. I didn't recognize you without that neon-orange safety vest you usually wear."

"Nicole's daughter is single. She wants to get your number for her."

Rob narrowed his eyes at me, as if saying, *Really? You're throwing me under the bus?*

"Really." I grinned at him. "Nic, go ahead and tell him about her."

Before she could launch into a spiel about her daughter, Rob gave her an apologetic smile. "I'm flattered, and I'm sure your daughter is wonderful, but I'm not looking for a relationship right now." He gave me a side-eye. "As Kim already knows."

I returned his glare with an innocent *Who, me?* look. A part of me felt bad for a crestfallen Nicole, but a tiny part was also clapping with approval at his gentle rebuff.

Choosing not to overanalyze that thought, I began to balance the register, while Nicole vacuumed the store and Rob went to fix the door handle. The cool summer evening greeted us as we stepped out of the store, and as we waved goodbye to Nicole, I could hear the faint sounds of live music from the rooftop entertainment area at Port Benedict Plaza.

"I skipped lunch, so I'm starving," I said. "How long is this strategic wedding meeting going to take? Can we do it over dinner?"

He cocked an eyebrow at me. "Are you asking me on a date?"

"Save it, Carmichael." I smirked at him. "Your flirtatious banter might work on other girls, but not me."

"Is that so?" He gave me a slow smile, and I wondered if it was the breeze or that grin that made me shiver a little. "Anything I can do to change your mind?"

"I might have to get back to you on that."

"Make sure you do." His smile got bigger, and I decided that it was definitely *not* the breeze. "Anyway, the purpose of tonight's meeting is to help you get ready for the wedding. I thought we could pay a quick visit to the hairdresser, and if you need any help, we can also choose your dress for tomorrow."

I stopped walking. "You mean like a makeover?"

He stopped with me. "If that's what you want to call it."

"No. We never agreed to any makeovers. I'm due for a trim, but other than that, I'm perfectly happy the way I currently am. And I don't need to buy fancy new dresses, because my closet at home is already overflowing as it is." Mostly with comfortable tops and jeans, but what he didn't know wouldn't hurt him.

"Yes, of course you're already perfect the way you are." Rob's tone was patient, as if he was persuading a toddler with a tantrum to calm down. "We're only going to make you look prettier and even more desirable for your potential partners. A trim sounds great, then maybe we can have a look at the dresses you have at home. *If* you want to." He twirled his hand and gave me a bow. "I'm here at your service."

"On one condition."

A curious smile lifted the corners of his mouth. "Let's hear it."

"I'll do it if you're also getting a haircut. If I'm going to be stuck at the hairdresser for an hour or so, the least you can do is keep me company."

"Is that all?" The smile turned into a huge grin. "From the look on your face, I thought you were going to ask me to jump through hoops of fire, or walk around the Waterfront in my underwear, or some other equally outrageous demand."

Out of nowhere, a high-resolution image of him wearing nothing but snug boxer briefs suddenly sashayed through my brain. *Crap*. Of course I'd never seen Rob in just his underwear or even shirtless in real life, but that tiny insignificant detail didn't stop my imagination from running rampant. I couldn't unsee the image now, no matter how many times I shook my head to dislodge it, because it had latched itself onto the apparently thirsty neurons in my brain. The only way I could probably remove it from their tight clutches was if I drove myself to the nearest hospital and begged the first neurosurgeon I could find to surgically eliminate those treacherous brain cells from existence.

"Kim? Did you hear me? Why are you shaking your head?"

"I'm, uh, tired. Feeling lethargic. Shaking my head keeps me awake." I mentally cringed. *That* was the best I could come up with?

"So honored my charming self is keeping you captivated."

"Barely." I avoided looking at him, because the mental image of him in his underwear was still in my mind, smugly strutting down an imaginary catwalk. And if I so much as glanced at him, I'd probably lose the plot by either laughing hysterically or demanding he strip down to his boxer briefs so I could compare my mental image with the real thing, before proceeding to drown him with my uncontrollable drool.

Damn it. I needed to get ahold of myself.

We grabbed a quick bite to eat, then went to my usual hairdresser, a small but popular Korean hair and beauty salon. I'd been coming to this place ever since I moved back to Port Benedict, and every single time, I always asked for the same thing—a trim and a highlight. Rob was ushered to the chair next to mine, and by the time our hairdressers were done, my hair had been trimmed a few inches, layered, and partially highlighted, while Rob's was styled into a neat, simple short cut.

"Well," I said, as my hairdresser took the barber cape off with a flourish, and I swiveled the chair in Rob's direction, "what do you think?"

He swept a slow gaze over my face. "You look great. The brown highlights bring out the color of your eyes."

My cheeks grew warm at his words. "You don't look so bad yourself."

"So." Rob gave me a curious look as we stepped out of the salon and walked toward the parking lot. "Have you finished reading the dossier? Decided who you're going to focus your efforts on?"

"Leaning toward Ben. He seems nice, and like you said, we have a lot in common."

"Good choice. Did you have a chance to look at the first date ideas? There's kayaking, paddleboarding, or sailing. Since, you know, he used to be a swimming instructor. Or if you prefer non-water-based activities, there's also mini golf, yoga, or axe throwing."

"We can go to Melly's yoga studio," I said. "Wait, he can't, that's women only. Axe throwing sounds good, too. I've never tried that. It might come in handy if the date doesn't go well. I can fling the axe at him and be done with it."

"You'd also be done with life." He thought for a second. "Let me make myself clear here: Bailing you out of jail isn't included in my services, okay?"

"That's mean." I gave him a sad pout. "True friends would bail each other out of jail."

"I'll come and visit, though," he said. "What about mini golf? That's always fun. Have you played before?"

"I haven't." That was a half lie, because even though I'd never played mini golf before, I'd briefly worked as a caddy back in college.

"Are you serious?" He gaped at me, looking scandalized. "It's heaps of fun. Perfect for first dates. You've seriously never played?"

I bit back a grin. "I promise, I've never played mini golf in my entire life."

"Unacceptable." Rob glanced at his watch. "If we hurry, we might be able to squeeze in a game or two. Let's go. We're going mini golfing."

I gaped at him. "Right *now*?"

"Yes. I'm gonna show you how it's done."

CHAPTER 8

If You're Not Keeping Score, What Even Is the Point?

The aim of the game is to finish the round in as few strokes as possible. There are nine numbered holes, and you need to complete each hole in order, without skipping any."

"As few strokes as possible, got it. Do I hold the club with my left or my right hand?"

That earned me a disgusted look. "You're joking, right?"

I popped my eyes wide. "Absolutely not."

Rob sighed. "You hold it with both hands. Your dominant hand is in front of your nondominant one. Like this." He gripped the end part of his club with his right hand, then placed his left one above it. "Every stroke counts as a point, and the player with the least strokes at the end wins. You're only allowed six strokes per hole before you must move on to the next one."

"Got it." I twirled my putter with my hand. "Those folks are moving on, so it's our turn now. Why don't you start us off and show me how it's done?"

We were at Ace Adventure Golf Park, a popular mini golf place half an hour outside of town. It was still bright at seven thirty, perfect to enjoy the outdoor course we'd chosen, that was winding and twisting around miniature man-made lakes, waterfalls, and sand pits. The place was buzzing, full of couples on dates and young families with excited kids. A family of five ahead of us had just finished the first hole, so we stepped up to take our turn.

"Watch and learn." Rob placed his red golf ball at the end of the green, then gripped his putter and bestowed his full concentration on it, as if that would help him score a hole in one. The ball slid smoothly on the green, before teetering on the edge of the hole, and finally falling in with a soft *plunk*.

"Impressive."

He suppressed a smile, trying his best to look modest but failing miserably. "Your turn."

"It's a lot of pressure. Don't know if I can live up to that excellent shot."

"You will, with practice. Here, I'll show you how to do the proper stance." He stepped behind me and placed his hands on my hips. "Good posture is the key. Try to keep your feet at least a foot apart, lining up with your shoulders. Use a putting stroke, which means you need to keep your swing below your waist and hit the ball with a firm yet smooth stroke."

Theoretically, I knew what to do. I'd watched enough golfers during my short caddying career and played myself several times, so golf stances and putting strokes weren't foreign, unfamiliar terms. But all my prior knowledge seemed to have mysteriously evaporated into thin air, and all I could focus on was how he was standing so close, with his annoyingly warm hands on my body, and how I was enjoying this a little more than I was supposed to.

Get a grip, Kim. You know better than to fawn over a cute guy with warm hands.

"Back up a little, Carmichael. Not too close. I got it." I aimed for the hole and swung my putter. The club hit the ball with a soft *thwack*, before smoothly sliding into the first hole. "Look at that! A hole in one. Are we keeping score?"

Rob was gaping at the hole, as if it had somehow sprouted an invisible hand that had reached out and pulled my ball into it. He gave me an accusing look. "You've played before, haven't you?"

"Well, I did use to caddy back in college . . ."

He scoffed. "Then hell yes, we're keeping score."

We ambled to the second hole, where the family of five was still playing, and the father was helping one of the children with their shot. Rob was watching the dad and the child with a smile, chuckling to himself when the little girl cheered each time her putter managed to even gently tap the ball.

"She reminds me of my niece and nephews," he said. "I know I'm biased, but they're just the most adorable kids you'll ever meet."

"How many have you got? You never told me about your family."

"One niece, two nephews." He glanced at me. "Didn't I? That I have five older siblings?"

"Yeah, but you never told me about your relationship with them. And your parents. Are you all close? Do you talk to them a lot?"

Rob stiffened a little. "Why do you want to know about my parents?"

His offhand remarks about his father popped back into my mind. "I'm sorry. You don't have to answer if you're uncomfortable. It's just that, I love hearing people talk about their big families, because I've never had that. Ellie and Jenna are the closest I have to sisters, so I'm always jealous of people with a lot of siblings."

"You can have mine. They're adults now, but they're still annoying." Rob smirked. "But no, I don't mind talking about them."

His eyes were back watching the laughing family in front of us. "I talk a lot to my mom and siblings. Alexandra, the oldest, is a retired athlete, and now hosts a podcast about women in sports. Amanda is a screenwriter. She's about to write and direct her first movie, a romance murder mystery set in the 1950s."

"Ooh." I whistled. "I'll watch that."

"My dad had wanted to continue with the 'A' names, but my mother vetoed the idea. Jennifer is a fashion designer, and she just launched her newest clothing line earlier this year. Kylie is the smartest of us all. She's the youngest adjunct professor of science in her department and has authored more than a hundred academic papers. Paul is only fifteen months older than me and is the CEO of a fintech startup."

"Your siblings sound super intimidating."

"Tell me about it. My mom's an interior designer, and my dad's an architect. So was my grandfather, who had started the family business. Carmichael Architects used to be one of the oldest, most well-respected architecture and design firms this side of the country."

The young family had just finished their turn, so we stepped up for our shots, and Rob motioned for me to go first.

"But things haven't been going so well lately. Dad used to run it with his sister, until my aunt retired a few years ago. She didn't have any kids, so it was down to me and my siblings to continue the firm, but none of us are interested in getting involved."

"But isn't what you're doing still in the same industry?" I tapped the golf ball lightly with my club, and it slid smoothly down the green directly into the hole. I smirked at the crestfallen look on his face. "Are you regretting asking me to mini golf?"

"Not at all. I'm just getting warmed up." He placed his ball on the ground. "Anyway, my dad had always wanted me to continue the family business, because he thought I could use a bit of direction in my life."

I frowned. "Why? What were you doing that he thought was directionless?"

Rob hit the ball and was quiet for a few beats before answering. "I dropped out of my architecture degree. Second year."

"I didn't know that."

"It's not something I go around telling people about." His laugh was dry as we headed to the next hole. "It's kind of embarrassing when the rest of your family is achieving great things left and right, while I was still trying to figure out my life, you know? And Lucy—she's my ex—she and her family used to always say that I had more to offer. That I don't take my life seriously enough. They think I should go back and finish my degree."

"But you don't need fancy degrees to be successful. There are people who dropped out of college and still did well in life."

"Yeah, but I mean, I *am* the least successful one out of all my siblings." His face was unreadable as he watched the parents in front of us cheering on their children. "I spent my entire childhood"—he paused to shake his head—"no, actually, my entire *life* having my dad compare me to them. Being told I wasn't as smart. Two of my sisters were always top of their classes, and my other siblings were always winning an award or two. I never did, because I was too busy goofing off and joking around instead of burying my nose in a book.

"Long story short, that's why I'd gone into architecture. Because I wanted to make my dad proud. But my heart just wasn't in it, so I decided to quit." The family of five moved on, and Rob thwacked the ball with a steely glint in his eyes that probably had nothing to do with mini golf. "Dad never forgave me for that. Not even today, even after more than ten years. I think he considers me a disgrace to the family, because I'm the only one without a degree and who hasn't had an article or ten written about me somewhere. For him, a college degree is an important measure of success, and dropping out of college meant I was a quitter and a failure who had let everyone in the family down."

"That's unfair." A white-hot surge of anger passed through me. I wouldn't call my own father parent of the year, but at least he never belittled me or my life choices (probably because he was never around). "You're not a failure because you chose your own path instead of doing what your father wanted you to. Does the fact that you have your own business mean nothing to him?"

"Absolutely nothing." His golf ball rolled into the hole with a satisfying *plunk*. "I'm actually working on a house flip with Alec. You know, buying old houses, then renovating and reselling them. We're about to finish the work on our first one."

"Rob! That's impressive."

"I'm not just a pretty face, you know." He gave me a small smile as I took my turn. "Dad isn't impressed, though. He's disappointed I'm not designing luxurious, award-winning homes for high-profile clients, like what he and my grandfather had done. To him, that was unacceptable." He paused for a beat, looking like he was debating whether to say whatever was on his mind out loud. "And after the breakup with Lucy, I've been wondering if maybe my dad was right."

I was quiet as we headed to the fourth hole. He obviously still had feelings for his ex, even if he claimed to have moved on. No wonder he wanted me to show up at the weddings with him.

The family of five was already finishing their turn, so we did ours quickly, whizzing through the fourth and the fifth holes as silence stretched between us. Rob was the first one to speak as we waited for our turn at the next one.

"My dad is offering me full control of his firm once he retires. With the caveat that I finish my degree." His laugh sounded bitter. "He said it's my final chance to make something useful out of my life, before it's too late."

"How do you feel about that?"

"I haven't said yes. Maybe he's right. I could probably be doing more with my life. What if this *is* my last chance to finally make something out of myself? Live up to my so-called potential?" Rob blew out a long breath. "Don't get me wrong, I love my job. I love building houses, working with my hands, and constructing something out of nothing. Taking people's plans, dreams, and visions, and making them all come to life. Seeing the thrill on their faces when they see their new houses for the first time, it makes all the hard work worthwhile. But I also feel like I need to make it up to my dad. Make him finally be proud of me. I mean, let's face it. I'm not"—he made a vague gesture with his hand—"making a *difference* in the world. I don't change people's lives by working in science or showcasing underrepresented voices in sports, like my siblings. I'm just . . . a builder."

He fell quiet as he stepped up for his turn.

"But you're making a difference in your own way. Don't waste your life doing something other people want for you, because you'll never be happy. Take it from me." I pointed at myself. "My grandparents had encouraged me to go into accounting, because accountants are always in demand. They weren't pushy about it, and I knew they were only looking out for me. But I've never enjoyed it, so after I graduated, I only spent a year working in that field, before deciding I'd had enough."

"Is that why you change jobs so often?" Rob tapped his golf ball, and we watched its trajectory as it went over a bridge before rolling down the slope toward the sixth hole.

"It's a long story."

"I just rambled about my life to you. The least you can do is tell me about yours."

"It all came back to my ex." I took a deep breath. "I met Leo my senior year of high school, and I thought he was The One. When we both got accepted into a college across the country, I didn't hesitate to leave home to be with him."

A group of golfers shuffled into the spot behind us, so I stepped up and took my shot. Then we walked toward the seventh hole and waited for the young family to finish their turn.

"When he proposed, it was like all the painful years I'd spent trying to balance cash flow statements were worth it, because I'd get to spend the rest of my life with him. I thought I'd get to have what my grandparents had: a lifetime full of love, laughter, and happiness. Until one day, when he suddenly decided I wasn't good enough for an up-and-coming, hotshot corporate lawyer like him."

"No. *He's* the one that's not good enough for *you*. He has BDE, remember?"

"I remember." I chuckled. "But that's how my job-hopping started. I just wanted to distance myself as much as possible from anything that reminded me of him. My old job, my old neighborhood, the city we went to college in. And I figured, if I couldn't trust the man I was supposed to share the rest of my life with, what hope did I have trusting some faceless corporate honcho whose sole purpose was to make record-breaking profits? They were only going to screw me over anyway, so I'd go before they could."

"I'm sorry you had to go through that with him."

"It's in the past. I've moved on. But my point is, you should work with your dad only because *you* want to. You've accomplished so much on your own, and you should be proud of that. Don't let him tell you otherwise."

His smile held a tiny bit of sadness in it, and it suddenly made me feel oddly protective of him. I wasn't used to seeing that look on his face, because the Rob I knew was always cheerful, confident, seemingly without a care in the world. Someone who, I had initially thought, was an older version of a frat boy who only cared about himself.

And I was slowly learning that I'd been completely, totally, way off the mark.

"What about the house flip you're doing with Alec? Why isn't he impressed with that?"

"He thinks we're wasting our time, because he says the residential property market is going through a slump now and prices are overinflated, so we won't be able to sell the property at a profit." He blew out a long breath. "Alec disagrees. We've done all the numbers, and he's confident we can sell it at a good price. But what if my dad's right? Then we will have wasted our time and money for nothing. It will only solidify his opinion that I'm not doing anything worthwhile with my life."

An idea began to form in my mind. "How long until you finish the renovations?"

"We're almost done. Maybe one week at the most. Why?"

"I can help you," I said, my tone rising with excitement, because the idea was cementing itself onto the walls of my brain and refusing to budge. "Remember I told you I worked as a property stylist once? It was one of the most fun jobs I'd ever done. I got paid to ogle pretty Pinterest boards, rent gorgeous pieces of furniture, and style a house like it was my dream home. Wait, I've got pictures to prove it." Pulling out my phone from my pocket, I waded through the thousands of photos in my camera roll—the ones I'd been meaning to sort through for ages—and when I found the ones I was looking for, thrust the phone into his hand with a gleeful grin.

I took my turn as he scrolled through the pictures, and because he was still looking through them when I was done, I grabbed his putter and finished his turn for him.

"Took me six strokes to do yours, sorry." I handed the putter back to him.

"Whatever. I'll still win." He returned my phone as we headed toward the eighth hole. "You've obviously got a knack for it. They look great. Very professional."

"Right? Styled homes are likely to sell faster, because potential buyers can visualize themselves being in that space. There's research showing that staged properties boost sale prices by at least five percent. But hiring a professional to stage a home can cost you a few thousand dollars," I said. "You're doing so much for me, so the least I can do is help you sell the house you're flipping. It'll save you some money, and all you need to pay for is the cost of renting the furniture. I'll even take professional shots of the house for you, because online photos of the staged home would attract more potential buyers to view the house in person."

"You really would do that for me?"

"I would. Because your father needs to be taken down a peg or ten."

Rob looked thoughtful as he took his shot, sending the golf ball cleanly into the hole.

"Okay." He finally nodded. "The sooner we can sell the house, the sooner we can recoup our investment. And I can prove to him that I'm doing something useful with my life."

"Great. I promise I won't let you down."

We were both quiet as we waited at the start of the ninth hole. The final hole took longer, because our golf balls had to zip through an underground tunnel before being sucked into a long PVC pipe and flung into a huge metal tub near the entrance. Rob was smiling to himself as we listened to the young kids begging their parents for another round.

The past hour had truly opened my eyes to this man standing next to me. Underneath his easygoing confidence, there was a loud insecurity that told him he wasn't good enough. It was heartbreaking to see, especially because I'd always had nothing but love and support from my grandparents. To hear how his dad had been belittling him most of his life was sad and infuriating, so I'd now made it my own personal agenda to do everything I could to help him realize that he *was* worthwhile, no matter what his obnoxious dad might say about it.

"You're up." Rob nodded at me when the family of five moved on.

I pushed away my thoughts and lined up my shot. "Are we still keeping score?"

"Yep. I'm winning, aren't I?"

I swung my club, sending the ball cleanly into the final hole. "No way. I scored more hole in ones than you, and I took six strokes to do your turn. *I'm* winning."

There was a long pause, and when I glanced at him, he was watching me with a big grin.

I rolled my eyes at him. "You know I am."

"Fine, you are." Rob chuckled. "Honestly, I'd love to see you kick Ben's ass if you played golf with him on your date."

"He might be secretly a pro at mini golf, for all I know. He'd probably kick my ass."

"Doesn't matter whose ass got kicked. As long as he falls head over heels in love with you, that's all that matters. And then my job here will be done."

He was right. Once I managed to prove to the lawyers that I had met Oma's requirement, I wouldn't need his help anymore.

Which should be a good thing.

Right?

CHAPTER 9

Not All Pets Are Created Equal

The minute I arrived at the wedding on Saturday, regrets began marching through my brain. I'd done a pretty good job of squashing the free-flowing doubts during the drive, but the stunning sight in front of me only amplified the voice in my head that said, *How is this any different from all the bad dates I've suffered through in the past?* What made me think that Rob could accomplish what a dating app, with all their sophisticated algorithms, couldn't? What if this was a massive waste of time, when I should have been coming up with ways to tackle the Goodwin issue instead?

Then my grandparents' faces innocently waltzed into my mind, reminding me and slapping me back to the reality of why I was doing this.

I'm here for them. So we can keep the yarn store.

Think of the food. And the music. And the wine.

This will be fun. Fun, fun, fun.

Maybe if I kept chanting those words in my head like a mantra, they would manifest themselves into reality. Wasn't that what the power of positive thinking was all about?

Feeling a tiny bit self-conscious as I didn't know anyone else, I cast my eyes around, looking for Rob. I took out my phone from my clutch and sent him a short message, letting him know I was here. Tucking the clutch back under my arm, I repeated my mantra and ran a hand down my dress to smooth it, even though it was perfectly fine. I didn't know why I was nervous, because I'd gone to lots of weddings on my own, and it was never a problem.

Maybe because there was a lot of pressure riding on this wedding.

Because I needed this, so very badly, to work.

Alamanda Farm was a beautiful ranch that had been transformed into a romantic, magical wonderland for the wedding. At the entrance, hand-painted wooden signs directed the guests toward the different places of interest: the chapel, the mobile bar, the barn—where the reception would be held later—and the bonfire. Colorful buntings with the couple's initials and strings of lights decorated the venue, making the place look otherworldly and enchanting.

The ceremony was starting in thirty minutes, so I willed my legs to get moving, following other guests who were walking past. Lush green archways entwined with colorful flowers lined the path to the timber chapel, which looked like it had been airlifted straight out of a fairy tale. A large antique door stood open, and gorgeous flower arrangements overflowed from the two large pots flanking the chapel entrance. Rows of white steel chairs were lined up inside, where some guests were already seated.

"Hey, Kim."

Rob was walking toward me, dressed in a dark suit and a crisp white shirt, turning several pairs of heads as he walked past.

"You look stunning." He gave me a once-over. "Ben won't know what hit him."

My stomach did an involuntary backflip. Not that I was keeping track, but so far he'd called me smart, beautiful, and stunning. *Is he flirting with me?*

I cocked my head at the people watching him instead, hoping to deflect the attention from myself. "Those people over there seem to think the same about you."

"Never mind them." His eyes were focused on mine. "What do *you* think?"

"Eh." I wasn't going to tell him that I agreed with those strangers. "You clean up well, I guess. At least you're not an eyesore."

His chuckle was a low rumble, giving me shivers in places I didn't know were even possible to *feel* shivers.

"Anyway, you've made a great choice. Ben's a good guy. When I introduce you two later, I want you to bring your A game and impress him like the world is ending tomorrow. Like your life and your future depend on it."

If only he knew how close to home that was. "I'll do my best."

"You better. By the way, a guy I was talking to saw you walking up and was wondering who you were. Should've seen his face when I said you're my hot date for the day."

"Hot date reporting for duty." I flipped my hair and offered him a coy smile. "At your service, for as long as you need me. For anything." I gave him an exaggerated wink on purpose. "*Anything* at all."

"Kim." He groaned. "What the hell was that?"

"It's a preview of how I'm planning to impress Ben." I popped my eyes wide, trying to look innocent. "What's wrong with that?"

"*Everything*. Are you being serious? Listen, you might want to dial it back a little, because Ben is going to run a mile in the other direction if that's how you—" He sighed when I burst into laughter. "Hilarious. Maybe you should consider a career as a stand-up comedian."

"I was just messing with you. Trust me, I know how to do this."

"Says the woman who gets duped into paying five hundred dollars for her date."

I smacked him lightly with my clutch. "Keep this up and your hot date is leaving."

"She can't leave." He placed his right palm on his chest in mock outrage. "I've got a hot date lined up for my hot date. They're supposed to hit it off, fall head over heels madly in love, and make beautiful babies together."

His hazel eyes were glinting with amusement, and for a brief second, they threw me for a loop. The colors reminded me of my favorite sweater that Oma had knitted for me when I was younger, and it was the coziest, warmest, and most comfortable item of clothing I had ever owned. I knew there was a shade of yarn in the store with that exact same color, and even though I should know all of them by heart, the name seemed to escape me right now.

Simply Sage? Burnt Olive? No. Golden Thyme?

I mentally shook myself. *Focus*. I was here for a specific purpose: to find a single man and fulfill my grandmother's last wishes. Not to stare at Rob Carmichael's twinkly hazel eyes, trying to figure out their yarn shade equivalent.

"Where's your ex?" I asked. "Is she here, too?"

"Haven't seen her. She's probably not here yet."

We found ourselves seats at the back of the chapel. An acoustic song began playing, and the groom walked into the chapel, smiling at the guests, nerves evident in his eyes. Then the pianist played the wedding march, and all the guests stood and turned their heads to watch as the radiant bride walked down the aisle, looking like a real-life princess in her stunning white dress, while her husband-to-be beamed at her. The ceremony was simple and sweet, with heartfelt vows written by the couple themselves. By the time the priest announced them as husband and wife, there were very few dry eyes inside the chapel.

Rob gave me a gentle nudge. "That was beautiful, wasn't it?"

"Yeah." I wiped my eyes with the pads of my thumbs. "They almost make me want to believe in happy endings. *Almost.*"

He chuckled. "This is only the first wedding. You'll change your tune by the fifth one."

Once the ceremony was over, guests were directed to the open bar for cocktail hour. Rob grabbed a couple of champagne flutes from a passing waiter and handed one to me as I took in the gorgeous setup. There were several mouthwatering options for the guests to nibble on: a charcuterie station brimming with piles of ham, salami, different types of cheese, fruits, olives, dips and crackers, all artfully laid out on wooden serving trays. There was also a raw bar, with oysters, cooked shrimp, and lobster claws. A pretzel cart, a cupcake table, a macaron tower, and a vintage mobile bar completed the lineup.

"Ben's over there." Rob tilted his head at a group of men chatting by the bar. "Ready to meet the love of your life and dazzle him with your charm and beauty?"

I didn't reply, as my anxiety irrationally snowballed into Herculean proportions. I knew this shouldn't be any different than all those online dates, but somehow it *was* different—because doing this with Rob meant that I had to put my trust in *him*. And I wasn't sure I could, no matter how nice he was, because the years and the heartbreak I'd gone through with Leo taught me that it was best to be cautious and keep relationships—all kinds of commitments, honestly—at arm's length. It was the safest thing to do, and it would save me from a lot of heartache.

I was in uncharted waters here, and I wasn't ready to plunge into the deep end. Not even to dip my toes in.

"Hey. I know your brain is racing a hundred miles a minute." Rob took my hands and squeezed them gently. "I promise, if Ben turns out to be an ass, we'll walk away immediately. No judgment, no questions asked. I've got your back, okay?"

I looked up and met his sincere hazel eyes, and a sense of calm slowly washed over me. *Opa was right. He does have kind eyes.* And Alec wouldn't be friends with Rob if he was untrustworthy. Plus, I didn't have the luxury of time, so I had to trust him and go ahead with the plan, because I was already here, and I didn't really have much of a choice, did I?

I took a deep breath. "I've got this," I said. "Let's do it."

"Good." Rob offered me his arm. "Humans can smell fear. Just relax."

"That's ridiculous." He felt warm, and solid, and dependable, and a funny sensation slid into my stomach at the feel of his arm underneath my fingers. "What does fear even smell like?"

He leaned closer and sniffed, his nose a whisper of a brush on my neck, and I sucked in a sharp breath at the almost-contact. "Like berries, with a hint of orange?" When I rolled my eyes, he chuckled. "Listen, and I'm not saying this to be nice, but if Ben isn't interested, he's an idiot."

"You know I'm not paying you to make these flattering comments, right?"

"You're not?" He widened his eyes in mock surprise. "Then the least you can do is compliment me back."

I gave him a brief once-over. "Fine. I think the suit makes you look smart."

"Hot." His grin was teasing. "You know you want to say that I look smoking hot."

"I know what I wanted to say, and it's not that."

"You sure? Those people earlier seem to think so."

"I'm not those people. I have twenty-twenty vision, and they all needed to get their eyes checked."

"Maybe they all have excellent taste." He lowered his voice to a whisper. "It's okay to admit if you agree. I won't tell anyone."

That made me chuckle. I knew he was just trying to make me

relax, and it was working, because I no longer felt like I was about to projectile vomit my breakfast.

"Carmichael!" One of the men in the group gave Rob a friendly nod, as his curious gaze landed on me. "How's it going?"

My mind raced back to Rob's dossier, trying to place him. He was the financial guy, the one who rowed and played football.

"Hey, Spencer." Rob shook the other guy's hand and exchanged greetings with the rest. "Everyone, this is Kimiko Halim, a good friend of mine." To me, he said, "Spencer is our resident expert on stocks and cryptocurrencies. That's Oscar, the next big thing in Hollywood. Tony over there is your go-to for excellent legal advice. And this is Ben. Kickboxing whiz, vet extraordinaire, ex swimming instructor."

I opened my mouth while instructing my brain to produce a witty greeting of some sort, but to my absolute mortification, nothing came out. My brain had seemingly checked out and gone to enjoy drinks at the open bar instead of doing its job of coming up with interesting, scintillating repartee. Or with any kind of coherent response at all.

This wasn't like me. *At all.*

Rob turned to me, as if he'd just had a thought. "Hey, that's something you have in common with Ben. Swimming. Kim used to be a competitive swimmer, right, Kim?"

"You were?" A flicker of interest crossed Ben's face, while the other men resumed their own conversation.

Smooth, Rob. Real smooth.

Alec was right: Rob *was* an excellent wingman. He guided the conversation effortlessly, he was awesome at hyping people up, and let's face it, his dossiers were top-notch. If his career in the construction industry fizzled out, he would probably make a fortune helping Port Benedict's single population find their forever match.

For those who believed in one, of course.

I sent him a smile, grateful he was here to save my sorry ass. "I was." I turned my attention to Ben, noticing that he looked cuter in real life than the picture in the dossier. Lush dark hair, thick eyebrows, gorgeous brown eyes, and biceps straining his white dress shirt, practically begging to be freed into the wild. "I stopped competing when I was fourteen, though, then came back and worked part-time as a lifeguard at the pool I used to train in."

"Kim also used to work at a zoo," Rob said to Ben. "She's a huge animal lover."

Oka-aayyy, that might be pushing it a *liiittle* bit too much. Sure, I loved dogs and cats, and the occasional hamsters and guinea pigs, but I'd rather impale myself on a million knitting needles than befriend lizards, or most species of bugs and reptiles, or—*ugh*—snakes.

"Really?" The flicker of interest on Ben's face morphed into a look of approval. "I love zoos. My parents used to take me and my sisters every weekend when we were kids."

He launched into a story of how the zoo had sparked his interest in becoming a vet, and I finally began to relax. Rob was right: His matchmaking scheme was a *brilliant* idea. Ben ticked all the boxes, and this was so much easier—and safer—than scrolling through an endless list of questionable men on a random dating app.

Rob was chatting with Spencer, the finance guy, and I could hear Spencer saying to him, "Sorry to hear about Lucy, bro. What happened?"

I glanced at them. Rob caught my gaze and gave me a quick smile, before answering Spencer, their voices low.

"What do you do, Kim?" Ben asked.

I returned my attention to him. "I run a yarn store in the row of shops behind Port Benedict Plaza."

"I know the place. I might have driven my mother there a few times. Don't think I've seen you there, though."

"It was my grandmother's. I've taken over the business these past eighteen months. She's no longer with us, unfortunately."

A look of sympathy crossed his face. "I'm so sorry for your loss."

This was actually going well. Ben was cute, seemed nice, and was obviously close to his family. So far, so good. I glanced at Rob and found him watching us before giving me a subtle thumbs-up.

But of course, if it seemed too good to be true, it probably was.

"What did you do before you took over the store?" Ben took a sip of his drink.

"Oh, this and that," I said. "I was in a few different industries. F&B, entertainment, and childcare, to name a few." That was a fancy way of saying waitress, cinema operator, and nanny, but Ben seemed to have bought it, because he looked impressed.

"Sounds like you've built quite an amazing career portfolio. What made you decide to leave it all and run your grandmother's yarn store? That must have been a huge change from all those exciting jobs you've done before."

"There's nobody else to run it if I didn't, and I couldn't stand and watch the store close down," I said. "It's been great, though, and I've been enjoying it."

"Really?" He gave me a doubtful look. "You don't miss the jobs you've had in the past? I mean, I can't imagine quitting the career I love so much to work in someone else's business, let alone a different industry altogether. Especially doing something as mundane as running a store—a *yarn* store, of all things. It would *kill* me." Ben gave me an awkward chuckle. "Sorry, maybe I shouldn't have said that out loud. My mom says I have zero filter."

One of the odd jobs I'd done in the past was being an extra in an indie movie, where I was part of a crowd witnessing a proposal scene. All the other extras understood the assignment: to ooh and ahh at every declaration of love, and swoon when the main character got down on one knee to propose to the love of his life.

Except me. I was the only one who had scoffed—loudly—at the supposedly romantic moment, and when the director yelled "CUT!" because I had ruined the take, I proceeded to explain why the scene was unbelievable. (He had to run across an entire airport and still managed to stop her just before she boarded the plane? Make it make sense.)

If Ben had zero filter, then I was told by the AD that I had zero acting talent.

So it was a huge struggle, having to maintain a friendly face with Ben, when all I wanted to do was throw my clutch on the ground and challenge him to a duel at dawn. Did he really imply that running my grandmother's beloved business was *beneath him*?

I checked myself. *Stop putting words in his mouth.* He was just making harmless conversation, wasn't he?

I shot Rob another quick glance. The other men were still chatting, but his attention was on me, and a crease was starting to form on his forehead. Probably because *my* forehead was starting to have deep ridges and valleys on its own.

Pull yourself together, Kim. Do not fuck this up.

Time for a subject change. "What about you? It must be fun working with all those animals. Do you have a favorite?"

"I love all kinds of animals. They're all magnificent."

"There must be one or two that you dislike. I mean, cats and dogs are adorable. Snakes aren't. Or critters like tarantulas and lizards."

"But lizards are beautiful, and they're fascinating." Ben's face broke into a wide grin. "And snakes *are* adorable. I have one as a pet. Her name is Custard, and she's the most exquisite albino ball python snake you'll ever see in your life. She lives in a vivarium in my bedroom, and she's the first thing I see when I wake up."

I flinched. Did he really say a pet snake?

In his *bedroom*?

No. Fucking. Way.

That did it. Didn't matter that he was cute and drove his mother to yarn stores. I could even tolerate his careless comment about my job. But some things had to stay sacred, and certain types of reptiles, especially snakes, didn't matter how "adorable" they might be, were immediate deal-breakers for me.

"Gosh! Will you look at the time?" I made a show of glancing at my watch, interrupting him as he waxed poetic about his beloved Custard. "I'm so sorry. It's late, and I haven't had my second glass of wine yet. It was lovely to meet you, Ben." I caught Rob's gaze and blurted out the first thing that came to mind. "Rob! I'm off to do some wine tasting."

I turned around and stalked across the lush lawn, ignoring his calls. He was breathless when he finally caught up with me.

"What happened? What did Ben do?"

I spun around, my eyes wide and probably looking a little wild. "Did you know that he has a pet snake?"

He looked taken aback. "I didn't."

"He does." I shuddered. "An *exquisite* albino snake called Custard, that lives in *his bedroom*."

"That must be a new thing." Rob frowned. "He never spoke about a pet snake whenever we saw each other, or posted about it on social media."

"And not just that, he was practically belittling my job and my grandmother's yarn store. What was I thinking?" I shook my head, exasperated. "I shouldn't be here wasting my time sipping wines and eating canapés when I should be focusing on how to stop Goodw—you know what? I'm grateful for your help, but I don't think this is going to work."

"To be fair, we didn't have enough time to prep for this wedding," Rob said, his tone gentle and reassuring. "I promise we'll do better with the second one."

"I think one wedding is enough for me."

"It's your call, but your soulmate might be at the next one, and if you don't go, you won't be able to meet him."

"But if there is such a thing as a soulmate, I'm going to meet him one way or another, right? And you wouldn't have to waste your time helping me with this."

"Kim." Rob reached out and caught my hand, anchoring me in place. "I thought you said this was important to you. Don't you want to fulfill your grandmother's last wishes? How are you going to do that by finding dates from the internet?"

Damn it, because he was right.

And didn't I promise him that I'd be there, so he didn't have to face his ex alone?

Plus, I didn't really have time on my side.

Looked like I had no choice but to soldier on.

CHAPTER 10

Dating Isn't That Different from Finding a Pair of Shoes

My phone trilled early the next day, saving me from a chaotic dream about lizards and champagne flutes and albino snakes. I groped around my bedside table for my phone and saw Rob's cheerful face popping up on my screen.

"Hey. Just calling to make sure you're okay."

"H'lo," I mumbled. "'Course am 'kay. Why wudden I be?"

His deep, rumbly laugh sent a sudden flood of fluttery feelings into my stomach, doing things to my insides that it had no business doing, and catapulting my eyes wide open.

What the hell.

"Did I wake you up? I'm sorry." The low chuckle came back, delivering more bursts of delicious tingles all over my body, as if I had repeatedly jabbed myself with multiple shots of dopamine. "I just wanted to check in to see how you're doing, because I felt bad after the wedding yesterday. It wasn't what I had promised you."

"No, but it wasn't your fault he kept pet snakes." I burrowed deeper into my blanket and pressed the phone to my ear. It was . . . kind of nice to have his voice wake me up in the morning. "I appreciate you checking in on me."

"Just part and parcel of my service." There was a pause, before he cleared his throat and said, "What time do you have to get to the store?"

"Soon." I briefly closed my eyes, not sure why I wasn't ready to hang up yet, just as an idea popped into my mind. "Hey, if you're free tonight, do you want to come over to my grandfather's for dinner? Think of it as me saying thank you for everything you're doing."

"Oh." He sounded surprised. "I'd love to. You sure I won't be imposing?"

I smiled into the phone. "I wouldn't have asked otherwise."

When I arrived at my grandfather's house after work that evening, Rob's truck was already parked at the front. He got out of his car, clutching a box from Twisted Sweets.

"You didn't have to bring anything."

"But I did. My mother always said to never show up empty-handed whenever someone invites you over. Ellie said you loved her matcha cinnamon rolls, so I got some of those."

I was impressed, because he made an effort to find out what I liked. "Thanks. That's very thoughtful of you."

Unlocking the front door, I walked into the house, with Rob following behind. The place was quiet, save for the basketball game on TV.

"Opa?" I left the containers of food on the kitchen bench, and Rob placed the Twisted Sweets box next to them. "I brought a friend."

My heart rate kicked up a notch when there was no answer.

"Opa?" I raised my voice while walking toward his bedroom. "Where are you?"

"Kim?" To my relief, my grandfather walked out of the laundry room, pulling out his AirPods from his ears. "Ada disini.* I didn't hear you."

"Hey, Opa." I went over and gave him a hug. "Had me worried for a second."

"I'm fine. I was listening to a book while folding some clothes." He stopped short when he saw Rob. "You brought a friend!"

"I'm Rob." He approached Opa and offered his hand. "Kim was kind enough to invite me over for dinner. I'm sorry to show up unannounced."

"Don't apologize. We always have plenty of food. And if my granddaughter invited you, you're more than welcome in my house." My grandfather tilted his head, realization in his eyes. "Did you say your name is Rob? I know who you are. I saw your picture on Instagram! You're the friend who helped Kim escape her horrible date, aren't you?"

Rob glanced at me, looking surprised. "That's me, sir."

"Please call me Thomas. And thanks for looking out for her."

"Of course. Can I just say, I've been enjoying your woodworking posts on social media."

"You have?" Opa looked pleased. "I'm glad to hear that."

"Are the others coming?" I began taking out plates and cutlery from the kitchen drawer.

"They can't make it," Opa said. "Their family of pet snakes escaped from the vivarium, so they had to find them before someone called one of those reptile wrangler people. And to make things worse, while they were combing the neighborhood, a wild raccoon bit them and they've had to be rushed to the hospital for urgent medical attention."

"What is it with snakes and this weekend?" I gave my grandfather an appreciative nod. "Ten out of ten, for both content and delivery."

---

* Indonesian, meaning: "I'm here."

My grandfather beamed at me, looking proud of himself. "That was good, wasn't it?"

"I'm sorry," Rob said, who was watching us, looking bewildered, as if we'd just announced that those same snakes and raccoons would be joining us for dinner. "Did you say you were expecting someone who has a family of pet snakes?" He leveled an accusing stare at me. "And you gave me grief about Ben and his *one* pet snake?"

"It's a joke. It's a thing we do every week. No actual animals are involved." I waved my hand at him. "I'll explain later."

My grandfather perked up with interest. "Who's Ben?"

"Just someone Rob introduced to me. Should we start eating? I'm starving."

But Opa wasn't one to be deterred so easily. "Tell me more about this Ben."

"He's no one. I met him at a wedding, and I'll never see him again. End of story."

Opa's gaze was now swiveling back and forth between Rob and me. "You two went to a wedding? Together?"

"Yes. *No*. I met him there. Can we *please* start eating?"

"Who did you meet there? Rob or Ben?"

"Both," I said, then immediately regretted my answer, because there was no way my grandfather was going to stop now until I told him the entire story.

"Kim mentioned how challenging it's been trying to meet someone," Rob chimed in. "I offered to introduce her to some people."

"That's very nice of you." Opa gave him a thoughtful look. "How are you going to do that? Do you work for one of those dating apps?"

I raised my eyebrows at him. "You know what a dating app is?"

"I don't live under a rock, Kimiko. Yes, of course I know what a dating app is."

"That would probably be an interesting place to work at, but no," Rob replied. "I've been invited to a few weddings this year, and Kim has very kindly agreed to go with me, so I thought she could meet a few of my single friends there."

Rob might not have noticed it, but I did, because I knew my grandfather and all his telltale signs very well. His entire body had straightened, his eyes were now focusing intently on Rob, and I knew that the gears in his brain were rapidly turning, considering and assessing the younger man. "What do you do, Rob?"

"I'm in construction, sir."

He didn't elaborate, so I explained to Opa, "Rob runs his own construction business. He was the one who did the renovation on Ellie's bakery. And he's just started a house flipping venture with Alec."

"That's impressive for someone so young. How old are you, early thirties?"

"Thank you. I'm thirty-four. I appreciate your kind words, but it's not that impressive, honestly." Rob gave Opa a polite smile. "I'm nowhere near what my father had accomplished at the same age."

But Opa shook his head. "Don't ever compare yourself to your father, or to anyone. Everybody's path is different, and what worked for your father may not work for you, and that's perfectly okay." It was a line my grandfather had recited so many times when I was growing up, whenever I felt down after hearing stories about my friends going on camping trips or weekend getaways with their mom and dad.

Never compare yourself to your friends.

Our family is unique, and even though your mom and dad aren't around like all those other families, you're still loved.

So very much.

Rob looked a bit taken aback, but he only nodded.

My heart broke at the look on his face. At the irony of the

situation. Because even though I'd grown up without my parents, I was always safe in the knowledge of how much my grandparents loved me. Rob had both his parents around, but the fact that he felt his father would only be proud of him and love him based on what he achieved was heartbreaking.

And somehow, I was glad he was here tonight, to hear those words from my grandfather.

We sat around the kitchen island, and I picked up the vase of freshly cut calla lilies and moved it to the dining table to make more room for the food.

"Gorgeous flowers," Rob commented.

"They are, aren't they?" Opa replied. "They're Emilia's favorite. My late wife," he added at Rob's questioning look. "I grow them in the garden myself."

"He used to bring her flowers all the time, just because. Even went through all the trouble of planting the lilies, because she loved them so much."

That earned me a curious look from Rob. "Sounds like you're not a big fan of flowers."

"I mean, flowers are pretty. But buying them is a waste of money, because one, they're expensive, and two, they wilt after a few days. You're better off using the money on more important things."

Opa sighed, having heard my argument far too many times. "That might be true, but it's also a simple gesture to show your partner how much you appreciate them. It's because of that boy Leo, isn't it?" Irritation flashed in his eyes as he said to Rob, "That's what he told her when they were together. She loves roses, but he never appreciated her enough to bring her flowers, and that was his excuse. He never deserved her. It's pathetic."

Rob sent me another look, and I only shrugged, as if saying, *He's not wrong.*

When the food was all gone, Rob helped me clear the dishes

and stacked them in the dishwasher, waving off my insistence that he was the guest. Then he sat and chatted with Opa, listening as my grandfather told him funny anecdotes about growing up in Indonesia and the culture shock he'd gone through after migrating overseas. The next thing I knew, a couple of hours had gone by, and Opa was showing off his latest woodworking projects to Rob.

"This is awesome." Rob was admiring a wooden couch sleeve with a cupholder. "How long did it take you to make it?"

"Probably half a day." Opa beamed at him, and I felt a sudden surge of affection for Rob for being so kind to my grandfather. "They're very simple to make. I can send you a link to the tutorial."

"I did a bit of woodworking in high school, but I was never any good at it. I only got into it to spend time with my dad. And it worked for a while, but—" He stopped himself from saying whatever he was going to say. "Then he got too busy with work."

"That's still a nice memory to have. Not many teenage boys are thoughtful enough to want to do something together with their father."

A sad look crossed Rob's face. "I don't think he shares that opinion, but thank you for saying that."

My grandfather opened his mouth, as if he was going to say something, but seemed to think better of it. "I'm going to call it a night." He climbed down from his stool and ambled over to the sink to place his empty glass there. When Rob made a move to stand up, Opa waved his hand at him. "No, please stay. Sit with Kim, chat with her, keep her company. Give her a break from putting up with a boring old man."

"Oh, Opa." I gave him a kiss on the cheek. "You know you're anything but boring."

"Still. I'm not as handsome as this fella here." Opa gave me a wink, and I could hear Rob's low chuckle from behind me.

"Good night, sweetheart. I'll see you tomorrow." Then he leaned closer and whispered for my ears only, "Orangnya baik, Kim."*

I only rolled my eyes while he laughed, before shuffling away to his bedroom. When I glanced at Rob, he was watching my grandfather with a thoughtful look on his face.

"Thanks for having me over. Your grandfather is great." He turned his attention to me. "You're a wonderful granddaughter. He's very lucky to have you."

"No. I'm the one who's lucky to have him. And I'm glad you came and chatted with him about woodworking, because I know nothing about that stuff. In fact, I couldn't remember the last time he laughed so much at dinner. You've spoiled him, because he's going to want to be this entertained every week now."

"Glad I could be useful. Just another productive weekend, right?"

"Except for the Ben debacle."

"I've been meaning to ask you about that, actually. You said you're doing this for your grandmother. That one of her last wishes was for you to settle down." When I nodded, he continued, "And you're okay with that? You never seemed to be a hundred percent enthusiastic about the idea. At the end of the day, this is *your* life. Do *you* really want to settle down?"

Warmth expanded through my chest, and I knew it wasn't because of the cup of peppermint tea I just had.

Rob was the only person—apart from Ellie and Jenna—who had asked me that question. Ellie and Jenna knew how much my grandmother meant to me. But Rob, though, I'd only gotten to know better these past few weeks, and he was observant enough to ask me that?

A voice in my brain whispered, *Maybe you should come clean*

---

* Indonesian, meaning: "He's a nice guy, Kim."

about the real reasons why you're doing this. About the inheritance clause.

I opened my mouth, only to close it again. *No, I don't have to.* My reasons for doing this shouldn't concern him. He was helping me find someone, and what I planned to do with that someone was none of his concern. He was just a means to an end, and once this entire charade was over, we'd part ways and I wouldn't need to have anything to do with him anymore.

"I don't know," I answered, probably the closest to a truthful answer I could come up with. "Honestly, settling down with one person for the rest of my life seems like such a reckless concept. I'll be trusting him, and only him, with my heart forever. Do you know how many things could go wrong during those forever years? How do I know I've chosen the right person? How do I know he isn't going to abuse my trust and break my heart?"

"Like your ex-fiancé," Rob said slowly.

"Exactly like him."

"Not everyone is like your ex, though. You *can* trust someone if it's the right person, and maybe you just haven't found yours yet. The way I look at it, dating is like trying to find the right outfit for the right occasion. Or trying on several different pairs of shoes before you find the one you really love." At my raised eyebrows, he dimpled at me. "Blame my metaphors on my sisters. My point is, you don't buy the first pair of shoes or dress you tried on, do you? You're not going to settle and spend your hard-earned money on something you don't feel comfortable wearing. It's the same thing. You don't settle for the first guy you meet, because you don't want to spend the rest of your life with someone you're not truly happy with."

"That's true."

"It is. And I believe there's someone out there for everyone, including you. You just haven't met him yet. Or maybe you have, but you just haven't realized it yet."

"Still, I'm going into this with zero expectations. The idea of being tied down in a long-term relationship isn't something I'm comfortable with, but that was what my grandmother wanted, and I'd do everything in my power to make it come true."

He was quiet for a few minutes, and I thought he was done with the conversation.

But then he asked, "Do you think you'll ever change your mind? About the idea of settling down with one person for the rest of your life?"

No. Because I didn't know if I could endure what I'd gone through with Leo all over again. "I don't know."

We shared a long look, and I was once again struck by the brilliant colors in his eyes, by the flecks of gold among the green.

I still couldn't find the yarn equivalent, and it annoyed the hell out of me.

Royal Fern? Leafy Willow?

Because that exact shade didn't just resemble my favorite childhood sweater anymore.

It was also slowly becoming my favorite color.

CHAPTER 11

Cynical Is Careful, Spelled Differently

I arrived bright and early next Saturday morning at the address Rob had given me. The house he was flipping with Alec was in an older neighborhood on the outskirts of Port Benedict, a single-story home with original red bricks, newly replaced roof tiles, and a freshly landscaped front yard. Rob said demands for houses in the area were starting to rise, and a lot of young families were moving in because the suburb checked all the important boxes: local schools, a small hospital, grocery stores, close to the freeways.

I parked just as he was tossing a rolled-up old carpet into a dumpster on the driveway. Grabbing the bunch of calla lilies from my passenger seat, I got out of my car and opened the trunk, hauling my camera bag and a box full of staging props.

"Hey. Wasn't expecting you for another hour," he said. "Let me help you with those."

"Thanks." I also grabbed a paper bag while he picked up two other boxes, then followed him into the house. "Nicole arrived earlier at the store so I could leave."

The smell of fresh paint lingered in the air as I walked in. Everything looked brand-new, and the open plan of the house made the place look inviting and spacious. I'd made a Pinterest board when Rob first sent me pictures of the house, and proposed a clean, minimalist vibe. Once he and Alec agreed on the look, I sourced furniture from a rental company and thrifted some items from the antique store next to Selma's bookshop.

The furniture was delivered yesterday, so there were dining chairs and barstools and floor lamps being placed haphazardly around the house. There was a beige leather sofa and a farmhouse-style coffee table pushed to one side of the living room. A long wooden dining table was in the middle of the dining area, with mirrors in Bubble Wrap and art prints stacked on top.

I waved at Alec, who was perched on top of a ladder installing LED light bulbs above the kitchen island. "Hey, Mackenzie."

"Hey, Kim." He lifted a hand in greeting. "Thanks for helping us out."

"No problem." I placed the boxes on the floor. "The place looks great. When is your first showing?"

"Early next week," Rob said. "Three showings a week, and an auction in four weeks, unless we get an offer earlier."

"I told you, we will," Alec said. "Back yourself up, Carmichael. Have faith in us. Your dad might have been in this industry longer, but he isn't always right."

I shot Rob a quick glance to see his reaction, but he only made a noncommittal sound.

We began to rearrange the furniture, pushing the sofa and the coffee table to the middle of the living room and setting the chairs around the dining table. I hung the art prints and the mirrors on the walls, arranged some pillows on the sofa, and placed a decorative wooden tray and a potted plant on the coffee table.

As Rob and Alec put up the blinds, I filled the vase I'd bought from the antique store with water, then placed it on top of the dining table. Opa had given me ten stems of calla lilies, which should bloom nicely just in time for the first showing.

"These were freshly cut this morning," I said. "They should last around a week or two, with fresh water every three days. Let me know if you need more and I can bring some over."

"Are those from Thomas's garden?" Rob asked.

I nodded, while Alec shot him a curious look. "Thomas?"

"Kim's grandfather."

"I know who he is," Alec replied. "Wonderful man. He's had me and Ellie over for dinner a few times. My question is, how do you know him and that those flowers might have been from his garden?"

"Because I've also had dinner at his house."

"Have you?" Alec directed his curious gaze at me, chuckling when I rolled my eyes at him. "Interesting."

We spent the entire day staging the rest of the house. By the time we were finished, I was exhausted, but the house looked amazing. All three bedrooms had been accessorized with cream-colored bedding, fluffy pillows, and throw blankets; there were potted plants in every room; and crisp white towels and jasmine-scented candles were featured in the two bathrooms. We had a black-and-white-striped ceramic serving bowl and some fresh lemons for the kitchen bench, and another wooden tray with a hand-painted porcelain teapot and its matching teacups next to it. Ellie had lent us some of her cookbooks for display in the kitchen, and I'd brought some of my own books for the bookshelf. Then I took out my camera and captured photos of the house after Rob had steam-cleaned the floor and made sure everything was pristine and spotless.

"I'll download the photos and send them over when I get home."

"Great." Rob had his hands in his pockets, watching me as I packed up my camera. Alec had gone to meet Ellie for dinner, so it was just the two of us left in the house. "Are you going back to the store? Or your grandfather's house?"

"Nicole is closing tonight, and my grandfather is with a couple of friends and their families tonight. I'll see him tomorrow."

"If you're free tonight, maybe we can go over the dossier for the second wedding." He shifted on his feet. "I know it's still two weeks away, but I feel like we should prepare early."

It was the thought of spending more time with him that had me nodding my head. "I'd love that."

We grabbed a quick dinner from Ocha Izakaya, my favorite Japanese restaurant, then drove back to the apartment I shared with Jenna, with Rob following in his truck. I unlocked the front door, switched on the lights, and led him inside.

"Shoes off, please." I pointed at a low shoe rack in the hallway, underneath a sign announcing the same thing. "Spare slippers are on the bottom rack. Sorry, it's an Asian thing. Both Jenna and I grew up with this habit and it's ingrained in every fiber of our being."

"Don't apologize." Rob took off his work boots and placed them neatly on the rack, briefly considered the choices of available slippers, then chose a pair of fluffy purple ones. "My mom used to do the same thing. My siblings and I often came home with dirt and mud on our shoes. She got so fed up with cleaning the floor, she always made us all take off our shoes as soon as we walked into the house."

"Very wise mom."

"Very busy, too, with the six of us."

"Your mother must be a superwoman." I headed to the kitchen and tossed my bag and keys onto the counter. "What can I get you? I have coffee, tea, or water. Maybe a bottle or two of kombucha in the fridge."

"Water's fine." Rob placed his keys on the kitchen counter and climbed on a stool, his eyes curiously assessing the apartment. "Yeah. My mom's the best."

"Do they live here? What about your siblings?"

"Some of them. My parents do." He nodded his thanks at the glass of water I handed him. "Should we get started?"

Okay, so someone didn't feel like talking about his family today. Hint taken.

He set his laptop on the kitchen counter, then navigated to a presentation that looked similar to the first one. I took the seat next to him, my arm lightly brushing his as I scooted closer to get a better look on the screen.

"When do you have the time to do all this? Don't you have a business to run?"

"This didn't take long. A guy from the first wedding will also be at this second one, so I've only given you two new options. And Alec and I sold our shares in Mackenzie Constructions to Goodwin Property Group, so I've got more time for other things."

"I seem to be hearing that name a lot recently."

Rob looked up from his screen. "What do you mean?"

"You know how Goodwin owns Port Benedict Plaza?" When he nodded, I went on, "All the shop owners in our neighborhood received a letter from them. They're offering to buy our buildings because they want to demolish the old shops in our precinct and build a swanky new tower in its place."

He stilled. "They do?"

"Yep." I turned to look at him. "You have networks and connections with the local property industry, right? Have you heard anything about this?"

"Don't think I have." He slowly shook his head. "You should speak to Alec. He knows the owner better than I do."

"Ellie's reaching out to her. Why did you sell your shares to them?"

"Alec and I are more of a silent partner in the company anyway, and we needed the capital to finance our house flip, so it made sense." He studied me. "Are you going to sell?"

"I'm not," I said. "But there are other businesses that said things have been slow since the Plaza revamp last year, and they're thinking of saying yes. So I want to bring more traffic to the strip, and hopefully convince them not to sell."

"Can I help? Two heads are always better than one."

"I don't pay you enough to be my matchmaker and my business consultant."

"You haven't paid me a single cent. And I grew up with sisters, I know how to multitask. Is the yarn store affected? Have you noticed a drop in business?"

"Not really. Maybe a little, but not significant enough to worry."

"Still, a bit of publicity would go a long way. Are you doing any promotions?"

"Mostly social media. But I suck at posting regular content." I thought for a bit. "My grandmother used to rave about this lady named Melinda Paulson, a Port Benedict local who's considered a legend in the arts and crafts community. She became super famous several years ago, thanks to her knitted dresses being worn in a hit romance movie. We stock her knitting books at the store, and they always sell out. Maybe I can reach out to her and see if she'd be willing to do an event in the store."

"I know someone at the Port Benedict tourism office. I'll ask if they can do a coverage of your shopping strip. Maybe highlight it as an iconic attraction of the city and include it in their must-visit list," he said. "I used to have a contact at the local newspaper, too. Let me find out if they're still there, and if they could also do a feature article about the area."

"Ooh, someone's very well-connected in the community."

He gave me a lopsided grin. "I can't help it if I'm a likeable person."

I snorted. "Forget I said anything. But yes, thank you, that would help a lot." I pointed at his laptop. "Which brings me back to my question. How do you find the time? Do you even sleep?"

"I don't have to. My entire existence is fueled by a continuous supply of energy drinks and multiple caffeine shots." He navigated his way to the start of the presentation. "Our second couple is Annabelle Mitchell and Riley Soo. Riley is an interior designer, and Annabelle is an architect."

I studied the picture of a serious-looking redhead and a smiling Asian woman. "How do you know them?"

"I met Annabelle when I was doing my architecture degree. Remember Spencer from the first wedding?" When I nodded, he continued, "He's friends with Riley, so he's also invited to this one. Spencer has lived and worked all over the country, just like you, and you both have financial backgrounds. Those shared experiences would be a good way of connecting with him. I think he deserves a second look."

"Sure."

"Next we have Elijah Thompson, thirty-eight, one of Annabelle's closest friends." There was a photo of a man standing barefoot on a beach, moodily staring down the camera. "A film editor and huge movie buff. And you love watching movies, so you two should be a great fit. The last one he worked on, *The Art of Living a Life*, had early Oscar buzz around it, but it fizzled out."

"Don't think I've seen that one."

"Critics are saying he should at least have gotten a nomination," Rob said. "Married once, but separated last year because both were too busy with work. Divorce was only finalized last month."

My mind immediately went to ex-obsessed Shane. "What if he's still hung up on his ex?"

"Last I heard, they got into a nasty custody battle over their dog. I don't think he's hoping for a reconciliation with her. He also loves a quiet night in, just like you, because he's been known to leave dinners and events early to catch up on his watchlist."

"Great. Anyone else?"

"I saved the best for last. Neil Cosgrave, Annabelle's cousin, a high school PE teacher and a certified nutritionist. Used to play competitive golf when he was younger, but didn't go pro because of multiple hip and back injuries. He's had three serious long-term relationships in the past, all ended amicably, and is now godfather to his exes' children. And here comes the best part." He flashed me an excited grin. "His dad used to work for the government, so he's lived all over the world, including six years in Indonesia. He even speaks the language fluently. He's perfect for you."

"I don't know how I feel about someone who might scrutinize everything I eat. I'm not ready to give up carbs and bubble tea."

"Anyone ever told you that you're picky?"

"I'm careful, not picky," I said. "Huge difference. You would be, too, after a ton of horrible dates. And he sounds too good to be true. There's got to be a catch."

"There's no catch. Are you always this cynical and distrustful of other people?"

"Like I said, let's learn to use the word 'careful.'"

"Same thing, just spelled differently. The fact that he's still friends with all his exes should tell you something about his character."

The smiling, dark-haired man in the picture looked like he'd be the kind of man who held doors open for seniors or gently moved a spider outside to save its life. "Let's give Neil a shot."

"Terrific. Now, in light of what happened at the first wedding, I recommend that you pick an alternative," Rob said. "The best-case scenario is for you to hit it off with Neil, but in case that doesn't happen, we can also approach the alternative, so you won't have wasted your time at the wedding. I'm not saying you should settle for a less-than-perfect match," he quickly added. "We're just keeping our options open."

"Let's go with the film editor. You said Spencer's parents want grandchildren, and I'm not ready for that."

"Great." Rob pulled up the next page. "The final item to highlight at today's meeting is the list of conversation starters. Which you obviously didn't read in the last dossier."

I gave him an innocent stare, like *I don't know what you're talking about.*

The list had questions like, *Where did you grow up? What's your favorite thing to do on a quiet weekend? What made you choose to become [insert subject's career]?*

"This is a lot to remember." I looked up at him. "Also a little bit insulting, actually. Do you really think I'm that incompetent at dating that I need a list of conversation starters?"

"Not at all," he replied smoothly. "But if you're like me, it might be useful to have one. It's a trick I do sometimes, when I'm meeting potential new clients or someone I hardly know. I'll have a list of neutral topics to break the ice, and they always work a treat. No more awkward silences, or uncomfortable small talk about the weather."

"You don't like small talk?" I tilted my head at him. "You don't seem like someone who has trouble making conversation."

"Oh, on the contrary. My special talent is making small talk. But I'm the youngest of six, so I tend to over-conversationalize."

"That's not a real word. You can't just go around making up new words."

"Why not? I think it should be a real word. Anyway, I used to get into so much trouble at school for talking too much. My mouth tends to run faster than my brain." His chuckle was dry. "My dad used to get really pissed with me for saying things he thought were inappropriate. Goofing around and telling jokes whenever we had our extended family over. Dad said I embarrassed him, and he was disappointed in me because I didn't take things seriously enough as a child."

"That's harsh." And the exact opposite of my grandfather, who always made sure to let me know that he was proud of me, no matter what I did.

Rob shrugged, as if saying, *That's my dad, let's move on*. "One of my sisters thought I should make a list of safe topics, to guide me with what I could or couldn't say, so I wouldn't get into so much trouble. It worked a treat. You could do the same thing with your dates. This list will help avoid an awkward lull in the conversation. I've prepared some generic ones, and some especially tailored to each candidate."

But I hadn't moved on. Forget the conversation starters, because I wanted to ask him questions about his dad. I wanted to give him a hug and reassure him that he wasn't an embarrassment or a disappointment. I wanted to tell him that even though I'd never met his father, I was already convinced the man was a nasty piece of work.

But I didn't do any of that, because it wasn't my place. So instead, I said, "You should really do this for a living. Your service is very thorough."

"I only do this for an extremely select group of people."

"Aww. Are you saying I'm one of your favorite people?"

"Let's not get ahead of ourselves, okay?" But there was a hint of a smile tugging on his lips. "I've also suggested a few date ideas, but mini golf is the obvious choice, since Neil used to play for a living."

"Perfect. It's like he and I are meant to be. We're practically soulmates."

Rob narrowed his eyes at me. "I detect a hint of sarcasm in your tone."

"What?" I placed a hand over my chest. "I would never."

He let out a low chuckle. "I'll email you the dossier, and let me know if there's anything else you need to go through with me before the wedding."

"Actually, I could use your help with choosing a dress this time. I don't know if the dresses I have would suit the"—I consulted his presentation—"*rustic elegant* wedding theme."

"Of course. Lead the way."

I led him toward my bedroom, acutely aware of the fact that he would be the first guy ever to set foot there. None of the men I'd dated in the past, or any other male friends, had ever been in my apartment, let alone my room. I pushed open my bedroom door, my gaze quickly sweeping the room to make sure it was presentable. My bed was made, albeit sloppily, no bra or underwear on the floor, and all my dirty clothes were in the laundry basket.

Excellent.

"You sure you're up for this?" I slid open my wardrobe. "Most guys wouldn't be happy having to sit through someone trying on clothes without being threatened with bodily harm."

"I'm not most guys." Rob sat down on my bed. "My sisters trained me well."

"Suit yourself. Don't say I didn't warn you." I mulled over my choices, before pulling out a floral A-line dress in soft pastel colors. "Does this look rustic enough to you?"

"It'll work. Let's choose several others, and we can go through them all."

I took out a few other options: an olive-colored wrap dress with butterfly sleeves, a simple blue midi dress, a soft pink pleated maxi dress, and the last one, one of my favorites because of its pockets, a rust-colored belted shirt dress. Grabbing all five by their hangers, I disappeared into my bathroom, put on the floral one, then went back into the bedroom, where Rob was frowning at his phone.

"Everything okay?"

"Yeah. Just a minor issue with one of the jobs we're . . ." He looked up, trailing off when he saw me striking an awkward pose in an attempt to model the dress. "That's cute, but I feel like it might be too casual for a wedding, especially if you're wanting to impress a potential suitor. What do you think?"

I did a half twirl in front of my full-length mirror, assessing myself. "Good point."

Going back into the bathroom, I took off the floral dress and slipped into the olive wrap dress, then went out to show him again. "What about this one?"

"No." His reply was immediate. "Again, beautiful dress, but you look like you're going to a formal dinner with the British Royal Family instead of a romantic country wedding. Next."

"Since when are you a fashion expert?"

"Since before I was born. Four older sisters, remember? It's embedded in my DNA."

For the next half hour, I tried dress after dress, none of which met his ridiculously high expectations. The first five I'd chosen had been unceremoniously dumped on my bed, and soon they were joined by three more, plus a very comfortable jumpsuit, all heaped into a tall, sad, unwanted pile.

"You do realize this is only the second wedding, and you're already vetoing all the dresses I have in my wardrobe?" I called out from the bathroom as I put on a pale red one-shoulder lace dress with pretty ruffles at the front and a high side split.

"My reasons are justified. None of them fit the theme," he yelled back.

"This is my last one, and it's one of Jenna's, so if you don't like it, tough luck, because I'm showing up in an old T-shirt and my ripped jeans." I reached behind me to zip the dress up, but the zipper must have gotten stuck on the fabric or a loose thread, because it refused to budge. I tugged on it a few times, but nothing happened.

"What's taking you so long? I'm falling asleep here."

"One sec." Yanking on the zipper repeatedly did absolutely nothing, and if I used more force, it might tear the delicate fabric. I let out a frustrated groan, then made a split-second decision to discard this dress and choose one of the earlier options. But before I could take the dress off, there was a knock on the bathroom door.

"You okay in there?"

"No. I can't zip the dress up. It's stuck."

There was a long pause, then, "Do you need help?"

I sighed. "I suppose I do. Come in. It's unlocked."

The door creaked open, and Rob walked in. "Let me see."

Lifting my hair out of the way, I turned around to face the bathroom mirror, watching as he stepped behind me, his face scrunched in concentration as he fiddled with the zipper, gently tugging and pulling on it, trying to get it to move up. His knuckles lightly grazed my exposed back, sending unexpected tingles down my spine. Those sleeper brain neurons that had been daydreaming about Rob in his underwear a week and a half ago abruptly woke up from their peaceful slumber and aggressively resumed their fantasizing. Like, no holds barred. It was as if they were trying their best to produce an R-rated movie just from visualizing him in very minimal clothing.

"It's snagged on the dress," he murmured, his voice low and gravelly, whipping those thirsty brain cells of mine into another enthusiastic frenzy. "Hang on, I almost got it."

I held my breath as a large, warm hand pressed on my back, sending heat all over my body. After another tug or two, he finally managed to pull up the stubborn zipper, ever so slowly. Once he finished zipping me up, one of his palms rested on my shoulder for the briefest second, before falling away.

His eyes met mine in the mirror, and the insides of my stomach flipped and somersaulted when his thick eyelashes flickered at me.

"You look pretty." His gaze trailed down the dress snugly hugging my body, before finding my eyes again. "I vote for this one."

I might have held his gaze a few seconds too long, and the bathroom suddenly felt a little too cramped and stuffy. Did I turn the heating on too high? "Okay."

And what happened to my voice? Why did I sound so throaty?

Rob grunted and took a few steps back. "I should go. Do you need help unzipping and taking off the dress?"

I knew that wasn't meant to be an innuendo, but it sure as hell sounded like one. "I'll manage," I croaked out. "Thanks for your help."

He nodded, then walked out of the bathroom and my bedroom without another word. When I heard the front door closing, I released the breath I didn't realize I'd been holding.

What the hell just happened?

CHAPTER 12

When It Rains, It Pours, and Sometimes All You Can Do Is Dance in the Rain

The next Monday, I donned a new sterile mask as I walked into the dialysis center. I signed my name on the guest register, greeted the nurses on duty, then went to find my grandfather.

A dark-haired, brown-eyed woman dressed in a white coat stopped me in my tracks. "Are you Thomas Halim's granddaughter?"

"Yes." I shook her hand. "I'm sorry, I don't think we've met before."

"I'm the new nephrologist here, Dr. Nguyen. Can we have a word in private?" She held up her palm at seeing the crease in my forehead. "Nothing serious, don't worry, but I do need to discuss something with you."

I followed her into a small office at the back. Taking a seat in one of the metal chairs in front of her desk, I folded my arms in my lap, trying not to show my nerves. "Is he okay?"

"He is. Thomas had his blood and urine tests last week, which is something we regularly do for all our patients to monitor their kidney function." At my nod, she continued, "The results came back fine, so we know his dialysis sessions are working well to remove waste from his body. But his hemoglobin levels aren't where they should ideally be, which means your grandfather has anemia. It's one of the most common complications for people receiving hemodialysis."

I tensed a little. Anything with the word "complication" in it couldn't be good.

"At this stage, his numbers are borderline, so it's nothing to worry too much about. But if left untreated, it can develop into severe anemia, and with dialysis patients, it can increase the risk of developing heart problems. I'll prescribe some iron tablets, but he needs to pay closer attention to his diet. Make sure he eats more iron-rich foods to help boost his hemoglobin levels. Until then, you might notice him getting tired easier and having very low energy."

My heart dropped as fear—and guilt—slammed into me. Was there something I could have done? I was the one helping him with grocery shopping and meal planning, but maybe I should have taken extra steps to make sure he was eating healthier.

My grandfather had been the picture of perfect health when I was growing up. He wasn't a smoker, nor a drinker, he exercised a few times a week, and his idea of a snack was an apple or a bowl of edamame. On paper, he was the last person you'd imagine being diagnosed with chronic kidney disease.

But he did have high blood pressure running in his family. His parents had it, so did his two brothers, and Opa himself was diagnosed in his thirties. The solution would have been straightforward enough: He'd been prescribed some tablets to keep his blood pressure under control. But—as I'd learned later—he'd been too busy focusing on working and raising his young family, especially being a first-generation immigrant in a foreign country, that he had neglected taking his medication regularly like he was supposed to. It had taken a toll on his kidneys, which had finally given up not too long ago, necessitating the thrice-weekly dialysis sessions to keep him alive.

"One last thing. I'm not sure if you've heard, but it was recently announced that the insurance co-pay is projected to go up by at least six percent next year. I thought I'd flag it for your attention so you can prepare your finances accordingly."

Fantastic. What was that saying again? When it rains, it pours?

I thanked her, then walked out to find Opa. Ann, one of his regular nurses, was chatting with him as she helped him stand up from his chair.

"There she is!" She beamed at me. "Thomas is ready to go. Just letting you know, his blood pressure is a tad low, and he says he feels a bit dizzy. Make sure you keep an eye on him for an hour or so until he feels better."

"Will do." I held one of Opa's arms to support him. "See you on Wednesday."

Opa shook my hand off and slowly ambled toward the front door. "I can walk by myself," he grumbled. "How far is the car?"

"Parked right outside. You sure you don't want my help?"

I received a grunt in response, but I knew better and let it go.

The fact that my affable grandfather was often grumpy on dialysis days hadn't escaped my notice. He never said anything, but I knew he still hadn't fully accepted how his survival now depended on a machine taking on the role of his artificial kidney. He'd complained once that it had felt like a prison sentence, because his previously active life had been reduced to sitting in a chair for five hours, three times a week, for him to be able to continue living.

I'd heard stories from Ann. About other patients in the center who'd had enough and decided to stop the treatment, then sadly passed within a few weeks. Because the heartbreaking fact of the matter was Opa's life—and those patients' lives in the center—depended on these sessions. Forgoing them would be akin to choosing to end their lives. And one of my biggest fears was for Opa to one day realize that he didn't want to keep on doing this anymore and decide to give up altogether.

Dr. Nguyen's words rang in my ears as I started the car. Opa was the only family I had left, and I couldn't bear the thought of a world without him. I knew he wouldn't be here forever, but while he was still here, I had to do everything in my power to make sure his medical needs were being met, including making sure that he was safe financially, enough to be able to keep doing his dialysis treatments.

And if I needed any reasons to fight for the store, this would be at the top of the list.

"Thanks for taking the time to be here, everyone."

"Appreciate you organizing this, Kim," Melly said. "I nearly had a heart attack when I got the letter."

"I'm not selling to Goodwin," Anahita immediately said. "Fucking greedy developers. They're not taking my store away from me. Not even when hell freezes over."

I'd gotten in touch with other business owners in the precinct, and some of them had agreed to meet tonight. Ellie, who had offered to host the meeting at her bakery, walked out of the kitchen and placed a tray of freshly baked goodies on the table. "I made some low-carb chocolate brownies and cupcakes. Help yourselves."

"Oh! I nearly forgot." Quinn, who had just opened their artisanal coffee shop a few months ago, reached for a large paper bag at their feet and took out two six-pack cases of retro-looking glass bottles. "I brought some banana-flavored lattes, our café's specialty."

Melly raised her eyebrows. "Banana and coffee? What does that even taste like?"

"Trust me, they're good." Melody, the owner of a K-pop album and merchandise store next to Quinn's coffee shop, grabbed one and twisted the cap open with more enthusiasm than necessary. "I had my doubts when Quinn first told me about it. But they convinced me to take one sip, and the rest is history. It's now one of my favorite drinks."

"This would be perfect for the Knotty Tea Society," I said. "They're always looking at trying new drinks, so if you want, Quinn, I can recommend this to the members."

They beamed at me. "That would be awesome."

"Hey, Anahita. I've been meaning to ask you," Melly said. "How's your daughter doing? I hope she's still not upset because of your dickhead partner leaving."

The other woman blew out a long breath. "She was miserable the first couple of weeks, but we got through it. Nicole gave me a knitting kit for kids, and it was wonderful, because my daughter really got into it, and it helped us to bond and take her mind off things. I can't thank you all enough for your support."

"Sorry I'm late, sorry!" Selma rushed into the store, her long hair wildly flying as she took the last seat next to Nicole. "Did I miss anything?"

"Got here just in time." I smiled at her. "Now that everyone's here, shall we get started?"

Seven pairs of eyes focused on me.

"As you all know, Goodwin Property Group is offering to buy the buildings on the strip with the plan to demolish them all and build a new high-rise. The antique shop owner next to Selma's bookshop has already said yes, and since Goodwin already owns some of the shop fronts, the renters of those stores will have no choice but to vacate and move their businesses elsewhere."

"My boss said he's also thinking of selling," Selma said. "He said there's no profit in selling secondhand books and he's better off taking the money from Goodwin. And if he's selling, then I'll be unemployed, and the job market is tough as shit these days."

"Same. My landlord told me yesterday that they're thinking of selling, too." Quinn made a face. "I've only just moved in a few months ago, and now I'll have to find another place."

"I took the liberty of reaching out to Jacqui Goodwin." Ellie swiped open her phone and scrolled through her email. "This is her reply: 'I understand that the proposal concerns the livelihood of many business owners, and that the precinct holds sentimental value for a lot of people, but the project isn't entirely within our control. It's a collaboration between Goodwin and the local government, and the city is investing a substantial amount of capital in the development.'"

"I'm still on the fence whether to sell or not, to be honest." Melody gave us a sheepish smile. "The demand for K-pop things isn't as high as it used to be. I could take the money and start something new elsewhere. Maybe even find a spot at the Plaza, if there's any availability, since it's gotten very busy since the renovation."

"You won't be the only one thinking that," Selma said. "The Plaza is the main draw. The rent here might be cheaper, but if people were given the option between leasing a space here and at the Plaza, most would choose the latter."

"I'm not surprised," Quinn piped up. "I like it here, and the vibes are immaculate, but when I signed my lease, the real estate agent said it had been vacant for over a year."

"That's because the foot traffic to this area is minimal," Melly said. "The huge parking lot separating us from the main Plaza building is a big drawback. Most people couldn't be bothered to walk all the way across to get to us."

"It's been better since Ellie's bakery blew up," Selma pointed out. "I managed to sell all our copies of *The Fundamentals of Molecular Biotechnology*, even the really ratty ones that looked like they've been through hell and back. But, like my boss said, it's still not good enough."

"It's not," Melly said. "True, I've had more people calling to inquire about yoga classes since Ellie's bakery became famous. But out of ten inquiries, maybe only two or three joined. We need to do more."

"This precinct had been a longtime fixture of Port Benedict," Nicole said. "It was a big part of my childhood. My parents used to take me here, back when the corner store used to be a toy shop. It has such beautiful classic buildings, too. It would be a shame to see it go."

"It's not going anywhere." There was determination in my voice. "We'll do everything we can to stop it. We need to help those businesses that are struggling. Encourage more people to visit our strip and remind them what made the place so special."

"Maybe we can rent one of those pop-up stalls inside the Plaza to promote our stuff," Anahita suggested.

"That's going to cost money." Selma shook her head. "I've only sold six textbooks in the past week, and my boss will say he can't afford to pay for another space when he can't even make a profit out of his current one, which is totally fair."

"What about making flyers and handing them out to people at the entrance of the Plaza?" Quinn suggested. "Anyone who brings one gets a ten percent discount or something? I can hand out free banana lattes with the flyers."

"And free banana bread! That'll go so well with the lattes."

"Ooh, yes! We can play some K-pop music to attract people."

"I can ask some of my students to do a yoga demonstration."

"I have an idea." I raised my voice a little so I could be heard among all the excited chatters. "What about holding a street festival? Here, at the precinct?"

Selma raised her eyebrows. "Like those Lunar New Year festivals in Chinatown?"

"Yes. There are studies about how street fairs boost the local economy. They promote the area, draw new visitors, which will bring new sales, and foster a sense of community pride. Here's what I have in mind." I opened my laptop and the pages of research I'd put together. "We'll have to apply for a permit to host a street and sidewalk event, but the process is straightforward, and it's all done online. We can block off the entire street, set up stalls, give out free samples, hold coffee-making classes or yoga demonstrations. We can also rent out stalls to other small businesses outside of this precinct, for people who want a cost-effective way to showcase their products, and that would help cover our costs."

Encouraged by everyone's nods, I continued, "You can run promotions, giveaways, whatever you like. All those things you were talking about, but within the convenience of our own stores, so visitors will have a chance to see for themselves all the wonderful things we have to offer. It's a great chance to elevate the profile of the area and bring more customers in, and hopefully that would encourage all the business owners *not* to sell to Goodwin. And if no one is selling, they can't go ahead with the project."

"I think that's a sick idea," Quinn said. "Anything to introduce more people to the goodness of banana-flavored coffees, I'm down."

"I like what you said about renting out the stalls," Melly said. "A friend of mine sells handmade jewelry, but she can't afford to rent a storefront right now. This is perfect for her."

"My sister-in-law would love that, too," Nicole piped up. "She makes these gorgeous leather wallets and coin pouches. I'll ask if she's interested."

"My cousin and his band can play for us," Anahita said. "For free, because he owes me a shit ton of favors. Some music and dancing would interest people to check out the festival."

We kept brainstorming and started divvying up jobs to get the ball rolling. Melly would come up with a budget, and Anahita was in charge of applying for the permit, while Melody volunteered to reach out to local small businesses that might be interested in renting a stall. Ellie was tasked with renting tables, tents, a portable stage, and all other necessary equipment, and my job was to find sponsors for the event. The rest of the group would be working together to reach out to the other business owners in the precinct and market the festival to the greater Port Benedict community.

I left the meeting feeling buoyed and optimistic. If the idea worked, we'd be able to save the precinct and the yarn store in the process.

And then all I had to do was make sure that I was its official owner.

CHAPTER 13

Two's a Company, Three's a Party

The sun was hiding behind the clouds on the day of the Soo-Mitchell wedding, casting a gloomy feel over the gorgeous winery we were at. The ceremony had been short and sweet, and the newlyweds looked radiant in sparkly, ethereal white gowns.

I stood up from my seat at the very back row and scanned the crowd, trying to spot Rob among all the other guests. I hadn't seen him since the zipper malfunction episode, even though we'd been texting every day, which was probably good, because I wasn't sure how I'd act around him when all my brain wanted to do was to constantly evoke the (sweet, sweet) memories of that evening.

"Kim! There you are." I looked up to see Rob walking over. He gave me a quick hug, surrounding me with his now-familiar sweet, minty scent. "I've been looking for you."

I reluctantly tore myself away from him and instructed my brain to behave. "I was late, sorry. The store was busy, and I couldn't just leave Nicole on her own."

"Don't worry about it." His eyes did a slow sweep of my body, and the corners of his mouth lifted into a smile. "Looks like we chose the perfect dress. You look amazing."

Before I could overanalyze his comment (even though there might be nothing to analyze—it was just a simple "amazing," wasn't it?), Rob gestured to the man standing next to him. "Kim, this is Neil Cosgrave. Neil, meet Kimiko Halim, a good friend of mine."

The man looked like he could play Prince Charming in a Hallmark movie, with wavy dark hair, deep dimples, and cornflower-blue eyes, looking so sickeningly wholesome with the backdrop of the vineyard and the rolling hills behind him. He smiled at me, momentarily blinding me with a flash of white teeth. "Lovely to meet you, Kim."

I accepted his proffered hand and shook it. "Likewise."

"Is that an Indonesian surname?" Neil gave me a curious look.

"Yes." I feigned surprise. "How do you know?"

"My family moved around when I was younger for my dad's work. We lived in Jakarta for six years. I had a friend with that same surname."

"What a coincidence. How long ago was that?"

"Twenty, twenty-one years ago, maybe?"

"And you still remember?" I gave him an admiring look. "Great memory."

"I used to speak the language, but I've forgotten most of it now."

"You did?" I dialed up my look of admiration a notch. "That's amazing."

I racked my brain for more things to say as we headed toward the reception area. What else did Rob have in his dossier? Should I attempt a conversation in Indonesian? But with my limited abilities, that'd probably be over after two sentences. What else should I talk about?

"Neil is a PE teacher," Rob helpfully supplied. "He was a

professional golfer in his past life. Weren't you even touted as the next Tiger Woods or something?"

"He's being too kind." Neil flashed me a modest smile. "I had a serious injury that derailed my golfing career. Now I only play for fun."

Yes, of course, I could talk about golfing, no problem. "Sorry to hear that. I used to caddy when I was younger."

A spark of interest flashed in Neil's eyes. "How long did you caddy for?"

"Less than a year. Ten months, I think?"

"Kim is also a beast at mini golf," Rob added. "I don't know why I kept agreeing whenever she challenged me to a game, because she destroyed me every single time. You two should play together."

I knew I should be glad that Rob was hyping me up to Neil, but somehow, an irrational part of my brain was telling me that *this doesn't feel right*. I didn't want to challenge Neil, or any other guys, and play mini golf with any of them. It was *my* thing with *Rob*, and I didn't want to share that experience with anyone else.

But both men were still looking at me, waiting for my reply. "We should. I might be able to show you a thing or two."

Neil grinned at me. "Is that so?"

"Maybe." I pushed away those pesky thoughts and fixed a flirty smile on my face—or at least, what I hoped resembled one. "It's not every day I get to beat a pro golfer in a game of mini golf."

Neil took the bait. "I'm not one to refuse a challenge, so you're on."

We stepped into the reception area and were instantly surrounded by the chatter of guests and the clinks of champagne glasses. There was a long grazing table in the middle piled with both sweet and savory options, next to a rustic market cart serving as the drink station, with buckets of chilled wine bottles, cocktails in mason jars, and glass dispensers of lemonade, iced teas, and fruit-infused water. A doughnut wall was on one side of the room, with a churro station on the other side.

"I have to say hi to a friend," Rob said. "Catch you both later."

He waved at someone across the room as he walked away, and both Neil and I watched as he greeted and hugged a gorgeous brunette, then gestured in our—*my*—direction, clearly telling the woman he was here with me. I craned my neck a little, curious to get a better look at her. That had to be his ex, right? Why would he be pointing at me otherwise?

"Would he be okay with us going golfing together?" Neil kept his eyes on Rob and the brunette for a few more beats, his eyes following their every move, before finally glancing at me. "Maybe we should ask him to come along with us."

"Oh. Sure, we can ask him, if you want to."

He flicked another glance at Rob and the woman, before shaking his head. "Or maybe next time. Are you free next week?"

We exchanged numbers and chatted for a few more minutes, before he excused himself to go to the restroom. Once he was gone, I let out a relieved breath. That went kind of well, didn't it? Neil seemed like a nice enough guy, and he was easy on the eyes, so it wouldn't be a hardship to spend time with him for the next few months.

Maybe this was a sign that things were finally turning around.

My stomach grumbled, reminding me that I hadn't eaten anything since breakfast. As I weaved my way through the crowd toward the long table of food, a page boy holding a plate full of chocolate cupcakes headed straight in my direction. One of the flower girls was chasing him, and for a minute, it felt like I was transported into one of those slow-motion movie scenes where you could see the imminent disaster hurtling toward the main character, but you knew it was too late to do anything. The young boy collided with me, dumping what looked like a ton of creamy, gooey chocolate ganache onto the dress I was wearing.

A dress that had been borrowed from Jenna's closet.

I gasped.

The page boy looked up at me and gasped.

It seemed like the entire room had fallen silent, and all signs of life had ceased, because everyone had stopped whatever they were doing and turned to gawk at the trainwreck that was unfolding right before their eyes.

Then someone started to cry, probably a baby in the crowd needing to be fed, or their diaper changed, or something equally critical. Would babies even be at weddings? Whatever it was, it was probably more important than a dress getting intimately acquainted with thick chocolate icing, and was that Oreo crumbs I spotted among the sticky chocolate goodness?

Both the page boy and the flower girl were still standing in front of me, their eyes wide, their mouths agape.

I knelt to their eye levels and smiled at the boy. "It's okay. Accidents happen, right?"

A relieved grin broke across his face. He mumbled a quiet, "Sorry," then ran off, the flower girl at his heels, while the rest of the crowd resumed their conversation.

"That was really sweet of you. Not getting upset at the boy."

I stood up and found Rob standing behind me with a smile and a handful of napkins. From the corner of my eye, I could see some of the guests still watching me, but he moved his body, so he was blocking their view.

"He was just being a kid." I took the napkins and tried to scoop the big blob of chocolate off the dress. In vain, might I add, because it only made things worse. Instead of removing it, I successfully made it cover a larger surface area, because it was now smeared entirely over the left side of my chest. "Being upset at him isn't going to make the stain disappear."

"Wise words. Need any help?"

"Sure." I didn't look at him as I continued to clean—no,

smear—more chocolate ganache on the dress. "Maybe if you have one of those white Magic Eraser thingies that can miraculously get the stain off. Or help me find the exact same dress, because this isn't mine. Or, failing both options, maybe you can just lick the chocolate clean."

A loud, awkward silence fell over us, while I paused my scrubbing, silently cringing inside. Did I seriously just ask him to lick me?

I stole a glance at him. He was watching me, biting his lower lip, obviously trying very hard not to burst into laughter.

No, no. Do NOT look at him biting his lips.

"That is *so* embarrassing." I groaned. "Please pretend I never said anything."

"Too late." His lips twitched. "I can't unhear that, and it'll stay with me for the rest of my life. Don't be embarrassed. It's kind of cute, actually."

My heart stumbled a little at his words, and suddenly the chocolate stain just became immensely fascinating. "You obviously have a warped sense of what can be classified as cute."

He only chuckled. "How did it go with Neil?"

"He's nice." The chocolate icing had now coated my entire chest, so I gave up trying to salvage the dress. "Oh, fuck it. I'll just buy Jenna a new one." I crumpled the dirty napkins into a ball and sucked the excess chocolate on my fingers to clean it off, before releasing them with a loud *pop*. "We might be going mini golfing next week."

There was no answer. I looked up to find Rob giving me a funny look, his eyes darkening a little as he stared at me. He swallowed, his gaze dropping to my lips and lingering there for a few seconds before finding my eyes again.

"I'm sorry," he rasped, "what did you say?"

"I said I might see him next week for mini golf."

"Right." He cleared his throat. "Great first date choice. It's fun, it's safe, and, uh, it won't cost you five hundred dollars."

"Do you want to come along? He did ask about you coming with us."

Rob raised his eyebrows. "You want me to third-wheel on your first date with Neil?"

"No, it's Neil who wants you to third-wheel on my first date with him."

He considered me for a moment. "Actually, now that I think about it, maybe I *will* tag along on your date. But in secret, so he won't see me. Just in case you need another rescue."

"The fact that you're offering to come along on a date with a guy you introduced, on the off chance that I might need a rescue, is a bit worrying." I grinned at him. "Then again, you *were* wrong about Ben—just saying—so I guess there is a possibility you could be wrong about Neil, too."

"I wasn't wrong about Ben. I just didn't know he kept pet snakes. And I'm not wrong about Neil, either, but I'll feel better if I know that you're having a good time with him. And that you're safe. I mean, if he plans to swindle five hundred bucks out of you, not that he will, I can be there to help you stop it before it happens."

My chest felt like it had expanded a hundredfold from the sweet gesture. "Sounds like you're having second thoughts about Neil."

"I definitely am not. Think of it as an extension of my service."

"Did you offer the same thing to your sister, brother, and cousins?"

"I didn't." A streak of pink crept up his cheeks. "Look, just say yes, okay? I promise I'll be discreet. He won't know I'm there."

"Fine. But only because I'm such a good friend, and I'd hate to deprive you of the fun of watching me defeat Neil."

He snorted, but his eyes were smiling. "Text me the time and the place. Anyway, I think we should also introduce you to Elijah as well." At my blank look, he clarified, "Your alternative? The film editor?"

"Looking and smelling like this?" I glanced down at my dress. "It's not a good look for meeting someone."

"You smell fine. Hang on, I think I see him." Rob placed his hand at the small of my back and steered me toward a man standing by the bar. "Hey, Elijah. Enjoying the party?"

Great. Of course I was going to meet a guy covered in melted chocolate.

"Not really." Elijah took a long pull of his beer, his eyes watching the front door like a hawk. "I'm about to go. Waiting for my ride to arrive."

"That's too bad." Rob turned to me, as if he'd just realized that I was standing next to him. "By the way, this is a good friend of mine, Kimiko Halim. Kim, this is Elijah Thompson."

Elijah gave me a once-over, not even batting an eyelash at the humongous chocolate stain on my dress. "Hey, how's it going?"

It was obvious he wasn't interested in chatting with us, because his gaze went back to the door, as if glaring at it would make his ride arrive quicker.

But Rob wasn't giving up that easily. "Elijah is a film editor, Kim. You might have seen some of his work."

"Wait. Are you *the* Elijah Thompson?" I pretended to look awestruck. "I know who you are. Didn't you work on *The Art of Living a Life*? Brilliant movie. You should have gotten tons of awards for it."

That earned me a look of approval from Rob, like, *Huh, that was pretty impressive.*

I flashed him a smug look in return. *Watch and learn, buddy. Watch and learn.*

Meanwhile, that caught Elijah's attention, because he was now appraising me with a mild look of curiosity. "Thank you. What did you like best about it?"

Uh-oh. I'd never even heard of it before Rob mentioned it.

Although I did praise his movie, so what did I expect? I brought this on myself.

"The entire thing is brilliant," I said. "It's so hard to pick a favorite part. Are you working on anything right now?"

"I am, but nothing I can tell anyone about. In fact, I'm heading to the studio after this to finish some stuff." Elijah's phone buzzed. "That's my ride. Great to meet you, Kim. See you around, Carmichael."

As soon as he was out of earshot, I turned to Rob. "That was a bit . . . rushed. At least now we have two viable options, don't we?"

"*You* have two viable options. They're both great guys, and hopefully one of those is your happily-ever-after."

I nodded, trying to muster up the enthusiasm that I was supposed to portray.

But I couldn't.

No matter how hard I tried.

CHAPTER 14

Oh, the Places You'll Never See!

After Elijah had left, Rob and I went to find some food, and my chocolate-stained dress was quickly forgotten. By 10 P.M., most of the guests had relocated to the dance floor, but Rob and I only watched from the deserted bar as the newlyweds did a conga line with their friends and families. The couple stole kisses every time they passed one another on the dance floor, clearly smitten with each other.

I would never admit to it, but seeing that had made me envious. I'd seen that kind of love in my grandparents—the kind that looked like true love—but I had never shared that kind of all-encompassing love with anyone, and it was something I probably would never experience in my life. Nobody, not even Leo, had ever looked at me the way my grandparents looked at each other, like the sun and the moon and the stars hung in each other's eyes. Like their world started and ended with the other person. I'd never know how it would feel to be so deeply in love with someone, to trust them, and to be happy and secure in the knowledge that they would be there for you through thick and thin, for better or for worse. Knowing that whatever you did, you were safe, because someone else would always be there for you.

"I can still smell you from where I'm sitting."

I turned to Rob, who was watching the conga line as he sipped his gin and tonic. "I thought you said I smelled good."

"I said you smelled fine, and that was a few hours ago, when the chocolate was still fresh. Now you just smell like stale cupcakes." Rob loosened his tie and rolled up his sleeves, exposing forearms that rendered me slightly mesmerized for a few seconds. "How's your grandpa doing?"

"He's good." I averted my eyes from his forearms. "Enjoying a night of card games and C-drama reruns with his friends, as we speak."

Rob was quiet for a few minutes as he picked up his glass and swirled the liquid around. "How did your grandparents come to raise you? You said you'd tell me the story of your parents some other time. Is this a good time?"

"I guess so." My eyes drifted to watch the conga line, which seemed to have gotten longer in just a few short minutes. "My mom died when I was a baby, and my dad decided that he didn't have it in him to raise a young child on his own. He left to pursue his career, so my grandparents raised me instead."

"I'm sorry." Rob looked disturbed. "Where's your dad now? Do you talk to him at all?"

"Every now and then." I shrugged, trying not to sound like it bothered me, because it didn't. "He's based overseas for his job, so he comes home maybe once, twice a year."

A sad look crossed his features. "I can't imagine how hard it must have been for you."

I waved a dismissive hand, because I didn't want, or need, his sympathy. "It never felt hard, because I never knew anything else. My grandparents are all I've ever known, and I'm just grateful to have them in my life, because if it weren't for them, who knows where I'd be right now. There's no point wasting my time being upset about my dad, or resenting him, because how can you resent someone you don't even know, right?"

It was what I'd told myself over and over again, but that wasn't the entire truth, because even though I *had* come to accept that my father was never around, I *did* resent him for not making more of an effort to be present in my life. Fine, so maybe he wasn't mentally and physically able to care for a young child while coping with the grief of losing his wife and juggling his super-important job. But that was thirty years ago. How hard would it be to reach out to his one and only adult daughter now, say, once a month, at the very minimum? Was that too much to ask?

Maybe that was another reason I couldn't trust men and relationships. How could I, when the very first one I was supposed to have with my own father didn't even work out?

But yeah, I had accepted the fact that there was nothing I could do about it. My life could have gone in a totally different, much worse direction, so instead of being angry and bitter about how things could have been, I chose to be grateful for it.

"You're a bigger person than I am," Rob said. "I probably would never be able to forgive my parents if they'd done that to me." His expression hardened. "I don't want to judge, because I'm sure your dad had gone through a lot, but I don't know how anyone could have done that to their own child."

My smile was thin. "I've stopped wondering about that ages ago." I signaled to the bartender behind us for another glass of wine. "Have you thought about your father's request?"

"I told him I'd try working in his office one or two days a week, as a trial run to see if it was a good fit. *Then* I'll think about going back to finish my degree."

"What did he say?" I thanked the bartender as he placed a fresh glass in front of me.

"He wasn't happy, because he doesn't like taking no for an

answer. Wanted me to come in full-time immediately." His smile was dull. "We haven't come to an agreement yet. How's the store? Did you get in touch with that knitting influencer you told me about?"

"No. I've tried to reach out, but none of her people responded to my emails. Her last public appearance was two years ago, and I heard she doesn't do in-person events anymore now, unless it's someone she personally knows."

"Let me ask around. Maybe someone I know would know someone who knows her."

The conga line was now gone, replaced by people dancing the macarena. Neil Cosgrave was in the group, laughing with a few other guests, looking like he was having the time of his life. Like he was genuinely enjoying other people's company, and vice versa.

That was a good sign, right?

"He's a nice guy." Rob followed my gaze. "Thank you for trusting me to do this for you. I know it couldn't have been easy, but I think you're very brave for doing this and putting yourself out there."

"You're getting too far ahead of yourself. I never said I trusted you."

"You don't?" He tilted his head at me. "You wound me."

"I haven't decided." I bit back a smile.

"Anything I can do to help you decide?"

"If I'm going to trust you, it has to happen organically."

"That's fair." He nodded. "Trust can't be given; it has to be earned."

"Exactly. Maybe you can start by telling me things about yourself. You know more about me than I do about you, so we need to level the playing field."

"Sure. What do you want to know?"

"Why don't you answer the questions you gave me in your

questionnaire?" I folded my hands in front of my chest. "Let's see. What is the one thing that's most important in your life?"

His answer was quick. "Easy. Being with my loved ones."

"What were some of your other questions? Oh, describe to me your ideal partner."

"I know you said the ideal man doesn't exist, but I think the ideal woman does exist. She wouldn't be ideal for everyone, but she would be for me. Someone with a zest for life, someone funny, loyal, and smart, and has similar values to me." He gave me a faint smile. "Someone who puts their family above everything else."

Was I being delusional if I thought he was describing me? Or was it wishful thinking? "Okay." I cleared my throat. "What about hobbies? What do you do in your spare time, other than setting people up and going to weddings?"

"It used to be sports when I was younger. Basketball, football, tennis, hockey. Anything that would keep me out of trouble."

"That shows." I made a vague gesture at his physique. "I mean, I can tell. You've, uh, obviously kept it up. Anyway, final question. Give me five fun facts about yourself."

He ticked off his fingers. "One, I'm addicted to coffee. At least four cups a day. Two, I love watching stand-up comedians, because they always cheer me up after a long day. Three, I played drums in high school, because I wanted to impress this girl I had a huge crush on. Four, I think pineapple on pizza is one of the most genius food inventions ever, and yes, I know that's controversial. And last one"—he leaned closer, his voice a low rumble in my ear—"I have five tattoos, and no, you can't see them, because they're in places you cannot see."

I couldn't care less about coffee, or pineapple, or pizza, or food in general, because all I could focus on was how he was so close and how it was giving me warm, tingly feelings all over my body, along with full-blown permission for my brain to go rogue and imagine the (oh so many) possible locations of the tattoos that I would never see in my entire life. What the hell did "places I cannot see" exactly mean?

He gave me a wide, innocent grin, and for a moment, all I could do was stare at his eyes, back to the puzzle of figuring out the shade of yarn of those hazel eyes.

Lemon Myrtle? Or Dark Lime?

I snapped myself back to the present and narrowed my eyes at him. "Okay, you really got me thinking with that"—I made air quotes with my hands—"'places you cannot see' line. I mean, that was really good. Maybe I'll steal that and use it on my date with Neil."

"Got you thinking, huh?"

"Only for, like, two seconds." More than two minutes, and still going.

"Good." His grin was teasing, like it was holding secrets that I would never be privy to, and I was suddenly, irrationally, jealous of whoever he had privately shared those secrets with. "But seriously, when you go on that date with Neil, make sure you unleash all your wit and charm. Go ahead and steal my line, as long as you make him fall head over heels in love with you, because you deserve your happy ending."

His eyes drifted across the room, and an affectionate smile lifted the corners of his mouth as his gaze snagged on someone across the room. The brunette that he was talking to earlier—his ex—lifted her glass at him in salute.

I knew I should probably ask how things went with her, but I had a weird feeling that I wouldn't like his answer.

And so, as the night went on, instead of thinking about Neil, my mind kept wandering to someone else. Someone I knew I shouldn't be thinking about, because I knew it would only lead to heartbreak. Someone who was my polar opposite, who wanted love and happy endings, while I didn't believe in one. And I didn't know if I could trust anyone enough to even consider thinking about it. Not even if it was him.

Because I knew relationships weren't made to last.

At least, not for me.

CHAPTER 15

The Meeting That Could Have Been an Email

"Ooh, Kim, your cute friend is back."

I looked up to see Rob walking into the Yarn Fanatics, his face lighting up when he saw me.

"He seems extremely happy to see you," Nicole observed. "Even my own husband doesn't look that excited when he sees me at the end of the day. Unless I bring food. Or a case of beer." She slid me a curious look. "Is there anything you'd like to share with us?"

Two other pairs of eyes pivoted my way. It was Thursday afternoon, almost the end of the day, and Ellie and Melody were going over some items for the street festival.

"I have nothing to share."

"That's not true. They've been going to weddings together," Ellie unhelpfully informed Nicole. "He's been helping Kim meet some single guys."

"But didn't you say *he's* single?" Nicole lowered her voice to a whisper. "Why do you need to meet other single men when you've got one right in front of you?"

"Because he still carries a torch for his ex," I said, also lowering my voice to a whisper. "I'm going to the weddings with him because he doesn't want to show up alone in front of her."

"You've never met said ex, though," Ellie pointed out. "Two weddings so far, and you've never seen her, have you?"

"She was at the last wedding, but we were never officially introduced."

"Maybe he's just making up that excuse to spend time with you," Melody said, her eyes widening. "That is *so* romantic! I love weddings. All the romance, the joy, the music, and the dancing. Is he a good dancer? He looks like he could be a great dancer."

"He is," Ellie said. "I've seen him dance, and believe me, he can move."

Our hushed conversation stopped as Rob came up.

"Hey." He beamed at me. "Sorry to show up unannounced. Are you busy?"

I couldn't help but smile back at him, even though I knew that Ellie, Nicole, and Melody were watching us with interest. "We're just going over things for the street festival. What's up?"

"I wanted to let you know that my contact at the tourism office got back to me, and he's interested in covering your shopping precinct. The guy at the local newspaper had left, but he said he'll find someone else to help us."

"That's fantastic." I didn't know it was possible for my smile to get bigger, but it did.

"That could probably have been an email, though," Ellie said to him. "Or a text. You didn't have to come all the way here to tell her that."

"I know." Rob shoved one hand into his jeans pocket, his face sheepish. "I finished early, and I was in the area, so I thought it would be easier to share the news in person." His other hand went up to rub the back of his neck. "And I wanted to see if you're free for drinks after work."

"She is," Ellie immediately answered. "In fact, she can be free now, since you're already here. Time is money, so no point in waiting around!"

"But Thursday nights are dinner nights with you and Jenna," I protested. "We were supposed to try that new bingsu place at the Plaza, remember?"

"We can try that tomorrow. Or next week. Or you can try that with Rob," Ellie said. "Wait, it's my phone. I think it's a text message." She made a show of pulling out her phone from her back pocket and swiping through her messages. "Oh no! Alec said he's not feeling well, so it looks like I won't be able to make dinner tonight anyway. I'm so sorry."

I gave Ellie a look. "Really?"

She chuckled. "Just go, will you?"

"I can do the closing." Nicole ducked under the counter and emerged holding my bag. "Have fun, kiddos!"

"What do you recommend?"

We were standing in the queue for the new bingsu café that I was supposed to go to with Ellie and Jenna tonight, staring at the laminated menu in our hands, while a Korean pop song played softly from the speakers above our heads. We'd been standing in the queue for the past ten minutes, and from the looks of things, we might be here for a while. There were around four or five other groups ahead of us, making the queue stretch past the shop next door. The place was tiny, with only three four-seater tables and two long tables in the middle of the shop, and they were all occupied.

"Apparently the black sesame bingsu is phenomenal," I said. "And I've been told the mango one is amazing, as well."

"Let's get one of each to share between us."

I didn't know why, but the thought of sharing a bowl of bingsu with him—or sharing anything, really—felt strangely intimate. In a good way. "Great idea."

Rob was still studying the menu, his face serious. "I wonder how black sesame mixed with mango would taste."

"What?" I gaped at him. "Who *does* that? You taste the black sesame by itself, *then* the mango by itself. You don't mix them together!"

"Why not? Everything will practically be mixed anyway once they're in my digestive system, right? It's a question of when, not if."

"Yes, but that isn't the proper way of eating desserts." I made a face. "Of eating anything! Would you mix, say, a glass of red wine and a cup of bubble tea? Or a plate of lasagna and a slice of tiramisu?"

He was watching me with a grin. "Didn't know you were so passionate about your food."

"Passion has nothing to do with it. It's called being kind to your tastebuds."

His chuckle was low, sending delicious shivers down my spine. "Okay, food police. I promise I'll behave."

Just then, his phone buzzed, and his eyebrows creased as he saw the caller ID. "I need to take this. I'll be right back."

The queue had only inched forward a tiny bit when he returned a few minutes later, looking troubled. "I'm sorry, but I need to go. That was my mother, and she needed a ride. My dad was supposed to pick her up from her appointment, but he didn't show up and he wasn't answering her calls. I can drop you back at the store—"

"Don't worry about me," I said, immediately leaving the queue. "I'll find my own way back. You just go look after your mom. Is she okay?"

"She's fine." He glanced at me. "Actually, do you want to come with? This won't take long, and we can find something to eat after."

"I'd love to." I didn't know why I said yes, only that I wanted to be there for him.

Twenty minutes later, we walked into a physiotherapist's office, and a woman limped up when she saw us walking in. She was holding on to a pair of crutches to support her right foot, which was wrapped in a tall black walking boot.

"Hey, Mom." Rob leaned over and gave her a hug, then helped steady her on her feet. "You okay to walk? The car is right outside."

"I should be okay. Thanks for coming to get me, sweetheart." The woman looked like she could be a carbon copy of Rob, with the same friendly smile and warm hazel eyes. "You must be Kim. I'm Michelle, Robbie's mother. I'm so sorry you had to cut your date short."

How did she know about me? "Please don't apologize. It wasn't a date or anything, we were just hanging out."

She flicked a curious glance at her son. "Right."

"Mom injured her ankle a couple of weeks ago," Rob said. "She was going down a staircase too quickly, lost her footing, then successfully tore her ankle ligaments."

I made a sympathetic grimace. "That sounds painful."

"Very much." Michelle laughed. "Moral of the story: Take your time going down the stairs. An extra two or three seconds wouldn't kill you."

"Shaving off two or three seconds might," Rob said, earning an eye roll from his mom.

His parents' house was a charming bungalow-style home with a covered wraparound porch, a short drive away from the physiotherapist. Rob parked the car in the driveway before going around to the passenger side to support his mom into the house. He helped her settle on the living room sofa, then moved around the house to put her bags away and get her a glass of water.

"Thanks again, honey," Michelle said. "You two should go. Have your dinner or whatever it was that I interrupted."

"When is Dad coming home?" Rob was frowning. "I don't know if I feel comfortable leaving you on your own. Maybe we should wait until he gets here."

"He texted, saying he's on his way." Michelle waved her hand. "Go. I'll be fine."

Just then, the front door slammed, followed by footsteps echoing on the tiled floor.

"Michelle? Are you home?"

An older, less lean version of Rob, with graying temples and sharp, calculating eyes, strolled into the living room, stopping short when he saw us. "Robbie. What are you doing here?"

"I drove Mom home. We're about to go." I noticed Rob was standing up straighter, and the laughter in his eyes had dulled a little. "This is a friend of mine, Kim Halim. My father, James Carmichael."

I shook his hand. "Nice to meet you."

His father eyed me with curiosity. "What do you do, Kim?"

"I run a small business at the back of Port Benedict Plaza," I said. "A yarn store that used to belong to my late grandmother."

"The row of old shops with that popular bakery? Can't imagine you get a lot of foot traffic there."

"Dad," Rob began, "can we not—"

"That's okay, Rob." I gave James a tight smile before answering, "The store has been there for a long time and we're very lucky to have a lot of loyal regulars. We're doing fine."

"I see." He considered me for a few seconds, before turning his attention to his son. "Why haven't you been at the office this week?"

"That's because I wasn't supposed to be at your office this week. I told you already, I'm working at a new job site this week. I can come next week on Friday—"

"That's not good enough," his dad said. "If you're going to take over Carmichael Architects one day, you need to put in more effort. Everyone else in the firm has been there longer than you have, and they're not going to respect you if you haven't paid your dues, especially if they all have degrees and you don't."

"James," Michelle said, wariness lining her face. "We have a guest."

I could feel Rob stiffening next to me. "Seriously, Dad? You're bringing up the degree argument again?" He gestured at his mom. "Shouldn't we be focusing on getting Mom better now, instead of worrying about my lack of a degree and how you want me to live my life? Where were you, anyway? Did you forget that you were supposed to pick her up?"

"Robbie, that's enough," his mom said, her voice tight, her eyes darting nervously between her husband and son. "And I'm fine, you don't have to worry about me."

"I had a meeting that ran late." James bristled. "You would know that if you had been at the office. And I'm bringing up your lack of a degree again because it's *important*. Do you really think your building experience alone is enough to run the firm? It's not, and you'll need to work twice as hard, and one or two days a week in the office isn't going to cut it. You'll need to be in there full-time."

"And I already told you"—Rob's voice rose—"I've still got my own busi—"

"Robbie. James. Please, that's enough." Michelle sounded distressed now, and there was something resembling panic in her eyes. "Can you two not fight with each other all the time? You both know how much I don't like it. Can we please arrive at a compromise that works for everyone?" She turned a pleading look at her son. "Your dad means well. If you can't do full time now, maybe two days a week? And that way we're all happy?"

Rob shook his head, looking like he was about to argue his point further, but his mom sent him another imploring look. He closed his eyes and sighed. "Fine. Two days a week."

Relief crossed his mother's face. "Thank you."

James only scoffed, before saying, "I expect to see you first thing Monday morning."

Rob mumbled a clipped goodbye, then grabbed my hand and

led me out of the house, not saying a single word as we got into his car and drove away.

"Hey." I turned in my seat to face him. "You okay?"

He expelled a long breath before answering, "I will be. My mother always gets very anxious and emotionally distressed whenever I have an argument with my dad. He can be very headstrong, while she hates confrontation and disagreements, always has ever since I was little. She doesn't like conflicts and can't stand anyone in the family fighting with each other. Her parents got divorced when she was a teenager, and she said they used to fight a lot, and I think that scarred her for life. To her, any form of conflict is a problem that might potentially tear our family apart." He sighed. "And it's hard, because she often avoids saying what needs to be said to keep the peace."

"So you give in to your dad a lot to appease your mom," I said. "And that leads to him walking all over you."

"Yeah. But I hate it whenever she's stressed out because I'm arguing with my dad. It feels like I'm disappointing not just him, but her, too." He stopped at a red light and glanced at me with a small smile. "I'm sorry you had to see that. And for ruining our bingsu plans. But thank you. I'm glad you were there with me."

"Don't thank me. I didn't do anything."

"You were there with me. That was more than enough."

The lights turned green, and he returned his attention to the road, but I couldn't stop thinking about what had just happened.

This was a guy who was willing to drop everything to help his mother, and did things that were probably going to be at his expense to help keep the peace in his family. Not because he couldn't stand up for himself and say no, but because he puts his family and their well-being first, above a lot of other things.

Above himself.

And I knew I shouldn't be finding that trait—*him*—attractive.

But damn it, I did.

CHAPTER 16

Laughter Is the Best Medicine—Unless You're Trying to Score a Hole in One

The day of my golfing date with Neil Cosgrave was another gloomy Saturday afternoon. The course was forty-five minutes away from the city, and by the time I got there, Neil was already waiting in the reception area, leaning against the wall as he scrolled through his phone.

The Greenhill Fairway golf course was bigger and newer than the one I'd gone to with Rob, offering mini golf courses, a driving range, and a full-sized golf course designed by a former PGA player. There were posters everywhere advertising discounted entrance fees for their first-year anniversary, which probably explained why the place was packed.

"Sorry I'm late."

"Not at all." Neil gave me a warm smile. "I just got here myself."

"Did you say your friend owns this place? It's enormous."

"Yeah, one of my old buddies from junior golf tour." Neil pointed at the map of the place above us. "They have two mini golf courses. An eighteen-hole indoor option, or the nine-hole outdoor one. What do you feel like?"

Major points to him for being courteous and asking for my opinion, instead of bulldozing his way and assuming what I'd like to do, like some of my dates in the past. "I vote for the outdoor one. It's shorter, so we'll have time for dinner after."

"Good choice." Neil directed his attention to the young woman manning the front desk. "Two for the nine-hole course, please."

I pulled out my purse, but he waved it away, ignoring my protests. "I'll get this one, and you can get the next one."

Extra bonus points because he was generous *and* confident, so sure that there would be another date.

But then Shane, Ben, and all the other terrible dates I'd had in the past suddenly came floating back into my mind, sending a bundle of hot nerves sliding into my stomach, along with the growing dread at the thought that I'd be spending the next hour or two with him, forty-five minutes away from anything and anyone familiar.

I glanced around, mentally mapping my exit routes, and did a double take when I saw a familiar group of people standing near the in-house golf shop in the furthest corner, not far from the restrooms.

Rob, wearing aviator sunglasses and a baseball cap, had his back to us, but there was no mistaking the way his hair was curling up and sticking out from under the hat. Next to him were Ellie, Jenna, and Alec, all wearing caps and sunglasses, looking like they were extras in a badly made spy-noir movie.

"I'm going to the restroom," I said to Neil, who was now chatting with the young woman about some tournament that had just happened last weekend. "I'll see you outside."

Without waiting for his reply, I sauntered over toward the restroom, and after a quick glance to make sure he wasn't looking, I stopped in front of the displayed golf clubs for sale, a couple of feet away from my friends.

"What are you all doing here?" I hissed at the group.

Rob walked over, pretending to inspect the selection of clubs. "Alec heard about this outing and thought it would be fun for them to tag along."

I glanced at Neil, who was still involved in an increasingly animated conversation with the attendant, then turned toward the rest of my friends, who were watching us with varying degrees of amused interest. "Really? Signing me up for online dates isn't enough for you guys?"

"We just want to be supportive," Ellie stage-whispered, while Alec flashed me a thumbs-up from next to her. "It'll be fun!"

Jenna mouthed, "For us."

"You're all sick in the head." But I was smiling, grateful that they were here, because even though they didn't have to, they all came to support me anyway. I might not have lots of siblings or a big family, but I had these people on my side, and that more than made up for it.

Out of the corner of my eye, I could see Neil collecting the clubs and balls from the young woman, who was saying a faint, "Enjoy the game!"

"I better go. Catch you guys later."

"Have fun!"

"Charm his socks off."

"Go and destroy him!"

"Hey, Kim." Rob was smiling at me. "You've got this. You're going to do great."

The ball of nerves that had settled in my stomach earlier began to dissolve as I walked away, and a sense of calmness came over me. *I* do *have this, because it's just another date, and I'm doing this for my grandmother, and everything will be fine.*

Neil handed me one of the clubs and a blue golf ball when I found him outside.

"Thank you. You ready for me to kick your ass?"

He grinned. "Let's see if you still sound that tough after I annihilate you."

"That's not going to happen in this lifetime, sorry. I'll be doing all the annihilation."

The course we'd chosen had a Wild West theme, so it was decorated with cacti of all shapes and sizes, broken-down wagons and stagecoaches, and mini replicas of abandoned saloons and log cabins. It was charming, very Instagrammable, and several people ahead of us were busy snapping selfies instead of playing.

"This looks fun," Neil said. "We should have asked Carmichael to come along."

If only he knew. "We should have. He would have enjoyed this."

"I think he would." Neil motioned for me to go ahead. "Would you like to start us off?"

"Sure." I placed my ball on the marked spot, took aim, and swung the club. The ball slid smoothly toward the hole, going in with a loud *plunk*.

Neil raised his eyebrows at me. "Starting off strong, aren't we?"

"I'm here to win." I walked to the hole and plucked my ball from it. "Your turn."

He placed his own plain white ball on the marked spot, sent the ball directly into the hole, and pulled out a tiny pencil and a scorecard from his back pocket. "Guess we're both here to win. One point each."

Okaayy. Good to know this wasn't going to be just another fun, harmless competition between friends. *Game on.*

It took Neil two strokes to finish the second hole. He then

motioned for me to step up, while wearing a satisfied grin on his face. I wasn't going to be outdone, so I aimed my ball, gave it a firm nudge toward the hole, and in it went. In one clean stroke.

The confident grin on Neil's face faltered a little.

Meanwhile, my friends were waiting for their turn at the start of the course. Rob, who was standing facing the other way, had apparently said something hilarious to the others, and they were now all howling with amusement.

Neil glanced over at the group and frowned with disapproval at Jenna, who was bending over with laughter. "Someone should have a word with those people. They're too loud."

"Oh, it's just a bit of harmless fun, isn't it?"

But he didn't reply, his eyes still on the group. "Does that guy look like Carmichael to you? The one with the brown shirt? Same build, same hair color."

Shit. "Kind of hard to tell from this distance, but I don't think so. That's a very common hair color, and there can be hundreds of men in the city who look like that."

"Hmm." Neil watched the group for a few more seconds, while I was mentally pleading with Rob not to turn around. "You're right. I guess we were talking about him earlier, so that's why my mind went there."

I let out a relieved breath. "Must be."

"How long have you known him?"

"Around a couple of years. He was a friend of a friend, and we've just recently been hanging out a lot more."

"I met him through my cousin. She's an architect, and Rob did a job for her a while back, and I was introduced to him when we all met for drinks after work one night. He seems like a great guy."

"He's an amazing guy," I said. "Smart, funny, and respectful. Probably one of the nicest and kindest men I've ever met." And I realized that I meant every single word.

Alec's laugh boomed from where my friends were, interrupting

Neil's reply. I glanced over quickly and smiled to myself, glad that they were enjoying themselves, but also wishing that I was there with them.

But Neil wasn't too impressed, because he cast another annoyed look at the group. "I might speak to my friend about putting in a policy to ban anyone with disruptive behavior."

"Is that really necessary?" I raised my eyebrows. "They might be a bit loud, but nobody else seems to be bothered. People are here to have fun, and those people are obviously just having a good time. I wouldn't call that disruptive."

"They're loud, and it's ruining other people's concentration. I'd call that disruptive."

"That hardly seems fair." My irritation kicked up a notch. "Maybe if they were being aggressive or threatening to other people, sure. But they're not."

"It's not fair that they're ruining *my* concentration," Neil said, the frown on his face deepening. "We're here to play golf, not to listen to people laughing like hyenas. If they want to do that, they should go to a large public space, like a park, so they couldn't bother anyone."

In less than twenty minutes, this date had taken a sharp turn for the worse. Maybe it was still too early to tell, but I had already crossed him off the list, because there was no way I'd put up with someone who was so unkind to others. To *my friends*.

As the date went on, Neil's competitiveness took over, and he became obsessed with winning the game. By the time we were halfway through the course, I had a slight advantage over him, with my six points to his nine, which he looked extremely unhappy about.

Then we got to the seventh hole, and it was especially tricky to navigate. It had an upward sloping tunnel, requiring golfers to hit the ball hard enough so it could shoot up the tunnel into a tiny cave, but not too hard because it would go straight into the pond surrounding the course. And from the way Neil was hitting his golf ball, it looked like he didn't get the memo. He thwacked the ball a bit too violently, sending it straight to the deepest, murkiest part of the pond.

"That was a terrible shot." Neil looked like he was ready to toss his club into the pond to follow the ball.

"We can ask for a new ball from reception."

"No. I must hit the ball from wherever it comes to rest. That's how you golf properly." He frowned at me. "I thought you said you were a caddy. You should know this."

"But this isn't—you know what, never mind. Yes, of course, you should totally do that."

I felt a perverse kind of satisfaction as I watched him wade into the pond to find the ball, with water and mud splashing over his light blue sneakers and khaki-colored chinos.

My phone chimed with a text from Rob.

You okay? Where's Neil?

I glanced in his direction. He gave me a small wave, his eyebrows raised in question.

He went to hunt for his missing golf ball.
btw, your disruptive laughter made Neil lose his concentration.
He wants to get you all banned from this place.
Also, tell Alec he laughs like a hyena.

I saw him smiling to himself as he typed his reply.

Let me guess, are you kicking his ass?

"Found it!" Neil's triumphant voice cut through the air. I tore my eyes away from Rob and turned to see Neil sloshing his way out of the water, waving the ball in his hand. His chinos and sneakers were destined for the trash bin now, judging from the way they dripped generously with pond sludge.

"I thought you were supposed to hit the ball from where it had landed," I said, unable to stop myself. "Isn't that what you do in proper golfing?"

Neil's face fell, before a determined look returned to his face. "Nobody saw." He nodded at the people behind us. "We don't have to say anything, and it'll be our secret, right?"

If I hadn't already crossed Neil off earlier, I definitely would have now.

I hurried through the final two holes, keen to get this date over and done with. By the end of the course, I managed to score eleven points, while Neil had twenty.

"I don't understand," he was grumbling as he snatched his ball from the ninth hole. "You said you've only caddied, so how were you able to beat *me*?"

I shrugged, but didn't offer a response. He bristled, before stalking off toward reception. I followed him, quietly amused at how he was such a sore loser and how it was such a contrast to how gracious Rob was. By the time we were walking to the parking lot, Neil looked like he'd calmed down and had gotten over the fact that he'd just lost to a total amateur.

But then he had to open his mouth.

"I'm feeling a bit under the weather. That's why I wasn't playing my best."

"Of course." I gave him a polite nod.

"Maybe we can do a rematch one day."

"Maybe." *Not a chance in hell.* "We should skip dinner if you're unwell."

"Great idea." We stopped next to my car, and he stood there, hands shoved inside his pockets, looking at the ground, then at my tires, at the roof of my car, anywhere but me.

"Thank you for a fun afternoon," I said. "Enjoy the rest of your weekend."

Unlocking my car, I pulled out my phone to text Rob, but Neil cleared his throat.

"I've been wanting to ask you," he said, "do you know if Carmichael is single?"

I turned around to face him. "He is. Why do you ask?"

The tiniest hint of crimson tinted his cheeks. "Ah, I'm thinking of asking him out for coffee sometime. You two seem close. Has he ever said anything . . . about me?"

I didn't know whether I should stay and answer his questions or march back to where my friends were and smack Rob in the head, because obviously his research was faulty.

Again.

Neil Cosgrave didn't go on this golfing date because he was interested in me. He did this because he was interested *in Rob* and wanted to ask me about *him*.

Honestly, I didn't see that coming.

Neil was still waiting for my reply, looking hopeful, and my heart went out to him.

"I'm sorry, but he's never mentioned anything to me," I said, as gently as I could. Because no matter how ultra-competitive and irritating he might have been, right now he was putting his heart on the line, being vulnerable in front of me, someone who was practically a stranger to him, and I knew that wouldn't have been an easy thing to do.

Neil nodded, his face now beet red. He mumbled his thanks, then speed-walked to his car without another look.

Great. I spent my Saturday afternoon on a date with a man who was pining for my friend.

Taking me back to a big, fat zero.

CHAPTER 17

Third Time Isn't Always the Charm

Here's the plan," Rob said. "Elijah's been working overtime the past two weeks because his team is finishing the final edits for their movie. He always finishes at the same time: ten P.M. on weekdays and four P.M. on the weekends. So when he walks out of that building in five minutes"—Rob pointed to the high-rise across the street—"you're going to casually bump into him and initiate conversation."

It was the week after the golfing date with Neil, and Rob had the brilliant idea to sneakily ambush the film editor. That was why I was here, on a Saturday afternoon, staking out the building where Elijah worked from the Starbucks across the road. My latte was long finished, because we'd been sitting at a table by the window, watching the building entrance for the past forty-five minutes, like vultures hunting for their next prey.

"How do you know all this?"

"I did my research."

"Must I remind you that your research hasn't been too reliable so far?" I turned to face him. "First Ben, then Neil. I mean, how did you miss that one very important fact about him in your *research*?"

"I wasn't expecting that." Rob looked sheepish. "He's always dated women ever since I've known him."

"I should have clocked it from the way he kept asking questions about you." I tilted my head. "You know what you need? Someone to fact-check your dossier. A second pair of eyes to confirm the information is accurate. When this is all over, you should hire me to be your fact-checker. We could probably build an actual business doing this."

"I promise I'm usually better than this. None of this ever happened when I was helping my siblings and my cousins."

"Hold up." I raised my eyebrows at him, deadpan. "Are you implying that *I'm* the problem here?"

"That's not what I'm saying, it's just that . . ." He trailed off with a sigh. "We just haven't been having the best luck, but you're not the problem. If anything, those guys should be thanking their lucky stars because you're interested in them."

My cheeks felt warm. I shouldn't have liked it when he said things like that, but I did.

Too damn much.

"And haven't you heard? Third time's the charm. Point is, you're going to accidentally run into Elijah, and that's when you strike."

"What if he decides to work through the night? Or took today off?"

"He won't have taken today off because his aim is to win an Oscar before he turns forty. I'm willing to bet my firstborn child—"

I snorted. "I hate to break it to you, but you don't have one."

"—that Elijah has spent his entire Saturday working in that building, because there's nothing that he wants more than getting his hands on one of those little golden statues. Remember, he loves his movies, so use that to break the ice."

"Yes, I know, this isn't my first rodeo."

"I'll be here, ready to assist at the first sign of distress from you. You won't have anything to worry about, though. Elijah can be a bit intense when it comes to his work, but he's a total sweetheart. Third time's the charm," he repeated. "Okay, here he comes."

I glanced up to see Elijah walking out of the front door, his messenger bag slung across his body, his attention glued to the phone in his hand.

"Go." Rob gave me an encouraging nod. "You've got this."

I reluctantly stood up, not at all keen on leaving my imaginary safety bubble with him. Walking out of Starbucks, I pulled out my own phone and pretended to stare at it as I strolled in Elijah's direction, before gently bumping his shoulder.

"Sorry, I wasn't watching— Oh, hey." I stopped in front of him and feigned surprise. "Elijah? From the wedding last weekend?"

He looked up from his phone, startled. His eyebrows were furrowed, like he was trying to place me or my name, before clearing up a few seconds later.

"Kim, right? Rob Carmichael's friend? The one with chocolate on your dress?"

"That's me," I said, relieved that he at least remembered my name, and that made me relax a little. *Good start*. "Fancy running into you here! Do you live in the area?"

"I work there." He gestured at the building behind him. "You?"

"I was just there to see a friend." I waved a hand at the Starbucks behind me. It wasn't exactly a lie, because I did sit down and have coffee with Rob. "Do you work on weekends?"

"Yeah. We're under a deadline to finish edits on a movie. I would have kept working, but I usually have dinner with my parents on Saturdays."

Okay, bonus points for being close to his family. Not that it would have mattered because I wasn't in this for the long haul, but it was nice to at least know that.

"You've got such a cool job. It must be so fun to work with movies all day long."

A smile formed on his lips. "It's the best job in the world."

"I'd be interested in hearing about your work sometime." I fluttered my eyelashes a little. "I've always been so fascinated with how movies are made."

"Sure." His eyes lit up with excitement. "I'm always down to talk about movies. I've got half an hour before I need to go. Do you want to grab a quick cup of coffee and chat?"

"I'd love to."

Rob was still inside, sitting where we previously were, but his shoulders were hunched, and his cap was pulled low over his head, so Elijah didn't seem to realize as we walked past.

I ordered my second latte, then joined him at a small table near the back.

"How long have you been a film editor?"

"More than half my life." His eyes took on a faraway look, as if he was reminiscing about the past. "I started fresh out of high school, worked as a gofer for an indie movie director while studying part-time, then slowly moved up to where I am now. I've been lucky to have collaborated with some of the best directors and actors in the industry."

"That's amazing. You must have seen thousands of movies, working in that industry for as long as you have. Do you have a favorite?"

"*The Exorcist*. I think that should be everyone's favorite movie."

"I've never seen *The Exorcist* before."

There was a long, painful pause following my announcement. Elijah was staring at me with a mixture of disbelief, judgment, and disgust.

"Did you really say you've *never seen The Exorcist*?" He enunciated the last few words slowly, as if he was explaining quantum physics to a group of three-year-olds. "Are you being serious right now?"

"I am. I've never seen it."

He looked scandalized. "How has anyone never seen the greatest movie of all time?"

"Horror movies aren't really my thing." I gave him an apologetic smile. "Tried it once, discovered I'm not a fan of the nightmares it gave me for the next few weeks."

"At least tell me you've heard the theme music." He hummed a song I'd never heard before. "'Tubular Bells'? By Mike Oldfield? It's a classic tune."

When I shook my head, the baffled look on his face turned feral, as if my ignorance of his beloved movie had somehow unleashed the dormant monster inside his psyche, who had been waiting for the right moment to strike at a poor, random soul who had innocently commented on a movie genre they weren't a fan of.

Me. I was the poor, random soul.

"You know horror movies aren't real, right? You can't be afraid of something that doesn't actually exist. And *The Exorcist* isn't just 'a horror movie.' It's a masterpiece. Did you know it was nominated for ten Oscars? Ten! It's a powerful, spellbinding tale of possession. It *transcends* movies. They just don't make films like that anymore these days."

Oh Lord.

I listened as politely as I could, as Elijah launched into a long explanation of how the movie was the top-grossing R-rated horror film for almost half a century, while I mentally drew a thick red line to cross out his name from the list of potential suitors. I had nothing against people who liked horror movies, but Elijah seemed a little too . . . intense.

"Horror is, by far, the best genre out there. Way better than thriller, sci-fi, action, or drama, and definitely better than romance. It's a delicate balance to achieve, because it must be chilling and thought-provoking at the same time. It must be unsettling enough to evoke dread and fear, but it must also have memorable plots and characters, instead of just relying on shock value. And the best ones? They will do all that and make you question your own reality."

"Fascinating." I glanced at my watch. "Didn't you say you only have half an hour?"

"I can spare a few more minutes." He whipped out his phone and opened YouTube. "I'm always excited to share my love of the genre. Let me show you my favorite scene from the movie. It's when the main character, Regan, vomits on—"

"I think I might've forgotten to lock my car." I stood up so quickly, my chair nearly rammed into the person sitting behind me. "I have to go."

"Wait, it's only a short video, it won't take too much of your time."

"It was nice meeting you, Elijah."

But he seemed to have made it his personal mission to convince me to join the other side. "At least let me show you one clip. Trust me, this movie changed my life, because it made me want to do what I'm doing now." He caught my right wrist, trying to force me back into my seat. "Or if you're free tomorrow night, come by the studio. I have the fiftieth anniversary ultimate collector's edition, and I'd be more than happy to show you the entire movie."

I yanked my hand away, but he was stronger. My next instinct was to throw my latte in his face, or maybe kick him in the nuts, but before I could do any of it, there was a gentle squeeze on my shoulder.

Rob was standing next to me, but his attention was on Elijah. His usually warm hazel eyes were now cold, and there was a tick in his jaw as he gave the other man a curt nod. "Let her hand go. You're hurting her."

Suddenly Elijah and his death grip on my hand was the least of my concerns, because all I could focus on was the way Rob was standing so close next to me, and how his low, authoritative voice was stirring something up in my belly.

It seemed to shake Elijah out of whatever trance he was in, because his eyes grew larger, and he quickly dropped my wrist as if I'd been licked by fire and he had to save himself from being burned.

"Sorry," he mumbled. "I got carried away."

Rob's glare stayed on him for a few more beats, before he turned his attention to me. "We should go. Ellie called, said something about a wine tasting emergency at her store."

"Of course. Thanks for a great chat, Elijah. See you around."

I grabbed my bag and sprinted out of the place to my freedom.

The minute we walked out of Starbucks, Rob took my wrist, the one Elijah had been clutching, and examined it. "Are you okay? Did he hurt you?"

"I'm fine." His warm hand holding mine felt wonderful. "He didn't hurt me."

"That was out of line." Rob looked angry. "He shouldn't have done that. I'm sorry."

"You don't have to apologize for him." I halfheartedly pulled my hand away. "But I'm seriously wondering if I should even keep on trying. You kept telling me that they're all good guys, and they are, but they're also not what I'm looking for."

"I know." He grimaced. "I'm sorry the afternoon didn't go well. But we've still got a very good chance of finding someone at the next three weddings."

"Should I even go?" But I knew I had to, because I didn't have a better option. Plus, he'd done so much for me, and I already promised that I'd be there for him.

And, maybe, *maybe*, if I really wanted to be honest with myself, I was kind of enjoying spending time with him at those weddings.

More than those guys I was supposed to be wooing.

"You should. We'll find your perfect man, I promise." He cleared his throat. "What's up for the rest of your Saturday night?"

"Something quiet. Some Japanese takeout and maybe a movie or two."

"Oh." He shoved his hands into his pockets. "I'm making some pizza tonight, if you want to come over. I figured after what you'd just gone through, I owe you a nice dinner."

"You? You can make pizza?"

"From scratch. Made the dough myself and everything."

"You don't have any plans?" I raised my eyebrows. "It's Saturday night."

"Why do you sound so surprised?"

"Because you seem like the type who would have exciting plans for their Saturday nights, instead of staying in and making pizza."

"Are you saying pizza isn't exciting?" He flashed his dimples at me. "I don't know what kind of person you think I'm supposed to be, but yes, I often stay in on Saturday nights and make pizzas. Tacos, sometimes. My lasagna's gotten rave reviews, too. From my mom mostly, but she's quite particular with her food, so I think you can trust her opinion. Also, define 'exciting plans.'"

"I don't know. Parties? Clubs? Dates with gorgeous people? Fancy dinner with friends?"

"That's what I'm trying to suggest. Dinner with a friend, although it won't be too fancy. It'll be homemade pizza. You can choose what toppings you want, though, so I guess that's pretty fancy, right? I'll even throw in a pint of ice cream, and we can call it a party."

He watched me, waiting for my reply, while the cogs in my brain belatedly kicked themselves into gear, and a wild thought crossed my mind.

Is he asking me on a date?

"Are you asking me on a date?"

The grin he sent my way lit up his entire face, and for a minute I couldn't seem to remember my own name.

"Call it what you want. It can be two friends spending time with each other, or it can also be me apologizing because of the horrible afternoon I've put you through."

Of course. Why on Earth did I think this could be considered a date? He was still hung up on his ex, after all.

"So? Is that a yes on the pizza?"

Logically, I knew I should say no.

"Sure. Pizza is always a good idea."

CHAPTER 18

Homemade Pizza Counts as Fancy Dinners

Rob lived in a renovated two-bedroom townhouse not far from the flipped house he'd been working on. There were pictures of his family around the house—some framed ones hung on the living room wall, a few sat on the bookshelf, mostly photos of him with his siblings and his mother.

Noticeably missing were photos of him and his dad.

"Nice place."

"Thanks." The tiniest look of pride colored his cheeks. "My grandfather left all his grandchildren a bit of money when he passed away a few years ago, enough for a house deposit. I found this place for practically a song, because it was so old, and the interior of the house was in appalling condition. I gutted the inside and slowly fixed it. It's not big, but it's mine."

I glanced around, impressed. "You did all this yourself?"

"Yeah. Finished it six months ago. Took me a bit longer than expected, but at least I was saving on rent, because I lived here while I was renovating. That was what had given me the idea to start the flipping business." He tossed his keys and wallet on the kitchen island and began rummaging in his fridge. Several wedding invites were stuck to the door, next to Polaroid snaps of him with his niece and nephews. He took out a large, covered bowl and a few smaller containers, then placed them on the kitchen bench. "I made the dough last night."

I hopped on a kitchen stool. "Ellie would have loved this. She's a big pizza fan."

Rob washed his hands, then uncovered the bowl, took out a big ball of dough, and sprinkled some flour on a wooden board before placing the dough on it. "I've made some for her and Alec." He began to gently push in the center of the dough with his fingertips. "My mother used to make pizza often, because it was something all six of us kids would eat without complaining. She taught us to make it ourselves. My sisters didn't really care, but me and my brother were keen to learn, mostly because we thought this could impress girls."

Not gonna lie, the way his fingers were working on the dough was pretty hot.

"Do you want to learn how? Maybe this would help impress some of the guys you're trying to win over."

"Ah, no. You don't want me touching things you might want to put in your mouth."

He looked up at that, humor twinkling in his eyes. "I don't?"

"That wasn't supposed to be an— Oh, fine, show me what to do."

I washed and dried my hands, then came over to his side of the kitchen.

"Start by rolling the dough over your knuckles. Use your fists, and work to form the dough into a circle."

He stood next to me, watching as I placed the dough over my fists to shape it into a larger circle. It wasn't easy, because no matter how long and how hard I tried to make the dough larger, it seemed to stay the same size, and I finally gave up after the dough flopped down onto the kitchen counter for the third time.

Rob chuckled. "Let me show you."

Before I could move aside, he stepped behind me and grasped my wrists, gently guiding me to turn the dough around.

"You'll want to leave it a bit thicker on the edges for the crust." He kept directing my hands in a soothing rhythm, patiently rotating the dough in a circle. "I usually make it a bit bigger, because it'll shrink back a bit."

But I wasn't paying attention to the dough, or what he was explaining, because the only thing I could focus on was how he was standing behind me. His firm body, his now-familiar scent, the heat of him surrounding me, and how it all just felt . . . right?

"Watch this." He flicked his wrists and tossed the dough lightly, sending it airborne, like what professional pizza chefs would do, then did another toss, his forearm brushing my shoulders as he did so, before setting down the pizza base.

"Okay, now you're just showing off."

"Is it working?"

Hell yes, it's working. "Performance wise, I'm impressed. But I'll reserve judgment until I taste the final product. For all I know, the pizza might not even be edible."

"Tough crowd tonight." His low chuckle rumbled in my ear, sending shivers all over my body. "Now we do the sauce." He stepped away and handed me a tub of tomato paste. "Then the toppings. You're the guest, so you get to choose. I've got mozzarella cheese, pepperoni, ham, mushrooms, olives, and onions."

"No pineapple? I thought you're a fan of pineapple on pizza."

"That can be on our next pizza dinner."

I ignored the swirls in my stomach at the promise. "Let's do pepperoni, cheese, and mushroom."

"Excellent choice." He slid the pizza into the preheated oven and set a timer. "I've got some drinks in the fridge while we wait. Help yourself."

I chose a can of lemonade and watched as he washed and

chopped some lettuce, then added it into a bowl with some quartered cherry tomatoes, sliced bell peppers, and red onions.

"How about a movie while we're eating?" He tossed the salad and took out a bottle of dressing from the fridge, then carried them into the living room while I brought the plates.

"Sure. What kind of movies are you into?"

"I'll watch anything with a good plot." He took out the pizza when the oven dinged. "I know you're into classics, so we can do that if you like."

"Let's see what our options are." I plopped down on the sofa, picked up the remote, and flicked through the movie choices.

"Why classics?" Rob placed the pizza on the coffee table, then folded one of his legs underneath him and sat down next to me. "What drew you to classic movies in the first place?"

"It was something I used to do with my grandparents." A smile tugged the corners of my mouth at the memory. "We used to have family movie nights on the weekends. My grandfather would go to our local Blockbuster on Friday nights after work, pick up a couple of movies, and we'd watch them on the couch with my grandmother's homemade popcorn, sweet Indonesian iced tea, and chocolate chip cookies. That was how I got my love of movies. Her favorite actress was Audrey Hepburn, so that was what my grandfather often borrowed, but it wasn't always classics. We used to watch anything and everything, and I think I might have watched too many movies I wasn't supposed to for my age. No one really cared about movie ratings or content warnings or parental guidance in those days."

"Which ones did you watch that you weren't supposed to?"

I grinned. "All the Bond movies, for starters. Opa is a huge fan. *The Godfather*, all three of them. *E.T.*, *Raiders of the Lost Ark*, *The Terminator*. Seriously, I could go on and on."

Rob chuckled. "Sounds like you had a far more exciting childhood than mine."

I smiled. "It might not be perfect, but it was the best."

"Is there anything in particular you feel like watching right now?" His eyes were riveted on my face. "We can find one that you used to watch with your grandparents, if you like."

I was touched he offered. "We don't have to. It's been a long day, so maybe we can do something light and funny."

Rob thought for a while, before nodding. "I know. What about a rom-com? Actually, yes. Why don't we do that?" He leaned closer and pointed at the remote in my hand. "May I?"

His shoulder brushed mine, distracting my brain from forming a coherent response. "May I what?"

He grinned. "My mission tonight is to show you a funny, entertaining, *romantic* movie. Think of it as part of my services. We want you to believe in happy endings, don't we?"

"But those movies aren't real." My fingers grazed his as I handed him the remote, and I had to suppress the shiver that went through my body. Quickly diverting my attention to the food, I picked up a slice of pizza and bit into it, and almost moaned at how good it was. "Oh, wow. This is amazing. The crust is so light and fluffy."

"Glad you like it." Rob was flicking through the selection of films on Netflix. "*When Harry Met Sally*? It's a classic, and it's one of my favorites."

"That's also Ellie and Jenna's favorite. I've seen it way too many times."

"How about *27 Dresses*? It's light and funny, like you wanted, but it also has heart."

"Yeah, but that was one of the first movies Leo and I saw when we started dating."

Then I vetoed *While You Were Sleeping* ("The premise isn't realistic enough for me."), *Romeo + Juliet* ("I thought you said we're going to watch *funny* movies?"), and *Notting Hill* ("Sappy Hugh Grant doesn't do it for me. He's hotter in his villain era."). After

I nixed *The Proposal* ("It's going to remind me of Betty White. Too sad."), Rob looked like he was about to force-feed me the remote alongside the pizza, but only sighed and gave it back to me instead.

"Fine. You choose."

"Let's find a non-romance flick." I scrolled through the choices. "What about the first Hunger Games?"

"I wouldn't call that light and funny." Rob took a bite of his own pizza. "You do know it's also a love story, right?"

"I don't know which movie you're talking about, but it's not *The Hunger Games*."

"The love triangle between Katniss, Peeta, and Gale? How Peeta has had a crush on Katniss forever and how he'd risk his life for her? It's a fucking love story."

I pressed play. "But at least there's gore and death to balance the love and kisses."

He groaned. "You're impossible."

"No, I'm realistic." I covered my yawn as the title sequence of the movie began to play. "Because those sickeningly happy, overly sappy romantic movies give false expectations to single women everywhere, teaching young people to expect a perfect, swoony, heartbreakingly handsome partner. But nobody in real life could live up to the characters in those romance movies. People like that aren't real. So why would you spend two hours of your life watching something that you'll be invested in, only to be disappointed when you realize that nothing like that would ever happen in your own life?"

"But aren't we trying to make it happen in your real life now?"

"It hasn't happened yet, has it? I think we need more movies showing single women thriving even without a partner in their lives. And you know what the best part of being single is?"

"I'm sure you're going to tell me."

"You don't have to check in with or answer to anyone, or plan your life around them, and be constantly mindful of someone else's needs and wants other than your own."

"That sounds like a pretty sad and selfish way to live a life. And lonely."

"It's not. I'm not lonely, because I still have wonderful people in my life that care about me," I said. "And that way, you don't have to sacrifice your life or your identity for another person. Nobody expects anything from you, nobody can hurt you, and vice versa. If you're hurt, you only have yourself to blame."

"I think you won't have to ever sacrifice any part of yourself if you're in a fulfilling relationship with the right person." He was watching me, looking thoughtful. "All healthy relationships will have a good balance of give and take from both partners. Not because you have to, but because you want to, because you care about the other person."

"I haven't seen that in real life."

His gaze stayed on me for a few brief seconds. "Seriously, if I ever have the chance to meet your ex again, I'm going to have some words with him."

As we finished our food and settled into the movie, my day finally caught up with me, because my eyelids started to droop as I watched Peeta confess his love for Katniss to the audience. And the last thing I remembered before succumbing to exhaustion was thinking that Rob wasn't wrong.

Even a damn dystopian movie had to have romance in it.

CHAPTER 19

It Doesn't Cost You Anything to Be Kind

The next thing I knew, I woke up in a strange bed, surrounded by a few fluffy pillows and a thick blue duvet, with sunlight streaming down my face. I sat up, my eyes roaming around the space, and it dawned on me that I was in Rob's bedroom.

It took me a few minutes to orient myself and remember what had happened last night. Which was . . . nothing? I was still wearing my clothes from yesterday, and there were no signs of someone having slept on the other side of the bed last night.

Nope, not willing to acknowledge and analyze why that fact had ignited a tiny spark of disappointment within me.

Instead, I fell back on the bed and pulled the duvet over my face, and was rewarded with the comforting smell of fresh mint and crisp apple. And because I was probably out of my damn mind, I burrowed my nose in one of the pillows, surrounding myself with his scent.

Enough, Kim. Pull yourself together.

Pushing away the duvet, I got up and grabbed my phone,

which Rob must have left on the bedside table. It was almost seven thirty, so I had to make a move if I wanted to go home and have a quick shower before opening the store.

But before that, I probably could spare a few minutes to snoop around.

His room was neat, simple and minimally furnished. A colorful abstract oil painting hung on the wall, next to a black-and-white canvas print of his family. I stood there for a while, studying the picture. His parents were smiling at each other, while the siblings had their arms around one another, all laughing for the camera.

The tiniest sliver of envy went through my body, because I never knew—and would never know—how it felt to have a childhood like that, to have grown up being surrounded by so many siblings and so much love. And the fact that Rob was close to his family had somehow made him even more . . . interesting.

Interesting? I mentally kicked myself. Nope. Not going to go there.

I slipped into the bathroom to wash my face, and when I finally ventured outside, he was already puttering in the kitchen, and the smell of fried bacon permeated the house.

"Hey. You're up." He had on a ratty gray T-shirt and pajama pants. His hair was sticking out every which way, which, if I wanted to be honest, made him look kind of adorable. "Coffee? I'm making hash browns and cheesy scrambled eggs."

"Coffee would be great." I climbed on one of the kitchen stools.

He turned around and opened a cabinet above his head to look for a mug, and his T-shirt sleeves rode up to expose his biceps. There was a small tattoo of a crab on his upper left arm, and a tiny scale on his upper right arm. I'd never seen them, because they were always hidden behind his sleeves. There were two other little ones peeking out of the waistband of his pants, one on his left hip and another on the right, but I couldn't make out their full shapes.

He said he had five tattoos. Where was the other one? My

mind wandered to all the potential places it could possibly be. If he had those two peeking out of his pants, maybe the other one was in the same vicinity . . .

Stoooooppp. His tattoos are none of my business.

I took one last good look before filing it all away in the back of my mind.

Meanwhile, oblivious to me silently going bananas over his tattoos, Rob had chosen a brown pod and popped it into one of those sleek-looking coffee machines. He pressed a button, some whirring sounds followed, and the next thing I knew, he handed me a cup of steaming hot coffee. "Oat milk latte, one sugar. Have I got that right?"

"Yes." I gaped at him. "How do you know?"

"That's what you always ordered. Whenever we're at Ellie's bakery, and yesterday when we were staking out Elijah."

I opened my mouth, then closed it again.

Not even Leo knew what my coffee order was. He used to say it was because he wasn't a coffee person and he couldn't tell the difference between a latte and a mochaccino, and I had naïvely believed him.

That should have been my first clue that he wasn't who I thought he was.

"By the way," he said, "last night was amazing."

I froze, the mug halfway traveling to my lips. "I . . . what do you mean?" My brain was racing a hundred miles a minute. *Did we do something?*

"It was, hands down, the best night of my life." He sipped his own coffee, his sultry gaze glued to me, while I tried not to stare at his lips. "You were incredible. That thing you did with your mouth"—his voice became huskier—"was unbelievable."

What? I couldn't remember anything. Was I really *that* out of it last night? My cheeks suddenly felt a bit warm, because if we *did* do things . . .

Then I glanced at the sofa, and there were pillows and a blanket on it, clear signs that it was his makeshift bed last night.

"Okay, yes, nothing happened." Rob burst out laughing. "You don't have to look so horrified. But seriously, I had tons of fun last night. Can I point out, though, that you fell asleep not even halfway through the movie. And you call yourself a fan of movies?"

Relief coursed through me, but also a tiny, uninvited thought of disappointment crept in. And it didn't escape my notice that this was my second thought in that way this morning, and how it all had to do with him. Or, rather, how it had *nothing* to do with him.

Why am I even thinking about this?

"You looked exhausted, so I didn't wake you up. You didn't even move a muscle when I put you into bed. Just kept snoring away." He smirked. "That's what I meant when I said 'that thing you did with your mouth.' You snore."

I never, ever swooned over a guy, but a mental image of him carrying me into his bedroom and putting me into bed danced into my mind and refused to leave my brain, and it was all I had to do not to sigh and melt into a puddle right then and there.

Get your shit together, Kim.

"Sorry. I usually snore when I'm tired."

"No need to be sorry." A small smile lifted his mouth. "It's kind of cute, actually."

Gaahhh. Focus, focus, focus.

"No one is cute when they snore." My cheeks now felt like they were on fire. "Uh, do you have a spare toothbrush I can borrow?"

"There should be some in my bathroom cabinet. Let me get them for you."

"I can find them." Anything to get away from him for a few minutes so I could recompose myself. I went back to his bathroom and rummaged in the drawers, but all I could see were some first aid items, spare razor blades, and extra tubes of toothpaste.

"Did you find them?" Rob called from outside.

"Not yet!"

I tried another drawer and was startled a few seconds later by his deep rumble echoing in the bathroom. "Let me have a look."

Surprised, I took a few steps backward and turned around, only to bump into him.

"Sorry," I mumbled, at the same time he said, "Oops."

What followed was an awkward dance of us trying to maneuver our way around each other. I took a couple of steps to my right, as he took a couple of steps to his left, rendering us facing each other again. Then we both took a couple of steps in the other direction, and finally, I took a couple of steps backward as he awkwardly moved forward. My back was pressed against the sink, and we were standing so close, if he did even the tiniest shuffle in my direction, we'd be practically plastered against each other.

He stared at me, and I stared back at him.

Neither of us made any effort to move.

"I'm sure I have a spare somewhere." His voice was gruff.

"Can't see any." My own voice came out a little bit raspy.

His eyes were intent on my face, before his gaze dropped to my lips. The air in the bathroom suddenly felt tens, even hundreds of degrees hotter. After a beat—or maybe forever—Rob inhaled a deep breath, the muscles in his jaw ticking.

"Might be in this one." He reached up and opened a cupboard above me. The underside of his arms brushed my head, and I sucked in a breath at the contact.

What the hell. I had to put a stop to whatever this was.

Without waiting for the toothbrush, I ducked under his arms. "Don't worry about it. I need to go home before opening the store anyway. Thanks for letting me stay the night."

Then I fled before I could change my mind.

* * *

By the time I arrived at Opa's house for dinner that evening, whatever moments I had with Rob in the morning had been aggressively shoved into the deepest, darkest corners of my brain, because I'd spent the entire day replaying it more often than I should have, and it had made for, by far, the least productive day in my entire life.

"Hi, Opa." I gave him a hug. "How's my favorite grandfather today?"

"Baik, dong."* He gave an awkward chuckle.

I tilted my head. That was the same laugh he used to use when I was growing up, when he surprised my grandmother with impromptu birthday trips, or when he didn't want me to know that he'd bought me the bicycle I'd wanted for Christmas.

Like he had something to hide.

"That's a suspicious chuckle." I narrowed my eyes. "What's going on?"

"Nothing." He grabbed his wallet and phone and led me outside. "You got my message, right? I made a booking for six thirty at Java Spice. We should go now if we don't want to be late."

"But we never have to book at Java Spice." I unlocked my car. "You know Oom Tanujaya will always have a table for you."

"It's Sunday evening. He might be busy. Better safe than sorry."

"Hmm." Something was up, but I knew he would never admit to anything. "Rob sends his regards, by the way."

Opa's face lit up. "When did you see him? I sent him a link for a sale on woodworking tools yesterday. Did he say anything about that?"

---

* Indonesian, meaning: "Good, of course."

"No." I raised my eyebrows as I navigated the traffic. "You have Rob's number?"

"We exchanged numbers when he came for dinner."

Of course they did. Two outgoing extroverts who loved nothing more than making friends and meeting new people. Why was I even surprised?

"We've been talking about the woodworking expo next month." Opa had a big grin on his face. "He said he used to go with his dad, so I asked if he wanted to go with me."

"I took you there last year," I pointed out. "Didn't remember you looking this excited when we went."

"I *was* excited. You didn't remember because you spent the entire time sitting down at the food court reading your book. Anyway, I'm glad you connected me with Rob. He's a wonderful young man. Polite and well-mannered."

"He is." I returned my focus to the road.

"Hard worker, and from the sounds of it, very close with his family."

"You're not wrong."

"He's funny, too. And patient with older people like me. Signs of a good person."

"I agree."

"Handsome, too, wouldn't you say?"

I sighed. "I know what you're doing, and it's not going to work, okay?"

My grandfather chuckled, knowing that he'd been busted. "Why not?"

Because Rob believed in that far-fetched fairy tale called love and happy endings, and I didn't. Because I had more pressing things to put my energy into, and a relationship that might not last was *not* on the list.

But I'd be lying if I said that he hadn't been occupying a rent-free space in my brain since this morning. Maybe even earlier, if I wanted to be truly honest. As much as I'd like to pretend otherwise, it felt like something had shifted between us, even though I had no business thinking of him in any way other than as a friend, and I didn't know what to make of it.

"We're here." I changed the topic, hoping Opa wouldn't push the issue. I found an empty spot next to a black rental sedan, then helped him out of the car. We walked into the tiny restaurant, and Opa made a beeline for a table at the back as he lifted his hand in a wave.

I followed his gaze, thinking that he was probably waving to the owner, but my steps faltered when I saw the person sitting at the table.

It was my father.

My hand shot out to catch one of Opa's arms. "Why is he here?"

"He texted me last night. He's in town for a meeting."

That right there was proof that my relationship with my father wasn't the best. Why didn't he text me as well? The fact that he didn't tell his own daughter that he was visiting should speak volumes, shouldn't it?

"He always does this." My voice was flat, void of any emotions, because you couldn't have emotions about someone who wasn't a part of your life, could you? "Waltzes into our lives and graces us with his presence whenever he's in town and has nothing better to do."

"He's only here for a day. And he's your dad, so let's give him some respect, okay?" Opa's voice was gentle but firm. "Your mom and Oma would have wanted you to have a good relationship with him. You can be nice to your own father. Don't let me down."

It was a view my grandparents strongly believed in, having been raised overseas in a conservative Asian country where most parents are put on a pedestal, regardless of whether they deserved it or not. Seniority was everything, and if you were a parent, you deserved unequivocal respect from your children, no matter what.

I didn't think my dad deserved unequivocal respect from me, but I knew this wasn't the time to show that.

"Dad." My father enveloped Opa in a hug, then directed his attention at me.

I wouldn't be surprised if strangers mistook my dad as my older brother. Despite the twenty-five-year age difference between us, he didn't look a day older than mid-forties. His dark hair, always styled into a neat, short cut, had grown longer since the last time I saw him, probably five or six months ago now. There were a few sprinkles of salt and pepper at his temples, the only sign that he was a few years away from turning sixty.

"Kim," my dad said, leaning in to hug me, "good to see you."

I stopped myself from echoing the sentiment. I was fine with the fact that he was never going to be present in my life, but what I was *not* fine with was being expected to play the role of the doting daughter without ample notice.

"Are you surprised? I asked Dad not to tell you that I was coming." My father smiled. "You look wonderful. I've missed you both."

Did he really say that he'd missed us? *Me and Opa?* That was a blatant lie, wasn't it? It had to be, because otherwise he would be here with us, wouldn't he, instead of living on the other side of the world for his job?

Be nice, Kim. He won't be here for long. Think of him as just another random person, and you don't really care whether he's here to stay or not, do you?

But deep down, I realized that I *did* care. That he wasn't here to stay. That he breezed into town only whenever it was convenient for him, and we were supposed to welcome him with open arms and pretend like it was just another day in our wonderful, totally functional family relationship. My grandparents used to assure me that even though he wasn't here with us, he always carried a piece of me in his heart. It was probably true, because I'd get birthday cards every now and then, or Christmas gifts via my grandparents. So I knew they were right. My father wasn't a terrible person.

He was just . . . unavailable.

Physically and emotionally.

I'd reasoned to myself how it wasn't entirely his fault. How he was young when my mom died, and it was probably too much for him to deal with his grief while being saddled with the burden of raising an infant on his own. Some people thrived at being single parents, but my dad obviously wasn't one of those people.

It still didn't make things any easier.

I glanced at Opa. This must have been hard for him, too, because this was *his* son who had chosen not to be involved in our lives. Opa had lost his wife, and in a way, he had lost his only child, too. And he probably loved his son too much to be angry about it.

Fine. If he could sit through the evening and be kind to my dad, then I could, too.

Be kind, Oma used to say. *It doesn't cost you anything to be kind.*

I bit the inside of my cheeks to keep my bubbling irritation in check and muted the negative thoughts swirling in my head. "You look well."

"I've been trying to exercise more, eat healthier and all that. Anyway, enough about me. How's everything going, Kimmy?"

And that there was the *real* reason why I hated that nickname. That was my father's special moniker for me, as if a cutesy nickname would make up for all the time he wasn't around, and things would magically be fine and wonderful between us.

"We're good. Everything's going well." I hoped the subtext was clear: *We're doing great, even without you here.*

"I'm glad." For a brief second, a sad look crossed my dad's face. "Your mom would have been so proud of you."

I mumbled my thanks and focused my attention on the menu, even though I can recite everything by heart.

"How long are you here for?" Opa asked.

"I'm flying back to Singapore tonight."

Opa only nodded, his shoulders slumping a little.

"I'll probably be back in town again next month. Might stay a bit longer then."

My head snapped up so fast at that, I might have heard the reverberating crack my neck made. "What do you mean, longer? Like, two, three days?"

Dad cleared his throat. "More like two or three months."

Silence fell on the table following this announcement. Opa looked wary, as if trying to decide whether he'd heard his son correctly, and I knew exactly why.

"Are you sure?" I blurted out. "You said the same thing eighteen months ago."

Opa had been overjoyed then, and I was cautiously hopeful, thinking that we would *finally* have him back. That after Oma had passed, my dad would realize that he needed to spend more time with his father, with me, because we were the people that really mattered in his life, and that we would finally, somehow, be a normal family. Well, spoiler alert: It never happened. Something about a new role that was too good to pass up. It had left Opa heartbroken, and me pledging to myself to never believe anything that my father said, ever again.

"It's different this time." He let out an uncomfortable laugh. "I'm definitely staying."

My grandfather relaxed a little. "That's great, Daniel. It will be good to have you home."

A million things were running through my mind. The main one, I wasn't going to lie, was dread. If he really was sticking around this time, that would be the longest stretch of time I'd ever have to interact with him. The longest he'd stayed with us in the past was five weeks, when I was fourteen, because he was recovering from a broken arm and the news channel he'd worked for wouldn't have him back until he had fully recovered. I'd never had to put up with him longer than that, and to be honest, I wasn't looking forward to it.

"Why so long?" I blurted out. "What about your work?"

Opa directed a frown at me, and for a moment, an avalanche of guilt followed my question, replacing the dread.

But my father didn't seem to notice my tone. "I've got some time off coming up, and I thought it would be nice to spend it back home. I've been thinking about getting a place here, so I have somewhere to stay when I'm in town."

Time off? My dad? And he chose to spend it with us?

And he wanted to get a place here?

Something wasn't right, and I didn't like it. Because his being here for a long period of time would only lead to one thing: hope. The tiniest hint of hope that my father and I might have a chance at a normal father-daughter relationship, and when that eventually fizzled—because it would—it would only lead to more disappointment.

Our food came, and Opa asked my dad questions about his work and life in Singapore. I wasn't listening, because my mind was too busy recalibrating, trying to adjust to the fact that for the first time ever in my entire life, there was a strong possibility that I'd have my dad around for a couple of months.

Should I be thrilled about it?

Because I wasn't.

My grandfather didn't seem to mind, though. Opa was chuckling at one of my dad's stories, looking like he was thoroughly enjoying seeing his son again. I was happy for him, but that didn't mean I had to feel the same way, right?

But I didn't want to ruin the night for Opa, so I kept quiet and nodded and made perfectly acceptable replies whenever someone spoke to me. Mostly my grandfather, because my dad didn't even try to initiate conversations with me or ask questions about my life, which had made me even angrier. I barely survived the rest of dinner, and by the time my father hopped into his black rental an hour later, my chest felt tight, and I was mentally drained from the interaction.

"I'm sorry I didn't tell you," Opa said as we watched him drive away. "He said he wanted to surprise you, because it had been a while since he came home."

"Please just tell me next time. That kind of surprise doesn't really do anything for me."

"I know." There was a pause before he spoke again. "He's making an effort to start a relationship with you, Kim. Wouldn't you want that? At the end of the day, he's still your dad."

"Maybe biologically," I said. "But not in every other sense of the word. You and Oma are the only parents I've ever known. And sure, a relationship with him sounds nice, but I'm not holding my breath. I'm lucky I've got you, and that's enough for me."

There was a long pause before my grandfather finally replied. "I'm lucky to have you, too." He gave me a small smile. "In fact, have I ever told you that you're my favorite granddaughter?"

"I better be." I linked my arm through his. "Can we talk about something else? What do you say we go for a walk? Go get some desserts?"

Opa smiled at me. "I would love that."

CHAPTER 20

Practice Makes the Heart Grow Fonder

The Waterfront was still busy this time of night, with soft jazzy music coming from a few of the restaurants, and chatter of their customers in the outside dining area. It only took us ten minutes to walk from Java Spice to Ellie's new bakery, and the sweet smell of pastry greeted us the minute we walked in. Ellie usually worked at this shop on the weekends, because they stayed open until late, and sure enough, she was behind the counter serving a customer.

"Oh, look. Rob's here. We should go over and say hello."

My head swiveled in the direction my grandfather was pointing. Rob was sitting at a table talking with Alec, their faces serious, as if they were contemplating the bigger meaning of life.

"Maybe next time. They look like they're discussing something important," I said. It had only been several hours since I saw him last, and even after I'd spent the entire day overanalyzing what had happened at his house, I still wasn't ready to see him again.

"I'm sure it'll be fine. It's just a quick hi."

I made a lunge to grab my grandfather, but he was already

calling out to Rob as he approached their table. Both men looked up at Opa's voice and stood up to greet him. My grandmother would have applauded their impeccable manners, but right now I just wanted to grab my over-friendly grandfather by the shoulder and haul him the hell out of here.

I should have, but I didn't.

Instead, I went over to the counter to order some drinks and a slice of blueberry cheesecake, Opa's favorite, then joined them at the table. My grandfather was already chatting with the two men, taking the seat next to Alec, and leaving the empty spot for me next to Rob.

I gave my grandfather a side-eye, because he knew exactly what he was doing.

Rob gave me a smile as I sat down. "Long time no see, stranger." He frowned a little at the look on my face, then leaned closer and lowered his voice. "Hey. You okay?"

"I'm fine."

His gaze searched my face. "You don't look fine. You look upset. What's going on?"

"It's nothing. My dad is in town, and we just had dinner with him."

Rob gave me a long look, and one of his hands reached out to give me a quick squeeze. "I'm sorry. Do you want to talk about it?"

"Not really. Not now."

He nodded. "If you needed someone to vent to, I'm all ears. I hope you had a nice time with Thomas, at least."

My gaze drifted to my grandfather, who was laughing and talking with Alec, and I smiled a little. "I did." And Rob was right. As long as my grandfather had a lovely time, and he did, that was the only thing that mattered. "Thanks for reminding me."

"He looks happy." Then Rob leaned over to me and murmured in a low voice, so only I could hear him, "I like that smile. It's a good look on you."

Before I had a chance to respond, he grinned at me, then joined the conversation between Alec and my grandfather, leaving me to stare at him while my cheeks warmed, and the insides of my stomach slowly melted into a puddle of gooeyness.

But I realized what he'd done: That little comment had helped me to relax. The tightening in my chest had loosened, and I knew everything would be fine, because I wouldn't let the dinner, or my dad, or the fact that he might be here to stay, bother me.

Ellie brought a tray with my order, dragged a chair from the empty table next to ours and sat next to me. "Since when is your grandfather best friends with Rob?"

"Since Rob came over for dinner last month. Alec didn't tell you? He heard about it when I helped them at the house they're flipping."

"He never mentioned it. Why haven't Jenna and I heard about this?"

"I'm telling you now. It's no big deal."

"Not a big deal? Are you joking?" She gestured at Opa, who was laughing at something funny Rob must have said. "Look at them. They're literally the definition of bromance."

I shrugged. "I don't know what else to tell you. He's the grandson he's never had?"

"Kim." Ellie stared at me, her eyebrows hiking up her forehead. "You've never invited anyone else to your grandfather's house for dinner."

"That's not true. I've invited you and Jenna."

"Let me rephrase. You've never invited any *men* to your grandfather's house for dinner."

"Also not true. I've invited Alec several times."

Ellie folded her arms across her chest. "You know what I mean."

I knew what she was getting at, and I had to put a stop to it before it snowballed further into inaccurate speculations. "It was just a way of saying thanks for everything he's doing for me. That's it."

"I helped you with a flat tire once," Alec said, and I looked up to see that the three of them had stopped talking and were shamelessly listening to our conversation. "Never even got as much as a cupcake as a thank-you."

I glanced at my grandfather, who was biting back a smile, and Rob, who was watching me with an unreadable expression on his face. "Seriously, Mackenzie?"

"Dead serious. And for jump-starting your car, patching that hole in the wall at your store, and being the designated driver more than once whenever you ladies had a night out."

I flipped Alec the middle finger as he collapsed with laughter.

"I'm kidding. Or maybe not." He grinned at me. "Hey, Ellie said you managed to sign three major sponsors for the festival? That's great work."

"Thanks." I returned his grin. "There's been lots of interest from small businesses wanting to rent stalls, too, which is awesome."

"You know what . . ." Opa looked thoughtful. "I follow this local woodworking influencer on social media, and I've seen him put things up for sale sometimes. I can reach out to him and see if he's interested in renting a stall at your festival."

"That'll be wonderful." I beamed at him.

"Is he going to be at the expo next month?" Rob asked.

"He will. He's fantastic. We'll have to stop by his booth."

"Wait, you're going to the woodworking expo together?" I looked at Rob and my grandfather. "I thought you were still talking about it."

"We are," Opa replied. "We're going to the Friday session, because it'll be less busy, and we'll have more time to chat with the exhibitors."

"But you have dialysis on Friday afternoons."

"We'll go in the morning, and I'll drop him off at dialysis after," Rob said. "I'll take half the day off, because we think Friday morning will be easier for Thomas to navigate the expo. It'll be less crowded, and easier for him to walk around."

Both he and my grandfather looked at me, with big grins on their faces, as if waiting for my approval. For a moment, I was taken aback, because this was one of the rare times after Oma had passed that I'd seen Opa being truly enthusiastic and looking forward to doing something that he loved.

And it was all thanks to Rob.

I'd told him on his matchmaking questionnaire that I wanted someone who would make me feel safe. Someone who would be there for me, and someone who would appreciate Opa as if he was their own family. He'd done all that, and so much more. Not only had he befriended my grandfather, but he also looked after him, even though he didn't have to.

"Sounds like a solid plan." I slowly nodded.

"How's it going with the weddings?" Alec asked Rob. "Found anyone nice for her yet?"

"Working on it. Kim's going through the dossier of the potential suitors for the next one."

"What do these dossiers look like?" This came from my grandfather. "Kim's told me about it, but I've never actually seen one."

At my nod, Rob pulled out his phone and showed Opa the last one he'd emailed me.

"It's very thorough," Opa said. "I can see how it helps make things easier for Kim. Do you know who you're going to approach, sweetheart?"

With that, several pairs of curious eyes swiveled my way. Rob's gaze was intent on mine, and it suddenly dawned on me that there was nothing I wanted less right now than to have to choose a total stranger and pretend to be interested enough in them to fake a relationship for a few months.

Someone cleared their throat, and I realized that everyone was still waiting for an answer.

"Uh." My brain scrambled back to the list of men, and I blurted out the first name that came to mind. "Aiden Cho. The Brit."

I stole a quick glance at Rob, trying to gauge his reaction, but his face was inscrutable.

"Aiden, Aiden . . ." Opa was still holding Rob's phone, and he scrolled through the dossier to find the profile. "Ah, here he is. Thirty-three years of age, works in private equity, the only child of a Chinese Singaporean father and an English mother. Grew up in London, went to college in the States. His interests include go-karting and ice-skating." Opa looked up at me. "Sounds promising. You'll have to brush up on your skating skills, sweetheart."

"Rob used to play hockey, so he's a great skater," Alec said. "An excellent driver, too. The perfect person to take you to practice your skating and go-karting skills."

"I think that's a great idea," Opa said. "Practice makes perfect."

"You'll need more than one practice session," Ellie said. "You want to make sure you hook him right in with your skating and your expert go-kart driving."

"Please stop. You guys are not subtle at all."

There were smiles and chuckles around the table.

"Don't mind them." Rob grinned at me. "But it wouldn't hurt to schedule a couple of skating practices, so when you go on those dates with Aiden, you'll have the best chance of impressing him."

As the rest went back to chatting with each other, I realized that Rob had done so much more than looking out for my grandfather.

He had also made sure that he was always there for me.

True to his word, Rob took me to skating practice the week after, during which I mostly sat on my ass on the floor while Rob spent the entire time trying to pull me up. We then decided that since skating wasn't my strongest forte, we'd try go-karting, since

Aiden's family ran a go-kart racing track in the UK. I'd never raced go-karts before, but I could drive, and they were practically the same thing, right?

Right now, two nights away from the third wedding, we were at a packed indoor go-karting place, and I was putting the helmet over my head as we waited to do our laps.

"That's not tight enough." Rob pointed at the helmet strap under my chin. "Can I help?"

When I nodded, he reached and fiddled with the strap, and I watched him from behind the visor as he gently pulled and tugged at it, trying to make it fit snugly against my neck, his brows furrowing with intense concentration.

"Aiden used to spend his weekends and holidays working at his family's racing track when he was growing up," Rob said, his eyes focusing on the helmet buckle under my chin. "I think this date idea is going to really appeal to him."

But Aiden was the furthest thing from my mind, as I watched Rob step back to reassess what he did. Because deep down I knew that being with Rob right now, this so-called practice session, was really just an excuse for me to spend more time with him.

And I had a feeling I would prefer this, any day, over anything and anyone else.

"I hope you're ready." He fastened his own helmet over his head. "Because I'm going to smoke your ass."

"In your dreams, Carmichael."

He grinned as he jumped into his kart. "No, pretty sure I'm going to do it now."

We did twelve laps, and I purposely let him be in the lead earlier, while still tailing him closely. That made him cocky, thinking that he was a surefire bet to win the race, even giving me a smug grin during a turn around a corner, yelling, "See you at the finish line!"

Just as we started the final lap, I pressed my accelerator and steadily overtook him. He sped up a little, and I picked up my speed to match his. We rounded a corner, neck and neck, and that was when it happened.

I was too focused on winning, and I didn't realize there was another kart right on my tail. When I sped up around the corner to overtake Rob, that third kart went faster as well, making a sharp turn in the narrow corner. But something must have gone wrong, because the driver lost control of their kart and then they were heading straight for me. In my panic, I turned my steering wheel a little too abruptly to avoid the collision, and the next thing I knew, my kart was spinning around, and within seconds, I crashed into the rubber barrier at the sides of the track, sending me to a complete stop.

My heart was beating rapidly, and I took a few deep breaths, trying to compose myself.

"Kim!" Rob leapt out of his kart and raced toward me. "Are you okay?"

"Fine, I'm fine." I took off the helmet and shook my head. "I'm okay."

"Are you sure?" He crouched in front of me and placed a shaky hand on my chin, examining me with the tiniest look of panic. "How's your head?"

"Head's fine." I gave him a small smile. "Good thing you helped me with my helmet earlier, huh?"

One of the attendants came over to check on us and make sure we were okay, then escorted us off the track while someone else drove our karts away. All the while Rob kept checking to make sure I was okay, and it wasn't until we left the karting arena that he was finally convinced I hadn't suffered a concussion or life-threatening injuries.

And it wasn't lost on me that by doing that, he had also ticked another box from that matchmaking questionnaire.

Somehow, he never failed to make me feel safe.

CHAPTER 21

Let's Talk About the Concept of a Platonic Relationship

The venue for the third wedding was a breathtaking, renovated eighteenth-century convent that looked as if it had been plucked off the pages of a magical fairy tale. The estate was probably around twenty acres, with manicured gardens, a beautiful chapel, and a grand, old mansion with heritage architecture, which had been converted into a function space, where the reception was held. It gave off a tranquil vibe and painted the most romantic image for the wedding.

Rob's cousin, Evie, was the bride, and this union was another success story of Rob's matchmaking efforts. The ceremony was small and intimate, but the reception was a full-blown celebration, and the ballroom was packed with people wearing pretty dresses and sharp suits.

I smiled my thanks at a server who was bringing drinks around and chose a champagne flute, as I watched Rob, who was squatting down to talk to his niece. Today he wore a white shirt with the sleeves slightly rolled up and gray dress slacks that snugly hugged his long legs, with his gray suit jacket draped over his left arm. He had picked me up earlier, and from the moment we arrived, there was no shortage of high fives and backslaps from various members of his extended family.

It was so lovely to see, because I'd never experienced anything like that. His cousins, aunties and uncles, and everyone he ran into always stopped to talk with him. He chatted with all of them and asked questions about their jobs, their kids, about anything and everything in the other person's life. A few of his married cousins brought their young children along, and they gave him high fives and called him "Uncle Robbob," and it was impressive how well-versed he was in monster trucks, *Bluey*, and *Mario Kart*.

It was fucking adorable.

I waited until he had finished talking to his niece, who was squealing with excitement as Rob promised to come by to watch the My Little Pony movie with her.

"I didn't know you speak fluent Toddlerese," I said as his niece ran off to find her parents.

"I'm an expert. They don't call me the funcle for nothing."

"You're great with your niece and nephews," I said. "And they all obviously adore you."

"They're the best." His face turned wistful. "I can't wait to have kids of my own one day. It'll be so much fun making memories with them and sharing all the important milestones of their lives—their first steps, first words, teaching them how to play catch, going on road trips together."

An image of Rob as a father suddenly popped into my mind, and I didn't know why the thought made me a little hot all over. "I think you'll make a wonderful dad."

"I don't know about that, but I sure as hell will do my best." He broke into a grin. "For now, I get to play with them and give them back to their parents when they're tired and cranky. There's a perk to being the only unmarried sibling in the family."

"Are they all here?" I glanced around the room, nerves suddenly churning in my stomach. "Your siblings?"

"Yeah. Amanda flew in this morning, and Alexandra drove down yesterday. They'll be here for a week, which is nice, because I haven't seen them both in a while." He lowered his voice, as if sharing a secret. "My siblings often have no filter, so if they say something that offends you, ignore them and move on."

"Got it."

"They don't do it to everyone, only to the people I introduce to the family. Make sure those people pass muster."

"That sounds scary." It sounded *wonderful*. I would *kill* to have siblings who would put someone through the wringer to make sure they were good enough for me.

"It's not, but they can be a lot. But you can handle them." He grinned at me. "By the way, watch me tell them off, it's really sexy."

I rolled my eyes. "Yeah, right."

Rob raised his eyebrows, his eyes dancing with amusement. "That sounds like you don't believe me. That I can be sexy? Or that I can tell my older siblings off? Because I can totally do both."

"Okay, fine, I believe you." I bit back a grin. "You're always sexy in everything you do. Your walk is sexy, your laugh is sexy. You even make breathing look sexy. Happy?"

"It'll be more convincing if you look a bit more enthusiastic when you're saying it."

"I can even *feel* your sexiness from a mile away. Whenever you enter a room. When I'm talking to you on the phone." I dropped my voice lower, trying to sound sultry, although to my ears, it was so low I could probably have passed for a creepy serial killer. "Even your text messages ooze sexiness."

Rob was laughing now. "Okay, you can stop."

"But what if I don't want to stop? What if I want to explore and find out what other parts of you are sexy?" I bit on my bottom lip—not aiming for a suggestive look, but more to stop myself from laughing—then stepped closer, leaving only a few inches between us, and slowly trailed my fingers up his arm. "And, oh Lord, these arms. And your hands. They're probably the sexiest part of your body. And your long, lean fingers. Imagine the things you can do with them. The pleasure you can bring. *Damn.* Just the thought gets me so hot and bothered." I made a low moan and leaned in, my lips only a whisper of a breath away from the shell of his ear, as my fingers moved to trace a path on his chest. "*So hot.* I bet you work out so many times in a week, because this hard, strong, lean body doesn't become drool-worthy on its own, am I right?"

He sucked in a breath, and I had a feeling that my little stunt might have backfired on me, because we were practically chest to chest, and the feel of his warm skin underneath my fingertips was doing wild, unexplainable things to my insides, and I didn't want to stop, because touching him felt like the most natural thing in the world, and I found myself wishing that we were somewhere else right now.

Somewhere private.

Just the two of us.

So I could find out what those strong hands of his could actually do.

There was no reply, so I glanced up, and Rob was watching me, his gaze burning into mine, looking like he was sharing the same thoughts as me.

I cleared my throat and took a step back. "There. Convincing enough?"

"Fuck yes." His laugh was low and husky, sending more chaos churning inside my stomach. "I can't remember who was trying to convince who of what, but I'm sold."

"Great." I needed a few minutes to catch my breath. "I'm going to the restroom, okay?"

"Yeah." He let out a long breath. "I guess we should probably find Aiden when you come back, huh?"

Oh. I hadn't even thought about Aiden because I'd been having too much fun spending time with him. "Good idea."

When I returned a few minutes later, he was surrounded by a group of people who were laughing and talking over each other, in a way that showed they were completely comfortable with one another. I recognized their faces from the photos in his house, so I began to walk away, not wanting to disturb him, but it was too late. Rob gave me a wave, and the people he was talking to all turned to watch me, looking curious. When I blinked next, he was already heading in my direction, followed by his mom and all five of his siblings.

"Everyone, this is Kim, a good friend of mine." He tugged on my hand and pulled me closer to him. "Kim, these are my siblings. This is Alexandra. The tall blonde is Amanda, and the one next to her is Jennifer. That's Paul, and Kylie, and you've already met my mom."

His mom took one hand off her crutches and pulled me into a hug, and there were choruses of "Hello, Kim" and "Good to meet you" and one baffled voice saying, "She's already *met Mom*?"

"Lovely to meet you," Alexandra said. "When Robbie told the group chat he's bringing a date to the wedding, we all got very curious."

Rob made a strangled sound from next to me. "She's not my date. I told you all already, I'm helping Kim meet some single people. I'm introducing her to Aiden, Evie's friend."

"You're single," another sibling—Amanda?—pointed out, a smirk on her face, before giving me a grin, telling me that they were just winding him up.

"Listen." Rob raised a finger. "I can show up at a wedding with a woman that is my friend and we don't have to have a romantic relationship between us. Can we all take a minute to let that concept sink in?"

"We can. We just choose not to," the last sibling he introduced, Kylie, answered with a serious look on her face. "We spoke on the phone, Kim. When you asked for references for Rob's matchmaking experience."

"Yes. And Paul, too."

The man who looked like he could be Rob's twin nodded. "We did."

"We've heard so much about you," the brunette—Jennifer?—quipped. "You're the first woman he's brought to a family event since Lucy, so we all went into a collective flip-out."

His ex. The *other* reason I was here.

"Paul did a bit of digging into your background and we all approve," Amanda said.

"Nothing too extensive," Paul assured me when he saw me flinch. "Just a routine background check to confirm you're not a deranged psycho who might hurt our brother."

"I'm not going to hurt him. We're not in a relationship or anything." I snuck a quick glance at Rob. "We're just friends."

"That's how the best relationships start." Amanda nodded. "As friends."

"But remember, Robbie," Kylie chimed in. "You don't need a partner to live your life, and there's absolutely nothing wrong with that, okay?"

"What are you talking about? This is Robbie," Paul said. "He's the hopeless romantic, remember? He's going to find someone. It's not if, it's when."

His mom gave me an apologetic smile. "Robbie's never offered to matchmake anyone outside of our extended family before. So of course there was a huge fuss when he told us that he's helping you find someone."

"Maybe I've decided to expand my services to the wider community," Rob replied. "Make other people's lives brighter by helping them find their soulmates."

"But why would you pair Kim off with someone else when you can ask her out yourself?" Amanda said.

"I agree with Paulie," Jennifer said. "Who wants to bet that Robbie's going to be the one getting hitched next?"

"How can you be so sure? He doesn't even have a girlfriend yet."

"She's going to be his girlfriend, dumbass. Look at how he's looking at her. He's next."

How he looks at me? I glanced at Rob, who was watching his family with a mixture of exasperation and amusement on his face.

"I agree. And a mother's intuition is never wrong."

"Maybe you can do a double wedding with Cousin Clare. Have you heard? She proposed to her boyfriend last month."

"Can you just elope? I'm getting tired of weddings, honestly."

"Everyone needs to calm the fuck down." Rob raised his voice a little, although a smile was playing on his lips. "Kim and I are just friends, okay?"

"But you don't usually bring female friends to family events." Amanda was giving me furtive looks she thought I didn't catch. "Not after Lucy. Oh, I'm so glad Evie didn't invite her."

"Go away," Rob said, but without any heat to his words. "Find someone else to annoy."

She gave him a pout. "Is that how you treat your favorite sibling?"

Paul flashed me a sympathetic smile. "I apologize on behalf of my sisters. Robbie and I have no choice, we're stuck with them. You know the saying, 'You can choose your friends, but you can't choose your family'? Underneath all this craziness, we're normal and lovable."

"Who are you calling crazy, Paulie?"

The siblings started talking over each other, earning looks from the other wedding guests around us, and with that, I fell in love with his family. They might be loud and opinionated, and Rob might act like he was annoyed with his siblings, but it was obvious that they all loved and supported each other. I stole a glance at him, and he had one arm around his mother, while his other hand was gesturing wildly, trying to emphasize his point.

I had to admit, I was secretly enjoying this side of him I'd never seen before. There was a lot to be said about how someone treated their mother, and seeing the way he interacted with his mom and siblings told me all I needed to know.

And honestly, I really, *really* liked what I'd seen so far.

Suddenly the group went quiet, as Rob's father strode our way.

"Hey, honey." Michelle gave the man a hug. "You made it."

"My lunch meeting finished earlier than expected." He gave her a kiss and turned his attention to the rest, his eyes briefly pausing on me, before turning to his youngest son. "Robert. I've only seen you at the office once this week."

"Dad, it's the weekend," Kylie said. "Are you seriously talking about work?"

James threw her an impatient glance. "Yes, because Rob has been slacking off again."

"I'm not slacking off." Rob glanced at his mother, who was vibrating with a nervous energy next to his dad. "I've just been busy with work."

"With that old house you're renovating? Didn't I tell you it's not a good investment?" His father let out a scoff. "Why are you still wasting your time on that ridiculous little project? You need to start taking your life more seriously."

I gaped at him. Did he just say 'ridiculous little project'? Did he really not know what his son had been up to?

"Rob's fine, Dad," Alexandra said. "He's doing perfectly well on his own."

"Honey, we're at Evie's wedding." Michelle hooked her arm into her husband's, her smile tense, as panic flickered in her eyes. "Can we please not make a scene? We can talk about this another time."

Rob slid his mother another look, then sighed with reservation. "Fine, Dad. I'll come Monday morning. Okay?"

"Make sure you do." James fixed him with a glare. "Because that's what you said last week, and you never did."

"Excuse me," I interrupted. "I don't think you know much about your son."

Silence fell over the group as their gazes pivoted toward me.

"Your daughter is right." I gestured at Alexandra. "Rob is doing very well on his own. You're aware that he runs his own construction business, right? He renovated my friend's store last year and turned it into an amazing, state-of-the-art bakery. That house he's remodeling, have you seen it? It's gorgeous. It would make a wonderful home for anyone to live in for many years to come. You also know that he owns a stake in Alec Mackenzie's company, don't you? And it's partly owned by Goodwin Property Group?" Fine, so I might have conveniently left out the fact that they'd sold their ownership, but whatever. I was on a roll here.

Rob's dad was scowling at me, irritation displayed across his face. "This is a family matter. You don't know what you're talking about—"

"I do know what I'm talking about," I cut him off. "But you obviously don't. Your son is an amazing guy, a hard worker, and he *is* successful in his own way. The least you can do is appreciate what he's done in his life, instead of belittling him for his choices."

I glanced at Rob, wanting to reassure him that I was there for him no matter what. He was staring at me, his eyes popped wide in disbelief.

Nobody said anything following my speech, and the loud silence in the group was deafening, even though we were in the middle of a party. Michelle looked frazzled, while Rob's dad was shooting daggers my way, which annoyed the hell out of me, so I lifted my chin and returned his glare. My grandparents had always emphasized the importance of being polite and respectful to people older than me, but this man was condescending to Rob, and he didn't deserve even an ounce of politeness and my respect.

James gave a quiet scoff and said to Rob, "Monday morning. Don't be late."

He turned on his heel and walked away, leaving the rest in awkward silence.

"Wow." Paul was staring open-mouthed at me. "You have balls of steel."

Michelle closed her eyes and exhaled. Before I could say anything, she turned to me and grasped my hands, her expression apologetic. "I'm really sorry. He's been stressing over a major project at work."

"You have nothing to be sorry about," I said. "I apologize if I made you uncomfortable."

"That doesn't give him an excuse to be an ass, Mom," Kylie said.

Michelle sighed. "I know, honey. I'll see if I can talk to him tonight."

"Thank you for standing up for Rob," Alexandra said to me. "You're good for him."

I nodded, but my attention was on Rob. He was still staring at me. The disbelief had turned into gratefulness, and there was a fiery look in his eyes, as if he was about to grab me and drag me into a secluded corner and do delicious, unspeakable things to me.

What? Where did that thought come from?

Amanda said to Rob, "I like her. She's now my favorite person in—"

He cut her off, his attention still riveted on me. "I see our target by the drinks table, and I'm on matchmaking duties, so Kim and I are leaving, okay?"

He placed a hand at the small of my back and led me away without waiting for his family's answer. As soon as we were out of earshot and a safe distance away, he stopped, turned me around to face him, and pulled me into a tight hug.

"Thank you for saying all that," he murmured. "It means a lot."

"Anytime. It's the truth, and you don't deserve to be treated like that."

We stood like that for a few minutes, and it was such a wonderful place to be in, surrounded by his warmth and his comforting scent, and right now, the prospect of having to meet and charm another man really wasn't appealing at all. I wanted to stay like this the entire night, and I didn't want it to be with anyone else but him.

He was the first to pull away, looking as reluctant as I felt. "I guess we should go and find Aiden?"

I slowly nodded. *Remember what you came here for.*

When we found him, Aiden Cho was chatting with an older woman who seemed to be thoroughly enchanted by him.

"That's the bride's grandma," Rob said. "She seems to be enjoying his company."

"I guess it's a good sign. He's patient with older people." Which was exactly what my grandfather had said about Rob.

"True. Patience is an important virtue."

A man was standing next to the woman, wearing a fond smile as he watched her chuckling at everything Aiden was saying. "Is that her husband?"

"Yeah. They've been married for fifty years, and it's one of the strongest marriages I know. That man is so secure in their relationship and even though she might be giggling like a schoolgirl at some handsome young man, he knows her heart is only reserved for him."

No wonder Rob was such a firm believer in true love, because his entire family was full of examples of solid, loving marriages.

When the couple walked away, Rob nodded at me. "That's our cue. Let's move."

Aiden was looking at his phone when we approached, and Rob gave him a friendly pat on the back. "Aiden. Great to see you again, man. How's things?"

"Oh, I can't complain." Aiden gave him a friendly smile. "It's such a lovely day for a wedding, isn't it? Evie and Jason look so happy. And I heard you played a huge part in getting them together."

"They're perfect for each other, so I didn't really have to do much." Rob gestured at me. "This is Kim, by the way. Kim, Aiden is one of Evie's college friends."

"Nice to meet you." Aiden tilted his head at me. "I feel like we've met before."

"Have we?" I gave him a polite smile. "Maybe I just have one of those faces."

"Oh, I know!" His face broke into a huge smile. "Are you a friend of Jenna Ng? Were you at her company's Christmas party last year?" When I nodded, he continued, "My firm consults for them, and her bosses were kind enough to invite us to their year-end get-together." A warm smile crossed his face. "I was actually trying to talk to you that night, but I had to leave early, so I didn't get a chance to introduce myself."

From next to him, Rob made a subtle thumbs-up gesture, before mumbling that he was going to get more drinks, then disappearing among the crowd.

I spent the next half hour talking to Aiden, and he was polite and funny, and his posh English accent made him sound like he had the intellectual ability to quote the entire dictionary off the top of his head. And the best part was, he seemed to be genuinely interested in *me* and not someone else, like Neil was.

Aiden Cho was, undoubtedly, *the* perfect boyfriend material for the next few months.

And I knew I should be feeling a lot more enthusiastic about it, but somehow, I wasn't.

"It's been wonderful meeting you, Kim," Aiden said. "Maybe we can catch up for drinks or dinner sometime?"

"I'd like that."

"Brilliant." He handed me his phone. "If you want to give me your phone number, I'll send you a text."

As he walked away, I glanced around the room to find Rob, wanting to share the news with him, and saw him talking to his father across the room. Rob was gesturing wildly with his hands, and after a few minutes of what looked like a heated exchange, he stormed off, looking annoyed, while his father stood there shaking his head.

Rob was standing in a corner when I went to find him, nursing a drink and wearing a scowl on his face.

"Can I join you?"

"Always." He glanced at me. "How did it go with Aiden?"

"Went great. Never mind that, are you okay? I saw you with your father."

He shrugged, clearly struggling to keep his emotions in check. "Just my dad being my dad. You know that major project my mom mentioned? He wants me to drop everything I'm doing and work for him full-time, because he needs all hands on deck."

"Why? He doesn't have other employees in his firm that could work on it?"

"I have a lot of experience that he can utilize." Rob sipped his drink, his eyes taking on a faraway look, as if he was anywhere else but here. "Being involved with that project will bring tons of exposure to his firm, which they really need right now. It's so massive that everyone who's a part of the project was asked to sign an NDA." He turned to me, looking troubled. "He can be infuriating sometimes, but he's my dad, and he means well. What if he's right? That I'm just wasting my life away? And all the hard work that Alec and I did to renovate that old house wasn't good enough?"

"I've seen the house. You two did an amazing job."

"But it's been a few weeks, and we haven't had any real interest yet." He drained his drink. "You've met my siblings. They're all successful and accomplished, making a difference in the world, and here I am, still without a real sense of purpose."

"Listen to me." I grabbed the sides of his face, making sure he was listening. "You. Are. Good. Enough. Who cares what your siblings are doing? Success looks different for everyone, and there are no right or wrong ways to define it. Didn't you tell me that you loved building things and making something out of nothing? That you loved seeing how happy people are when they finally get to see what you've built for them? *That's* your purpose. You *are* making a difference with what you're doing."

"Yeah, but—"

"No buts." My tone was more forceful than I intended. "You need to understand that you are doing something worthwhile with your life, and don't let your dad tell you otherwise. You don't need his approval. Don't let him, or anyone else, minimize everything you've achieved, no matter how big or small."

He stared into my eyes for a few beats, and I was suddenly aware of how close we were to each other. My hands were still cupping his face, and somehow in the past few minutes, he'd placed his empty glass on a table next to us, and his hands were both grasping my waist.

His gaze briefly lowered to my lips, before finding my eyes again.

I quickly dropped my own hands from his face and took a step back. *What am I doing?*

He wanted forever. A family and kids and the whole nine yards.

And I was here for a totally different purpose.

So whatever this was, whatever thoughts and feelings I was starting to have for him, it couldn't—it *mustn't*—go any further.

CHAPTER 22

It Takes Four to Slow Dance

As the wedding progressed and the alcohol flowed, the party became rowdier, and the four-string quartet that was playing romantic classical music earlier had been replaced by a DJ. We sat at our table, watching the guests on the makeshift parquet dance floor. A few of Rob's siblings and their partners were dancing, and so were his parents, swaying cheek to cheek even though the DJ was playing an upbeat pop song.

Rob was watching them with a mixture of affection and resignation on his face. I could only guess what was going through his mind: It was probably admiration for his parents' love but also a hefty amount of frustration at what his father was putting him through.

"This is getting to be a habit." I pointed at him, then at myself. "Us chatting and people-watching while everybody is dancing. Why aren't you out there with everyone else? I thought you were supposed to be a good dancer."

"I like chatting and people-watching with you. What's wrong

with that?" He turned to me and raised his eyebrows. "Who said I was supposed to be a good dancer?"

I shrugged. "Ellie might have mentioned it in passing."

He wriggled his eyebrows. "Have you been talking about me with your friends, Kim?"

"In passing, Robbie. In passing. Don't flatter yourself." When he only chuckled, I went on, "My grandfather said hi. He's very excited about the woodworking expo next week. Thanks for taking him."

"My pleasure. Thomas is great. He reminds me of my late grandfathers."

"I owe you one." I raised my drink at him. "I love him more than anything, but I would commit horrible things to avoid going to woodworking exhibitions."

"You sure you don't want to come along? Spend some quality time with your two most favorite people in the world?"

"You mean my *only* favorite person. Stop including yourself."

"That hurts. Deeply." He gave me a sad pout. "After all the weddings and the wild dates we've been through together? What do I need to do to be included?"

Leaning closer, I lowered my voice and whispered in his ear, "I guess that's for me to know, and for you to find out."

When I looked up, his face was only inches away, and his eyes were fixed on mine, so close I could clearly see the gold flecks in them and the brown rings surrounding them.

And for the life of me, I still couldn't find the right yarn equivalent to his eye color. It wasn't Green Meadows, or Forbidden Forest. Cypress Green?

"I accept that challenge." His gruff reply made me warm all over. "I *will* find out."

He grabbed his drink and downed it in one go.

We didn't say much after that and watched the newlyweds and

the guests tear up the dance floor instead. Evie and her new husband were smiling from ear to ear, and once again, something resembling envy speared my heart.

"They look good together." Rob was also watching the couple.

"They do. Your siblings sounded so sure you'll be the one getting hitched next."

He snorted. "That's because I'm the last single adult in the family, so they're not wrong." He paused and gave me a long look. "But I guess they know how much I've always wanted a family of my own."

Just then, loud hoots and cheers caught our attention. The groom was lifting the bride *Dirty Dancing* style on the dance floor while the rest of the guests formed a circle around them.

"Heads up, my sisters are coming, and they don't usually take no for an answer."

Sure enough, Amanda was marching in our direction, followed by Jennifer.

"Why are you guys sitting here?" Amanda was yelling to be heard above the loud music. "You two should be dancing!"

I was about to say no, but she was laughing as she grabbed my hands, and it was hard to resist. She led me to the dance floor, while Jennifer went for her brother, making Rob chuckle as he twirled her around.

I wasn't a terrible dancer, but I wasn't a decent one, either. My go-to dance move was bobbing my head up and down while swaying my body left and right. It probably looked awkward, but as long as I was enjoying the music and feeling the moment, right?

But just as I started to get into the vibe of the music, Amanda suddenly grinned at me. "Later, babe."

The next thing I knew, she did a shimmy and inserted herself in between her siblings, then pulled Jennifer's hand and whisked her away.

Leaving me alone with Rob.

"Your sisters are sneaky!" I raised my voice to be heard above all the noise.

"Sorry." He laughed. "But I think it means they like you."

I suddenly felt uncharacteristically shy, and whatever confidence I had earlier with my awkward dance moves had been reduced into nonexistence. "I'm not a dancer. No one should ever see me dance. It might scar them for life."

"That can't be true. Anyone can dance."

He grabbed one of my hands and spun me around. It was hard not to return his infectious grin, and against my better judgment, he managed to twirl me, dipped me, then gave me another spin, just as the lights were dimmed and a new song started. There was a sudden shift in the air as the slow, seductive guitar notes of "Señorita" began to play, and people around us began pairing up.

"I might sit this one out."

Rob extended his hand to me, a smile playing on his lips. "You're not going to leave me standing alone, are you? Let's not make this weird."

"I'm not being weird. I told you, I don't dance."

"You just did, with me. It's just one song, Kim. I don't bite. Or"—he tilted his head toward the other end of the dance floor, where his sisters were doing a terrible job at pretending not to watch—"do you want to explain to them why you're deserting their brother all alone on the dance floor?"

"Your siblings are frightening." I sighed. "One dance. And don't complain if I step on your feet, because you brought it on yourself."

He gave a low chuckle as he took my left hand and pulled me closer, his other hand settling on my waist. Shawn and Camila crooned about dancing for hours, and couples all around us were leaning into their partners, swaying to the music, probably murmuring sweet nothings into each other's ears. But I wasn't paying that much attention to anyone else. I was too hyper-focused on this man holding me, on his hard body pressed so close against mine. Too aware of his warmth, how my head fit just right tucked into the crook underneath his chin, and how comforting it felt. How no one else existed but him and me.

"There you go," he murmured. "It's not that scary, is it?"

It wasn't scary, no.

It was *terrifying*.

Because all I could see was him. His calming presence. How much he was starting to mean to me, and how much he was becoming a part of my life, and the scariest thing was, how much I wanted him to *stay* a part of my life and how I kept on feeling things I knew I *shouldn't* be feeling. I was falling for him, even though I knew I shouldn't be, because it could potentially shatter my heart into a billion pieces.

Because he was, very likely, still holding out for his ex.

Because he wanted love and family and picket fences and that wasn't what I wanted.

Because those things weren't for me.

I looked up and locked eyes with him, and I couldn't tear my gaze away. His face was so close to mine, and I noticed how the faint stubble on his jaw suddenly looked a little too appealing.

"Kim," he said, so softly I almost couldn't hear him, "I won't hurt you. Trust me."

After the past few weeks, I knew I could. He had earned that trust, and more.

And somehow, that scared the hell out of me.

The DJ had segued into a new, upbeat dance tune, and everyone else around us erupted in wild cheers. But we stayed where we were, staring at each other. His gaze drifted to my lips again, and my heart thundered loudly as he slowly lowered his head, pausing for a beat, as if giving me a chance to back out.

I didn't have a chance to decide, because one of the guests who was dancing too enthusiastically bumped into us, abruptly stopping whatever trance I was in.

"Thanks for the dance." I dropped his hands as if they were on fire and took a couple of steps backward. "I'm going to find something to drink."

He shoved his hands in his pockets and nodded, his eyes still on me. "Sure."

I gave him one last look, then turned around and walked away, quietly shaking my head.

Go back, a voice urged inside my head. *You can trust him. Tell him everything.*

Tell him how you feel.

No. What would I even say?

Maybe I should be honest and come clean about the reason I was doing this entire thing. Take a page out of Ellie's book and ask him to fake date me until I inherited the store.

No. The risks were too high. What if it backfired on me? I almost kissed him, for goodness' sake. What if these feelings I wasn't supposed to be feeling got even deeper, and it ended with me being hurt?

I checked myself, preventing my brain from continuing down that line of thought, and got off the dance floor as fast as I could.

And as I took one last look at the ballroom, I saw him standing there, watching me leave.

CHAPTER 23

The Ideal Place to Question Your Life Choices Is 8,000 Feet Above the Ground

Aiden texted me the morning after Evie's wedding to set up a coffee date, which then turned into a handful of lunches over the next two weeks. So far, so good: He was delightful, polite, and it didn't hurt that he had a charming accent. If there was someone I had to fake being in like with for the next few months, I could do a lot worse than Aiden Cho.

Plus, he was the distraction I needed to stop myself from thinking about Rob, because I couldn't afford to dig myself a deeper hole by spending more time than I should thinking about him. It would only make it easier for me to fall for him, and I could *not* fall for Rob Carmichael. For anyone.

It was as simple as that.

At one of the lunches with Aiden, I casually brought up the topic of a bucket list—which I didn't have, but he did, according to Rob's dossier—and Aiden got very excited. He was planning to tick skydiving off his list next, and it was something I'd always been very curious about (although, to quote Jenna, "Why the hell would you want to jump out of a perfectly good airplane?"), so I'd agreed to go on a jump with him.

Today was a rare sunny Sunday, the perfect weather for our skydiving session. I'd arrived at the drop zone ten minutes before our assigned time, and Aiden was nowhere to be seen. I pulled out my phone, thinking that I'd let him know I'd arrived, only to find out that my battery was flat. Before I could even send him a text message, it went completely dead.

I rolled my eyes at myself, then stuffed my phone back in my bag.

The small hangar where we were at was busy, full of other skydivers and the instructors and several long racks of what looked like harnesses on both sides of the hangar. My pulse was pounding with anticipation, because I'd been checking out (too many) skydiving videos on YouTube to get a feel of what I was committing myself to, and the more I watched, the more excited I was for today's jump. I checked in and was given paperwork and waivers to sign, then sat with a group of five other jumpers to go through the safety brief.

Meanwhile, Aiden was *still* nowhere to be seen.

A feeling of unease crept into me. What if something had happened to him on the way here? He had no way of reaching me, so he wouldn't have been able to let me know if he needed help or anything. And if I wanted to be perfectly honest, the thought of doing the jump on my own, without a friendly face around, felt a bit daunting, no matter how pumped I was.

We were five minutes into the safety briefing when a familiar face dashed in, his frantic gaze searching the area before finally finding me. Relief took over his face, but before he could come over, one of the instructors stopped him. I watched as he explained something to the other man, my forehead creasing when

I saw him scribbling his signature on the same waiver forms that I'd signed minutes ago.

Why was he here? Where was Aiden?

Rob squeezed into a spot next to me, and I breathed in his familiar, comforting scent. We hadn't seen each other since his cousin's wedding two weeks ago, although I'd been texting him updates on things with Aiden.

"Hey." He scooted closer, leaning down so he was whispering into my ear. "Aiden called me. He was freaking out, saying over and over again how he couldn't do this. Your phone is off, and he couldn't call to let you know he was backing out of the jump. So I thought I'd drive out here to take his place and do the jump with you."

I whipped my head toward him, my eyes popping wide. "But . . . why?"

"Something about him being scared of heights, I think."

"No, I mean . . . why are you here to do the jump with me?"

He shrugged. "Because I know how much you've been looking forward to this, and I didn't want you to be disappointed that Aiden wasn't here."

I stared at him, my mouth gaping open, as the orientation video droned on in the background about the basics of skydiving safety, trying to wrap my head around what he'd just done. Because this wasn't something most people would normally offer to do. My throat felt thick, and my chest felt like it was going to burst into a million confetti pieces of gratefulness.

This man had practically dropped whatever he was doing and gave up his Sunday to hurl himself out of a perfectly fine airplane so I wouldn't be disappointed.

He did that voluntarily.

For me.

Rob nudged me, his eyes riveted on the safety video. "We should be listening to that."

It took me another few seconds of gawking at him, before I slowly swiveled my head toward the screen, and yet another few seconds before my brain could process what the video was explaining.

After the briefing was over, we were broken up into smaller groups. Our instructors explained what the possible risks involved were, what to do if the chute didn't open and how to deploy the reserve parachute, what to expect during the jump, the free-fall body position, and proper landing procedures.

As the briefing went on, panic began to creep in. I'd done my research, and I knew that statistically this was supposed to be safer than driving—something about the odds of dying in skydiving to be one in two hundred thousand, while the odds of someone perishing from a motor vehicle crash was one in ninety-three. But hearing the things that could also happen still pricked my heart with fear.

Then I glanced at Rob, and I could feel my worries quietly fading away. And somehow I knew, that whatever happened, it would all be okay, because he was here with me.

Once the briefing was over, we got fitted with our jumpsuits, harnesses, and goggles. Rob's face was slowly turning pale, as if the reality of what he was about to do was just starting to sink in.

I leaned over and whispered to him, "Starting to regret coming over?"

"Not at all." But his ashen face said otherwise.

"You sure you want to do this?"

He turned to me. "Do *you* want to?"

"Yeah, but not if—"

"Then we're doing it." He gave me a firm nod. "Face your fears and all that jazz, right?"

"Okay." I reached for him and enveloped him in a hug. "Thank you. For giving up your Sunday and doing this with me."

There was a low chuckle as he wrapped his arms tighter around me. "Always, Kim."

We stood like that for a few minutes, our arms around each other, as gratitude and affection for this man poured into me.

He'd promised Ellie that I would get my swoony moments.

And this, to me, was one of them.

Rob and I piled into a small plane with four other jumpers and our instructors. Mine was called Mark, a gray-haired guy sporting a hip man bun. The small aircraft slowly climbed higher as I sat in an awkward position behind him, while my brain rapidly churned, excitement blending with fear as I questioned my poor life choices. I could have been standing on solid ground right now, safe and sound, yet I had to go and be all curious about this sport, and here I was. I brought this onto myself.

Almost ten minutes later, we were flying over the gorgeous blue stretch of Port Benedict Bay. Mark turned to me and made final checks on my harness and goggles, and when the pilot gave us a thumbs-up, one of the other instructors closest to the door pulled it open. He and his jumper scooted over to the edge of the plane, and when I blinked next, they were both airborne, their loud, unhinged yell piercing the air. I watched with a mixture of fascination and dread as their bodies became smaller, until they were nothing but tiny dots floating in the sky, and then, a white parachute popped open.

"You good?" Rob yelled at me over the loud drone of the plane. "Ready to do this?"

"I don't have a choice, do I?" I yelled back.

"You do," he shouted. "You always have a choice. We'll tell them you changed your mind. They'll understand."

"No. I'm doing this." No matter how terrified I might be right now. "It'll be fine. And if it's not fine, I'll be dead anyway, so it won't really matter. If I die, can you tell my grandfather I loved him?"

"You're not going to die!" He was shaking his head. "I need you to be alive so we can go celebrate after this!"

"What are we celebrating? That we're still alive?"

"I'll tell you when we're on the ground." He gestured at his instructor, who was now shimmying toward the door.

"Tell me now! I need something to distract me."

They were almost at the edge of the plane door now.

He grinned. "We have an offer on the house."

My mouth fell open. "That's awesome! Congrats!"

"Thanks." He gave me a thumbs-up. "I'll see you on the other side."

With that, he and his instructor were gone. I watched as their bodies floated farther away and their parachute popped open, and relief went through me at knowing that he'd be okay.

Then it was our turn.

Mark must have seen the frightened look on my face because he started yelling some encouragement that totally went over my head, because I was too busy questioning myself and my sanity. It was worrying how I had willingly surrendered a few hundred dollars of my hard-earned money to fling myself out of a moving airplane, from 8,000 feet above the ground that humans should be walking on. That *I* should be walking on. What was I thinking? What if something happened to me? *Who's going to look after Opa?*

"Kim!" Mark was yelling, trying to get my attention over the loud sounds of the airplane and the wind howling in our faces. "You still good to go?"

I only nodded. "It'll be over in a few minutes, right?"

"It'll be over in no time. You won't even realize."

Sure, especially if I was lying flat on the ground, too busy being *dead*.

"We're going in three!"

I made the mistake of glancing at what was below, and my stomach lurched into a jumble of vomit-like sensations. The bay on our right was a never-ending spread of blue, while the ground on the left looked like a collection of green patches, resembling a real-life Google Map in satellite mode. Aiden had the right idea—maybe not the freaking out part, but the part where he didn't show up.

Bucket list, my ass.

Mark was now counting loudly, "One . . ."

If I survived this jump, my first phone call would be to my lawyer to update my will. I would leave all my Earthly possessions to Opa, Jenna, Ellie, and Rob. And no, I didn't have time right now to analyze why he was included in the list of people I was leaving my things to.

"Two . . ."

I had to say goodbye to Opa first, though. Was it too late to call him now? Wait, I couldn't, because my dead phone was with the staff on the ground. *Where I should have been.*

"Three!"

And with that, all my thoughts flew out together with my jump, and the next thing I knew, I was free-falling at probably a hundred miles an hour toward the cold, hard ground, with Mark strapped to my back. He was hooting in excitement as I closed my eyes, mentally crossed myself, and recited multiple Hail Marys while trying not to visualize the inevitable crash that would happen when our bodies hit the ground. Would it hurt? Would I die instantly? Would I see my entire life flashing before my very eyes? Would there be anything left of my shattered body?

"Kim!" Mark was yelling. "We're okay! You're doing great!"

Oh, what the hell. If I was going to die in the next five minutes or so, I might as well use these last few moments of my life to enjoy the scenery, right?

So I opened my eyes.

And I realized that I was soaring through the beautiful blue sky.

The wind was rushing all around us, and the churning in my stomach had evaporated into thrill and exhilaration. I thought I could see some birds whizzing by, along with the two bright blue-and-yellow parachutes below us, gliding gracefully toward the ground. I spread my arms and legs outward like what they'd told us to do in the briefing, and I could feel Mark tugging on something. Then our own parachute popped out, slowing down our fall.

This was amazing. It was *incredible.* It was like seeing the world from a fresh new perspective, because the view was beautiful, and totally unlike anything I'd ever seen before. There was nothing separating me from the ground except for the crisp fresh air whistling around us, and a sense of awe and peacefulness came over me as we quietly floated down, and somehow, everything felt right in the world.

Before I knew it, we were descending toward the designated landing area. Things got pulled into focus, and I could make out the shapes of houses and cars, and the field that was our target. I even found myself wishing that it had gone on for a bit longer.

Once we landed safely, Mark unclipped the harness that had tethered us to each other and helped me remove my gear. I thanked him profusely, then ran to find Rob, who had landed earlier and was chatting with his own instructor. When he saw me running in his direction, he nodded at his instructor and walked toward me.

"We made it!" I jumped up and wrapped myself around him in a hug. "We're alive!"

His hands went around me. "Of course we're alive." His laugh sounded like music to my ears. "Did you think that we wouldn't be?"

"I didn't know what to think. It was incredible!" I pulled away and grinned up at him. "Thank you so much for coming and being here for me. I probably could have done it on my own, but knowing I had a familiar face, that I would at least see someone else before I plunged to my death, made everything so much better."

"You weren't going to plunge to your death."

"You can say that now, because we're safe. Had we plunged to our deaths, you would have said something else entirely different. Seriously, you don't know how grateful I am. I was going to include you in my will and everything."

He chuckled. "Anytime, Kim. I'm always here for you."

Hearing that triggered something inside. I didn't know what came over me, but I suddenly had the overwhelming urge to grab his face and kiss him.

So I did.

And honestly, it was probably the best first kiss of my entire life.

Maybe it was because I was grateful that we were both alive. Or because I felt an overwhelming emotion of gratitude because he had given up his day to be here with me. Or maybe it was the sum of all that and more. Whatever it was, I channeled all those emotions into the kiss and shoved all the other unimportant thoughts into the back of my mind. Because this wasn't the time to think about anything at all. This was the time to *feel*. At how soft his lips were, how *good* they felt against mine, and how the small moan that came from him stoked a craving I didn't know was inside me. I wouldn't think about how he groaned and closed his eyes, or how one of his hands went up to frame my face, and the way his other hand went around my waist to pull me closer, pressing our bodies together, and how he deepened the kiss, devouring my mouth as if I was going to be his last breath. I wouldn't think about how his touch was driving me wild and how I suddenly had an all-consuming urge to drag him into a private space and do more, *so much more* to the rest of him.

No feelings involved, Kim. Remember?

The sound of an airplane propeller, followed by someone shouting in the distance, kicked some sense into me. My eyes sprang open, and I abruptly pulled away from him.

His eyes opened, too, and I didn't know if I was brave enough to even *try* to identify the emotions that were swirling in those hazel eyes.

"I'm sorry," I whispered, not meeting his gaze. "I don't know what came over me. It was . . . maybe it was the adrenaline rush."

Rob didn't answer.

"I'm sorry," I repeated. "I shouldn't have done that."

"Kim, you mean a lot to me—"

No feelings involved. I didn't fit what he was looking for: someone to build a long-term relationship and a family with. A person to start his forever with.

I *couldn't be* what he was looking for.

So I cut him off before he had a chance to finish his sentence, finally meeting his eyes. "You mean a lot to me, too. I'm not going to risk our friendship because of one adrenaline-fueled kiss. It will never work between us anyway, right? You want happy endings and I still have a long way to go before I get there."

He opened his mouth, then closed it again, his expression unreadable.

"I better go." I made a vague gesture toward the area behind me. "Thanks again for being here, Rob. I'll see you around."

I walked away without giving him another look, while reminding myself that I should not, *could not*, in absolutely no scenario, fall for him.

Because he believed in love, and I didn't.

Because falling for him—for *anyone*—would probably only hurt me again, and it wasn't a chance I was willing to take.

But I had a sneaking suspicion that it was probably too late.

Because deep down, a part of me might already have fallen for him.

CHAPTER 24

Raise Your Hand If You Think Second Chances Are Overrated

Monday mornings at the yarn store were usually less busy, and the morning after the skydiving outing was no exception. Nicole was running the Knotty Tea Society at our corner nook (today's beverage of choice: banana-flavored lattes from Quinn's café), while I'd been staring at my laptop since we opened, using this little window of quiet time to try to go over the plans for the street festival. "Try" being the operative word, because my mind kept drifting back to what had happened with Rob yesterday.

The kiss had been playing on a continuous loop in my brain for the past twenty-four hours, each time the images more vivid than before, like I was reliving and replaying the moment over and over again on a Dolby cinema screen. I found myself reaching for my phone more than once last night, debating if I should call or text him, although I wouldn't really know what to say.

Stop it. There were absolutely zero benefits to be gained from overthinking and overanalyzing him and/or the kiss. Relationships weren't my forte, and he was still hung up on his ex, wasn't he? Wasn't that why he wanted me to go with him to the weddings?

A soft *ping* alerted me to a new email. It was from Rob's contact at the Port Benedict tourism office, wanting to schedule an appointment to come and talk to a few business owners on our strip for their article. I replied to the email, then sat back and stared at my phone.

Maybe I could use this as an excuse. I could call Rob to say thanks and see if he'd bring up the kiss first. Or maybe *I* should bring it up first. No, because what would I say?

Hey, I really enjoyed our kiss yesterday, but I don't know what to do about it, because we want different things in life. You got any thoughts?

Sighing, I refocused my attention on my screen and the street festival planning. At least things were lining up nicely on this front: I managed to secure another sponsor for the event, the permit for the festival was approved a few days ago, and the list of people wanting to rent the stalls was nearly full.

I still didn't know if what we were planning would work. If it would help bring more people to visit our strip, or if it was just a massive waste of time. Ellie spoke to the owners who were thinking of selling, to see if they would like to take part in the street festival, but so far only two had said yes.

I blew out a long breath. What if we gambled on the wrong strategy? What if this entire thing turned out to be nothing but a spectacular flop?

Maybe there was another angle we could approach this from.

I opened a new search page, then typed in "Port Benedict Plaza shopping precinct." There were over ten pages of results, nothing I hadn't seen before: a Google Map of the area, followed by the official website of Port Benedict Plaza and a list of its social media accounts and official pages from retail brands that had a presence in the shopping center. I kept scrolling, my finger aimlessly tapping my touchpad, when one of the search results caught my interest.

It was an article written by a self-proclaimed amateur architectural historian, detailing a comprehensive history of this area. According to the author, the cluster of shops that became Port Benedict Plaza and our strip of shops were built over one hundred years ago. It had the distinction of being one of the first business districts in town, and our row of brick buildings had apparently even involved a prominent architect of the time in its design.

Before I could dig any further, the front door swung open and someone walked in, their face obscured behind the humongous bouquet of pink roses they were carrying. I saved the link to the article and closed my laptop.

"Hi there. Can I help you?"

The bouquet was lowered, and Aiden flashed me an uncertain smile.

"Hey!" I raised my eyebrows in surprise. "I wasn't expecting you."

"I know." He gave me a sheepish smile. "I just wanted to apologize again for yesterday. I felt terrible leaving you on your own, but I was panicking and I couldn't think straight. I couldn't sleep the night before, because I got so anxious about doing the jump." He paused, looking embarrassed. "I'm deathly afraid of heights, and a friend told me going skydiving would help me overcome the phobia, but no. It's too bloody much."

"Don't worry about it." I waved him off. "Rob drove out and jumped with me, so I wasn't alone. It's all good." His name brought back memories of the kiss again, and I had to shake my head, desperately trying to dislodge thoughts of him from my mind.

Focus. On this man with the gorgeous bouquet in front of you. He's here, not Rob.

"He did?" A frown briefly flashed across Aiden's face, but it was gone the next second, as he handed me the bouquet. "These are for you. I know this doesn't make up for yesterday, but I hope it's a start."

"These are beautiful. How do you know they're my favorite?"

He cleared his throat. "Rob gave me a tip about the roses."

My stomach did somersaults. And backflips. Possibly even some cartwheels.

Instead of getting butterflies in my stomach from Aiden's romantic gesture, like I was supposed to, I was too hyper-focused on the fact that *Rob remembered about the flowers*.

"I know I messed things up yesterday," Aiden was saying, and I had to force myself to focus my attention on him. "But I'm here to ask for a second chance, and if you'll still have me, I'd love to take you out for coffee or dinner sometime. Although if you said no, I would totally understand." He tilted his head at the door. "Say the word and I'll go, no questions asked."

A part of me knew I should be saying yes. He was making an effort, because who wouldn't have a fear of heights, right? Plus, he was definitely the top choice on the list of potential suitors (let's face it, he was the *only* one on the list). Someone nice enough to spend the next several months with, but one I wouldn't fall in love with.

If only my thoughts weren't all consumed by someone else and *that damn kiss*.

I gave myself a mental kick in the butt and smiled at him. "I'd love that."

"Wonderful." His face lit up with a smile. "What about dinner tonight?"

I gestured at my laptop. "We've got a big event coming up, and I'm planning on working on that for the rest of the week. Can we do Friday night?"

"Absolutely. It's a date."

Once he left, I reached for my phone, composed a text message to Rob to let him know about the date with Aiden—fine, it was an excuse to get in touch with him—and sent it before I could second-guess myself.

His reply came a minute later, a short Thrilled for you.

That's it? That's his response?

But honestly, what did I expect? For him to stop me going on the date and profess his undying love for me? *I* was the one who had kissed him first and then walked away first, too, while I knew perfectly well that he was still holding a torch for his ex.

I had only myself to blame.

During our dinner on Friday, I casually mentioned go-karting to Aiden. He'd jumped at the idea and suggested that we try a place after, one that was bigger and busier than the one I'd gone to with Rob. We did our first twelve laps, and because Aiden was having so much fun, he coaxed me into doing another twelve. By the time we were finished, it was almost nine, and as we returned our helmets to the track attendant, Aiden leaned closer to me.

"I had a really great time."

"So did I."

"I'm going away for a conference tomorrow," he said. "Can we get together for dinner when I'm back? Saturday next weekend?"

"I'd love to, but I can't. It's my grandfather's eightieth birthday and we're having a surprise party for him that night."

"That's lovely." Aiden's face turned wistful. "I haven't seen my grandparents and the rest of my family for over a year. They're back in London, and I haven't been able to take time off because of work. I miss them a lot."

He seemed so dejected, and an idea popped into my head. "Would you like to come? There'll be cake." I knew how hard it could be living away from your family, because I'd experienced that firsthand, having missed my grandparents when I was working all around the country. Inviting him was the kind thing to do.

"To your grandfather's birthday?" He looked taken aback. "I don't want to impose."

"I wouldn't have asked otherwise."

"Then I'm in." He gave me a warm smile. "If there's cake, I'm always in."

Aiden had an early flight to catch, so we said our goodbyes not long after, and I took out my phone as I walked back to my car.

My heart nearly stopped when I saw my screen. There were five missed calls and four messages from Rob in the past two hours, each one sounding like he was getting increasingly worried and frantic about my well-being.

My heart was beating quicker as my thumb hovered over his number. Should I call him back? Our last conversation was a few days ago, when I updated him about the date with Aiden, and he'd given his curt three-word answer.

But my friends were his friends. Avoiding him long-term wasn't sustainable.

He picked up on the first ring. "Kim! Are you okay?"

Okay, so it sounded like he was going to pretend that the kiss hadn't happened. Fine, I could play along.

"Hey." My tone was cool, belying the chaotic storm inside at hearing his voice. "Of course I'm okay. Why wouldn't I be?"

"Thank goodness." He sounded relieved. "Ellie said you were going go-karting with Aiden, and I got worried when you didn't respond to my first text message. I thought something had happened."

I unlocked my car. "What did you think was going to happen?"

"You had a crash when we went, remember? And you were with Aiden, and after what he pulled last time at skydiving, my mind went to the worst-case scenario. I thought maybe you had another incident and Aiden abandoned you again, and I didn't know which track you guys are at, and I was tempted to call all the karting places in town—" He stopped himself and took a deep breath. "Alec thinks it'd be a bit stalkerish. And Ellie, too. But I mean, bad things could have happened. There's been serious incidents caused by go-karting before, you know."

He's been freaking out because he thought something had happened to me?

"I'm fine. Everything's good."

There was a pause. "I'm glad." He cleared his throat. "So the date went well?"

"Yeah. He's funny, and kind, and nice. I had a great time."

But he's not you.

"Right." There was another pause. "Guess we chose the right person this time."

"Guess we did."

"Great." He cleared his throat again. "I better go. Say hi to your grandfather for me."

Opa. I still wouldn't have a clue how I'd act around Rob, but I knew I had to invite him to Opa's birthday party. "Wait. Are you free next Saturday night? It's his eightieth birthday, and we're organizing a surprise party for him at the yarn store. I know he's grown fond of you, so it'll mean a lot to him if you can make it."

"I'd love to, but I have something with my dad that night." He sounded genuinely apologetic. "It's an event for that major project that he's been working on."

I shouldn't have felt disappointed, but I did. "Maybe you can drop by after. If you want."

"Of course." He was quiet again. "I'm thrilled things are working out for you and Aiden. I guess my work here is done."

"Yeah." I knew this would eventually happen, but somehow, those words weren't what I wanted to hear. "I guess it is."

CHAPTER 25

The Measure of Love Is to Be There Without Measure

My grandfather never liked people fussing over him. He never missed my birthday or Oma's, always making sure to bring home flowers for her birthday, or cupcakes with pretty sprinkles for mine. But he never celebrated his own, and whenever Oma tried to make a fuss, he'd wave her off and say he didn't need anything fancy, as long as his two favorite people in the world were there with him. Oma once told me that it stemmed from growing up in a modest family in Indonesia, and when they migrated overseas, he had to be very careful with his money to make ends meet.

But he'd turned eighty today. It was a huge milestone that had to be celebrated. So I decided that he was having a party, and the response to the invitations I sent out had been heartwarmingly positive. His friends and old coworkers had all jumped at the chance to celebrate him, and it warmed my heart to see how much he was loved by the people in his orbit.

The best surprise, though, was when I invited my dad. I'd done it out of courtesy, because I knew he was overseas, and the odds of him coming were minuscule. But he replied, saying that he was flying out to Tokyo that week for work, and since he had some time off, he'd make the trip back home to celebrate Opa's birthday. I wasn't holding my breath, but if my dad really *was* coming, that would make Opa's day.

As a cover story, I told my grandfather that instead of having our weekly dinner tomorrow, we were having it tonight instead to celebrate his birthday. He was wearing a big smile on his face when I picked him up at six.

"Selamat ulang tahun,* Opa." I gave him a hug and a peck on his cheek. It was one of the more common Indonesian phrases that I knew how to say, and I always made sure to wish my grandparents happy birthday in the language.

"Thank you." He beamed at me. "Delapan puluh!† I'm old, Kim."

"Age is just a number. Didn't you say that to me once?" I unlocked the car and opened the door for him. "Our dinner reservation is at seven, so do you mind if we swing by the store quickly? I forgot my laptop, and Nicole needed help with an online order."

"Of course." He settled into his seat as I navigated the car to the yarn store. "How was your day?"

"Busy, but good. We had someone from the tourism office come today for a tour of the precinct, and he's going to write an article to highlight the businesses, which is awesome. Someone else from the local paper is supposed to come too next week, to chat with all of us."

"Is that the person that Rob reached out to?" He adjusted his

---

* Indonesian, meaning: "Happy birthday."

† Indonesian, meaning: "Eighty!"

position to face me. "He texted me to say happy birthday, by the way."

My heart thumped a little quicker, and possibly even multiplied a thousandfold at the mention of his name. I was *that* pathetic. And he remembered to text my grandfather?

"Who texted you, the guy from the tourism office?" I played dumb. "That's nice of him."

Opa let out a soft scoff. "You know perfectly well who I was talking about. I invited him to come to dinner tonight."

"Did you?"

"Yes. And last week as well. Both times he said he was busy."

"Maybe next time."

"I said that to him, and his reply was, and I quote, 'It's probably best if I don't come over while Kim is around.' Why did he say that? Did you two have a fight?"

My heart dropped a little at hearing that. "No, and I don't know why he said that. Why don't you ask him?"

"Maybe I will."

"Maybe you should." I made a right turn into the Plaza complex and found a spot right in front of the yarn store. I told everyone to park a block or two away so Opa wouldn't suspect anything, so the street was empty. "We're here."

My grandfather shook his head. "If you think I'm going to forget the conversation, I won't. This isn't over. We'll talk more later."

"There's nothing to talk about. He's probably just busy." I turned the engine off and unbuckled my seat belt. "I don't know how complicated the online order is, or how long I'll be. I think you should go in, too."

"Okay." Opa heaved himself out of the car. "I need to use the restroom anyway."

I suppressed my grin, glad he bought my excuse. Unlocking the front door, I pushed it open and stepped aside to let my grandfather through.

"I forgot my bag in the car," I said. "You go in, I'll catch up with you."

"First your laptop, now your bag. When did you become so forgetful?"

I grinned. "When, indeed."

The second he stepped inside, someone flicked on the light switch at the back of the store, and everyone yelled, "SURPRISE!"

Loud cheers followed by bright lights drenched the store, and Opa's eyes widened as he took in the sights before him.

The entire store was decked out with balloons and buntings, and it couldn't have looked more festive. It was a team effort: Ellie, Jenna, and Nicole helped me rearrange the store after we closed yesterday. The long wooden table in the middle of the store had been repurposed as a refreshment station, covered with a checkered tablecloth, brimming with plates of food and drinks. Ellie had made cupcakes, kue lapis—Opa's favorite Indonesian layer cake—and some cookies in the shapes of champagne flutes and birthday gifts, while Jenna spent last night helping me inflate balloons and make party buntings. Alec had picked up the food I ordered from Java Spice, and Nicole had arranged to rent some folding chairs for the guests.

Opa was still staring at the scene in front of him, his eyes wide, his mouth forming an O. Everyone was clapping and cheering and taking pictures of my shell-shocked grandfather, and then people started coming up to wish him a happy birthday, shaking his hand, giving him hugs. His friends and their families, his old coworkers, and some of his neighbors came. There were a few families from the Indonesian community in the city, several patients from his dialysis center, Dr. Nguyen, and some of his nurses.

While Opa was busy talking to the guests, I snuck away to check my phone. My father's flight was supposed to have arrived in the morning, but I hadn't heard anything from him. My last text to him a couple of hours ago was delivered and read, but there was no reply. I sent him another text, then went into my message thread with Aiden and shot him a message too, to check if he had trouble finding the place. I hadn't seen him since the go-karting date, but he posted an Instagram story that he was back in town, so I assumed that he was still coming tonight.

But just as I finished sending the text to Aiden, a reply came in from my father.

Won't be able to make it tonight. Flying last-minute to Beijing to cover a story.

What?

Anger and disappointment slammed into me. Fine, maybe he wasn't able to turn down a work assignment, but couldn't he at least have told me the minute he knew he couldn't make it—*before* I had to ask where he was? Wasn't that just common courtesy?

I should have known this would happen, and I shouldn't have gotten my hopes up. Was I expecting too much for my father to show up for *his own* father? He was never there for either of us his entire life, so it was my own fault for expecting him to do so now.

I glanced at Opa, who was laughing and chatting with his friends. Good thing I hadn't mentioned that I invited Dad, because he didn't deserve to be disappointed on his birthday.

Blowing out a long breath, I cast my eyes around the room. Ellie was chatting with Nicole, and Jenna was at the other end of the room talking to someone else. Without thinking, I opened my WhatsApp thread with Rob.

Hey. I know you're at your event, but I just needed to vent. My dad was supposed to be here for my grandfather's surprise party, but guess what?

He couldn't make it. Too busy for his own father.

My own fault, though. Shouldn't have expected too much from him.

The only thing I can expect from him is disappointment.

The two blue checks appeared almost immediately.

I'm sorry. Are you okay?

Is Thomas okay?

Anything I can do to help?

No, there was nothing anyone could do. My father was probably beyond help, and I should really pull myself out of this funk, so I didn't ruin Opa's birthday night.

I only replied with a thumbs-up emoji, exited the chat, then checked on Opa.

Thirty minutes later, just as I was replenishing the drinks, the front door swung open. Rob walked in and caught my eyes, then made a beeline for me. My stomach flipped, and whatever resentment was brewing in my chest at my father suddenly didn't appear all that significant.

"Hey." I couldn't help the smile that was tugging at the corners of my mouth. "I thought you had an event with your dad."

"I left. Told him I wasn't feeling well." He returned my grin. "He probably didn't believe me, but he wasn't going to make a spectacle in front of his new business partners, so he had no choice but to let me go."

Gratefulness and appreciation for this man welled up inside of me. My father might not have shown up for Opa and me, but Rob did. He had dropped whatever he was doing, again, to be here for me.

"Thanks for coming. It'll mean a lot to my grandfather." *And me.*

"I wouldn't miss this for the world." He was watching me. "Are you okay? About your dad not coming?"

I nodded. "Please don't say anything to my grandfather. He didn't know I invited him."

"I won't. I should probably go find Thomas." He held up a brown paper bag. "Got him a woodworking book."

"He's over there with his doctor." I gestured to where Opa was chatting with Dr. Nguyen.

He gave me one last look, before finally glancing in the direction I was pointing at, and color drained from his face.

"Why is Lucy here?"

"Lucy?" I frowned at him. "As in your ex? What do you mean?"

He pointed in my grandfather's direction. "Lucy. My ex. Lucy Nguyen."

I followed his gaze, and my eyes widened. "Dr. Nguyen is *your ex*?"

"You didn't know?"

"How should I know? We've always only called her Dr. Nguyen. She's new, and I have no idea what her first name is." Something else dawned on me. "Wait. If she's your ex, then who was the woman you were talking to at Annabelle and Riley's wedding? When I was talking to Neil, you chatted with a brunette, and I thought *she* was your ex."

Confusion stretched across his face, before clearing up the next second. "That's Annabelle's older sister. We got to know each other when Annabelle and I were in college. Did you think she was Lucy?"

"Uh, yeah. You said you didn't want to go alone to the weddings because of your ex, and then you talked to her and looked really friendly with her, so I assumed . . ." I trailed off. I never asked him who she was because I didn't want to know the answer. Because I didn't want to know who the woman that he had been so deeply in love with was.

Turned out I'd known who she was all along.

"She's not." His gaze softened as he stared at Lucy. "I haven't seen her for a while."

A kaleidoscope of emotion washed over me as I watched him go puppy-dog eyes over her. No, I wasn't jealous, because I didn't have any right to be jealous over this man, no matter what I might or might not feel about him.

"You never told me. What happened between you two?"

"Her family didn't like me." He finally tore his gaze away from her. "Everyone in her family is a medical professional. Her dad is an endocrinologist, her mom an OB-GYN, and her younger brother was studying to be a surgeon. Everyone wanted her to be with someone as accomplished as her. Someone earning as much as or more than her. Who's also in the medical field. Not"—he gestured toward himself—"a builder who doesn't even have a college degree."

What the hell was wrong with her family? They sounded just like his dad. Rob ran his own business, made a good living for himself, and was one of the most patient, kindest people I'd ever met. Why did it even matter that he didn't have a degree or a job at some fancy hospital?

"She said she didn't want to end our relationship. But her family was adamant, and her parents threatened to disown her if she kept seeing me. They didn't give her much of a choice."

She didn't give herself much of a choice, I wanted to say. Not that I would do it, but wouldn't you go through hell on Earth, throw yourself in front of a speeding train, hang on to the sides of a sinking door in the middle of the ocean, do whatever it takes for someone if you really loved them?

"We'd been together for a while, and I really thought she was The One." His attention was back on Lucy. "I knew how her family felt about me, but I thought as long as the two of us were united against them, we'd be fine. I was willing to do whatever it took to change their minds. But she wasn't even willing to put in the work, to fight for me, for our relationship. She chose her family over us."

"Are you still in love with her?" Deep down, I didn't want to hear the answer, but maybe hearing it would do me good, because it would curb all these feelings I was developing for him.

"No." But his eyes were still on her. "I should go over and say hi."

I watched as he approached the group, gave Opa a hug and the gift, then turned his attention to his ex, who seemed to be equally surprised to see him. Opa was listening to their conversation, his head going back and forth between the two, and at one point, he glanced at me with questions in his eyes.

It didn't matter that his ex was here, I told myself. Even if he seemed to be stunned—and maybe still a little bit smitten—to see her. Because Aiden was supposed to be here, and I wasn't supposed to feel anything for Rob, right?

"They're getting along really well." A familiar face appeared by my side. Ellie was watching the group around Opa with interest. "Your grandfather seems to really like Rob."

"You should have heard him talk about Rob after the woodworking expo. It was Rob this, Rob that, can we have him back for dinner, for lunch, for Christmas and New Year's and all the public holidays. I think if he could have Rob as a grandson instead, he would've jumped at the chance."

"Rob does have that way about him." Jenna's voice materialized from my other side. "He's fun and infectious and he grows on you. Wouldn't you say he's grown on you, Kim?"

I gave Jenna a side-eye. "I know what you're getting at."

"You've been spending a ton of time with him," Ellie pointed out. "And sometimes spending a lot of time together with another person can lead to certain feelings."

"No feelings are involved in any way, shape, or form." I wasn't going to tell them about that skydiving kiss, because that would only confirm to them that I *was* having feelings.

Or maybe I didn't want to confirm that to myself.

"Did he get that memo, though?" Jenna asked. "Because I've seen him looking at you when he thinks nobody notices."

"No, he doesn't."

Ellie sighed, while Jenna only chuckled.

"Honestly, Kim, for someone so smart, you can be a bit clueless," Jenna said. "He. Looks. At. You. Often. And if he can't find you, he looks a bit panicked, like he's afraid he might lose you in this crowd. Then, when he finds you again, he looks relieved, like he's glad you're still within reach, and he'll have this little smile lifting his mouth, like he can't believe that he gets to share the same space with you."

"Stop it. You're exaggerating."

"See for yourself."

I followed Jenna's gaze, and sure enough, Rob was glancing in our direction. He sent us a brief smile, before returning his attention to Opa and Dr. Nguyen.

"See what we mean?" Jenna sounded satisfied.

"As you can tell, we've been spending an unhealthy amount of time watching you two," Ellie said. "Alec is thrilled, because he's been rooting for you guys to happen."

"Nothing is going to happen. We're just friends. And his ex is here."

Jenna frowned. "Who's his ex?"

"My grandfather's new doctor. I mean, look at her." Both my friends turned to watch Rob, who was grinning from ear to ear when Dr. Nguyen—Lucy—threw her head back with laughter at something he said. "She's stunning, successful, and smart. The perfect trifecta. And look at how he looks at her. Does that look like someone who might be interested in me? No. He's obviously smitten with her. He wants me to come to the weddings because of her, which means he's still in love with her."

I looked away from the nauseatingly perfect view, as I realized that the sinking feeling in my heart was . . . jealousy?

No. I shouldn't be jealous, because that meant I was entertaining the idea of a relationship with him, and that was out of the question. But everything happened for a reason, right? Maybe I was meant to invite Lucy so she could be reunited with Rob, because she was the one he was supposed to end up with. The one he was meant to grow old with.

"I saw Alec chatting with her, but I didn't know who she was," Ellie said. "She's gorgeous. Seems like a nice person, too."

"Right?" I said. "Would you blame Rob for being infatuated with her?"

Our chat was interrupted by high-pitched microphone feedback. Nicole was tapping the microphone, while Alec was fiddling with the portable karaoke machine I'd rented yesterday. Opa loved singing, and his face lit up with excitement when he saw what was happening.

For the next hour everyone sang and cheered as the guests took turns singing their favorite songs, while I kept an eye on things and made sure we didn't run out of food and drinks. At some point during the night, Rob roped me into doing a song, and everyone was probably a little drunk, because I was met with whistles and raucous applause when I finished.

"Great job." He grinned at me as the person after me began belting out an '80s pop song. "Maybe a bit pitchy, but excellent job overall."

"I don't know who you're calling pitchy, but it wasn't me."

"Really?" He chuckled. "Funny, she sure does look a lot like you." He glanced around the room. "Where's Aiden? Has he been here and left and I didn't realize it?"

"Um. Good question."

I checked my phone, but there was no reply from him, even

though my message had been delivered *and* read. It was total and utter silence. He never showed up, and I didn't even realize because I'd been too busy laughing and singing karaoke with Rob.

He'd made me forget about Dad and Aiden and saved the night from going downhill.

Pushing my father and Aiden out of my thoughts, I went to find Opa, who was sitting by the drinks, looking tired but like he was having the best time of his life. "Are you enjoying yourself?"

"I am, sweetheart. Thanks to you."

"Should we make a move?" It was almost ten, and Opa was usually in bed by nine.

"Maybe a few more minutes. I'm having so much fun." He waved a hand. "Don't worry about me. I just need to sit and rest for a while. Go enjoy yourself."

I eyed him, but he waved me off again, repeating that he was fine.

The guests started to trickle out soon, and half an hour later, everyone was gone, and the only people left were Rob, Ellie, Alec, Jenna, and Nicole.

"You should take your grandfather home," Ellie said. "He looks exhausted, and you've been on your feet all day prepping for this party."

"Ellie's right," Alec said. "We can do the cleanup."

I shook my head. "You should all go. You've done more than enough. I'll drop him off at home and come back to clean after."

But before anyone could reply, a loud *thud* interrupted us, and when I turned around, my heart practically dropped to the ground.

Because my grandfather was lying motionless on the floor.

CHAPTER 26

The Best Superpower Is the Ability to Sleep Anywhere

The next few hours were the worst, the slowest, and the most excruciating time of my entire life. Everything that happened after Opa collapsed was a blur, and I only vaguely remembered the paramedics bundling my grandfather into the ambulance, followed by Rob and Alec ushering me into my car as Rob took the keys from my shaking hand. He drove to the emergency department in record time, probably breaking every speed limit to get there as quickly as possible.

The ER doctors immediately wheeled my grandfather away for assessment, while I rattled off his details and medical history to the nurse. That was over two hours ago, but every time I went up to the nurses' station to check, the answer was always the same: They had nothing to tell me yet.

"Latte, one sugar." Rob handed me a paper cup, then sat next to me. "Got that off the vending machine, so I can't vouch for its quality." He sipped his own coffee and grimaced. "Oof. Drink at your own risk."

"Thanks." I blew on the liquid, but my attention was fixed on the nurses' station.

"You look exhausted. I can wait here if you want to go home and get some sleep. I'll call you if I hear anything."

"No." My eyes widened. "*You* should go home. You should have left with Ellie and Alec an hour ago. Take my car. I can call an—"

"Kim." He cut me off. "I'm staying. Are you hungry? Do you want me to find you something to eat?"

"I don't think my stomach can handle anything right now."

"You didn't have much to eat earlier, did you? Every time I saw you, you were either talking to someone, or getting something for your grandfather, or replenishing the drinks, or doing some other stuff."

"I was?" Was he watching me the entire night?

"You were. I think there's a twenty-four-hour McDonald's nearby, or"—his eyes narrowed at the snacks vending machine at the opposite end of the waiting room—"maybe we can find things in there that tickle your fancy?"

"I'm fine." I glanced at the nurses' station again, as if doing that every two minutes would make them tell me about Opa's condition quicker. "You really should go home. I'll be okay by myself."

"No way. You think I'm going to miss out on horrible hospital coffee and stale vending machine chocolates? We're going to have another party, right here, right now."

"I think I'm all partied out." I squinted at the clock on the wall. It was almost one in the morning. What was taking the doctors so long?

"Fine, party pooper." He shrugged. "I'll still stay and keep you company. I've got nothing else better to do anyway."

"Uh, you do. Ever heard of this thing called sleep?"

"I can sleep anywhere, in any position. It's my superpower." He slouched in his seat and folded his hand across his chest. "I can sleep like this." Then he propped his chin on his hand. "Or like this." Then he lay down on the empty seats next to him. "And like this." He made a move to get up and down to the ground. "I can even sleep on the cold, hard floor."

"Seriously?" My hand shot out to stop him. "With all the germs down there?"

He grinned. "I'll just douse myself with disinfectant when I get home."

I smiled, knowing that he was trying to cheer me up. "Thanks for being here. I really appreciate it."

"Wouldn't want to be anywhere else."

My heart stuttered. He shouldn't be saying things like that, and I shouldn't be liking it. I was perfectly fine to stay here on my own, but knowing he was around for support was somehow reassuring.

"How did it go with Lucy? Was it good to see her again?"

"A bit awkward, but better than I thought. Who would have guessed she's your grandfather's doctor?"

"It's wild," I agreed. "Maybe seeing her again is a sign." I should keep my mouth shut, but I couldn't seem to stop myself. "For you two to give it another try."

"That's not really important right now, is it?" He gave me a look. "We've got more urgent things to think about."

But somehow, it *was* important. Because if he was going to work things out with her, maybe it was exactly what I needed to hear. Because that would get me off the illusion that something could happen between us.

"You wanted me to come along to the weddings because you didn't want to show up alone in front of her," I insisted. "That means she's still important to you."

"No." He shook his head, very slowly. "I mean, she used to be, but she isn't anymore. And seeing her tonight confirmed that." He blew out a long breath. "I think . . . she used to tick all my boxes, and I was probably more in love with the idea of settling down with someone like her, instead of actually being in love with her. But she's the past, and it's time to move on." His gaze lingered on me before he shifted his attention to the coffee in his hand.

My heart thundered a little harder, because did he mean what I thought he meant?

Was he implying that he'd moved on from Lucy . . . with me?

Or was I being delusional?

Just then, my phone buzzed in my pocket, and it was a message from my dad. I'd texted him on the way to the ER, thinking that he would want to know that his father wasn't well.

OK. Keep me posted on his condition.

That's it? His father was fighting for his life in the hospital, and that was his reply? A blunt, emotionless text message? "Keep me posted on his condition"—what, would it have killed him to show a bit more sympathy, maybe even the tiniest ounce of concern? Pick up his damn phone and *call*, maybe?

I almost threw my phone across the waiting room in disgust.

What did I expect, though? My dad, Aiden, they were all the same. None of them cared enough to be there for the people in their lives. Fine, I could let Aiden off the hook, since we were barely seeing each other anyway, but my dad? What could be more important than being there for his own family?

"Are you sure you're not hungry? I think there's a packet of Doritos and some Snickers calling our names in that vending machine. It would be rude to ignore them."

Except this man.

He was different, because he cared enough to constantly show up and be there for me.

Because I was important to him.

Rob must have mistaken the bewildered look on my face, because he patted my hand, as if trying to reassure me. "Thomas will be fine. He's told me so many stories about the challenges he'd had to go through when he first came to this country. He's a fighter. He'll get through this."

I slowly nodded. "He has to."

"Family of Thomas Halim?"

I looked up to see a doctor who had admitted Opa standing by the nurses' station.

Finally. "Yes." I jumped up. "I'm his granddaughter."

She shook my hand. "He's awake. He's fine, but we'll need to keep him overnight for observation. If all goes well, we should be able to discharge him tomorrow."

"So he's okay?" I let out a long breath of relief. "What happened?"

"We did a complete blood count, and his hemoglobin level is extremely low. We've given him an iron infusion and he'll need a stronger dose of iron tablets, but otherwise, he's okay. He should be back to his normal self in a few days." She nodded at the corridor behind her. "You can go and see him now, if you like."

My grandfather had his eyes closed when we walked into his room. His arm was hooked up to an IV line, and a patient monitor was steadily and quietly beeping next to his bed. Fear flooded me at the sight, because he never looked this frail before, and it shattered my heart to see the man I'd looked up to my entire life struggling with his health.

Not wanting to wake him, I turned around to tiptoe out, when Opa called my name.

"Have you two been here all night?"

"Hey, Opa." I walked over and gave him a hug. "How are you feeling?"

"Capek."* He opened his eyes, exhaustion lining his face. "You both should go home. Get some rest. There's nothing you can do here anyway."

"I'm staying," I said. "Just in case you need anything."

"I'm in a hospital." He gestured at the nurses bustling around outside. "There are people here who could help me if I needed anything. Come back when you've had some sleep." He turned his attention to Rob. "Thanks for keeping her company."

"More than happy to."

"I still think I should stay," I insisted. "Rob doesn't have his car, so I'm going to drop him home and then come back, okay?"

"No. You both should go. I'm fine," Opa said. "I just want to get some sleep. I'm sure the nurses will call you if anything happens." He closed his eyes again. "Go home, Kim. I'll see you tomorrow."

---

* Indonesian, meaning: "Tired."

CHAPTER 27

He Thinks About Her All the Time

Twenty minutes later, we arrived at Rob's house. I killed my car engine and turned to look at him, only to find him already watching me. It was just after two in the morning, and he looked as exhausted as I felt. I'd been determined to stay and keep Opa company, but his doctor had assured me that they were keeping an eye on him 24-7, then gently pointed out to me that I needed to be well-rested to be able to look after my grandfather.

"Thanks again for staying with me at the hospital the entire night."

"Stop thanking me. I'm glad Thomas is okay."

We sat in silence for the next few minutes, the only sounds inside the car were our breathing and the increasingly loud drumbeats of my heart.

"It's late. You should go inside. Get some rest." I stifled a yawn. The adrenaline I was running on the entire night was finally depleted, and exhaustion ruthlessly seeped into my bones.

"I should." But he didn't make a move. "You shouldn't be driving. You look like you're about to fall asleep right now."

"I'm fine. I'm going to crank up the music really loud so I don't fall asleep at the wheel." At his horrified look, I quickly added, "I'm kidding! Jeez, no one has a sense of humor anymore these days."

Rob considered me for a few beats before nodding decisively, as if confirming his thoughts. "You know what? It's not a risk I'm willing to take." He reached across the console and pulled the car key out of the ignition. "You're staying. I'm not taking no for an answer."

"What? No. Give it back." I tried to grab the keys from his hand, but he was quicker and was already out of the car. He opened my door, gently tugged me out, then locked the car as he guided me toward his house. "Rob! I have to get some sleep and a shower and open the store in the morning and then go back to the hospital. I need to go home."

"You can shower and sleep here. I'll ask Ellie to text Nicole to open tomorrow morning." He ushered me into his house, before closing the door and turning to me, looking serious. "Please, Kim? I'll feel better knowing that you're okay. You can take my room like last time. I've got T-shirts and shorts you can use and yes, fresh supplies of spare toothbrushes."

If I wanted to be totally honest, the idea of crashing at his house sounded wonderful. I was bone-tired, and the immediate possibility of snuggling in a comfortable bed was so incredibly appealing. I knew I should say no, because I should be getting some rest in my own bed, instead of in *his* house, this guy I was not supposed to be falling for.

I suppressed another yawn. "Okay. Thank you."

"Do you want something to drink? Eat?" He flicked on the lights in his kitchen. "I can make you a grilled cheese sandwich. Or a cheese omelet. French toast?"

"Probably not a good idea. I'll be snoring by the first bite."

"Right." He led me to his bedroom, found a spare T-shirt and shorts, then handed me a new toothbrush. "Yell out if you need anything else. Get some rest. I'll see you in the morning."

But as I watched him starting to walk away, everything that had happened in the past few hours caught up with me. The realization of what Opa had just gone through was a harsh eye-opener of how short and fleeting life could be. How fragile everything was. How things could be fine one minute, and how quickly it could all change. It was scary and daunting and overwhelming, and a blunt reminder to cherish everything—and everyone—important in your life. To hold on tight to them, because you didn't know how long you had with them. Your time together might be limited, and you wouldn't even know what you had lost until it was too late.

I blinked once, twice, trying to keep those pesky tears that were threatening to burst at bay. "Wait." The small, uncertain voice didn't sound like my own. "Can you stay?"

He froze, and it took him a few beats before he turned around. When he saw my watery eyes, his eyebrows shot up in surprise. "Hey. What's wrong?" He covered the distance between us in two strides and wrapped me in a tight hug. "It's okay. Thomas is fine. You're fine. It will all be okay."

"But things aren't fine. He's not well, and I was so scared for him, and nothing else is going right. I don't know if our street festival plan is even going to work, and for all I know, we're going to flop in the most spectacular way, and then Goodwin will buy all of us out, and I'm going to lose the store. And I was so pissed at my dad, because I thought he was going to do the right thing at least once in his life, but he didn't, he fucking bailed on us again, and I'm just so sick of everything . . ."

And as if those weren't enough, I was falling hard for this man, when I wasn't even supposed to have any feelings for anyone, at all, and I didn't know how to stop myself from falling for him.

Or maybe I didn't *want* to stop myself from falling for him.

"I'm sorry about your dad." Rob tightened his arms around me. "Things will be okay. Everything will work out."

I rested my face on his shoulders, as tears quietly rolled down my face. He didn't say anything as he held me, his hands making soothing motions on my back.

"Let's get you to bed," he said. "You've had a long day, and you need to rest."

"Can you please stay? I don't want to be alone."

He nodded, calm and steady. "I'm here."

Ten minutes later, I came out of the bathroom to find him sitting on the bed, freshly changed into a white T-shirt and a pair of blue shorts. I climbed onto the bed and got under the covers next to him.

"We'll put a pillow in the middle," he said. "I'm a considerate bed-sharer. I promise I won't hog the covers or kick—"

But I was too tired, so before he could even finish his sentence, I curled my arm around his torso and closed my eyes.

And let sleep take me away.

I woke up with a start a couple of hours later, and my immediate thought was to go back to the hospital to check on my grandfather. I groped for my phone on the bedside table and saw that it was only four in the morning. There were no text messages, no phone calls from the hospital, and that meant he was okay, and I breathed a sigh of relief.

I tossed my phone back on the bedside table, and that was when I became aware of where I was and who I was with.

So, *so* aware.

Rob had one arm around my stomach, the weight comforting, and his warm body was snuggled close behind me, his front to my back, our bodies fitting perfectly, and the rhythmical sound of his breathing filled the silence. I shifted a little, trying to adjust my position, but that only alerted me to the fact that my bottom half was grazing a certain part of him.

Lifting his hand, I quietly shimmied out of his embrace, then slipped out of bed and went into the bathroom. Because my bladder was bursting and, ugh, morning breath, right?

When I returned, the bed—and the room—was empty, and a weird disappointment crashed into me. Steeling myself, I squashed those feelings and reached for my phone to make a quick call to the hospital. The nurse on duty assured me that Opa was still sleeping, and he was fine, and I would be the first to know if anything changed.

I hung up just as the door flung open, and Rob came in, looking sleepy and disheveled.

And so, *so* gorgeous, he took my breath away.

"Hey." I was acutely aware of the deafening thuds of my heartbeat. "You're awake."

I was silently cringing inside. At myself. *Well done for stating the obvious.*

"Yeah." He looked as unsure as I felt. "Bathroom trip. Did you sleep well?"

"I did. Uh, did you?"

"Like a baby."

"I just called the hospital." I waved my phone at him. "My grandfather's okay. But I should probably go home and get changed. I haven't told Nic—"

"She's opening the store. Ellie texted." He tilted his head at the bed. "It's still early. You should get a couple more hours of rest."

But something in the room had changed. He was staring at me, and the atmosphere in the room seemed to grow heavier, thicker, like there was something unspoken hanging in the air.

I sucked in a breath when Rob took a few steps closer, his eyes intent on mine. He stopped in front of me, his gaze dropping to my lips, before they went back to my eyes, and for a second, or maybe it was my imagination, he looked like he was about to lean down.

Like he was about to kiss me.

Instead, he lifted a hand to tuck a strand of hair behind my ear. "You really should go back to sleep," he murmured. "Recharge your battery. How are you going to look after Thomas if you don't have anything left to give?"

He might be right, but there was *no way* I could go back to sleep now, not with him standing there, or with the way he was looking at me.

You can trust him.

You're safe with him.

So I threw all caution to hell, let the walls around my heart crumble to nothingness, and stood on tiptoe to press my lips to his. It was a soft, tentative kiss, testing the waters. Rob let out a low groan, and his hands went up to frame my face. He pulled me closer, and gently deepened the kiss, his lips coaxing mine open, and I thought, *Kissing him feels like an extension of my oxygen.* Like I would cease to breathe if we stopped. Like the world would stop spinning on its axis if our lips were separated.

He broke the kiss and rested his forehead on mine. "Do you know," he said, his voice rough, "that I haven't stopped thinking about that first kiss? That I think about you all the time? You're my first thought in the morning, and my last one at night. And honestly, I don't know what to do about that."

My breath stuttered at his words.

"I haven't been able to stop thinking about you since you kicked my ass at mini golf. And when you stood up for me to my dad, that was it for me. I knew I was gone for you. It was *killing* me having to find single guys for you to date."

Was it possible for a heart to swell and multiply into a hundred times its size? "You never said anything."

He brushed his lips against mine, a whisper of a kiss carrying the promise of a lot more. "I had to prove myself to you first. Make you realize that those guys aren't right for you."

I flashed him a teasing grin. "And you think you are?"

His smile was slow, confident. "I *know* I am. But that's for you to decide."

Well, lucky for both of us, I had already decided.

I looped my hands around his neck and pulled him closer. His lips came crashing down on mine again, and then he was kissing me like his life depended on it. He let out a low groan as I nipped on his bottom lip, his tongue thoroughly exploring, and then he spun me around and walked us backward, pressing me against the closed door.

"Are you really, truly sure"—he broke the kiss—"that you—"

I shut him up by kissing him again, pulling his body against mine, my hips flush with his, and I groaned as he rocked his hardness against me, sending heat pooling between my legs. His lips kept devouring, tasting, while his hands slid under my T-shirt, stroking the sides of my body before cupping my breasts, and I let out a low moan at the feel of his strong hands against my skin. Our mouths were hungry, like we couldn't get enough of each other, and then one of his hands snaked lower, past my hips, into the waistband of my shorts, then my panties, my breath hitching when his fingers found their way inside. He stroked, patiently, maddeningly, his fingers working faster as my breathing got shallower, while his lips traced a path along my collarbone. I came apart in seconds, moaning and clinging to him like I would crumble to the floor if I didn't hang on to him for dear life.

"That's it." His eyes were molten lava, fixed on mine. "Come for me, Kim. I've got you."

When I finally got my breath back, he was already occupied with his next move—easing my top over my head, along with his own T-shirt, and tossing them both on the floor. Then he lifted me up, hooking my legs around his, before his lips went back on mine, then on my neck, tracing a path down to my chest.

"Just in case you haven't noticed," I breathed out, "there's a perfectly fine bed just behind us. Large enough for two. It might be, you know, more comfortable."

"On it." He was a man on a mission, carrying me a few feet toward the bed, and we were both laughing as we stumbled onto it. I straddled him as my lips explored his jaw, his neck, my hands hungrily mapping a path across his shoulders, his chest, and his arms. The feel of his body beneath mine was addictive, his hardness against my softness, and I was intoxicated by the way we fit so perfectly and how everything felt so right and so incredibly good, like this was what we were meant to do all along.

Like we were meant for each other.

"Kim." His whispered words were reverent. "I can't believe I get to be here with you."

"Me too." I dragged myself against his hard outline, teasing a groan out of him. "I can't get enough of you."

He pulled me closer and busied himself by taking a nipple into his mouth and gently sucking it. My hiss was incomprehensible, and a satisfied smile passed over his face as he switched his attention to the other breast. His hands tugged on my panties and shorts, and the next thing I knew, he flipped us over and pulled them all off. I watched, my mouth going dry as he lowered his own shorts, before climbing his way back up on the bed, his body towering over mine.

"Hi," I said, suddenly feeling shy.

"Hey." His smile was gentle. "How's it going?"

"Good." *Really, really good. Super fantastic. One of the best days of my life.*

"Only 'good'?" The smile turned into a smirk. "Looks like I need to work harder."

Then his lips were back on mine, then everywhere, mapping

every inch of my body, while the hard outline of his dick pressed into my stomach, and the only thing I could do was groan and mumble unintelligible moans because I had next to zero brain cells left. I reached down and curled my fingers around him, eliciting a soft growl from him.

"Kim," he rasped. "Slow down. I don't want our first time to be over in seconds."

"Rob." I never begged, but I was practically begging him right now. "I just want you. Now. Please."

There were still a few brain cells left over that managed to register the sounds of his bedside drawer closing and foil ripping, and the way his breath hitched when my other hand reached for the protection and slowly rolled it on him.

"For the final time," he breathed out, "are you absolutely su—"

"For fuck's sake. Does this look like I'm having second thoughts?" The hand that was curled around him started to move, stroking him, teasing him, guiding him toward me. He gave a low groan, before brushing himself against my entrance, hot and hard, then he gently slid inside, easing himself deeper, giving me everything he had, until there was nothing left to give. His hands grasped mine, and it felt as if our heartbeats thudded into one as he moved against me, slowly and then faster, his breath hot against my mouth. My name was a prayer on his lips, whispered over and over again as we both started to lose control. And when we did, as I stared into the greenish brown of his eyes, the name of the yarn equivalent for those eyes finally came to me.

Vintage Jade.

His eyes are called Vintage Jade.

CHAPTER 28

More Kissing, Less Talking

I never went back to sleep, because we spent the next couple of hours in bed chatting.

"Tell me about your tattoos." My head was resting against his chest, as I traced the shape of the tiny crab on his upper left arm.

"They're for my siblings. This one is the sign for Cancer. For Alexandra. The scale"—he gestured at the one on his upper right arm—"is Libra. For Amanda and my mom. These ones"—he pointed at the scorpion on his right hip and the ram on his left one—"are Scorpio, for Paul, and Aries, for Kylie."

I noticed he didn't say anything about his dad. "And Jennifer?"

"My upper thigh. Two fish, for Pisces. Can we stop talking about them? Discussing my siblings is at the bottom of the list of things I'd rather do right now." He lowered his voice and whispered in my ear. "Because I've got other things I'd like to do to you. Dirty, filthy things. I can't get enough of you screaming my name when I fuck you."

"Well, since you asked so nicely." I reached for him and

pulled him on top of me. "Let's get on with it. Less talking, more doing."

I took a shower when the sun was up, and by the time I finished, I could hear Rob whistling off-key in the kitchen. Everything felt so domestic. So normal. As if waking up in his bed after a lazy weekend to the smell of him cooking was the most normal thing in the world. As if we'd been doing it forever instead of a few hours.

And somehow, that made me feel so, so content.

I walked out to the kitchen to find him. "Morning."

Rob looked up and gave me the biggest smile. "Hey." Before I could reply, he went around the kitchen island, pulled me close, and gave me a lingering kiss, long enough to make my toes curl. "Got your coffee ready. Breakfast is almost done. Give me a few minutes."

He gave me another kiss, then went back to what he was doing. I hopped on a kitchen stool and watched as he scrambled some eggs and grated some cheese into the mixture. Then he plated everything and pushed one toward me: homemade hash browns, cheesy scrambled eggs, sliced avocado, with crispy bacon slices, cherry tomatoes, and sautéed mushrooms.

My stomach growled in anticipation. "This smells good."

"It's simple, but it's my breakfast specialty." He grinned as he took the stool next to mine. "My siblings and I used to take turns making breakfast in the mornings. We each have our own thing. Alexandra has her banana pancakes. Amanda has a killer chocolate waffles recipe, and Jennifer is known for her breakfast tacos. Kylie has probably fifty different recipes of healthy smoothies, while Paul's go-to is his cinnamon French toast."

"Your family is awesome. I would kill to be able to have those kinds of memories."

"It's not too late." His tone was nonchalant. "You can still make your own memories with your own family, right?"

And right then, suddenly the concept of having to commit to someone to build my own family didn't seem too scary anymore. It might be hard work, but it seemed plausible if you had the right person to share it with.

Like him.

Because he's the right person for me.

"Have you heard from the hospital?" He was oblivious to my Earth-shattering revelation. "I can't go with you to pick Thomas up, because I need to meet Alec at the flipped house to clean up a few things. But do you want to come over for dinner tonight? I'll make lasagna, which, if you remember, has gotten rave reviews from my mother." He shook his head, as if he was realizing something. "No, actually, I can bring the food over to your grandfather's house, so we can keep him company."

A smile took over my face. "I would love that."

I left his house feeling like I was on cloud nine, almost scared to believe that things might be different this time.

But maybe it *was* different this time around.

Because it was Rob. Because he was always there for me, in a way that no one ever was before. And he'd made me realize that there could be more in life than what I had right now. That maybe a healthy, loving relationship wasn't such a far-fetched idea after all, and there was nothing wrong with wanting that. That if you were with the right person, it was okay to give them all of you and everything you had, because you know you would be safe with them.

And I knew, without a doubt, that I was safe with him.

Opa needed to stay another night because his hemoglobin level wasn't quite where the doctors would have liked it to be, so I ended up spending the rest of Sunday with him at the hospital. The IV line was still hooked up to his arm, but he seemed less tired than he was yesterday. He was almost back to his old chatty self, and his doctor assured me that he should be well enough to be discharged on Monday.

The rest of the week followed pretty much the same pattern—yarn store during the day, driving Opa to his dialysis sessions, and meetings with the other business owners in our precinct to finalize the festival plans in between. My nights were reserved for Rob, laughing and chatting and exploring each other.

Aiden finally texted back, apologizing for ghosting me at Opa's party. His reason was so ludicrous that I wasn't sure whether he was joking or not—he said he got spooked because I invited him to meet my grandfather, and he thought things were getting too serious too quickly. I could only laugh, because he spoke about missing his grandparents, and here I was thinking I was trying to be kind.

On Friday, I went to pick up Opa from dialysis as usual. Dr. Nguyen—*Lucy*—was waiting for me when I walked into the center and beckoned me to follow her into her office.

"Thomas is almost finished with the session, so I'll be quick," she said. "We did a follow-up blood test today, and the results came back normal. His hemoglobin level has gone up, so the iron infusion and the new iron tablets are helping. Our renal dietitian met with him today to discuss meal plans tailored for his specific nutritional needs. We'll see how he goes, and we'll schedule another test in two weeks."

"Sounds great. Thanks for the update."

"My pleasure. Thank *you* for inviting me to celebrate his birthday. I had a great time. By the way," she said, her tone way too nonchalant, "I was surprised to see Robbie there. How do you know him?"

"We have mutual friends," I said, not liking her oh so casual tone and this weird sensation bubbling under my chest. "He told me you two used to date for a while."

"We did." She gave me a rueful smile. "It didn't work out."

"I'm sorry to hear that." I wasn't, obviously, but what else could I say?

"My parents are very traditional," she continued, and I had no choice but to politely listen. "They have very strong ideas about who their kids should have as partners, and someone like Robbie wasn't who they had in mind for me."

Annoyance was starting to simmer in my veins. "And you agree?"

"No, but I can't go against my family's wishes. My parents had high hopes and expected a lot out of me, because I'm the eldest." Her eyes had taken on a faraway look, as if she was reminiscing about the past. "Rob had wanted to move our relationship further, but my family was adamant that he wasn't a successful enough person to be with someone"—she hesitated before continuing—"someone like me."

"A doctor, you mean?"

She looked embarrassed as she nodded. "They wanted me to be with someone in the same profession, who understands the long hours and the mental and physical demands of the job. They also think I should focus on my career before starting a family."

"And you'd rather listen to your family and give up a wonderful guy who was actually ready to settle down and spend the rest of his life with you?"

"I couldn't disappoint my parents. They've sacrificed a lot for me." Her cheeks grew redder. "And they were right. I had to concentrate on my career first."

Suddenly I didn't like this woman—and her family—too much. It wasn't fair for them to judge someone's worth—to judge Rob—based on what he does. It was people like them, like Rob's father, who had made society shallow with their standards, who had made Rob question his own worthiness when in fact he was doing just fine—*more than* perfectly fine.

But it wasn't my place to comment on that. "Rob is a great guy. Did you know he was there to support us when my grandfather was unwell at the party?"

Lucy blinked at me. "He was?"

"He stayed with me until we knew for sure that my grandfather was okay." And yes, fine, I probably shouldn't be thinking this way about the woman who was looking after my grandfather's health, but damn it if I wasn't perversely satisfied at the surprise and jealousy on her face. "I couldn't have done it without his support. He's an amazing person."

Lucy looked a little sad at that. "He is."

"I better go. Thanks again for letting me know about the test results."

She only nodded as I walked away, and when I snuck a quick look at her as Opa and I walked out, she was still standing at the same spot, looking confused and miserable. And that made me feel sorry for her, because she didn't know what she'd lost, and worse, she didn't seem to have the freedom to change her life, even if she wanted to.

And that made me even more thankful for mine.

CHAPTER 29

Lies and Relationships Don't Go Hand in Hand

Half an hour later, we arrived at Opa's house, and I did a double take when I saw a familiar truck parked outside.

"Rob's here." I turned to Opa. "Were you expecting him?"

"Yes. He said he was coming over to give me something." Opa gave me a pointed look before he opened the car door. "He's been checking in with me to see how I'm feeling, which is nice. His parents raised him right. I like him."

I suppressed a smile. "He *is* pretty cool." I hadn't had a chance to tell Opa about my developing relationship with Rob, although I knew he'd be super thrilled about it.

Rob hopped out of the truck as we walked over, then opened the tailgate and hefted out a large wooden item.

"Oh!" Opa brightened as Rob placed the item on the ground. "Is that what I think it is?"

"Yes, sir." He grinned at me as I watched them with a baffled look on my face. "When we went to the woodworking expo, Thomas mentioned he was thinking about making a mobile cart for his tools. I looked up some DIY plans online and found one for this beauty."

"You *made* that for him?"

"I did. Turned out better than I expected."

"It turned out *great.*" Opa beamed at him. "It looks incredible."

My baffled look turned into a grateful smile. "Thanks. That's very kind of you."

Rob grinned. "Wait. I've got something for you, too." He retrieved a bouquet of red roses from his truck, then gave me a quick kiss as he handed them to me. "These are for you."

What was it about this guy that made me want to kick my feet up and giggle like a teenager? "Thank you. They're beautiful."

I glanced at Opa to see his reaction. His eyes were wide, and the next second, he broke into a wide smile.

"I knew it! I knew something was going on between you two." His grin stretched across his entire face, and he reached for Rob's hand and mine, clasping both between his hands. "This is wonderful. Why didn't you say anything to me?"

"I was going to." I gave him a sheepish smile as we walked into the house.

"Your grandmother would have been so happy if she was still here. She would have loved you, Rob." Opa sat on the sofa, exhaustion and happiness lining his face. "And the best thing was, you managed to do it before the deadline in her will."

My heart lurched at that, and the bouquet nearly slipped from my grasp. I hadn't had the chance to tell Rob about the will. About the real reason I was looking for a partner.

Because falling for him wasn't part of the plan.

I glanced at him, and panic licked my spine at the look on his face. He was staring at Opa, a frown creasing his forehead. His eyes darted to me, before returning to my grandfather.

"What do you mean, a deadline in her will?"

Opa stilled, knowing that he'd said something he shouldn't have.

"Kim?" Rob's eyes flickered back to me. "What does it mean?"

"Uh." I scrambled for a reply that made sense, but my brain just wasn't cooperating, and I wasn't able to form any coherent thoughts.

"I must have remembered wrongly," Opa said in a hurried tone. "It's been a long day."

But I knew Rob knew something wasn't right. I had to come clean to him, because I didn't want to start off the relationship based on a lie.

I placed the flowers on the coffee table and took a seat in front of him.

"I was going to tell you, but I haven't had the chance," I said.

He stiffened. "What were you going to tell me?"

"You knew about my grandmother's last wish."

He only nodded.

"The request was included as a clause in her will." I took a deep breath. "If I could find someone to settle down with in two years, I'll inherit the yarn store."

"An inheritance." A look of understanding dawned on his face. "So that's why you're doing all this. This was all an act."

"*No*. Not anymore." I was struggling to find the right words to defend myself. "That was before I met you."

He shook his head, the understanding slowly transforming into disappointment, then hurt. "You were just using me."

Fear—the thought of possibly losing him—wrapped itself around my heart like a vice. "No, I wasn't. Please, I can explain."

His eyes turned cold. "I have to go." He gave Opa a clipped nod, then got up and stalked out of the house.

My grandfather looked horrified. "I'm sorry, Kim. I didn't know."

"I know you didn't. This is on me." I gave him a reassuring smile before running outside after Rob. He was already climbing into his truck when I went out, so I rushed over and knocked on his window.

"Give me a chance to explain," I said. "You have to believe me.

It might have started as an elaborate lie, but then I met you, and I swear it has turned into something more."

"Really?" His laugh was derisive. "When were you planning to dump me, Kim? Right after the yarn store became yours?"

"No. All those other guys you introduced to me, yes, I was planning to break up with them once I inherited the store." I was desperate to make him understand, to convince him that it was a silly, ridiculous plan that had nothing to do with him. "They were just a means to an end. But you're not."

He blew out a long breath. "Why should I trust you? You didn't trust me enough to tell me your real reasons for doing this. If you had, I would've made sure I didn't fall for you. No, you know what, Kim? Maybe you just weren't capable of trusting someone, of opening yourself up and letting someone else in. Of falling in love."

"That's not true," I stammered. "Maybe at first, because I didn't know if I could trust anyone ever again. But you, I know I can trust you. I know you're not going to hurt me. You're different."

"But *you're* not."

I paused. "What?"

"You're just like everyone else. Like Lucy. And my dad." The usual warmth in his eyes was gone. "People who put their careers first over the people in their lives, who are supposed to matter more. I thought you were different, but you're not. You were never interested in finding someone. All you wanted was the inheritance. You used me to get what you wanted."

Chills trickled down my spine. "Please, you have to believe me. Yes, it might have started that way, but you've changed my view of love and relationships along the way, and—"

"No. We're done here, Kim."

He gave me one last look before starting his car and driving away.

CHAPTER 30

It's Me. I'm the Terrible Blind Date.

The next few days were some of the worst of my life. I sent Rob a couple of messages, asking for another chance to explain things, but all of them went unread and unanswered. Opa said that Rob still checked in with him every day, but other than that, it was as if he—*we*—never existed.

He'd ghosted me, and I knew I deserved every bit of it.

Oma's will deadline was getting closer, so here I was, only two months away from potentially losing her legacy. I came clean about the will to Ellie and Jenna and apologized for keeping it a secret from them. They gave me a hug, then tried to encourage me, telling me that anything was possible. Anything could happen in those two months. They meant well, but I realized that I didn't really care.

Because Rob wasn't in my life, and that was all that mattered.

I had briefly, in a moment of madness, contemplated hiring an actor to be my pretend boyfriend. That was what I probably should have done from the very beginning, and my life wouldn't have intersected with Rob's, and things would probably have been a lot easier. But I nixed the idea seconds later, because the thought of having to pretend to be in love with a stranger for the next two months made my stomach sick to the core.

My friends convinced me to at least give things one last shot, so I did. Instead of jumping on a dating app, Jenna had set me up on a blind date with one of her coworkers, who was supposed to be one of the nicest guys she'd ever worked with.

The date turned out to be another disaster.

Only this time, it was my fault.

Jenna's friend—Colin—was all that she'd said he was. Handsome, polite, and a good listener. In fact, he was *too good* of a listener. Within half an hour of meeting him, I'd shared with him the entire sordid saga of how Rob was playing matchmaker for me and how I ended up falling for him. The poor man had to spend the entirety of our dinner listening to me pouring my heart out about Rob.

"I sent him a couple of messages to apologize." I pushed my mashed potatoes around the plate instead of eating them. "Maybe more. Like, five or ten. But he ignored them all. I don't know what else to do."

Colin shot a quick glance at the people at the table next to us, like he was pleading for help, then let out a long sigh, and it occurred to me that it was probably his fifth sigh in the space of thirty short minutes.

"I know where he lives. Do you think coming over to explain myself is too stalkerish?"

My date lightly smacked his forehead. "You know what? I think I might have left my fridge door open, and I just bought a big tub of my favorite Greek yogurt. I probably should go home so it doesn't go bad."

And that was when the first realization hit me.

I was turning into that horrendous date that other people would gossip about. I was reenacting my Shane the Nightmare Date from a few months ago, but this time, *I* was the Shane.

"Gosh. I'm so sorry." I groaned and placed my fork on my plate. "I shouldn't have agreed to this date in the first place. I'm sorry to have wasted your time. You're a lovely man, but I think my mind is elsewhere tonight."

And that was when the second realization hit me. I didn't want to date other people. I didn't even want to *pretend* to date other people. I only wanted Rob.

Because I was madly, *desperately* in love with him.

A few days later, a thick envelope from Goodwin Property Group arrived at the yarn store. It had another letter addressed to all the owners and tenants at our precinct, mentioning how several business owners on the strip had graciously agreed to their offers, and how they would like to share their plans in the hopes of convincing the rest of us.

I skimmed through the letter before fishing a thick bound document out of the envelope. It was a planning proposal of what the new multipurpose building would look like: retail spaces on the ground level, a ten-story residential area, hotels, offices, with an urban rooftop garden and a multistory parking lot. There was a short message from some bigwig at the City of Port Benedict expressing their excitement at this investment, saying how the development aimed to "transform the Port Benedict shopping precinct to complement the main Plaza building, while uplifting the lifestyle and living experiences of our residents." More things followed—a site investigation report, an urban design analysis, an artist's rendering of what the completed building would look like, even a waste management plan.

My heart skidded to a halt when I got to page thirty-nine and saw the name of the party responsible for the indicative concept plans for the project. Hands trembling, I flipped to the very end of the proposal, and scanned my eyes through appendix A, the architectural statements and plans. It had the construction documents for the project, and in the right-hand corner of the page was the name of the party that had been appointed to design the new development.

It was Carmichael Architects.

I dropped the proposal on the desk, as if it was on fire.

So Rob had known, all along, about the development plans for the precinct, and he pretended to know nothing about it? Anger and disappointment swirled inside my chest. He chose not to tell me, even though he knew how important this place was to me. I might have done him wrong by not telling him about Oma's inheritance clause, but he *lied* to me about this.

I didn't bother looking at the rest of the proposal. Shoving it and the letter back into the envelope, I stalked out of the office and told Nicole that I was going out for an hour, then dialed Rob's number as I walked to my car. He didn't pick up, which wasn't surprising. I called Alec instead, who picked up on the third ring.

"Hey, Kim." He sounded like he was in the middle of a construction site. "What's up?"

"I need to know where Rob is right now. You know how Goodwin is trying to buy out all of us? Do you know that his dad's company is working with Goodwin on that project?"

"What?" Alec sounded confused. "He never told me."

"You should probably rethink your choice of friends. If you don't know whether you can trust your best friend, who else can you even trust?"

"I'm sure he has his reasons," Alec said. "You've met his dad, right? Maybe he's just as much in the dark as the rest of us."

I scoffed. "He must know. Just tell me where he's at today."

Rob was where Alec said he would be. The site he was working on was a large allotment of land that had just recently been opened and subdivided into smaller plots. He was standing outside one of the half-built houses, talking to one of the guys on the crew.

I slammed the door as I got out of my car, clutching the Goodwin envelope in my hand.

Rob frowned when he saw me marching up the driveway. "What are you doing here?"

I pulled out the proposal and shoved it in his chest. "What the fuck is this?"

Color drained from his face.

"Your father's firm is working with Goodwin? Why the hell didn't you tell me? Why did you pretend that you knew nothing about it?"

"Oh, now *you're* angry at *me*?" His eyes flared as he shoved the proposal back at me. "You have no right being angry when you've also been hiding things from me."

"No." I glared at him. "You don't get to pull that card. This is different. You've seen how worried I've been about everything, how important this was to me because of my grandmother, and you chose not to tell me?"

"Has it ever occurred to you that I probably don't have a choice?"

"You chose *not* to tell me," I repeated.

"It wasn't my choice." He ran a hand through his hair, looking frustrated. "Everyone at Carmichael Architects had to sign an NDA when we submitted our interest. Something about Goodwin wanting to protect the intellectual property of the project. I couldn't say anything to you, even though it was killing me not to. Breaking the NDA could mean lawsuits and substantial financial consequences for my dad, and I couldn't do that to him."

I waved the proposal at him. "But you can do *this* to me."

Rob flinched. "I tried to convince him not to submit a tender for the project, but he wouldn't listen. It's a huge opportunity, and Dad was adamant that we had to be involved, especially after how difficult things were the past few years. It's his firm, not mine. I don't have a say in it."

"That might be true." My body was vibrating with fury. "But it's *your* life, not his, and *you* have a say in *that*, and you didn't have to be involved with any of this if you didn't want to. You never really wanted to work for him, anyway! Are you just going along with what your dad wants because you think he's right?"

He scoffed. "That's rich, coming from the person going along with her grandmother's wishes even though it wasn't what she wanted."

"It's not the same thing, and you know it. I did it because I loved my grandmother, and I wanted to honor her wishes. Not because I wanted anyone's approval. Do you really still think you're nothing but a builder, and working on this with him will make you worthy in his eyes? In *your own eyes*?"

"You don't know what you're talking about." His jaw clenched.

"But I do know! I know that you're an amazing guy. You're a hard worker. You're loved by your friends, and your family— screw your dad. You have a career that you love, that you're good at, and you don't need to prove yourself to anyone. You. Are. Good. Enough. Can you get that through your thick head?"

He opened his mouth, as if he was about to say something, but let out a long sigh instead. "I don't know. I'm trying. I really am. I'm sorry."

Disappointment welled up in my chest. "Me too, Rob. Me too."

And with that, I spun around and left him.

CHAPTER 31

The Right Google Search Can Work Wonders

"Are you okay, Kim?"

I looked up from my laptop and met Ellie's concerned eyes. We were in her bakery, and it was a cool mid-October night, two weeks away from Halloween, and one week away from the street fair—and the fourth wedding I was supposed to go to with Rob—so we were in the home stretch of finalizing things for the festival.

But I hadn't been focusing on the tasks I was supposed to be doing, because I'd been staring at the same email draft for the past fifteen minutes.

"You've been awfully quiet," Ellie said. "Want to tell me what's on your mind?"

"I'm fine. Just thinking about the festival."

"Are you?" She was completely ignoring the chalkboards for the signs and directions that she was supposed to be working on. "Did I tell you that Alec met up with Rob last night?"

Hearing his name still tore a fresh wound in my heart. "I don't need to know that."

"He looks miserable," Alec said from where he was sitting cross-legged on the floor, tying strings together to make buntings for the festival decorations. "Thought you might want to hear about that."

"Serves him right."

My two friends exchanged a long look. Alec sighed, abandoned his buntings, and straightened his legs. "You two are hopeless. He tells me he's fine, but clearly he isn't, because he's grumpy all the time. He misses you."

I pretended not to hear him and busied myself by typing a long nonsensical paragraph for the email, only to delete everything a few seconds later.

"We know, and you know, that you miss him, too."

"I don't." My reply came out louder than I intended. "I don't miss him, okay? I made a mistake, he made a mistake, we've both moved on."

"Neither of you have moved on," Ellie said bluntly. "He's cranky and unhappy, and you're snapping at people like you're about to bite their heads off. We care about both of you, and we want you both to be happy. Together or separately, I don't really care, as long as nobody is sulking like this. So tell us what we can do to help."

"There's nothing anyone can do. I lied to him, he lied to me, and I don't know if I can move past that. We're not even in an actual relationship, and he's already being dishonest." And it had hurt too much, because it was a reminder that he was just like any other men out there who had betrayed my trust.

Ellie sighed. "I'm sorry. I know how hard it must be. I won't even pretend to know what Rob was thinking, but it must have been hard for him, too, to be trapped between a rock and a hard place. Knowing what the store means to you, while at the same time knowing what his dad was doing and not being able to say anything about it."

At that, I looked up. "Is he still putting in hours at his dad's firm?"

"He is," Alec answered. "His dad has been pushing him to make the switch to full time, because he's very confident the Goodwin project will go ahead." He hesitated for a beat, briefly glancing at Ellie, before continuing. "I should probably also tell you that Lucy has been around."

A dull ache thumped in my heart at hearing that. "Has she?"

"He's mentioned that she's been texting, asking to meet him for coffee. I think she's trying to get back together with him."

Maybe this was all for the best. He was getting his life on track, proving to himself and his father that he could do more with his life, and now that his ex was back in the picture, he could finally start building that forever happiness that he believed so much in.

"Good for them. They make a good-looking couple."

Ellie exchanged a look with Alec.

Time to change the topic. There were more important things at play, so I needed to set aside my heartbreak and focus on the issues that matter more. "We should get back to work. This festival is all we've got to convince the other owners on the strip to turn down the Goodwin offer. We have to pull it off. If it doesn't work, we're all screwed."

And I really, *really* needed it to work.

Because I'd lost Rob, and I couldn't afford to lose my grandmother's legacy as well.

I left Ellie's bakery and drove home with the plan of showering and going straight to bed after. Jenna was away on a work trip, so the house was empty when I got home. I jumped in the shower and washed away the exhaustion of the day, but my mind was too awake to go to sleep after. I couldn't stop thinking about Rob, and the street festival, and Opa's health, and Rob, the redevelopment plans, and the yarn store.

And Rob.

Maybe an hour of mindlessly scrolling through YouTube and watching funny duck videos would help me relax and forget everything that was going on in my life. I opened my laptop while waiting for my hair to dry, and that was when I saw the link I'd saved from weeks ago—the link to the article written by the architectural historian. I clicked on it and reread the piece, my gaze snagging on the third paragraph of the article.

The historian had claimed, based on their research, that our shopping precinct had been supposedly designed by an architect named Marion Mahony Griffin. Google told me that she was once an associate of Frank Lloyd Wright and was widely considered as one of the first licensed female architects in the world. She had even helped design Canberra, the capital of Australia, as well as several well-known landmarks across America and Australia. The historian believed that the brick buildings on our street were one of the earliest properties she had designed, allegedly not long after she graduated from MIT in 1894, although they admitted there were no public records substantiating this claim.

I stared at my screen, my brain turning over rapidly.

Does this mean there's historic significance to our area?

I opened a new page and typed "heritage sites" into the search box. Google spat out an extensive list of results, and before long, I'd gone down the rabbit hole of reading everything I could find about heritage sites and Marion Mahony Griffin.

One hour later, I finally resurfaced with a vague idea of what I might be able to do.

If the historian was right, that our row of shops had originally been constructed back in the 1890s, it would make the place over a hundred years old. Typically, sites older than fifty years would be eligible for listing in the National Register of Historic Places.

That, coupled with the fact that one of the most prominent architects in the world had designed the place, should probably be enough to stop any planned developments to the site.

The only problem was, how could I prove that the place had been designed by her?

I went back to the article, found the historian's contact details, and drafted an email. My heart was hammering behind my rib cage as I explained who I was and what I was looking for, then sent the email before I had a chance to overthink it too much.

Closing the laptop, I went to bed, not expecting to see a reply until Monday.

But when I woke up the next morning, there was an email from the historian sitting in my inbox. The thundering of my heart was deafening as I tapped it open.

They admitted that there were no official records to validate their claim. But they listed all the facts that made them arrive at the conclusion, and they all added up to a very strong possibility: The style of our brick buildings was called the Prairie School, which was a late nineteenth- and early twentieth-century architectural style usually marked by horizontal lines, flat roofs with broad overhanging eaves, and rows of large windows. Griffin was regarded as one of the founding members of the style, and this was the only cluster of buildings in the entire city of Port Benedict to have that distinctive design.

Attached to the email were scans of old, yellowing photographs of Griffin visiting the city and posing with a friend, who was one of the early owners of the current site of the Plaza. The historian strongly believed that Griffin had most probably designed the buildings as a favor to her friend and hadn't been properly credited as the person responsible for the designs.

My hands were shaking as I rushed to type a reply: *Would this mean that the precinct could possibly be classified as a heritage site, considering its famous architect?*

Their reply came twenty minutes later: *Absolutely.*

Well, fuck.

This could change *everything.*

I texted Ellie, who immediately called two minutes later.

"Kim, you're a genius." Her voice was overcome with excitement. "If we can pull this off, we might be able to convince everyone that they can't sell to Goodwin and that would stop the development plans!"

"We might," I said. "But from what I've read, it would probably take us a while to get the heritage application approved."

"That's okay. We'll get the process started as soon as we can. In the meantime, we should get in touch with Goodwin. I'll ask Alec to call Jacqui and tell her about this."

For the first time in the past two weeks, there was a flash of hope blooming in my chest, the first bright spark of something positive.

And it gave me the tiniest bit of hope that maybe everything would turn out okay.

CHAPTER 32

Everybody Needs Somebody to Love

The first day of the street festival was finally here.

Our usually quiet street had been temporarily transformed to resemble a busy, fun carnival ground. The entire road was closed to local traffic, there were banners and buntings put up along the street and strings of lights threaded across the trees, and there was a makeshift stage at the end of the road for performances throughout the three-day festival.

The local shop owners had been busy since the crack of dawn, helping to set up market tents and folding tables for the stallholders that had rented a spot. There was a huge variety of vendors: We had jewelry makers, candle and soap makers, scrapbook suppliers, and arts and crafts stalls. There were also food vendors, a face painting corner, a mini petting zoo, and Ellie had even managed to source a bubble tea seller. It was a fun mix of things, and it was heartwarming to see how people at the precinct came together to pull this weekend off.

My phone beeped with a calendar alert. I pulled it out of my pocket, only to see that it was a reminder of the fourth wedding I was supposed to go to with Rob tomorrow.

I ignored the painful twist in my heart. Maybe he'd be going with Lucy this time.

Well, whoever he was going with, it was none of my business, because I didn't have time to dwell on it and think about him right now. Pushing Rob out of my mind, I continued what I was doing—putting up flyers in the store to advertise the activities we were planning for the day. I was teaching a beginner's class on knitting (after having sat through several intensive hours with Nicole to make sure I knew what I was doing), while Nicole was running embroidery demonstrations and a workshop on beginner's amigurumi. She was talking to someone on the store phone while I finished putting up the signs. When she hung up, she gave me a funny look.

"Guess who that was."

"I don't know. The pope?"

"That was Melinda Paulson's personal assistant," Nicole said, sounding as if she was still in disbelief. "Melinda Paulson, the knitting influencer."

I turned around to gape at her. "What?"

"Exactly." Nicole nodded. "She said Melinda is available to come into the store to speak and give a short demonstration. She's available for an hour tomorrow and on Sunday, too, if we can squeeze her in."

My jaw became practically unhinged. "But *how*?"

"I asked, and the PA said she was only told to convey the message and arrange the schedule. If you're interested, we need to call her back and confirm before noon."

I wasn't one to look a gift horse in the mouth. "Fuck yes, we're interested. We can fit her in the morning, or in the afternoon, whenever she's free. Look, she can come whenever she likes, we'll work *our* schedules around her."

Nicole went to call them back, while I directed my attention to the people who were already starting to trickle in. For the next eight hours, we were up on our feet serving customers and answering questions, as the festival was in full swing outside. The street was chock-full of people visiting the stalls and the other stores on the strip. There were people lining up outside Ellie's bakery and Quinn's coffee shop, and Anahita's cousin and his band were playing on the makeshift stage at the other end of the street.

The next two days followed a similar pattern. We opened the yarn store an hour earlier than usual, and not long after, visitors began to show up. Melinda Paulson came for her session just after lunch, and it was probably the busiest I'd seen the yarn store since I started running it, and that was saying something. It was standing room only, and at least sixty people were crammed into the store, some even having to stand just outside the door. Melinda was warm and engaging, kept the audience hanging on her every word, and even graciously stayed to sign books and take photos after her session was over. We sold all her books and almost half our stock in one day, and none of that would have been possible if she hadn't been in the store.

"Thank you so much for doing this," I said to her once she was finally finished chatting with people. "My grandmother was a huge fan, and she would really have loved to meet you."

The woman smiled at me. "My pleasure. I don't do events anymore, but I owe Amanda a huge favor, so when she reached out to ask for my help, the least I could do was say yes."

"Amanda?" I only knew one Amanda, but surely she wasn't talking about the same—

"Amanda Carmichael. The screenwriter? We're represented by the same agency, and I met her at my last book launch a couple of years ago. I was going through some stuff at the time, and she connected me with her therapist, because she had been doing some work in the mental health space. It helped me tremendously, and I'll be forever grateful to her."

Rob's sister.

He had somehow made good on his promise to find Melinda Paulson, and that helped make the day—and possibly the festival—a success.

Even when he wasn't around, he was still there for me.

After Melinda left, I took out my phone and debated with myself whether I should send him a message. In the end, I did, because he did me a solid, and having Melinda come into the store made a huge difference. My text was read immediately, but no matter how many times I checked my phone throughout the day, he never answered.

And even though it shouldn't disappoint me that he was ignoring me, it did.

By seven thirty on Sunday evening, I was exhausted, mentally and physically. The last visitor had just walked out of our store, and the company we rented the equipment from had almost finished packing up the tents and makeshift stage.

In the three days that we held the street festival, we managed to sell nearly all our stock, and there was a long list of people wanting to join our knitting clubs. The other shop owners had similar reports in the group chat—everyone said their sales for the past three days had surpassed anything they'd done in the previous twelve months. A lot of visitors said it was a pleasant surprise to discover our shops and how they look forward to coming back in the future. A few of the vendors that had rented a stall even told me that they were interested in leasing the vacant shop fronts.

It was all good and well, but I hoped it was enough to convince everyone not to accept the offer from Goodwin.

"Kim?" Opa's voice shook me out of my reverie. "Did you hear what I said?"

My grandfather was much stronger and healthier these days, thanks to the iron supplements and his newly reconfigured diet. He had insisted that he help in the store on the last day of the festival, but it was getting late, and I didn't want him to over-exert himself, so we were driving back to his house right now.

"I'm sorry, Opa. My mind was somewhere else. What were you saying?"

"I was asking how things are with the heritage application. Have you heard anything?"

"We haven't. The historian thinks it might take a while to get the application approved. There's nothing much we can do until then." I gripped the steering wheel in frustration. "I'm sorry, Opa. I don't know if I've done enough, and I feel like I've failed you and Oma."

"You haven't," Opa immediately replied. "You've done your best, and if your grandmother were still here, she would have been so proud of you."

"You have to say that, because you're my grandfather."

"But it's the truth." He chuckled. "Your grandmother was just worried about you. I think she thought she was being helpful by asking you to run her store. She thought it would help you find your purpose."

"My purpose?"

His smile was sad. "You haven't had a long-term job for a while, honey. You were always moving from one new job to another, from one new city to another. Like you were searching for something but you probably didn't even know what. She was just worried about you. But you should know that whatever you do, even if we lose the yarn store, she would still have been proud of you. As long as you're happy and content and doing what you love."

I was quiet as I mulled that over.

"I *am* happy," I said. "Coming back home, and being here with you, was the best decision I've ever made. And I do love running the store, but I guess I've been so fixated on keeping it going, because I thought that was what she had wanted. I thought it would keep her legacy alive, and help with your medical bills, because I know they can be a lot."

Opa waved a hand. "Don't worry about me. I've got enough savings to look after myself. You need to think about your own future, and what *you* want to do with *your* life. Not what your grandmother or I wanted."

I nodded, swallowing the lump in my throat. Somehow, hearing my grandfather say that felt like a huge load had been lifted off my shoulders.

There was a white rental SUV parked in his driveway as we turned onto his street. My blood froze in my veins when I saw the man leaning against its door.

"What is he doing here?" I turned to Opa. "Did you know he was coming?"

"He arrived this morning. He said he had something he needed to talk to you about. Just listen to what he has to say, okay?"

"Why should I? Why are you listening to him still? Where was he when you were hospitalized?"

"Kim." Opa looked tired, and for a second a heavy dose of guilt came over me. "I know you invited him to the party. He texted me that night and said he was sorry he couldn't make it. Did you know he checked in with me every day after I was released from the hospital?"

I was taken aback. "He did?"

"He did. And as much as I would have liked him to be around more, the fact of the matter is his job takes him away from us. He has his reasons for accepting those overseas postings. But he's still my son. Your dad. He asks about you whenever we talk. He's trying."

Before I could reply, my grandfather was already opening the car door and stepping out, ending our conversation. My father gave Opa a hug, then directed his gaze at me. "Kimmy. Can I have a word?"

I let out a long breath. "Sure. But first of all, I hate that nickname."

He frowned. "I'm sorry?"

"I hate that you call me Kimmy. Please don't ever call me that again."

I turned around and followed Opa into the house without another word. My grandfather waved toward his bedroom. "I'll be in my room."

The first few minutes after Opa had closed his door were deathly quiet. I plopped myself down on the sofa, and watched my dad, waiting for him to start talking.

"I know you haven't been happy with me," he began. "I haven't been the best parent . . ."

"Or son."

". . . Yes, I know, and if you can give me a few minutes of your time, I want to tell you my side of the story."

I sighed. "Dad. You haven't been here for your own father for the past year and a half since he's been on dialysis. You haven't been here for him, for Oma, for me, and you've had the past thirty years to make things right, but you haven't made any effort to. Why do you want to suddenly tell your side of the story now?"

"Things haven't been easy, Kim." It was his turn to sigh. "You remind me so much of your mother. You look just like her, and seeing you used to remind me of what I'd lost. It made me think of her, and what my life, our lives, could have been if she was still alive."

That hurt more than I'd expected. Seeing me was painful for him, so he chose not to see me at all?

"And for a time, I was also angry at my parents. So I left."

I spluttered. "Fine, I can accept if you don't want to be around because I reminded you of Mom, but how can you be angry at *your* parents? They're the nicest people in the world. What did they do?"

"When Hana died, I was heartbroken, and all I'd wanted to do was bury myself with work," he said. "I decided that I could never open my heart and love anyone else again, the way I loved her. Not another woman, not my parents, not even my own daughter. It was easier to focus on my career instead of investing in relationships with the people that mattered in my life, so I wouldn't have to go through the heartbreak of losing anyone else, ever again. I thought I could protect my heart and myself that way."

I stared at him. Because I'd never heard this part before.

And because I'd never realized how we were *very* similar in so many ways.

"But my parents wouldn't let me. They tried to force me to be present, for your sake. They wanted me to move past my grief, as if nothing had happened. As if the love of my life hadn't just left me on my own, forever, to raise our child. They wanted me to be strong so I could"—he made air quotes with his hands—"'be there for you.' I love my parents, and I knew they only wanted the best for me, for you. I thought they were right. And for a while, I did it. I put up a brave front and went on with my life.

"But then it got to be too much. I just couldn't keep up the facade anymore. I wasn't okay. Being here"—he waved his hand around the house—"being in this city, seeing you, everything reminded me of her. So I accepted an overseas assignment, because I thought that distancing myself from you, from my parents, taking a break from everyone, was the right thing to do. For my own sake, and for yours, because you deserved a better parent than what I could give you at the time."

I took a deep breath. That had given me an entirely new perspective of my father. "Why are you back now?"

"I've been asked to retire. They've given me a twelve-month

contract for a desk job at the local Port Benedict office, so that was basically my notice."

Anger began bubbling up to the surface again. "So now that you're retiring, you thought you could go back to the family you've abandoned for so many years?"

"Kim." My father looked old and tired. "I haven't abandoned you. I might not be here, but I checked in with my parents every now and then. They told me everything that's been happening with your lives."

"Why don't you ever check in with *me*?"

At that, he was quiet. "If I wanted to be honest, I was scared."

I let out a low scoff.

"I know I messed up with you. And I didn't even know where to begin fixing it. I didn't think a casual text message once every month was the solution."

"No, but it could be a start."

"But would you have answered?" His smile was sad. "Or would you have ignored my message, or worse, given me a one-word perfunctory answer?"

I was quiet, because that was exactly what I would have done.

"All I'm saying is, I'm here to apologize. Being asked to retire puts a lot of things into perspective, and I realize now that staying away from you and from my parents isn't the answer. I will never not grieve your mother, but I've learned to live with it over the years. And if anything, it reminds me that I need to be present for you and for my father, before it's too late." He paused, suddenly looking unsure. "I know I'll have to earn your forgiveness, but I'm here, and I'm not going anywhere. And I want to work on our relationship. But if you're not interested, I'll understand."

Opa was right. Dad *was* trying. It might not be enough, but it was probably all he could give right now. We both had issues that we had to work through, but he was here, and he was trying to make amends. It didn't mean it was as easy as forgiving him and moving on with our lives, as if the past thirty years hadn't happened, but maybe, *maybe*, this could be the start to a—somewhat—normal relationship with him.

"I know you have a lot to think about," my dad said. "But I'll be around this time. And I really hope you'll give me a chance to make things right."

I was still sitting on the sofa half an hour later when Opa came to the living room.

"Where's your dad?"

"He left. Said he's staying at the Plaza hotel tonight." I made a vague gesture toward the front door, then looked up at my grandfather. "He's coming back to stay. How can you be so calm and so forgiving of a son who hasn't been here for you for so long?"

Opa sighed and took a seat next to me. "It hasn't been easy for your dad, Kim."

"It hasn't been easy for *all* of us. Yet you stayed. Oma stayed. You didn't leave."

"Because we love you too much. We love him too much. I forgave him a long time ago. I've lost your grandma, and I don't want to lose him, too. Being angry with him and confronting him will only push him away." He gave me a sad smile. "I know it's harder for you. I couldn't help but always think how your life would probably have been different, had you grown up in a real family with both your parents and maybe even some siblings."

I shook my head vehemently, prepared to go into a lengthy debate of why I wasn't missing out on anything. I didn't need my dad, or any imaginary siblings, because my grandparents were my *real* family. But Opa wasn't finished yet.

"Your grandmother and I have been truly blessed to be able to raise you. I knew Daniel was hurting and struggling when he lost Hana, and we had no right to stop him from doing what he wanted with his life. And you've always been such a wonderful child," Opa said. "Always so independent, even when you were younger. Even with what you've been through, you've always managed to accomplish so much without our help. I'm so proud of everything you've achieved. How you've jumped in and taken over the store without complaining." He heaved a sigh. "But there's a difference between being independent and putting up a wall so that no one can get close to you. We all need other people, and there's no weakness in that. You need to allow people in, to support and help if you needed any, and to learn when not to push them away."

I shook my head. "What does this have anything to do with dad?"

"It has *everything* to do with him. I know you think you can't trust other people because he left. Because he abandoned you first. And when Leo happened, it's like you cemented that thought in your head, that you will only get hurt if you trust someone and let them into your life." Opa reached forward and enveloped my hands in his. "Your grandmother knows this, too. I think that's probably why she included that ridiculous clause in the will. Because she—*we*—wanted you to have someone in your life. When I'm gone, I want to rest in peace knowing that you'll have someone to share your life with, someone to be there with you through thick and thin. You're a strong, independent woman. But everybody needs somebody. Even the strongest of us all."

"But I tried. I thought I could trust Rob. Turned out I couldn't. I don't know if I'll ever be able to go through anything like that again."

"You can." My grandfather gave me a small smile. "If it's the right person, you can."

CHAPTER 33

She Wasn't Expecting Him

It had been a few weeks since the street festival, and our precinct was noticeably busier.

The Yarn Fanatics had had an influx of new customers at the store, mostly visitors who came to the festival. All our knitting clubs were now at maximum capacity, and I'd had to create new clubs to make sure everyone who wanted a spot got one. There was now a club running every day of the week with the addition of Game of Knots, another book-club-slash-knitting-club, because the first one was so overwhelmingly popular; we had the Crochet Mafia, for those wanting to learn more about crocheting; and Fiber Friends, where the members knit things like socks and hats and blankets to donate to people in need.

Melinda Paulson had also agreed to come for another talk sometime before the end of the year, because she said she'd forgotten how much she missed doing events and meeting people who shared the same passion as her. And all the other shop owners on the strip agreed that their business had picked up considerably after the street festival. That, coupled with the article in the official blog of the Port Benedict Tourism Board and a recent feature about the festival in the local newspaper, helped boost business at the precinct considerably. And the good news was, that helped sway people who were on the fence about selling to Goodwin to turn down the offer.

The bad news was, the people who had decided to sell weren't changing their minds.

Ellie and I even met with Jacqui Goodwin, and even though she was sympathetic to our plight, she said the City of Port Benedict was the major investor in the project, and how her hands were tied because the city was adamant they had to push on with the plan.

So when her number showed up on my phone just now, I wasn't keen on answering, because I knew we would be repeating the same conversation.

"Hey, Jacqui," I said, trying my best to sound upbeat. "I hope you're calling with good news this time."

"I am, actually." A soft laugh followed her words. "Good news for you, at least. I don't think the city officials are too happy, but they can't do anything about it."

I paused. "I don't understand. What do you mean?"

"I just got off a phone call with a very unhappy city executive. They've been notified that the row of shops at the back of Port Benedict Plaza has now been listed in the National Register of Historic Places, which means they have been instructed by their bosses to stop the project. Permanently. I suppose you have something to do with this?"

What is she talking about? "We did submit the application for the register, but I was under the impression it would take a while to be approved. I wasn't expecting it to be this soon."

"Apparently someone with friends in high places pulled some strings on your behalf," she said. "Whoever it was, they did you a huge favor. We will be withdrawing our buyout offers officially in the next few days, but I wanted you to be the first to know."

"Are you being serious?" I couldn't believe what I was hearing. "But what about the people who had already agreed to sell?"

"We will still honor the offer and acquire their properties, but we won't be demolishing anything. In fact"—I could hear the smile in her voice—"I was thinking that we might be able to donate some of the development funds to help revitalize the strip. If all the owners are agreeable, of course."

Yes. I made a mental fist pump. "I think everyone would love that. Thanks for letting me know, Jacqui. I appreciate that." I hung up and did a happy dance around the store.

At least that was one issue out of the way.

Now all I had to do was figure out a way to inherit and own the place.

My mind drifted to Rob, wanting to share the news with him. I gritted my teeth and pushed him out of my mind, then reached for my phone to tell Opa the good news instead.

"That's wonderful!" My grandfather was thrilled. "I'm so proud of you. All your efforts have really paid off."

"I don't know how we had our application approved so quickly, but I'm glad it was."

There was a lengthy pause from my grandfather. "I might have told Rob about it."

I froze. "You what?"

"He said he knows someone in the local State Historic Preservation Office and told me he'd try to reach out to his friend there."

My jaw unhinged. "So you're saying that Rob helped us fast-track the approval process? This all happened because of him?"

"I'm not saying that, but I'm also not saying no."

But if he did that, that meant he went against his father. His dad had wanted this project to happen so badly, and if Rob had stopped the development from going ahead, it meant he was sacrificing his future and his relationship with his dad.

He had done this for me.

He had chosen *me* over his father.

Today was the day of the fifth and final wedding Rob and I were supposed to go to.

So obviously, I was going to ambush him there.

Jenna had objected to the idea that I was planning to make a grand gesture for Rob. "Why should you be the one making the effort? Didn't he make a mistake, too?"

That might be true, but he had sacrificed more for me. He had practically given up a future with his father for *my* future.

I owed him a fucking grand gesture.

The bride of the fifth wedding was a lawyer who used to consult for Mackenzie Constructions, so Ellie and Alec were also invited. They'd picked me up, and I spent the entire twenty-minute car trip mentally rehearsing my speech. It wasn't long or flashy, but it was genuine, and it came from my heart, so I hoped that was enough to tell him how I felt.

The wedding was huge, so it was easy for me to walk in unnoticed. Alec said the bride was a senior partner at a top-tier law firm, which was probably why there were tons of people invited. He had approached the bride, told her about me, and she was so excited at the possibility of a live rom-com-grand-gesture movie moment at her wedding, that she immediately went on stage to stop the band and beckoned me to come over.

Meanwhile, I was about to chicken out. Cold sweat coated my forehead, my palms were clammy, and I seriously felt like I needed to cry. Or vomit. And faint. Maybe all three, at the same time.

But Ellie gave me a gentle push toward the stage. "Go on. Do what you need to do."

I ran my hand to flatten my perfectly flattened skirt. "What if he's not here yet?"

"He texted me earlier. He's here somewhere." Alec nodded. "You can do this."

I took a deep breath. *Fuck it. I'm going for it.*

The bride was quietly squealing when she handed me the mic. A hush fell over the crowd, and several hundred pairs of curious eyes turned to watch me.

"First of all, congratulations," I said to the beaming bride, "and thanks for giving me a chance to say a few words."

She gave me two excited thumbs-up, followed by another squeal.

"Hello, everyone." I scanned the darkened crowd, hoping to spot Rob. "I apologize for hijacking your night. I promise I'll be quick." I found Ellie and Alec in the crowd, and they both gave me encouraging nods. "Uh, my name is Kim, and I'm here because I have a few words to say to a friend of mine, who is a guest at this wedding."

Quiet murmurs broke among the guests, and my gaze roamed the crowd again, only to find Leo and his fiancée on the left side of the room. Maybe all the lawyers knew each other in this city? He was frowning at me, and I realized with relief that I didn't really give a damn about what he might or might not think about me right now.

Because I knew that I had truly moved on this time, and whatever he did in the past no longer had a claim over me and my life. Over my future.

"First of all, I just wanted to say to that friend, that I'm sorry. For being dishonest, for hiding my real reasons for wanting to find a partner." I took a deep breath. "I know it was selfish of me for not telling you, and I'll need to work on rebuilding your trust, to give you a reason to believe in me again. But if you give me another chance, I'm willing to put in the work."

My gaze finally fell on him, standing in the darkened corner at the back.

With Lucy Nguyen by his side.

Looking so perfect and gorgeous together.

It felt like my heart had stopped and dropped to my shoes, and I could feel blood draining from my face. I stared at the two of them, my heart struggling to start itself back up, while my brain was racing a thousand miles a minute.

This is all for nothing. I was here for him, but he was here with someone else.

I didn't know how long I stared at him. The bride was nudging me, prompting me to continue my speech, but it took me a while to swallow the lump in my throat. My eyes found Ellie again, and she must have seen Rob and Lucy, too. But she gave me a firm nod and mouthed, "Keep going."

She's right. I'm already here. Go for broke.

"Those of you who know me would know that I never used to believe in love. In marriages, in happy endings, because of a terrible relationship in the past." My eyes found Leo again, and this time, he gave me a sad, apologetic smile. "But that friend changed my outlook on love. He showed me that it's not as scary as I thought to trust in someone. That it's okay to give myself and my heart to another person—to the right person, if he's earned that trust." My voice faltered a little. "Because the risk is worth it."

"You're doing amazing," the bride whispered.

My gaze snagged on Rob again. "To that friend, I wanted to say how much I appreciate everything you've done for me. You're the kindest, best person I know. You were always there for me whenever I needed you. You always had my back. I don't know how many times you've dropped whatever you were doing to come and support me. I mean, you were willing to give up your weekend to throw yourself out of a plane, thousands of feet above the ground, for me. Like, who does that?"

There were scattered chuckles from the crowd, while I took another deep breath to recompose myself. "And you were there not just for me, but for the people that matter in my life, too. Honestly, I wasn't expecting you, because I've already convinced myself that I wasn't going to fall for anyone else, ever again. Then you came along and turned my world upside down. My life is so much better and brighter and more wonderful and amazing and fun with you in it. And until I met you, I didn't know it was possible. I didn't know what I was missing. You've given me a glimpse of what a life shared with the right person could feel like. You've shown me, and made me believe, what I never thought would be possible. That love really does exist."

The bride *awwwed* from next to me.

"You should also know that you deserve all the love and happiness in the world. And you're good enough to do what you want with your life, and that I would never, not in a million years, ever sacrifice the person I love over a job, or a business, or a career . . ." My rehearsed speech had gone off the rails, and I was rambling. I tore my gaze away from him and turned to the bride. "Congratulations again. I wish you nothing but love and joy for the rest of your life."

Handing her the mic, I thanked her and jumped off the stage, wanting nothing more than to disappear into the ether. I did what I could, even though it was humiliating, because I went up there to tell him how I felt, only to find out he was here with someone else.

I quickly navigated my way through the crowd, smiling and thanking people who were saying as I passed, "Good for you," and "That's really brave." When I finally made it outside the venue, I pulled out my phone and sent Ellie a message to let her know I was leaving.

"Where are you going?"

I closed my eyes at the familiar voice, embarrassment flooding all over me.

"Hey." I turned around and waved my phone at Rob, plastering a cheerful smile on my face. "I'm going home. Just about to book my ride."

"That was a great speech." He was studying me. "Just making sure that you were talking about me?"

I swallowed, before nodding. "I think you were the only person who had volunteered to fling themselves out of a plane for me. Remember that?"

"Yeah. Fun times." He stood where he was, his hands in his pockets, his eyes still intent on mine. "Were you going to leave without saying anything to me?"

But I did say something to you. A lot of things. On the stage. "I didn't want to disturb you. You looked"—I waved a hand—"preoccupied." *With Lucy.*

He didn't say anything, just kept watching me.

"Um, I haven't had a chance to say thank you. For all your help. With Melinda, and for contacting the people on the tourism board, the local paper, and especially with the heritage application. For *everything.* I'm sorry if that made things difficult with your dad. But I owe you, and I hope I'll be able to repay the favor one day."

But he shook his head. "You don't owe me anything. You did all the legwork and got the ball rolling. I just made a couple calls," he said. "And don't worry about my dad. I had a long talk with him. Things are a bit strained between us right now, but he'll come around. My siblings will make sure of it." He smiled at that. "The most important thing is he finally accepts the fact that I'm not interested in continuing the family firm. He's in the process of selling the business now. And I owe it all to you. You've always believed in me, even when I didn't believe in myself."

"That's great. I'm thrilled for you."

He only nodded.

"You should go back." I gestured toward where the wedding party was in full swing. "Lucy will be looking for you. You should probably send her a text to let her know that you're outside. With me. Or no, don't tell her that you're with me. She won't be happy." I was rambling again, but I didn't know what else to say. "I don't know, whatever, you do you."

He still didn't move. "She knows I came out here to find you."

"Oh, shit. I'm so, so sorry." I winced. "I didn't know you two were back together. I wouldn't have shown up here otherwise. Trust me, I have absolutely no intention of ruining your relationship. Congrats, by the way. You two are perfect together. Look, I really should go."

"I'm not with Lucy."

What?

"We both got invited to the wedding, but I'm not here with her. I came alone, and we ran into each other."

My brain did a one-eighty. *He's not back together with her?*

Rob took a deep breath. "You know what you said back there, about building trust? I owe you an apology, too. I was wrong for not telling you about the project. I honestly thought I needed to do that for my dad, but I know now it's not an excuse. I should have been honest with you from the start."

I nodded. "We both should have been honest with each other from the start."

"We should have. And I'm willing to do whatever it takes to rebuild your trust. I'll put in the work, and then some."

I could only swallow the lump that had reappeared in my throat.

He took a step closer. "Did you mean what you said? That you believe in love now?"

My heart began to beat faster. "Maybe."

Another step, then another one, and he was now standing in front of me. "It's a simple yes or no question, Kim. Do you or do you not believe in love now?"

"Yes." I stared into his eyes, and the hopeful look I saw in them floored me. "I do. And I do love you."

"Finally." His face broke into a grin. "You don't know how long I've waited for you to say that. That wasn't hard, right? Admitting that you're madly head over heels in love with me and you can't live without me?"

I rolled my eyes. "Look who's talking. I think *you're* head over heels in love with me."

The grin softened into a smile. "I am. I have been for a while, and matchmaking you was the hardest, but also the best decision of my entire life." He took one more step, closing the distance between us, and took my face in his hands. "Please don't ever change your mind, because my life just isn't as fun without you in it."

As I kissed him, I realized that he had fulfilled the promise he made a while ago.

He proved to me that happy endings do exist.

EPILOGUE

Rob

You know, that could probably be us one day."

I turned to Kim, suppressing the smile that was tugging on the corners of my mouth. "You know, that's not what you would have said one year ago."

She *tsk*ed, a little impatiently, while her eyes were still preoccupied with watching my best friend twirl around one of her best friends on the dance floor. It was Ellie and Alec's wedding, and everyone was dancing the night away, except for, as usual, the two of us. Kim had been on her feet the entire day, job-sharing the maid of honor duties with Jenna, and this was the first chance she had tonight to sit down and rest. I could tell she was exhausted, although she probably wouldn't admit it until after the night was over.

"Well, that's what I'm saying now." Her gaze strayed to the edge of the dance floor, and she smiled to herself as she watched her grandfather dance with Ellie's mom. She had been watching him like a hawk, making sure that he wasn't getting too tired, but she had nothing to worry about—he had been chatting and laughing with everyone else, looking like he was having the best time of his life. "We've had a big year, haven't we?"

"We've had a *massive* year. I don't know how we even managed to fit everything in."

The past twelve months hadn't been just massive. They had been life-changing.

The guy who bought the house that Alec and I had flipped turned out to be a production coordinator on a popular home renovation competition TV show. He loved the work that we did on the house so much, he managed to convince his producers to bring us both on board as consultants for the show, and we even appeared for fifteen minutes in one episode to chat with the contestants and share our renovating experience.

The outpouring of positive feedback from the viewers on our fifteen-minute appearance was so overwhelming, that the producers sat down with us and floated the idea of starting our own home renovation show. They wanted to follow Alec and me as we hunted for our next property, renovated it, then searched for the right owners for the newly flipped house.

That was how *The Home Matchmaker* was born.

Our first episode had over two million viewers, and it became such a huge hit, the network immediately ordered a full season. Alec and I asked Kim if she wanted to stage the house once the renovation was done. She did, and her work received a ton of attention and so many positive reviews, that people started asking if they could hire her to stage the property *they* were selling. It eventually got to the point where she had to promote Nicole to manage the yarn store full-time, because all her time was now occupied by her property staging work.

I was thrilled for her. More than thrilled. Because after a few short months of doing it, it was obvious that she was meant to do the job. Her clients loved her work, and while she might have been perfectly fine working at her grandmother's yarn store before, it was clear that she'd found her true passion. There was an extra spring in her step now, which had probably made it easier for her to navigate her newly found relationship with her father.

To his credit, he seemed to be genuinely trying. He'd only missed probably one or two Sunday dinners with Kim, her grandfather, and me, and had even started teaching Kim to cook healthy nutritional meals for Thomas. Her grandfather was thrilled to have his entire family around, which probably also helped with his health, because he seemed to be happier and stronger than ever.

"I think I know how we managed to fit everything in," Kim replied. "See, there's this one guy I know that kept saying it's because of him, because he's a master multitasker, because of the four sisters he grew up with or whatever. I mean, sure, he's a hard worker, and that's probably why we managed to do everything that we did in the past year, but I personally feel he thinks a bit too highly of himself."

"I disagree. I think he deserved all the rave reviews and accolades people are throwing his way. He's got a great work ethic, he's good-looking, and honestly, have you noticed how photogenic he is?" I wiggled my eyebrows at her. "The cameras on *The Home Matchmaker* loved him. Viewers of the show loved him. Alec might tell you otherwise, but I think that's the real reason the show is number one six months in a row. Don't you think so?"

"I think he needs to stop referring to himself in the third person."

"But does that mean you agree that I've got a great work ethic?" I flashed her a teasing grin. "And what I said about the good-looking and photogenic part?"

That earned me an eye roll and a long sigh, and I burst into laughter as I pulled her closer and planted a quick kiss on her cheek, still marveling at how I now have the privilege to do that.

"You're lucky you're cute and I love you." Her eyes turned soft as she smiled at me. "Although I have to admit that you're right.

Because there's no way I could have pulled everything off on my own. Well, I guess I could have, but it wouldn't have been as much fun. It's been an amazing year, but my favorite part was getting to be with you, and having you by my side, and sharing all those amazing experiences with you. That was the best part of it all."

And this, hands down, was one of *my* favorite parts of being with this woman. I'd seen every facet of her personality since I'd met her. She could be the sassy Kim, the hardworking Kim, and the businesswoman Kim. There was a sexy Kim, the private version of her that only I got to see. The loyal friend Kim, where she'd do anything and everything for her best friends. And the filial side of her, where she took care of her grandfather—and even her father—without a word of complaint.

But my favorite version of her was this one. When she smiled at me and looked at me with so much love and trust in her eyes, like no one else in the world existed but us.

And to me, that was the perfect Kim.

Acknowledgments

Like most things in life, it takes a village to make a book. So you might want to get a cup of tea (or coffee, or a glass of wine, or whatever your beverage of choice is) and make yourself comfortable, because we could be here for a while.

First and foremost, the biggest thank-you to my brilliant editor, Erika Tsang, and my rock-star agent, Ann Rose. Erika, I won the editor lottery with you. Thank you for your invaluable insights, for always seeing the bigger picture, for pushing me to dig deeper, and for making this story shine. I'm still pinching myself that I get to work with you! Ann, you freaking rule. Best. Agent. Ever! I don't know what I'd do without you. Thank you for always believing in me, for being so calm when I'm freaking out about something, for being patient with my (often silly) questions, and for always making the time to chat and brainstorm anything and everything. Have I mentioned that you're the best?

I'm beyond lucky to have such an incredible publishing family looking after me. Monique Patterson, I'm eternally grateful, and I can't thank you enough, because this book wouldn't exist without you. To the amazing editorial, marketing, and publicity team at Bramble / Tor Publishing Group: Luisa Rozo, Tyrinne Lewis,

Cassidy Sattler, Ariana Carpentieri, Ryan T. Jenkins, Jacqueline Huber-Rodriguez, Esther S. Kim, and Nicola Ferguson, thank you a million times over. I am so thankful for all your hard work. Thank you to copyeditor extraordinaire Hayley Jozwiak, for stopping me from repeating so many words!

Jacqueline Li, I didn't think I could love another cover more than *Salty*, but you've truly outdone yourself with this one. Thank you for being super talented and for illustrating the most beautiful, the most perfect, so-gorgeous-I-can't-stop-staring-at-it cover.

To Alex Lloyd and the Pan Macmillan family, especially Clare Keighery, Chloe Patterson, and Tom Evans, thank you so much for all your support with *Salty* and especially for holding my hand when I was nervous with all the promotional stuff!

My HEA writers group—Alexandra Almond, Kylie Mulligan, Amanda Robinson, Jennifer Tomlin, and Paul O'Doherty. We first met online back in 2021 when the world was a scary, uncertain place, and I'm so glad we all stuck around after because my writing life wouldn't be as much fun without all of you in it. It's an honour to have you all as my friends and critique partners.

Thank you to everyone in the writing community, especially Anahita Karthik, Melly Sutjitro, Melody Thio, Anselma Prihandita, Quinn Huang, the Rosebuds, and the Australian 2025 Debut Crew. A massive thanks to Julie Tieu for my first ever blurb. Nicola Marsh, thank you for always being so supportive and encouraging and generous with your time and for sharing your experience.

To my wonderful group of friends: Idawati Zhang, Grace Pan, Melinda Bott, Nicole Whelan, Wanni Tendean, Sarah Hale, Michelle Plant, Caroline Setiadarma, Monica Djojoiswanto, Cindy Husein, Christine Tanuwidjaja, Lulu Budy, and Jesslin Chandra. To everyone at SJM (you know who you are). Thank you all for always cheering me on, it means the world.

I'm lucky to have such great support from my family: Chris,

Lala, Ken, and Al, and Tatah and Oom David. Thank you from the bottom of my heart for everything.

Ludi, Maxwell, and Jasper. Thank you for always believing in me. My two boys, thank you for continuously reminding me to lock in and for telling your friends that your mum is an author. I'm so proud of the young people you two are becoming! Remember that I'll always be here for you both, to be your biggest and loudest cheerleader and to support you no matter what.

My mother, who was one of the strongest people I know. She went through a lot of hardships and challenges throughout her life, and just like Kim's grandfather, spent her last few years on dialysis. But no matter what curveball life threw at her, she always bounced back, every single time, and faced everything with her head held up high. She was an incredible woman, and she taught me so much about strength, courage, and resilience. Thank you for everything, Mama.

Finally, and most importantly, to all the readers (I still can't believe I have readers!!), the booksellers, the reviewers, the librarians, the Bookstagrammers, and the BookTokkers. Thank you so much for picking up my books, for reading, reviewing, for posting about them and spreading the word, for reaching out to me with all your kind and encouraging words. I am endlessly grateful to each and every one of you. Thank you for being with me on this journey, and I hope to be able to share many more stories with you.

About the Author

Cynthia Timoti writes fun, sexy multicultural rom-coms with plenty of heart and snark, where happy endings are always guaranteed. She was born and raised in Jakarta, Indonesia, and moved to Australia when she was seventeen. She spent too many years working in finance, even though numbers aren't her strongest suit.

When Timoti's not writing, she's probably trying to make a dent in her TBR pile, hunting for the perfect cup of bubble tea, and collecting pretty notebooks that she'll never use. She currently resides in Melbourne, Australia, with her husband and two sons.